ISSUNBOSHI

A Graphic Novel

AN ONI PRESS PUBLICATION

ISSUNBOSHI

A Graphic Novel
by Ryan Lang

Sometimes we need to reach deep within to find the strength to do what the world needs us to do, to become who the world needs us to be.

Written, illustrated, and colored by **Ryan Lang**

Lettering by **Steve Wands**

Designed by **Sarah Rockwell**

Hardcover edition edited by **Amanda Meadows**

Softcover edition edited by **Gabriel Granillo**

Cultural consulting by **Chiaki Hirai**

Published by Oni-Lion Forge Publishing Group, LLC.

Hunter Gorinson, *president & publisher*
Sierra Hahn, *editor in chief*
Troy Look, *vp of publishing services*
Spencer Simpson, *vp of sales*
Angie Knowles, *director of design & production*
Katie Sainz, *director of marketing*
Jeremy Colfer, *director of development*
Chris Cerasi, *managing editor*
Bess Pallares, *senior editor*
Grace Scheipeter, *senior editor*
Karl Bollers, *editor*
Megan Brown, *editor*
Gabriel Granillo, *editor*
Jung Hu Lee, *assistant editor*
Michael Torma, *senior sales manager*
Andy McElliott, *operations manager*
Sarah Rockwell, *senior graphic designer*
Carey Soucy, *senior graphic designer*
Winston Gambro, *graphic designer*
Matt Harding, *digital prepress technician*
Sara Harding, *executive coordinator*
Kaia Rokke, *marketing & communications coordinator*

Joe Nozemack, *publisher emeritus*

🐦 📘 📷 onipress.com

ryanlangdraws.com
📷 /ryanlangdraws
🐦 /osiristheory

First Edition: May 2024
ISBN 978-1-63715-429-8
eISBN 978-1-63715-101-3

Printing numbers:
1 2 3 4 5 6 7 8 9 10

Library of Congress Control Number 2022932177

Printed in China

Dedicated to my wife, Helen, and my parents.

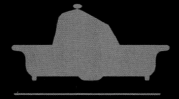

PROLOGUE

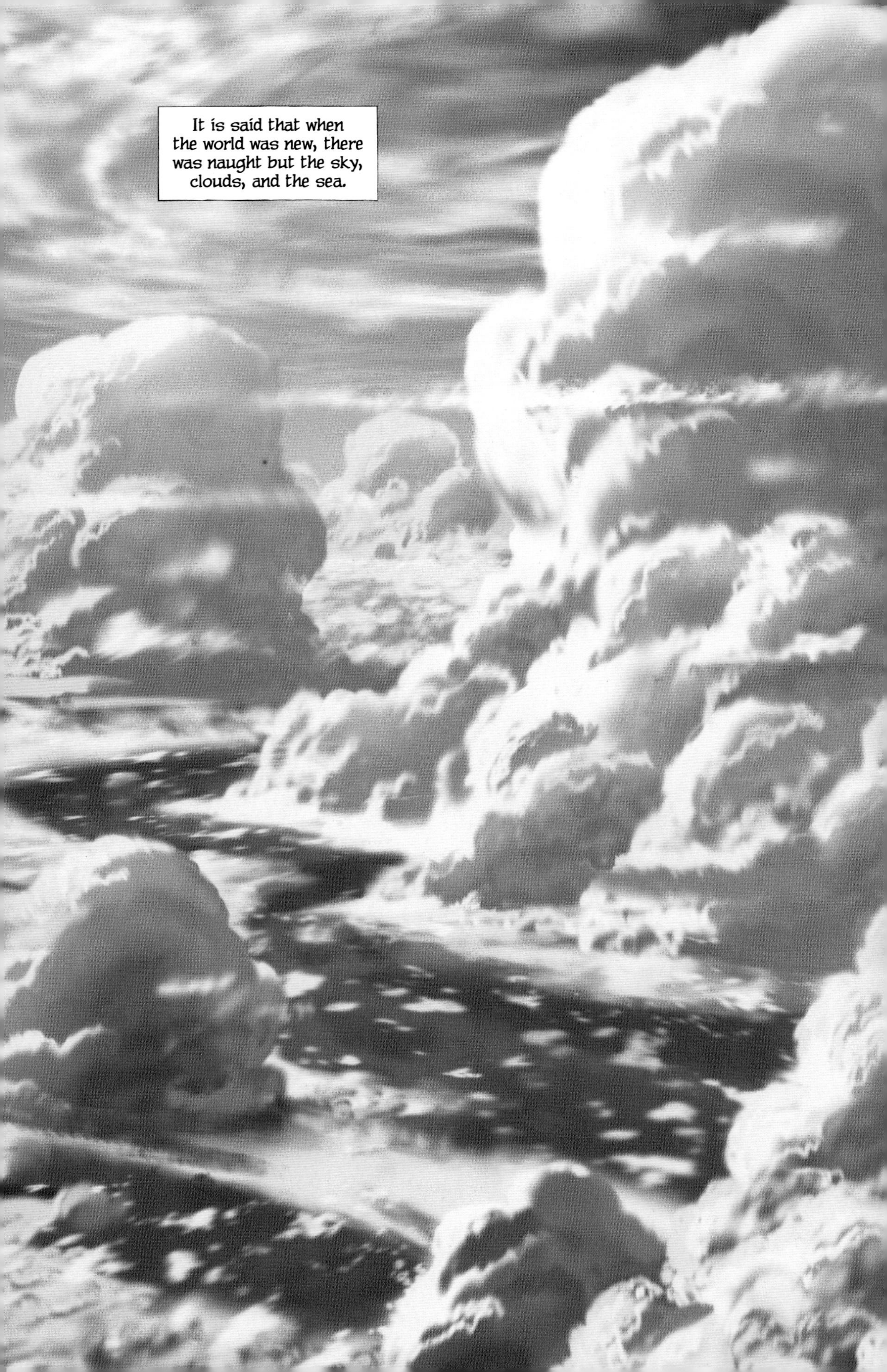
It is said that when the world was new, there was naught but the sky, clouds, and the sea.

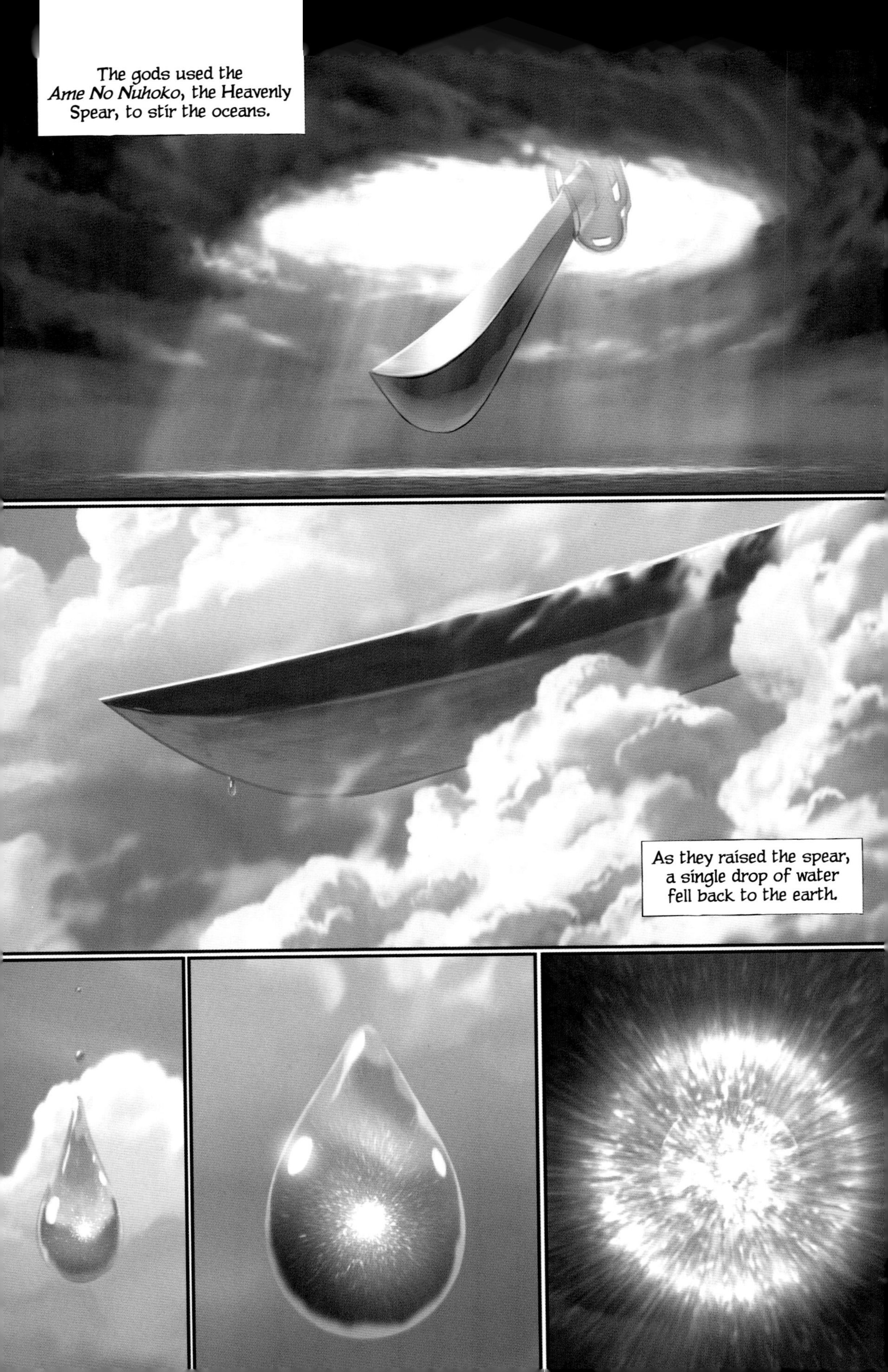
The gods used the *Ame No Nuhoko*, the Heavenly Spear, to stir the oceans.
As they raised the spear, a single drop of water fell back to the earth.

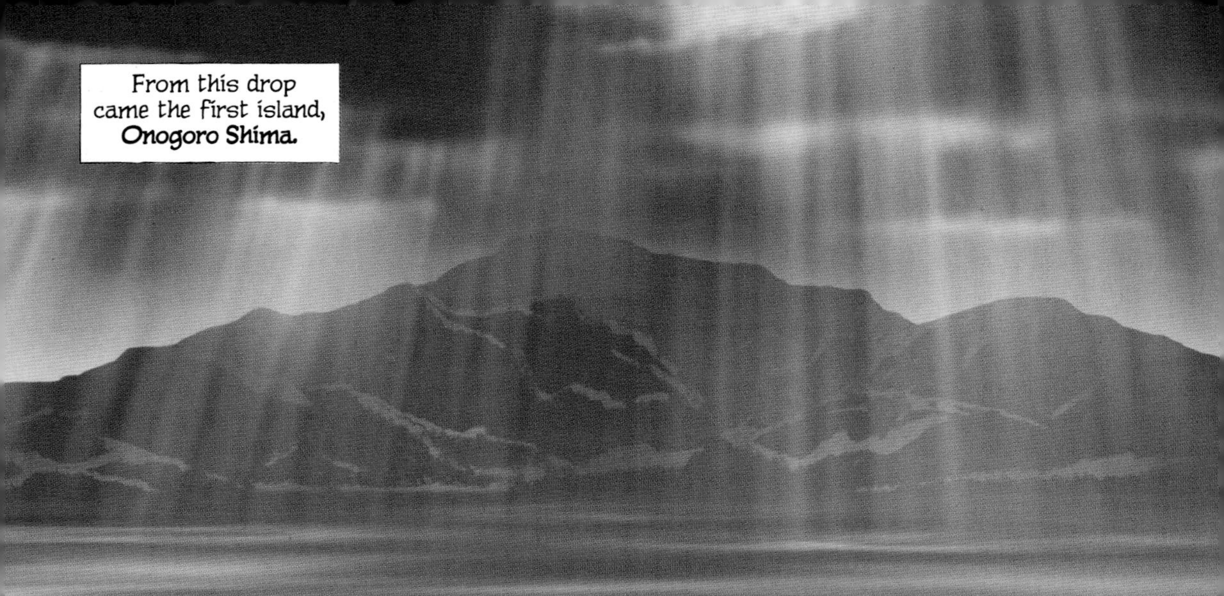
From this drop came the first island, **Onogoro Shima.**

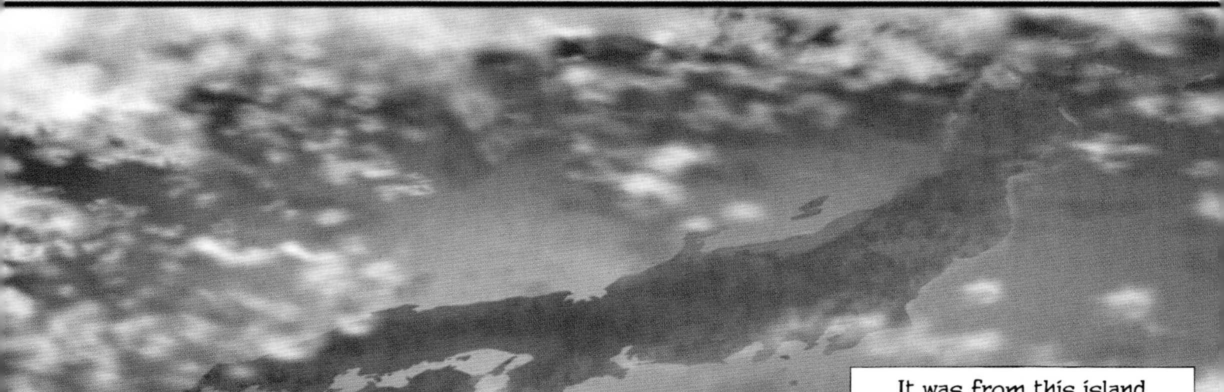
It was from this island that all the islands of Japan were eventually born. Legend does not speak of the *Ame No Nuhoko* again...

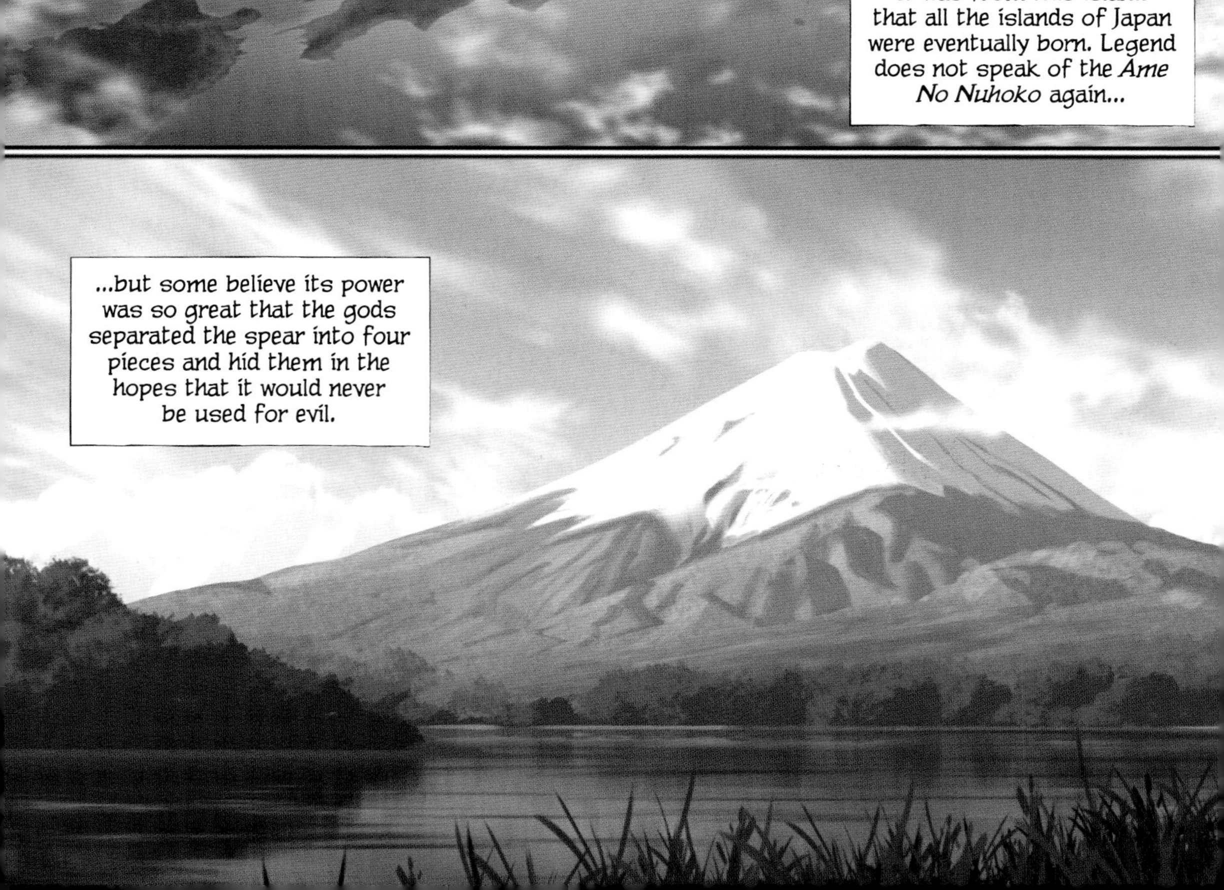
...but some believe its power was so great that the gods separated the spear into four pieces and hid them in the hopes that it would never be used for evil.

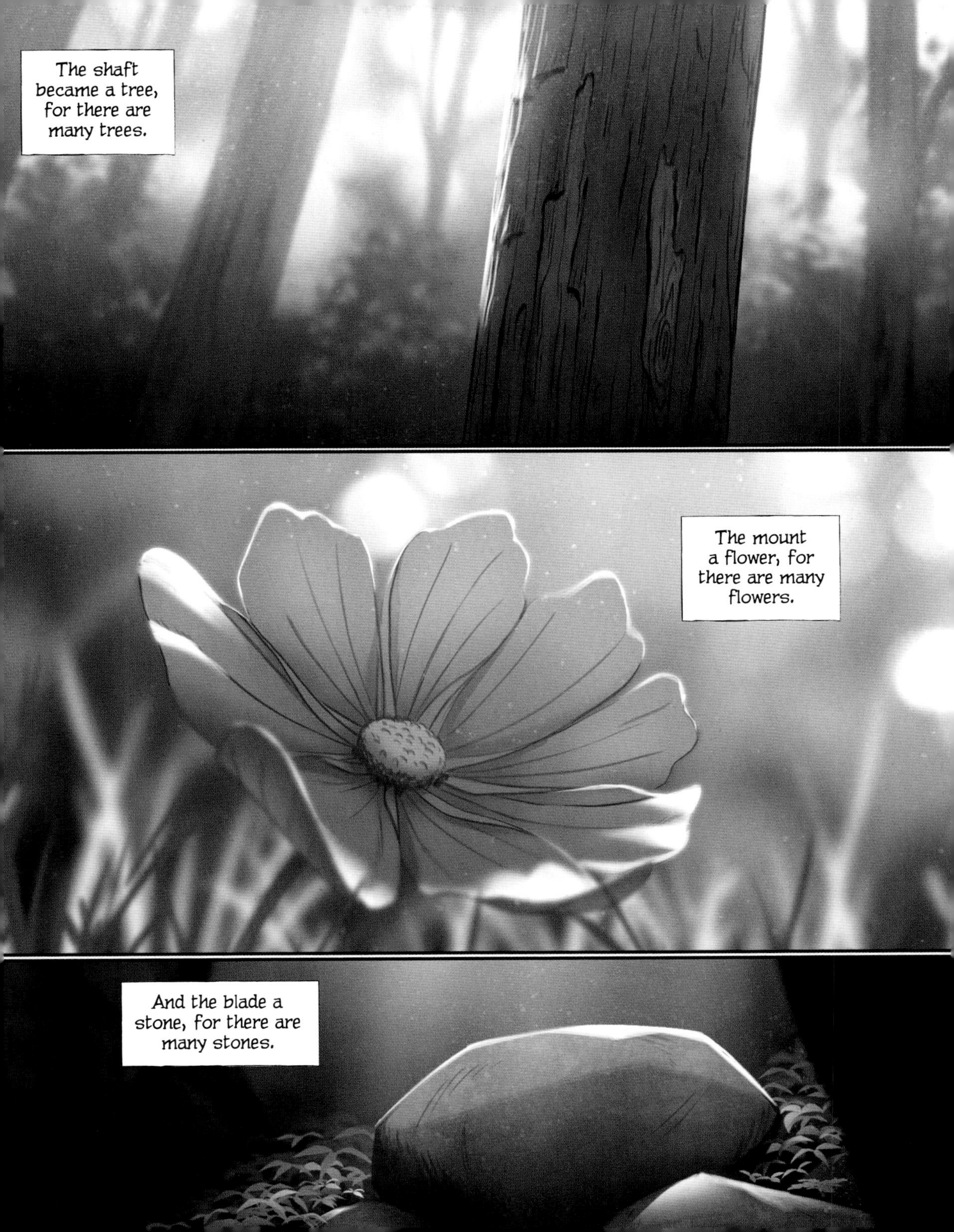
The shaft became a tree, for there are many trees.
The mount a flower, for there are many flowers.
And the blade a stone, for there are many stones.

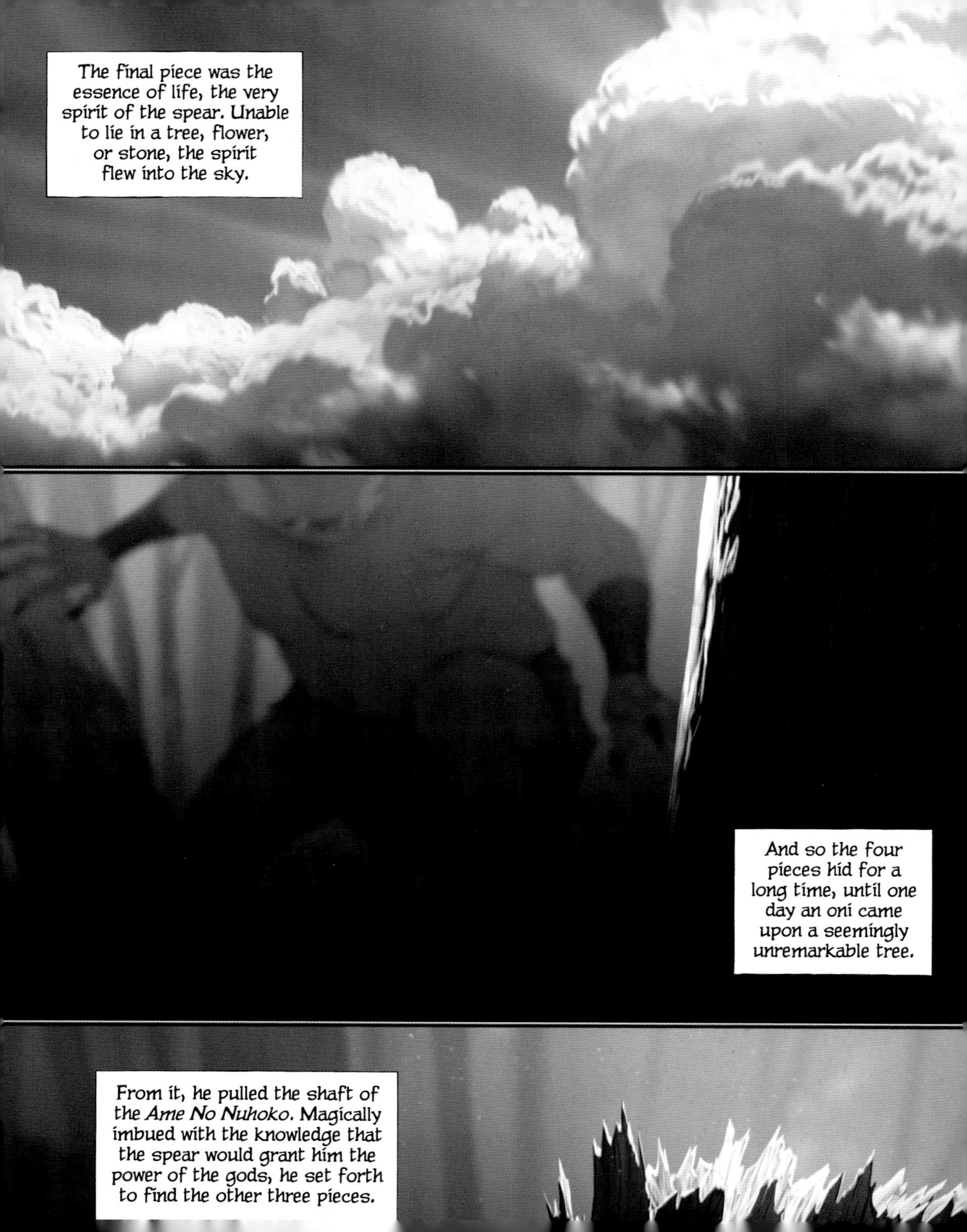
The final piece was the essence of life, the very spirit of the spear. Unable to lie in a tree, flower, or stone, the spirit flew into the sky.
And so the four pieces hid for a long time, until one day an oni came upon a seemingly unremarkable tree.
From it, he pulled the shaft of the *Ame No Nuhoko*. Magically imbued with the knowledge that the spear would grant him the power of the gods, he set forth to find the other three pieces.

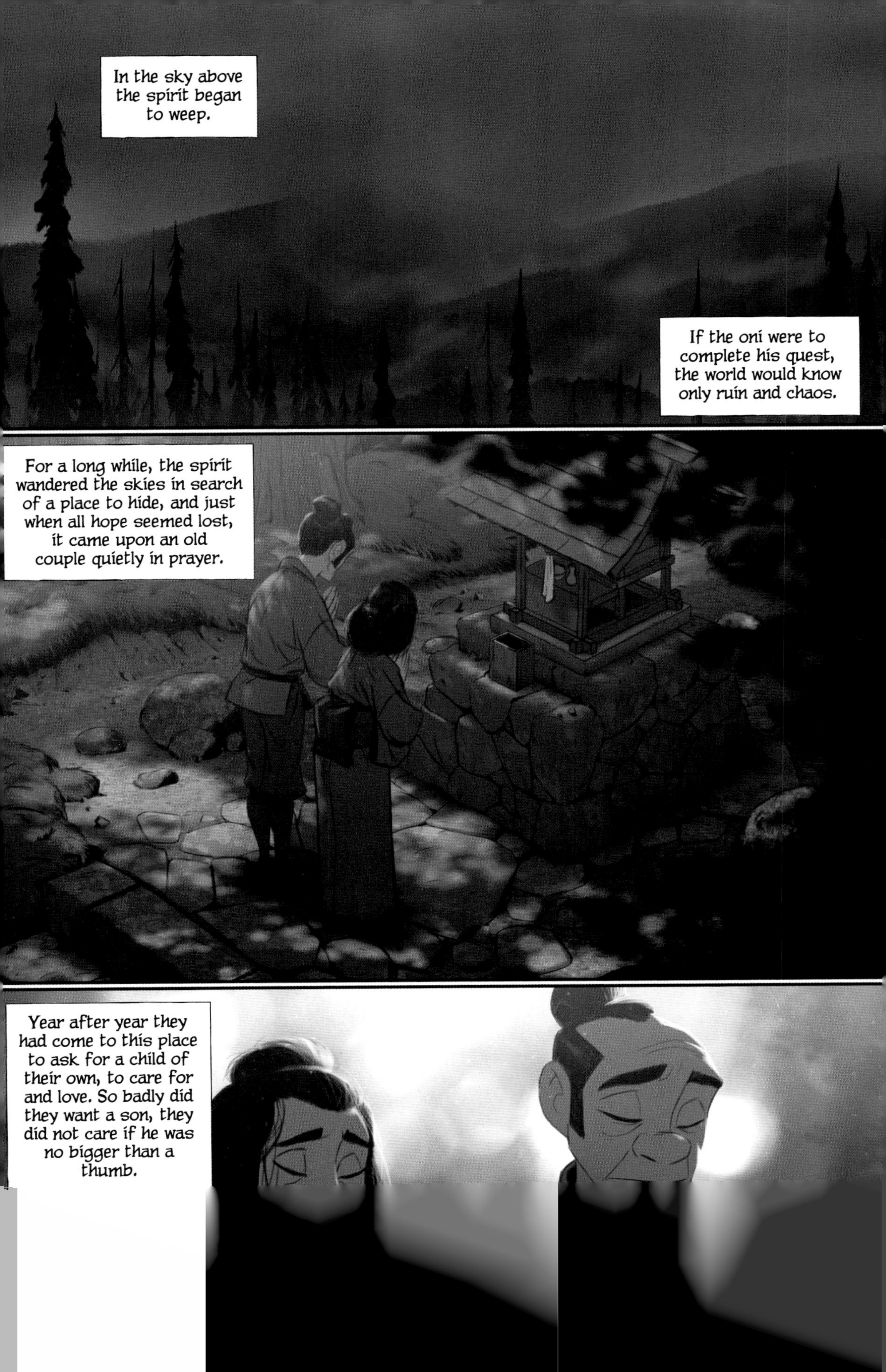
In the sky above the spirit began to weep.
If the oni were to complete his quest, the world would know only ruin and chaos.
For a long while, the spirit wandered the skies in search of a place to hide, and just when all hope seemed lost, it came upon an old couple quietly in prayer.
Year after year they had come to this place to ask for a child of their own, to care for and love. So badly did they want a son, they did not care if he was no bigger than a thumb.

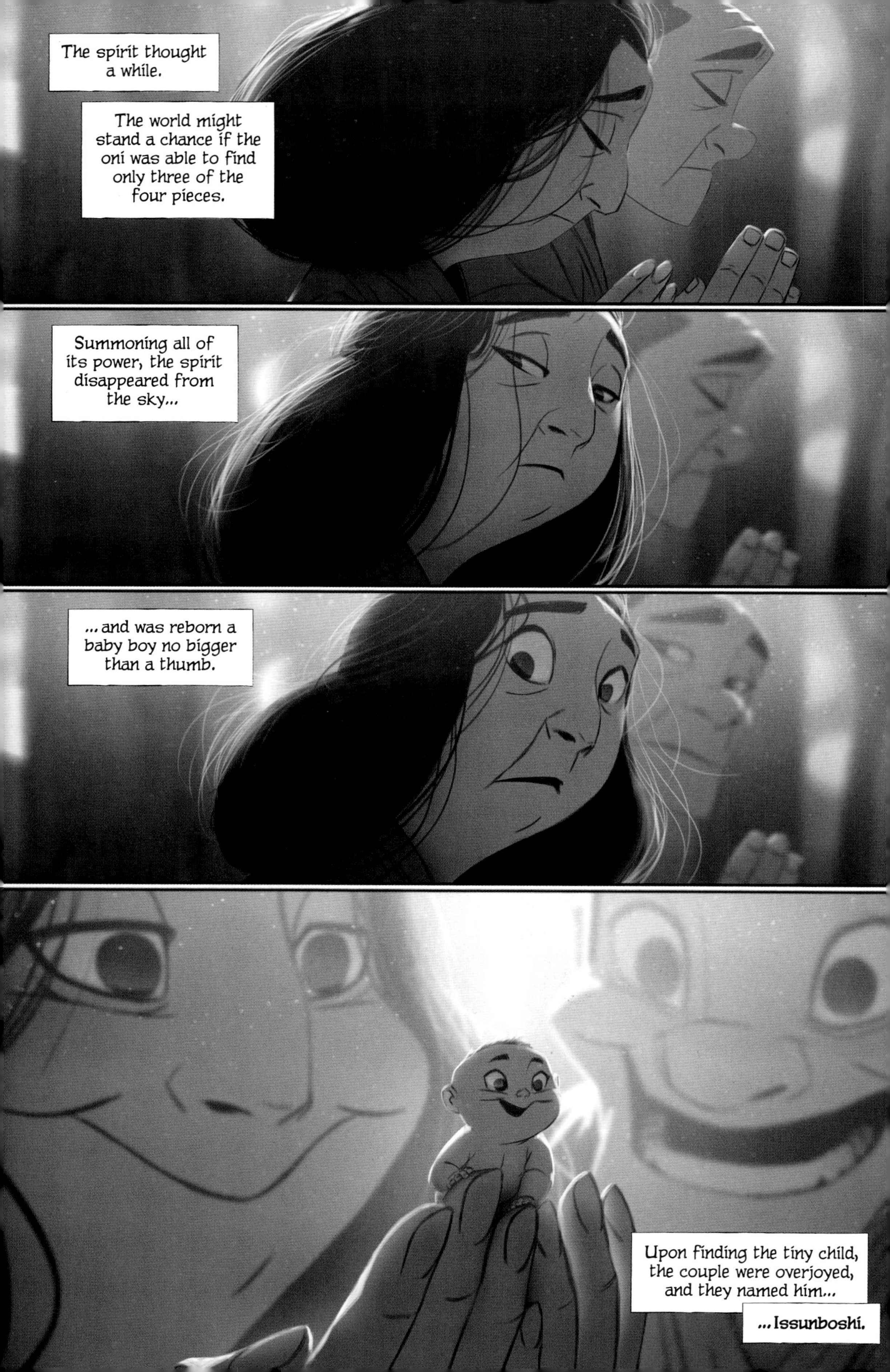
The spirit thought a while.
The world might stand a chance if the oni was able to find only three of the four pieces.
Summoning all of its power, the spirit disappeared from the sky...
...and was reborn a baby boy no bigger than a thumb.
Upon finding the tiny child, the couple were overjoyed, and they named him...
...Issunboshi.

ONE

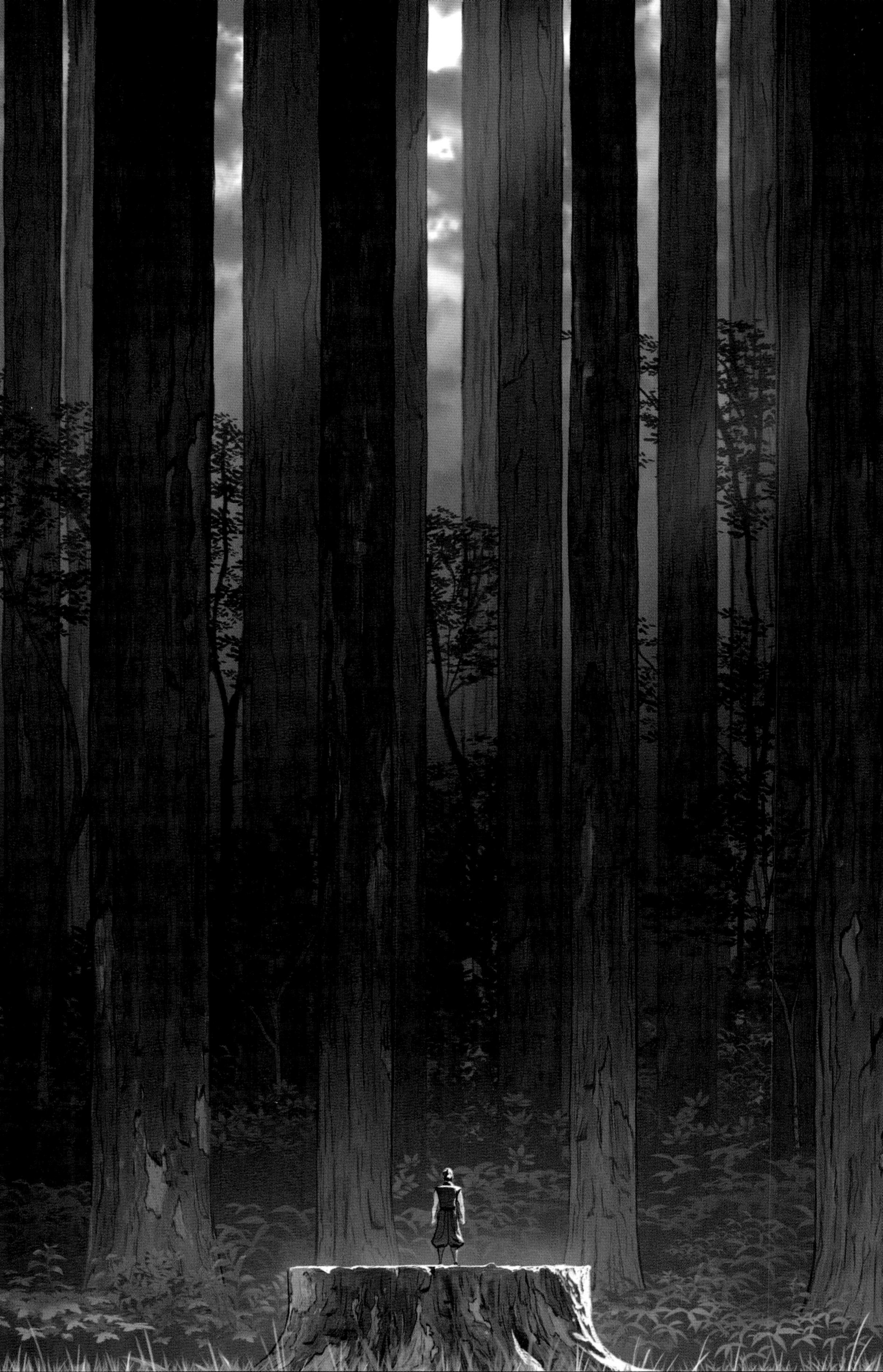

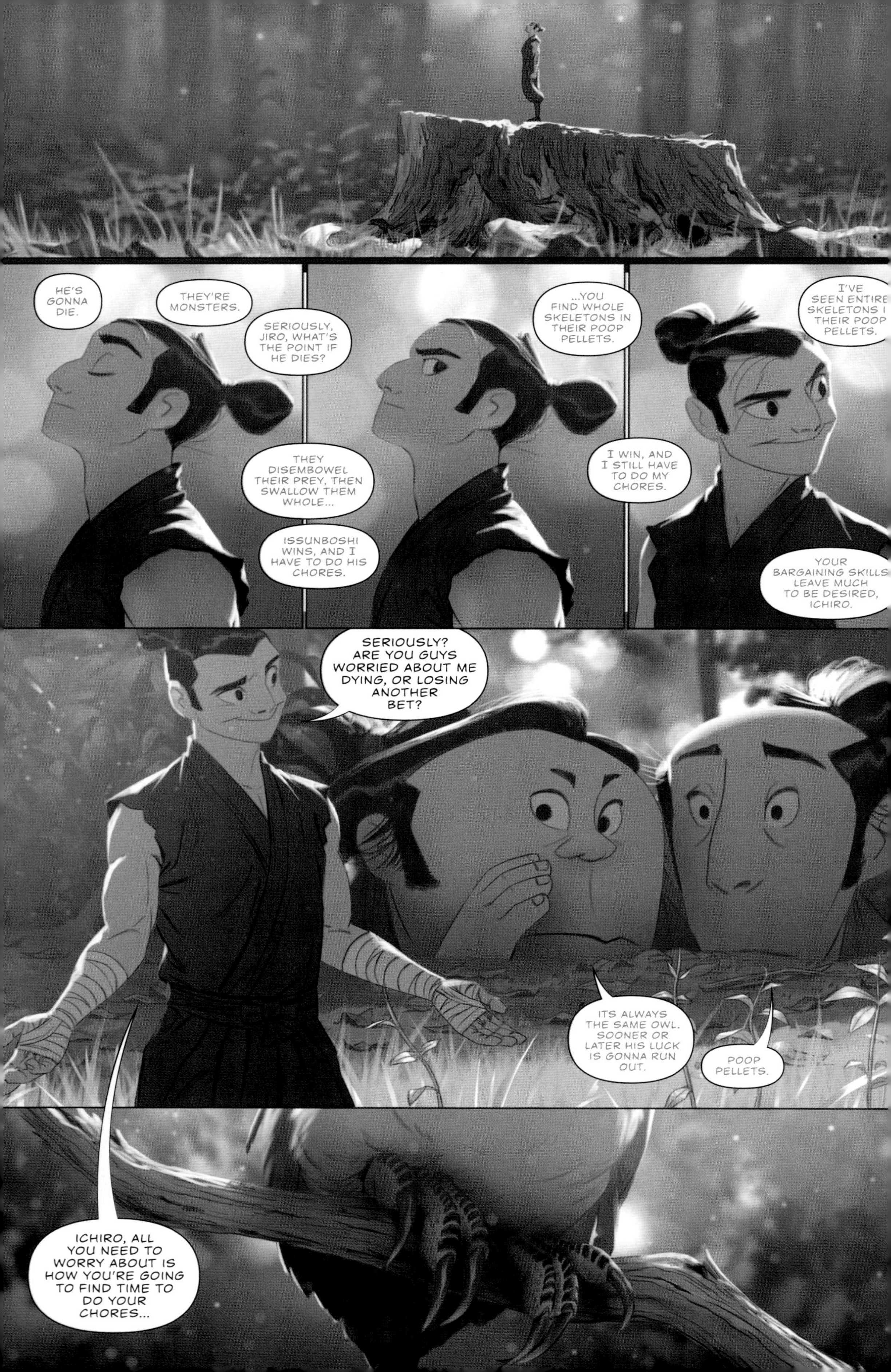
HE'S GONNA DIE.
THEY'RE MONSTERS.
SERIOUSLY, JIRO, WHAT'S THE POINT IF HE DIES?
THEY DISEMBOWEL THEIR PREY, THEN SWALLOW THEM WHOLE...
ISSUNBOSHI WINS, AND I HAVE TO DO HIS CHORES.
...YOU FIND WHOLE SKELETONS IN THEIR POOP PELLETS.
I WIN, AND I STILL HAVE TO DO MY CHORES.
I'VE SEEN ENTIRE SKELETONS I THEIR POOP PELLETS.
YOUR BARGAINING SKILLS LEAVE MUCH TO BE DESIRED, ICHIRO.
SERIOUSLY? ARE YOU GUYS WORRIED ABOUT ME DYING, OR LOSING ANOTHER BET?
ITS ALWAYS THE SAME OWL. SOONER OR LATER HIS LUCK IS GONNA RUN OUT.
POOP PELLETS.
ICHIRO, ALL YOU NEED TO WORRY ABOUT IS HOW YOU'RE GOING TO FIND TIME TO DO YOUR CHORES...

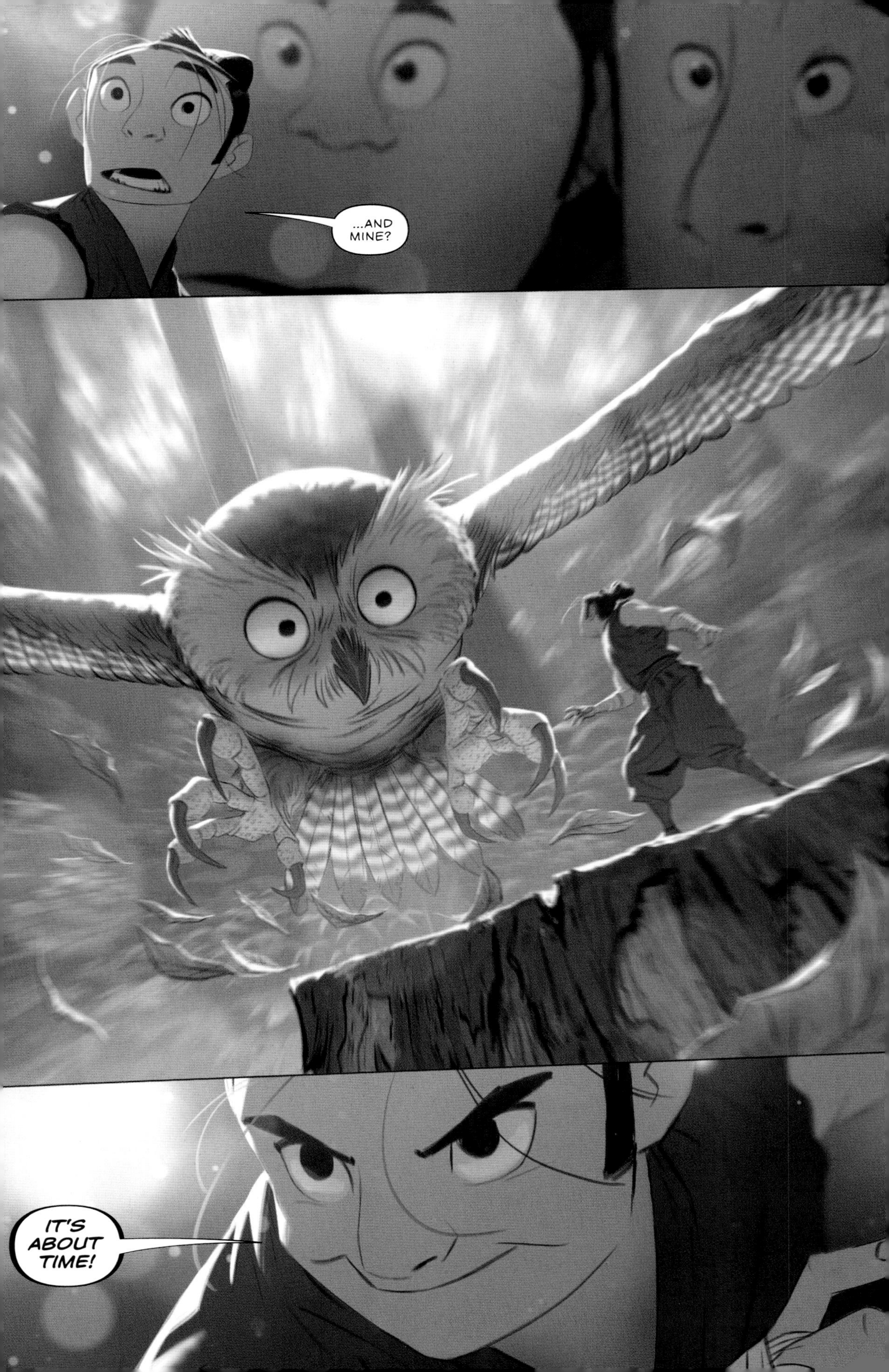
...AND MINE?
IT'S ABOUT TIME!

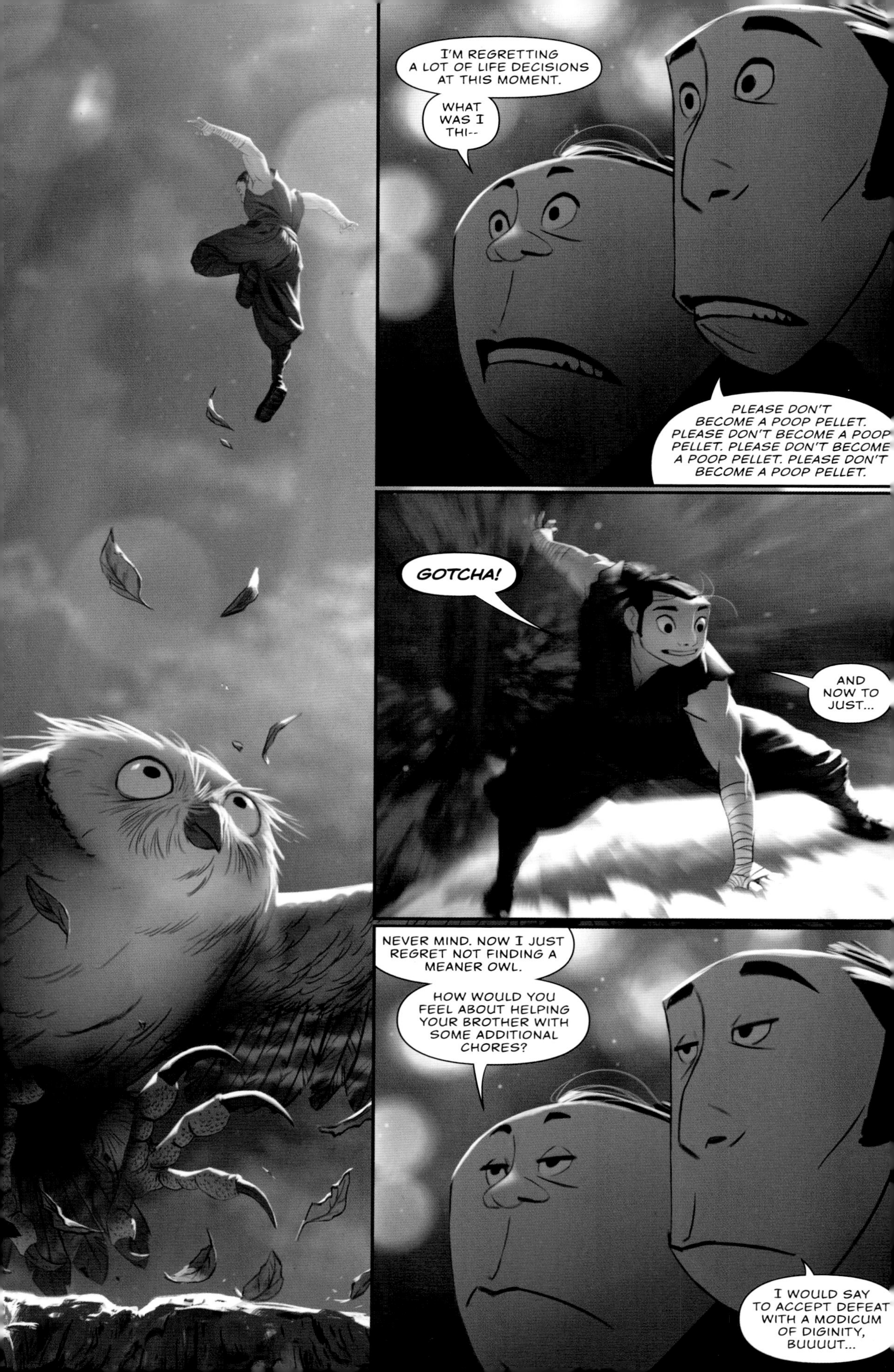

I'M REGRETTING A LOT OF LIFE DECISIONS AT THIS MOMENT.
WHAT WAS I THI--
PLEASE DON'T BECOME A POOP PELLET. PLEASE DON'T BECOME A POOP PELLET. PLEASE DON'T BECOME A POOP PELLET. PLEASE DON'T BECOME A POOP PELLET.
GOTCHA!
AND NOW TO JUST...
NEVER MIND. NOW I JUST REGRET NOT FINDING A MEANER OWL.
HOW WOULD YOU FEEL ABOUT HELPING YOUR BROTHER WITH SOME ADDITIONAL CHORES?
I WOULD SAY TO ACCEPT DEFEAT WITH A MODICUM OF DIGINITY, BUUUUT...

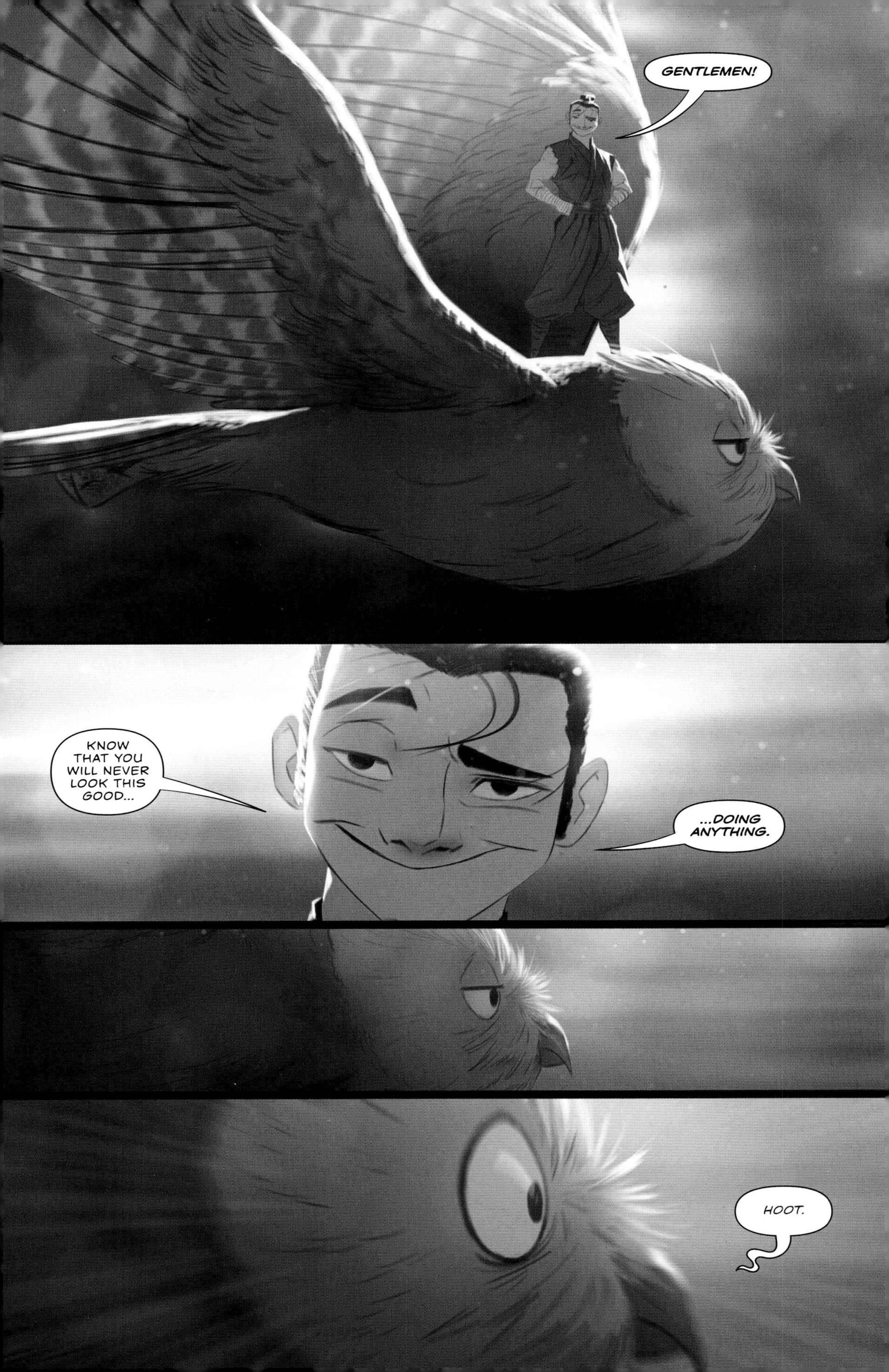
GENTLEMEN!
KNOW THAT YOU WILL NEVER LOOK THIS GOOD...
...DOING ANYTHING.
HOOT.

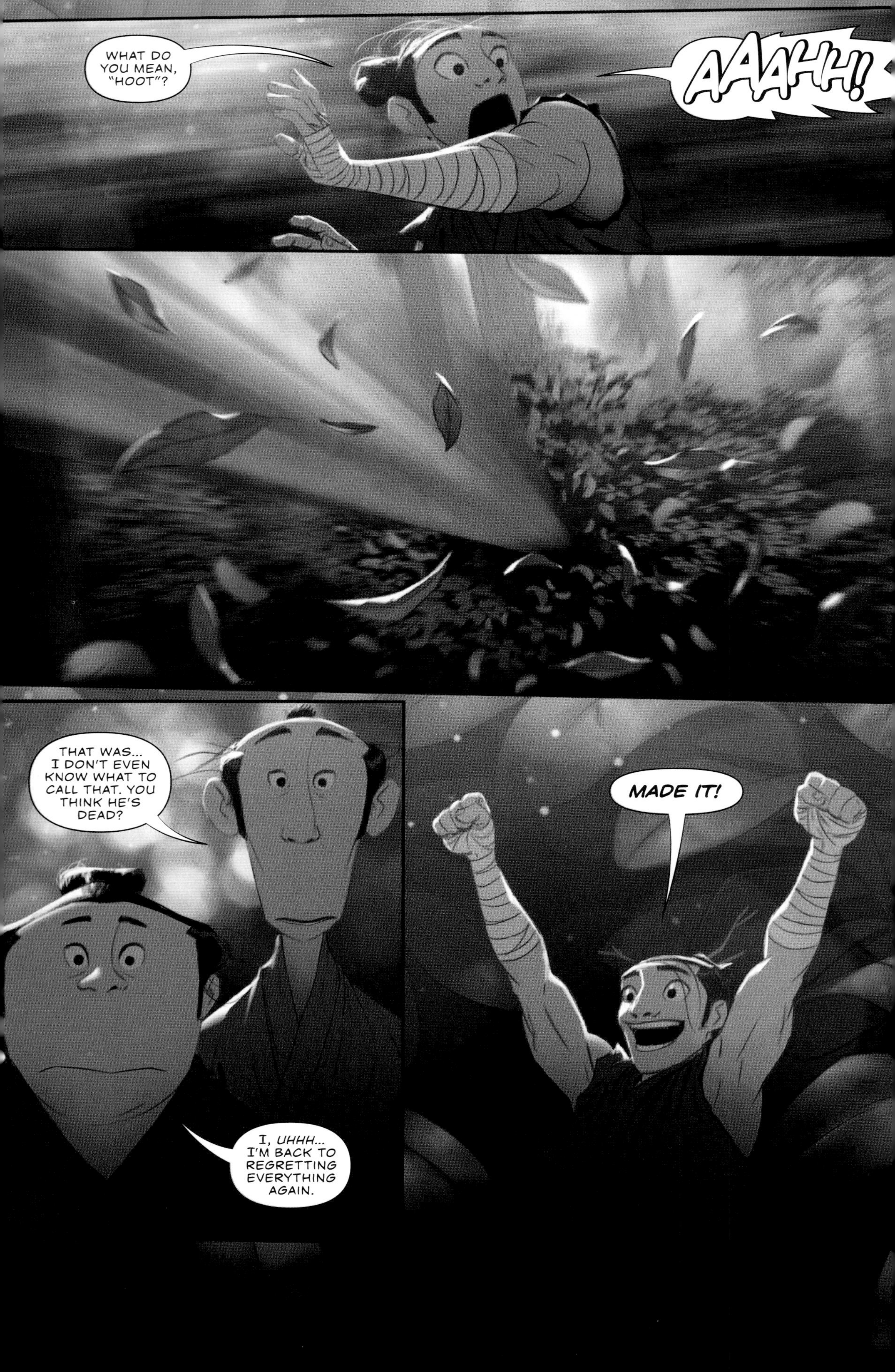
WHAT DO YOU MEAN, "HOOT"?
AAAHH!
THAT WAS... I DON'T EVEN KNOW WHAT TO CALL THAT. YOU THINK HE'S DEAD?
I, UHHH... I'M BACK TO REGRETTING EVERYTHING AGAIN.
MADE IT!

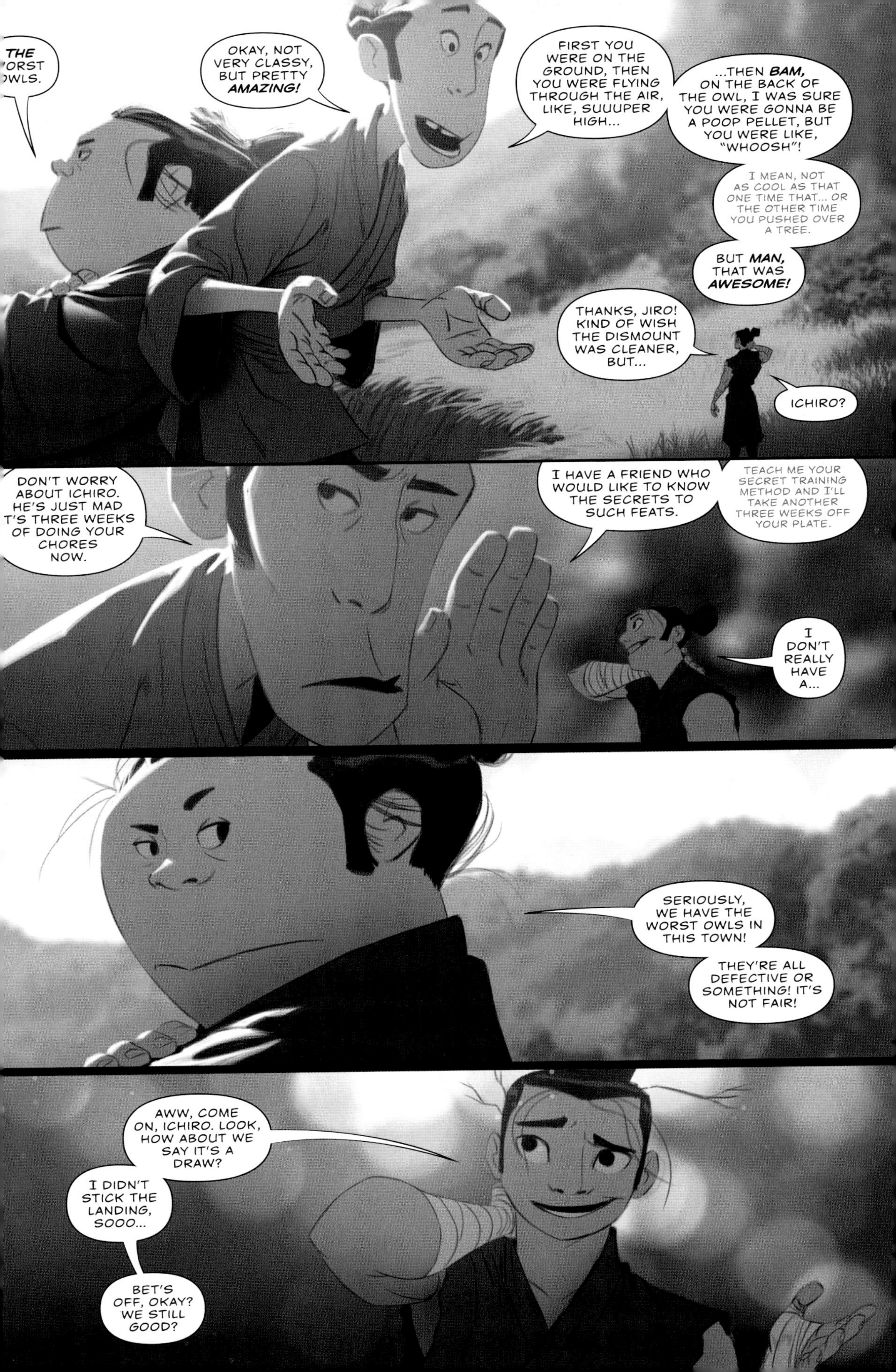
THE WORST OWLS.
OKAY, NOT VERY CLASSY, BUT PRETTY AMAZING!
FIRST YOU WERE ON THE GROUND, THEN YOU WERE FLYING THROUGH THE AIR, LIKE, SUUUPER HIGH...
...THEN BAM, ON THE BACK OF THE OWL, I WAS SURE YOU WERE GONNA BE A POOP PELLET, BUT YOU WERE LIKE, "WHOOSH"!
I MEAN, NOT AS COOL AS THAT ONE TIME THAT... OR THE OTHER TIME YOU PUSHED OVER A TREE.
BUT MAN, THAT WAS AWESOME!
THANKS, JIRO! KIND OF WISH THE DISMOUNT WAS CLEANER, BUT...
ICHIRO?
DON'T WORRY ABOUT ICHIRO. HE'S JUST MAD IT'S THREE WEEKS OF DOING YOUR CHORES NOW.
I HAVE A FRIEND WHO WOULD LIKE TO KNOW THE SECRETS TO SUCH FEATS.
TEACH ME YOUR SECRET TRAINING METHOD AND I'LL TAKE ANOTHER THREE WEEKS OFF YOUR PLATE.
I DON'T REALLY HAVE A...
SERIOUSLY, WE HAVE THE WORST OWLS IN THIS TOWN!
THEY'RE ALL DEFECTIVE OR SOMETHING! IT'S NOT FAIR!
AWW, COME ON, ICHIRO. LOOK, HOW ABOUT WE SAY IT'S A DRAW?
I DIDN'T STICK THE LANDING, SOOO...
BET'S OFF, OKAY? WE STILL GOOD?

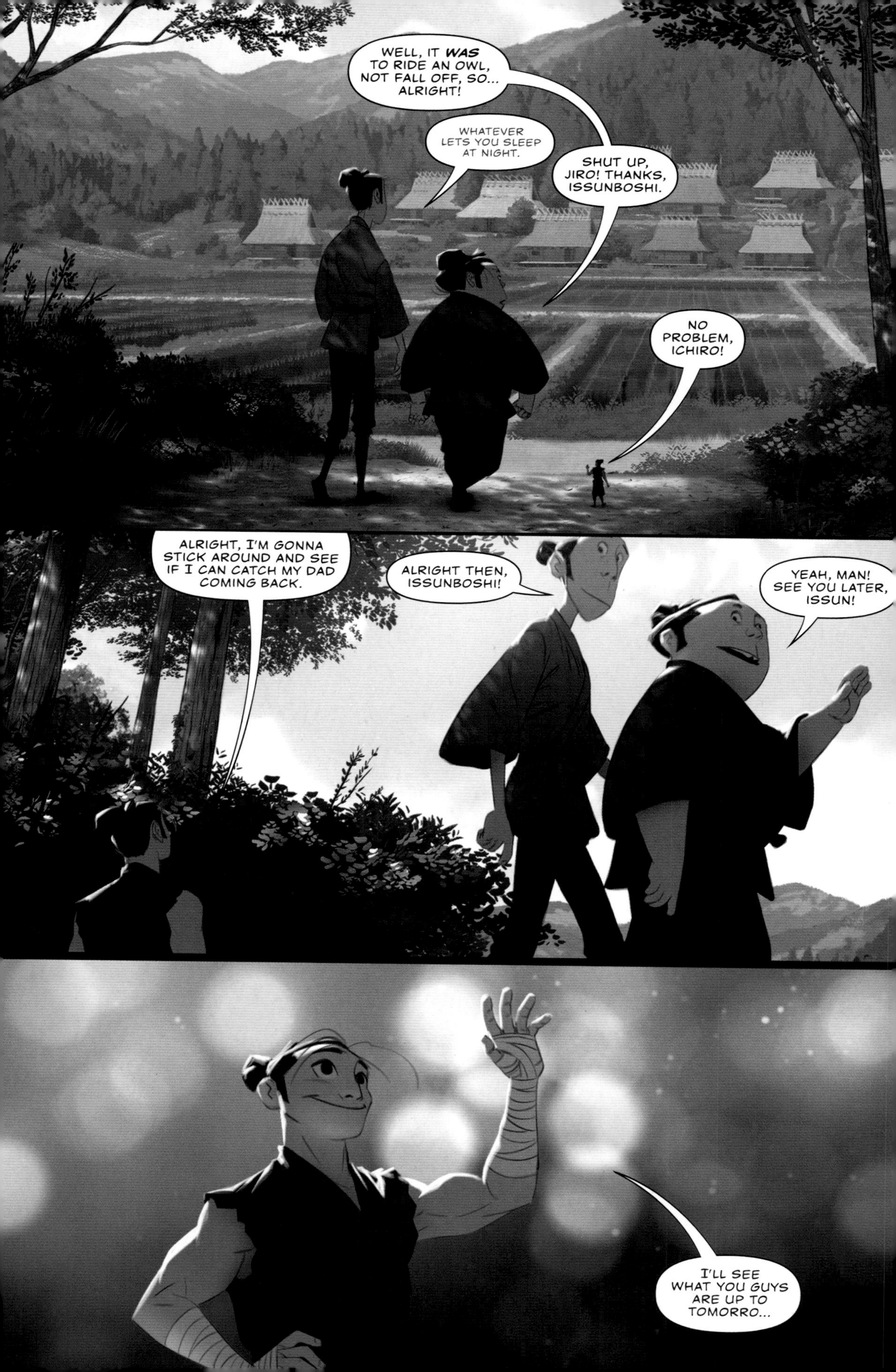
WELL, IT *WAS* TO RIDE AN OWL, NOT FALL OFF, SO... ALRIGHT!
WHATEVER LETS YOU SLEEP AT NIGHT.
SHUT UP, JIRO! THANKS, ISSUNBOSHI.
NO PROBLEM, ICHIRO!
ALRIGHT, I'M GONNA STICK AROUND AND SEE IF I CAN CATCH MY DAD COMING BACK.
ALRIGHT THEN, ISSUNBOSHI!
YEAH, MAN! SEE YOU LATER, ISSUN!
I'LL SEE WHAT YOU GUYS ARE UP TO TOMORRO...

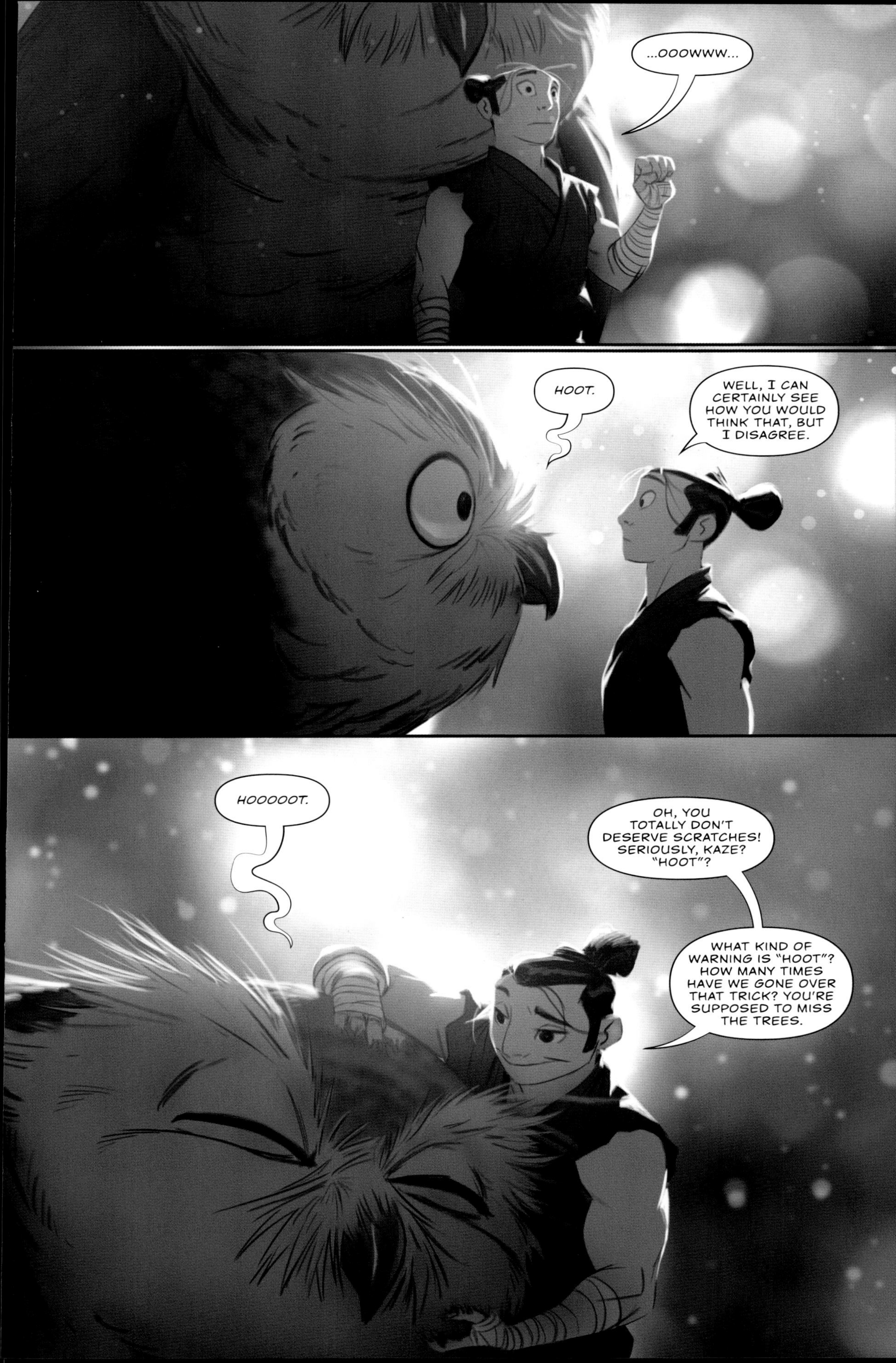
...OOOWWW...
HOOT.
WELL, I CAN CERTAINLY SEE HOW YOU WOULD THINK THAT, BUT I DISAGREE.
HOOOOOT.
OH, YOU TOTALLY DON'T DESERVE SCRATCHES! SERIOUSLY, KAZE? "HOOT"?
WHAT KIND OF WARNING IS "HOOT"? HOW MANY TIMES HAVE WE GONE OVER THAT TRICK? YOU'RE SUPPOSED TO MISS THE TREES.

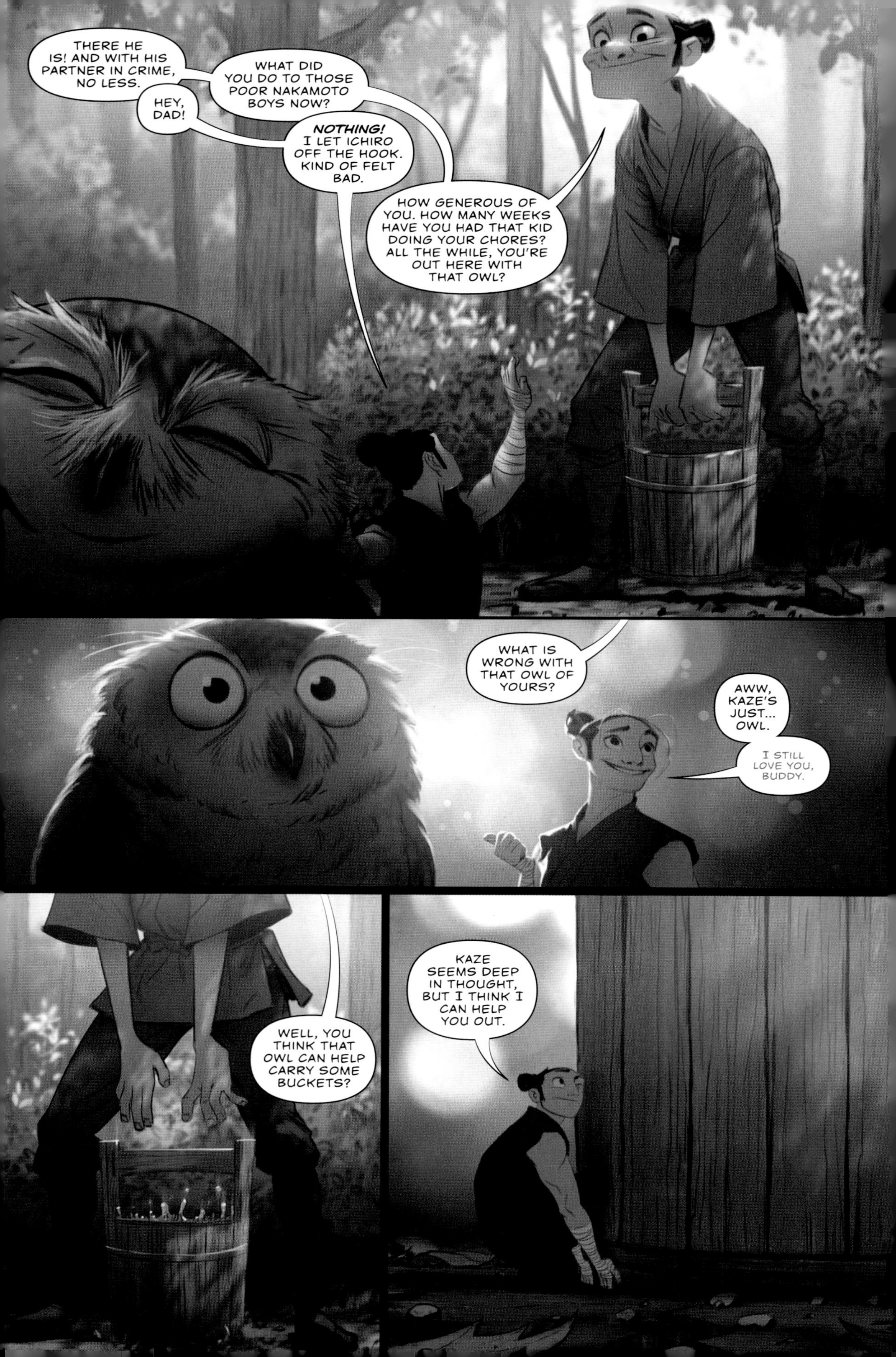
THERE HE IS! AND WITH HIS PARTNER IN CRIME, NO LESS.
WHAT DID YOU DO TO THOSE POOR NAKAMOTO BOYS NOW?
HEY, DAD!
NOTHING! I LET ICHIRO OFF THE HOOK. KIND OF FELT BAD.
HOW GENEROUS OF YOU. HOW MANY WEEKS HAVE YOU HAD THAT KID DOING YOUR CHORES? ALL THE WHILE, YOU'RE OUT HERE WITH THAT OWL?
WHAT IS WRONG WITH THAT OWL OF YOURS?
AWW, KAZE'S JUST... OWL.
I STILL LOVE YOU, BUDDY.
WELL, YOU THINK THAT OWL CAN HELP CARRY SOME BUCKETS?
KAZE SEEMS DEEP IN THOUGHT, BUT I THINK I CAN HELP YOU OUT.

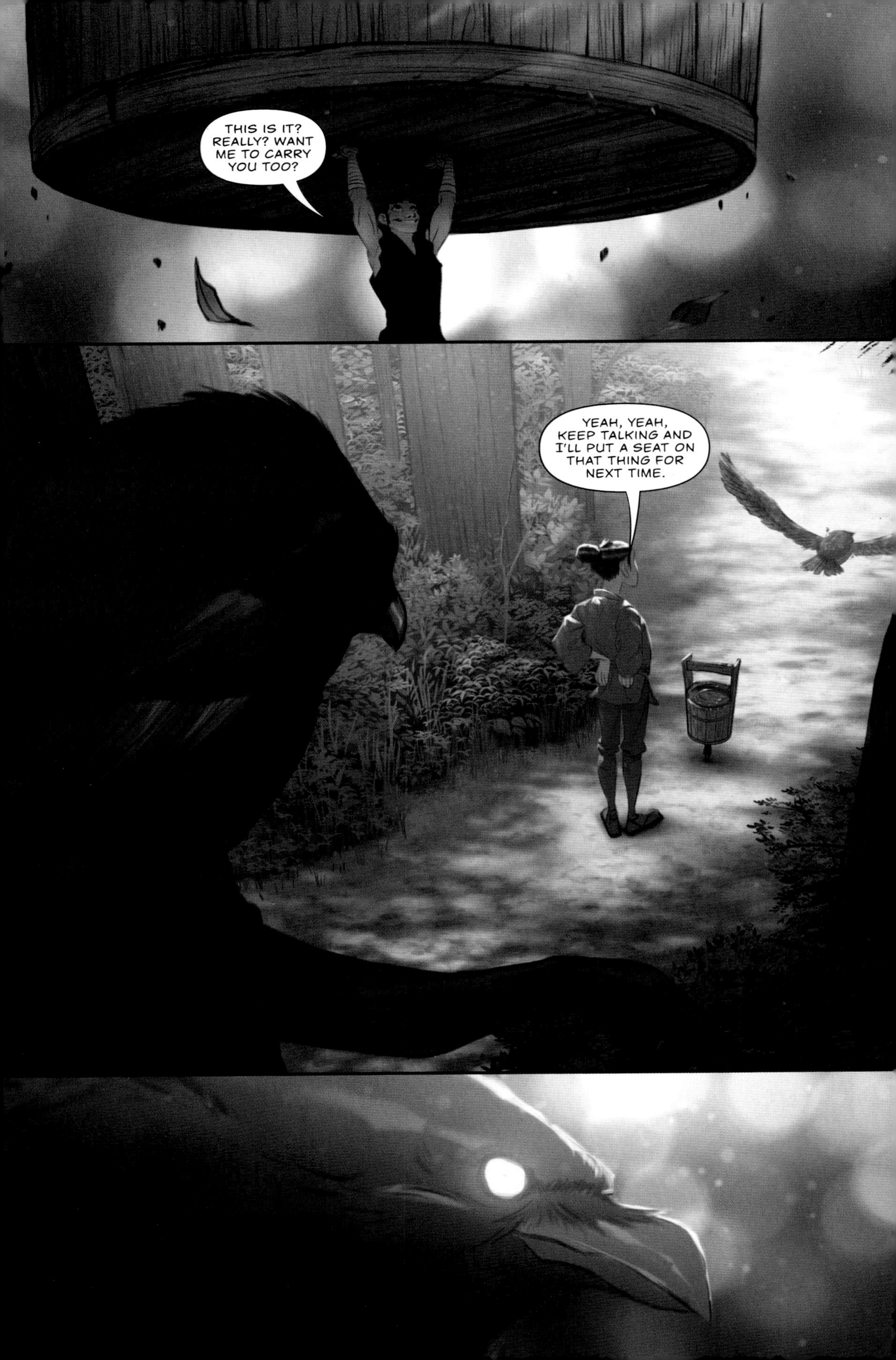
THIS IS IT? REALLY? WANT ME TO CARRY YOU TOO?
YEAH, YEAH, KEEP TALKING AND I'LL PUT A SEAT ON THAT THING FOR NEXT TIME.

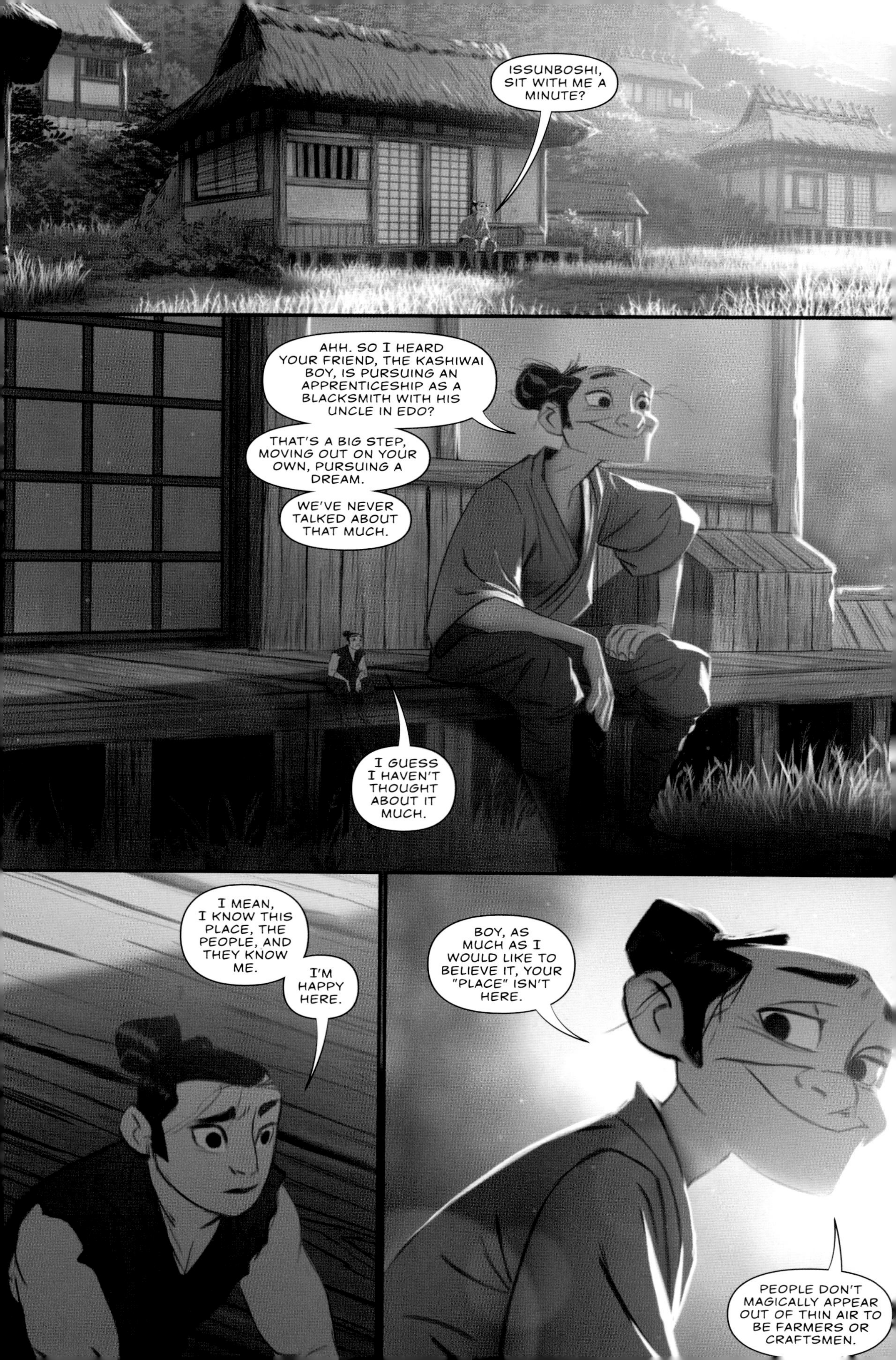
ISSUNBOSHI, SIT WITH ME A MINUTE?
AHH. SO I HEARD YOUR FRIEND, THE KASHIWAI BOY, IS PURSUING AN APPRENTICESHIP AS A BLACKSMITH WITH HIS UNCLE IN EDO?
THAT'S A BIG STEP, MOVING OUT ON YOUR OWN, PURSUING A DREAM.
WE'VE NEVER TALKED ABOUT THAT MUCH.
I GUESS I HAVEN'T THOUGHT ABOUT IT MUCH.
I MEAN, I KNOW THIS PLACE, THE PEOPLE, AND THEY KNOW ME.
I'M HAPPY HERE.
BOY, AS MUCH AS I WOULD LIKE TO BELIEVE IT, YOUR "PLACE" ISN'T HERE.
PEOPLE DON'T MAGICALLY APPEAR OUT OF THIN AIR TO BE FARMERS OR CRAFTSMEN.

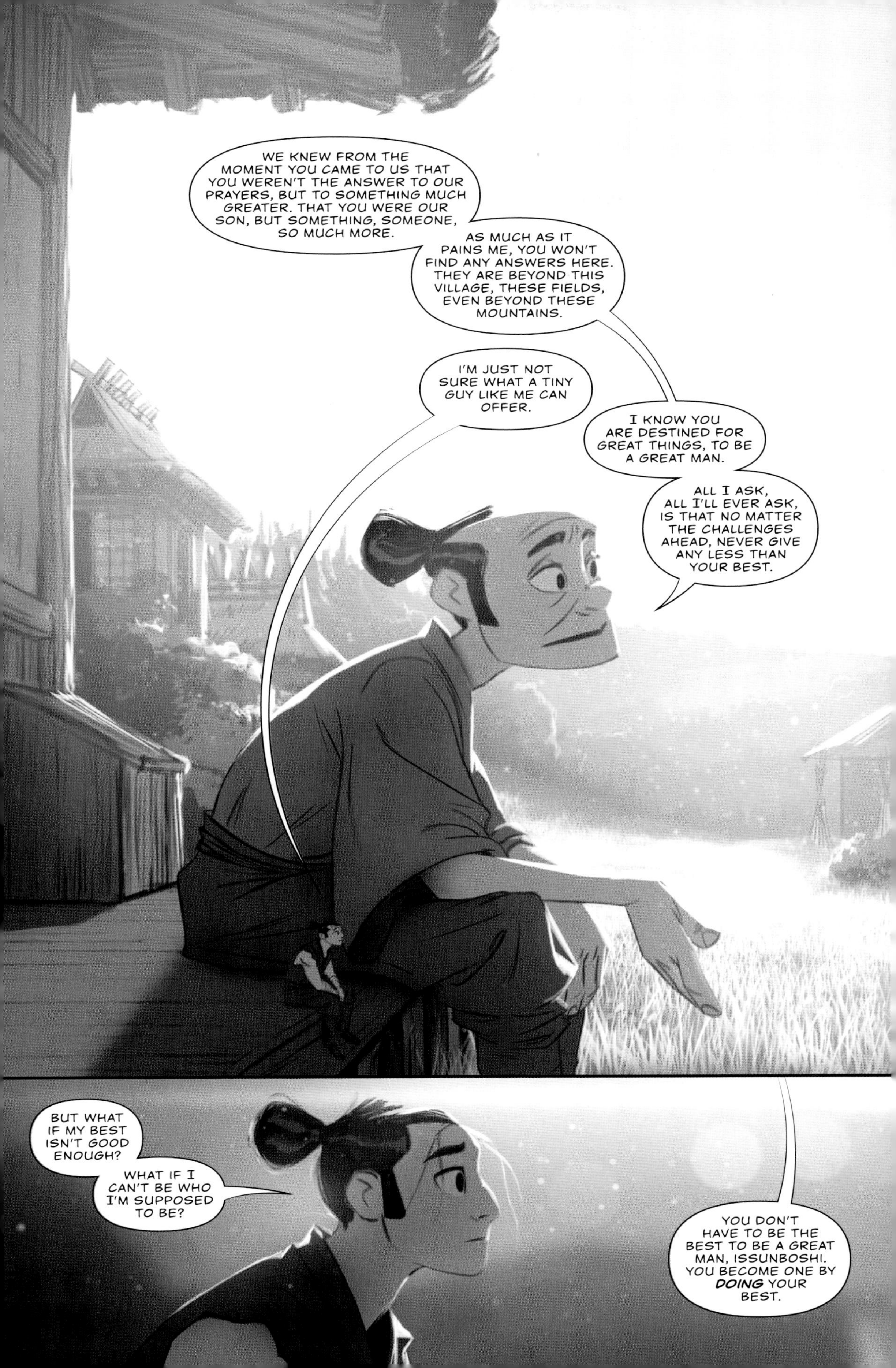
WE KNEW FROM THE MOMENT YOU CAME TO US THAT YOU WEREN'T THE ANSWER TO OUR PRAYERS, BUT TO SOMETHING MUCH GREATER. THAT YOU WERE OUR SON, BUT SOMETHING, SOMEONE, SO MUCH MORE.
AS MUCH AS IT PAINS ME, YOU WON'T FIND ANY ANSWERS HERE. THEY ARE BEYOND THIS VILLAGE, THESE FIELDS, EVEN BEYOND THESE MOUNTAINS.
I'M JUST NOT SURE WHAT A TINY GUY LIKE ME CAN OFFER.
I KNOW YOU ARE DESTINED FOR GREAT THINGS, TO BE A GREAT MAN.
ALL I ASK, ALL I'LL EVER ASK, IS THAT NO MATTER THE CHALLENGES AHEAD, NEVER GIVE ANY LESS THAN YOUR BEST.
BUT WHAT IF MY BEST ISN'T GOOD ENOUGH?
WHAT IF I CAN'T BE WHO I'M SUPPOSED TO BE?
YOU DON'T HAVE TO BE THE BEST TO BE A GREAT MAN, ISSUNBOSHI. YOU BECOME ONE BY *DOING* YOUR BEST.

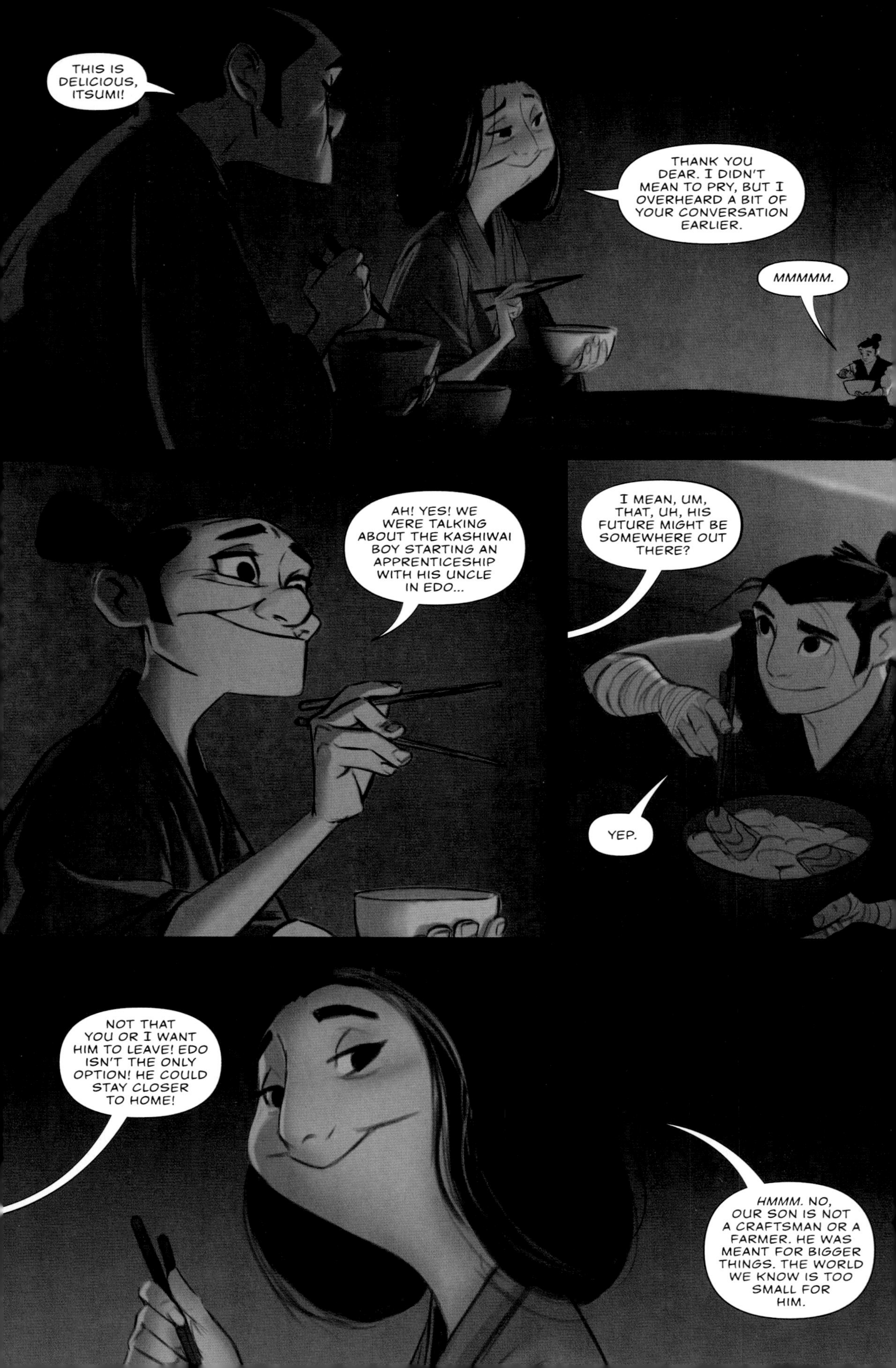
THIS IS DELICIOUS, ITSUMI!
THANK YOU DEAR. I DIDN'T MEAN TO PRY, BUT I OVERHEARD A BIT OF YOUR CONVERSATION EARLIER.
MMMMM.
AH! YES! WE WERE TALKING ABOUT THE KASHIWAI BOY STARTING AN APPRENTICESHIP WITH HIS UNCLE IN EDO...
I MEAN, UM, THAT, UH, HIS FUTURE MIGHT BE SOMEWHERE OUT THERE?
YEP.
NOT THAT YOU OR I WANT HIM TO LEAVE! EDO ISN'T THE ONLY OPTION! HE COULD STAY CLOSER TO HOME!
HMMM. NO, OUR SON IS NOT A CRAFTSMAN OR A FARMER. HE WAS MEANT FOR BIGGER THINGS. THE WORLD WE KNOW IS TOO SMALL FOR HIM.

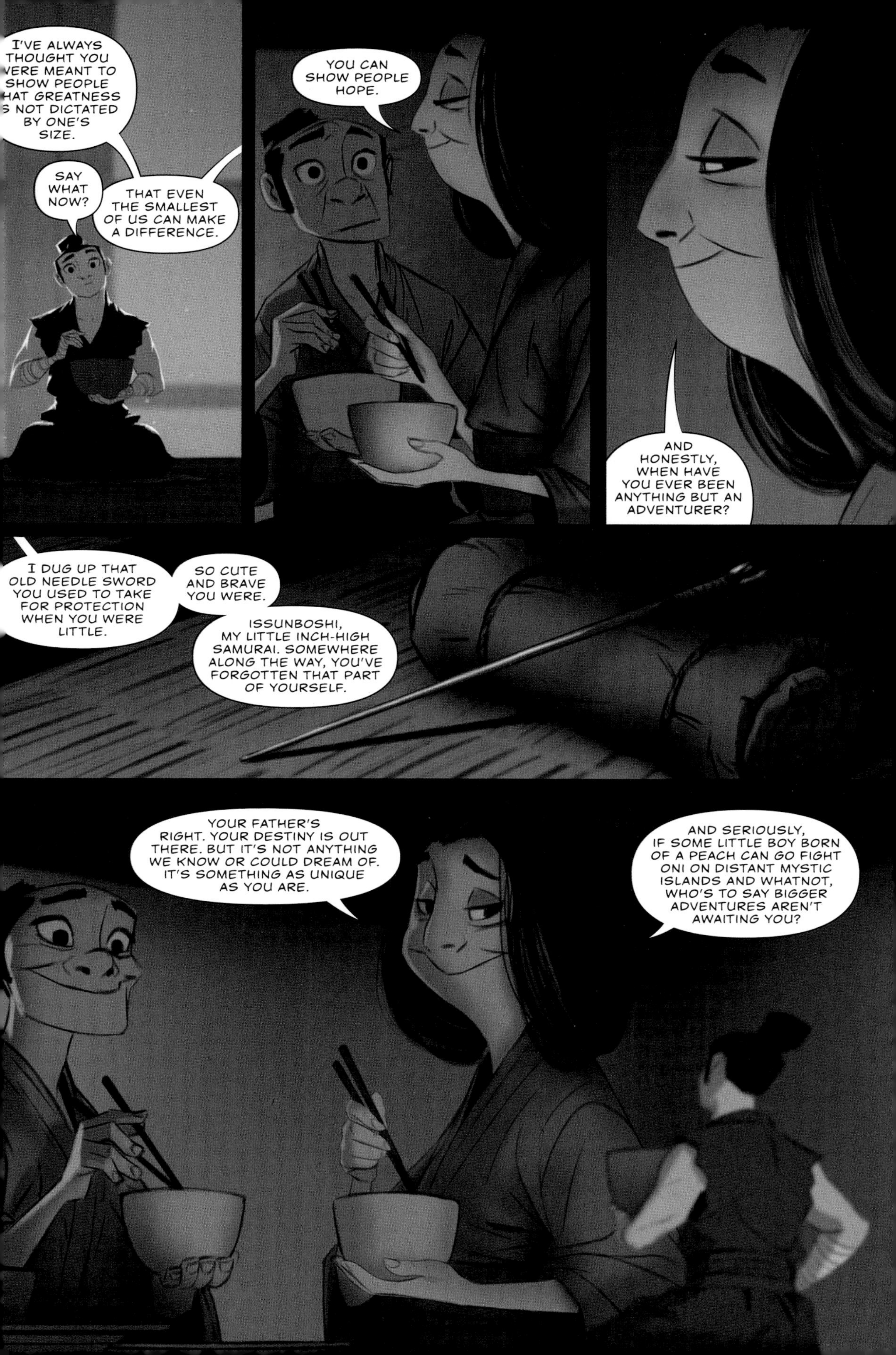

I'VE ALWAYS THOUGHT YOU WERE MEANT TO SHOW PEOPLE THAT GREATNESS IS NOT DICTATED BY ONE'S SIZE.
SAY WHAT NOW?
THAT EVEN THE SMALLEST OF US CAN MAKE A DIFFERENCE.
YOU CAN SHOW PEOPLE HOPE.
AND HONESTLY, WHEN HAVE YOU EVER BEEN ANYTHING BUT AN ADVENTURER?
I DUG UP THAT OLD NEEDLE SWORD YOU USED TO TAKE FOR PROTECTION WHEN YOU WERE LITTLE.
SO CUTE AND BRAVE YOU WERE.
ISSUNBOSHI, MY LITTLE INCH-HIGH SAMURAI. SOMEWHERE ALONG THE WAY, YOU'VE FORGOTTEN THAT PART OF YOURSELF.
YOUR FATHER'S RIGHT. YOUR DESTINY IS OUT THERE. BUT IT'S NOT ANYTHING WE KNOW OR COULD DREAM OF. IT'S SOMETHING AS UNIQUE AS YOU ARE.
AND SERIOUSLY, IF SOME LITTLE BOY BORN OF A PEACH CAN GO FIGHT ONI ON DISTANT MYSTIC ISLANDS AND WHATNOT, WHO'S TO SAY BIGGER ADVENTURES AREN'T AWAITING YOU?

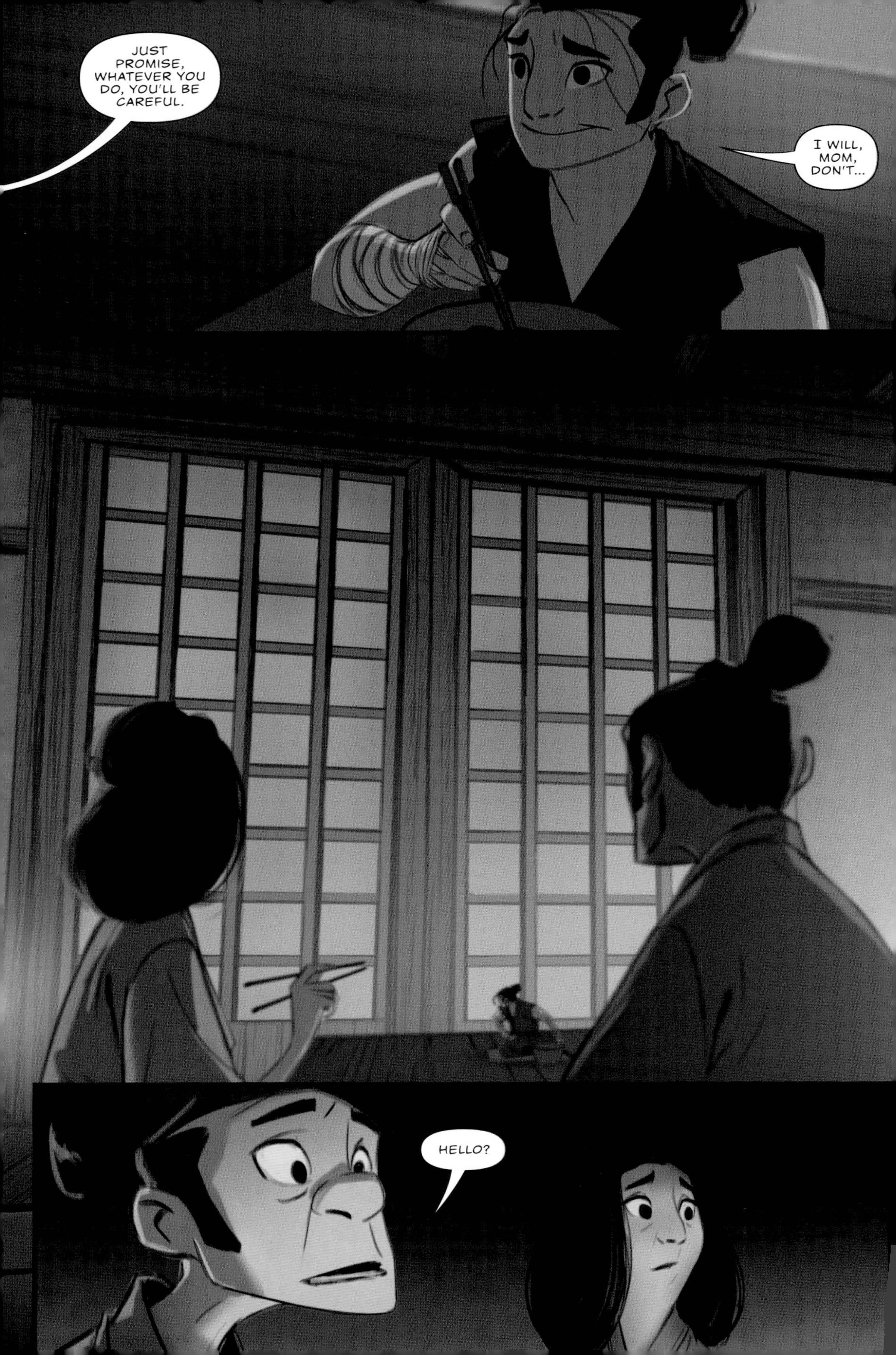
JUST PROMISE, WHATEVER YOU DO, YOU'LL BE CAREFUL.
I WILL, MOM, DON'T...
HELLO?

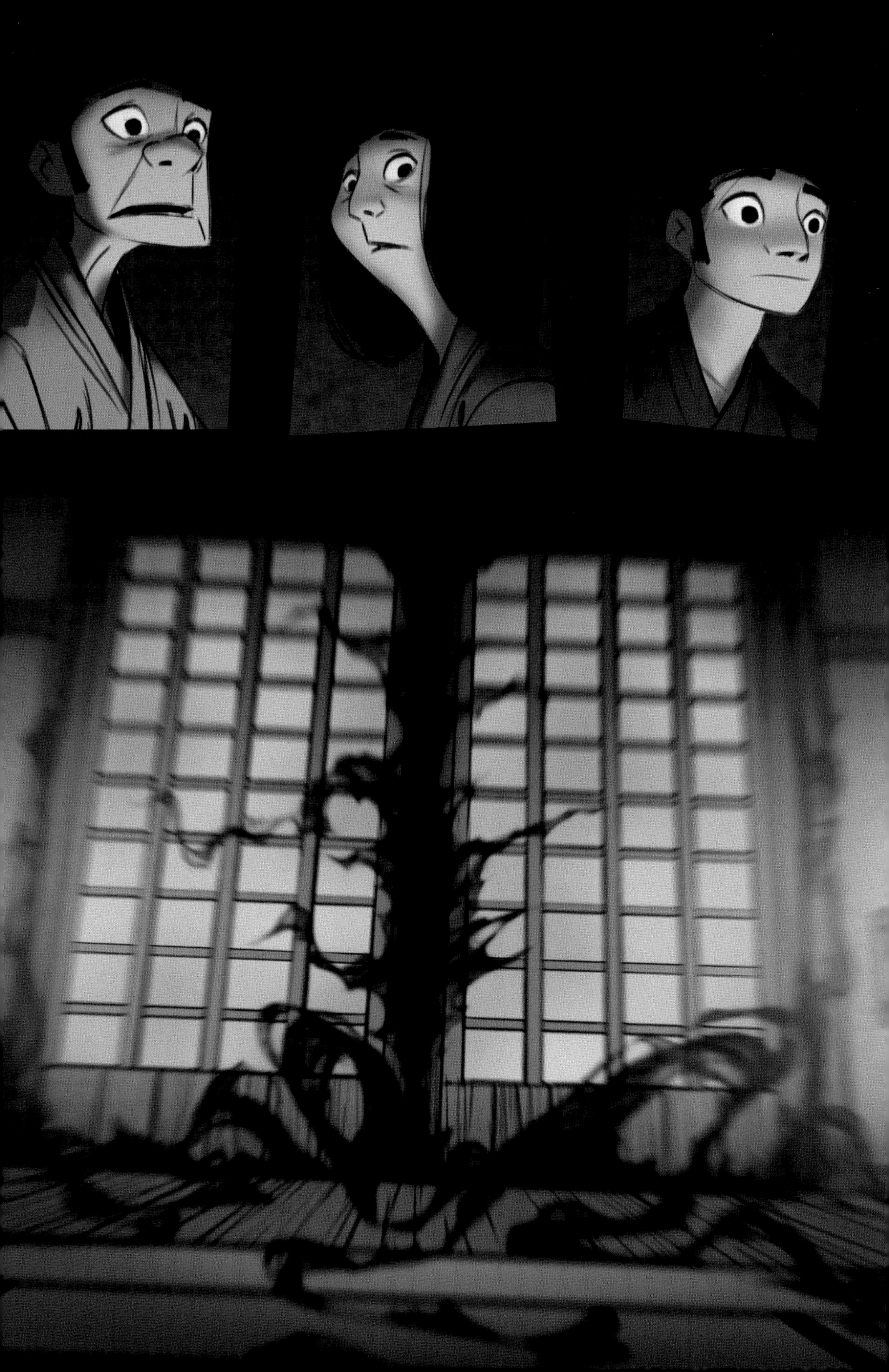

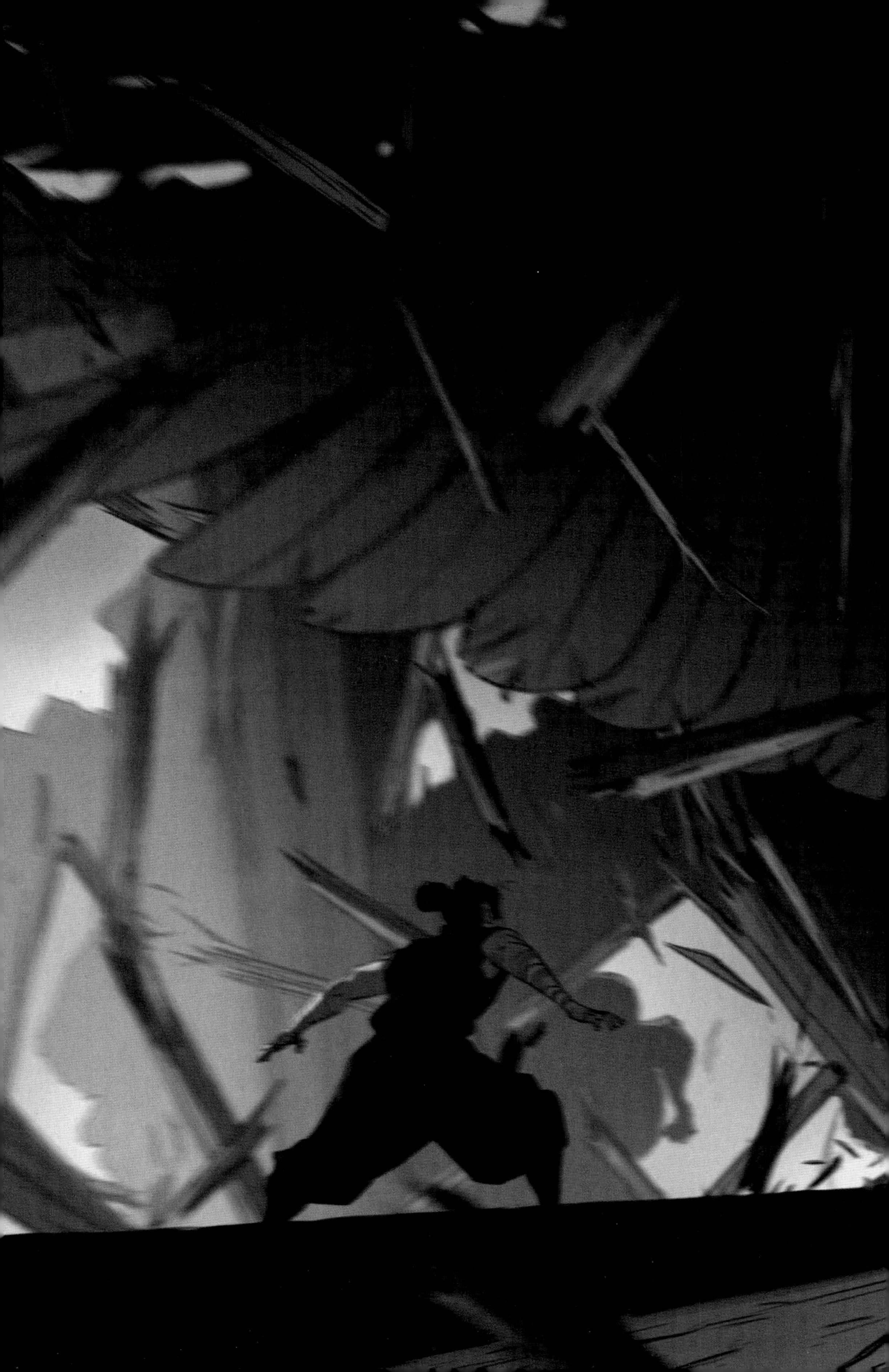

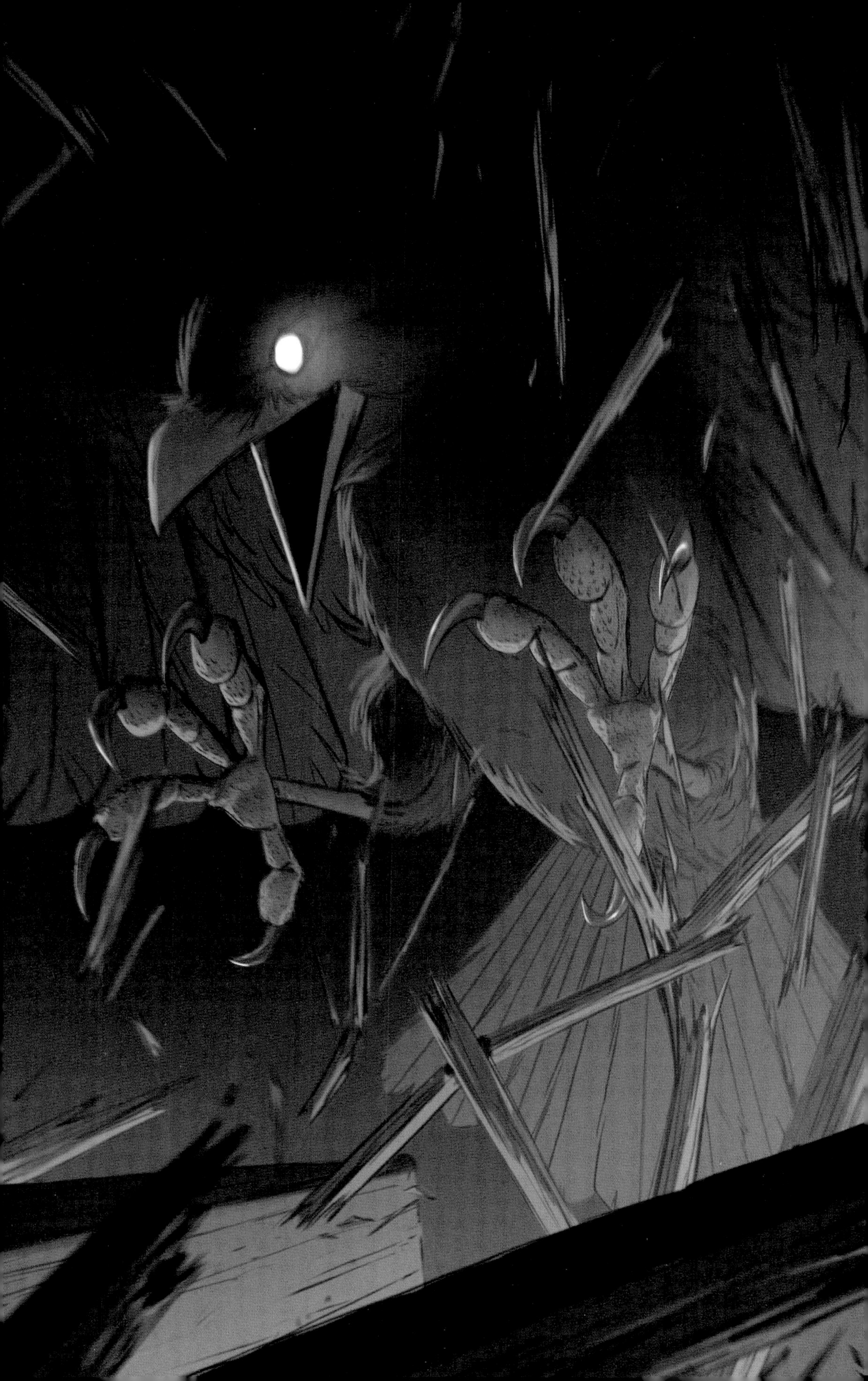

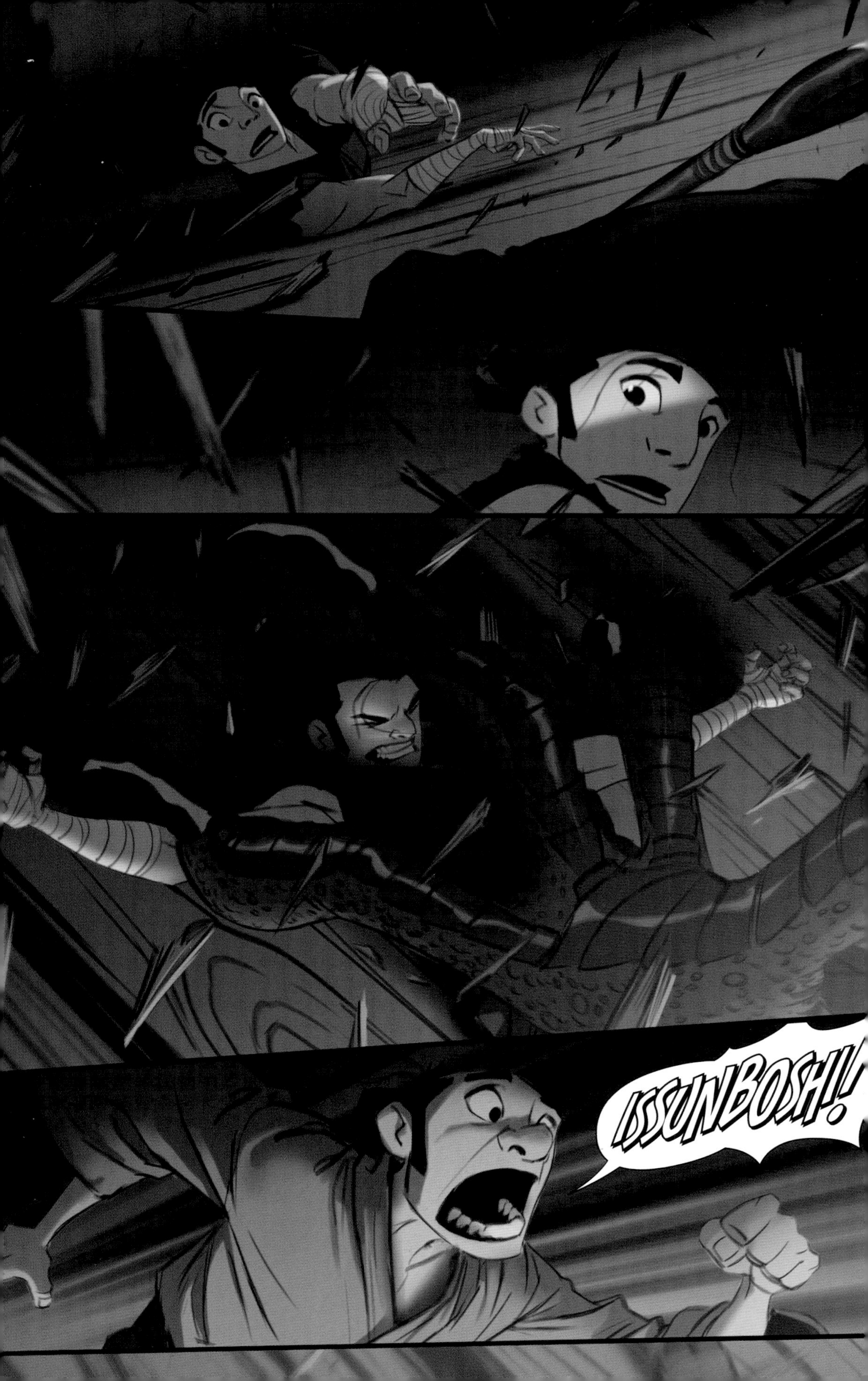
ISSUNBOSHI!

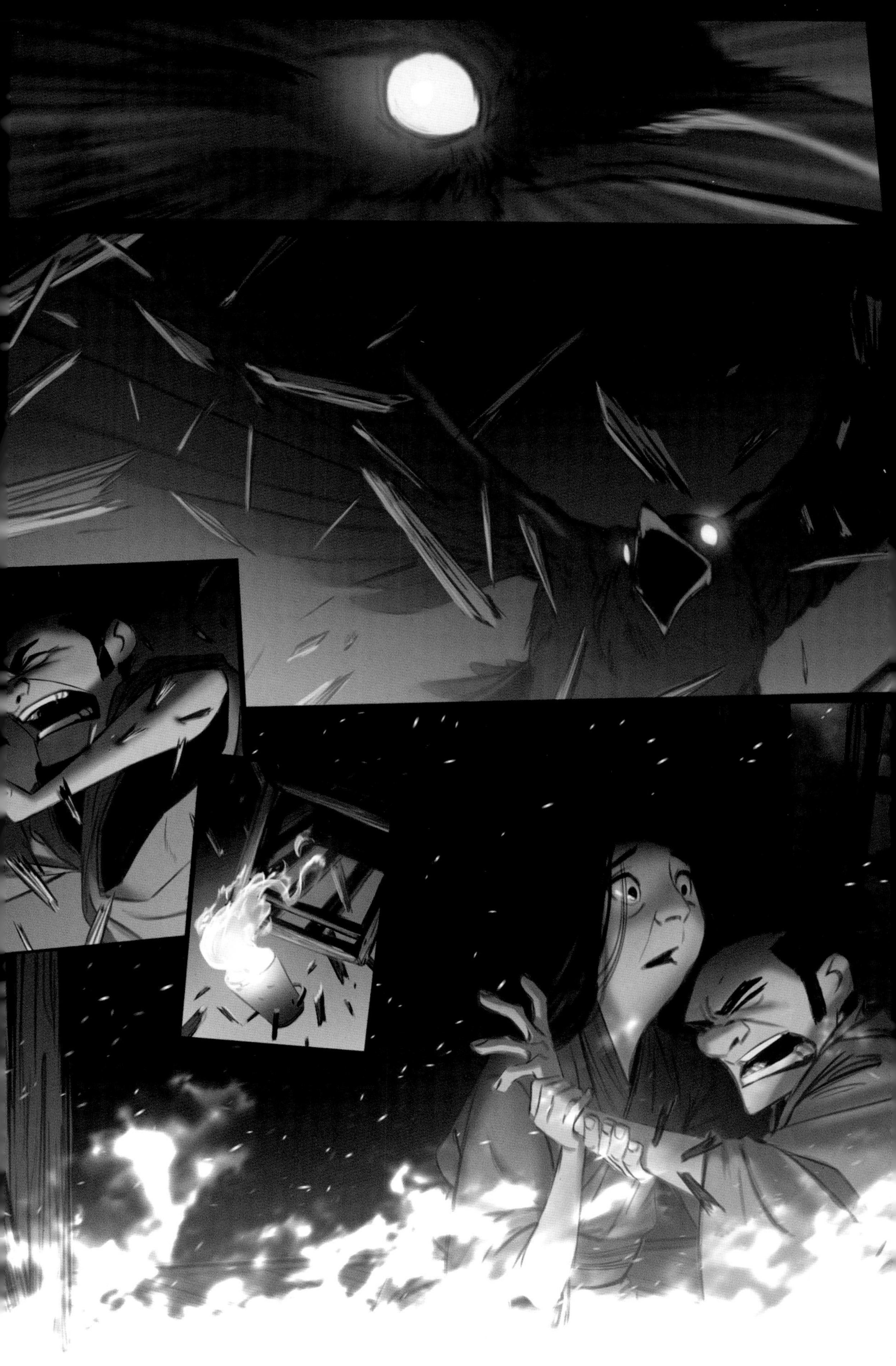

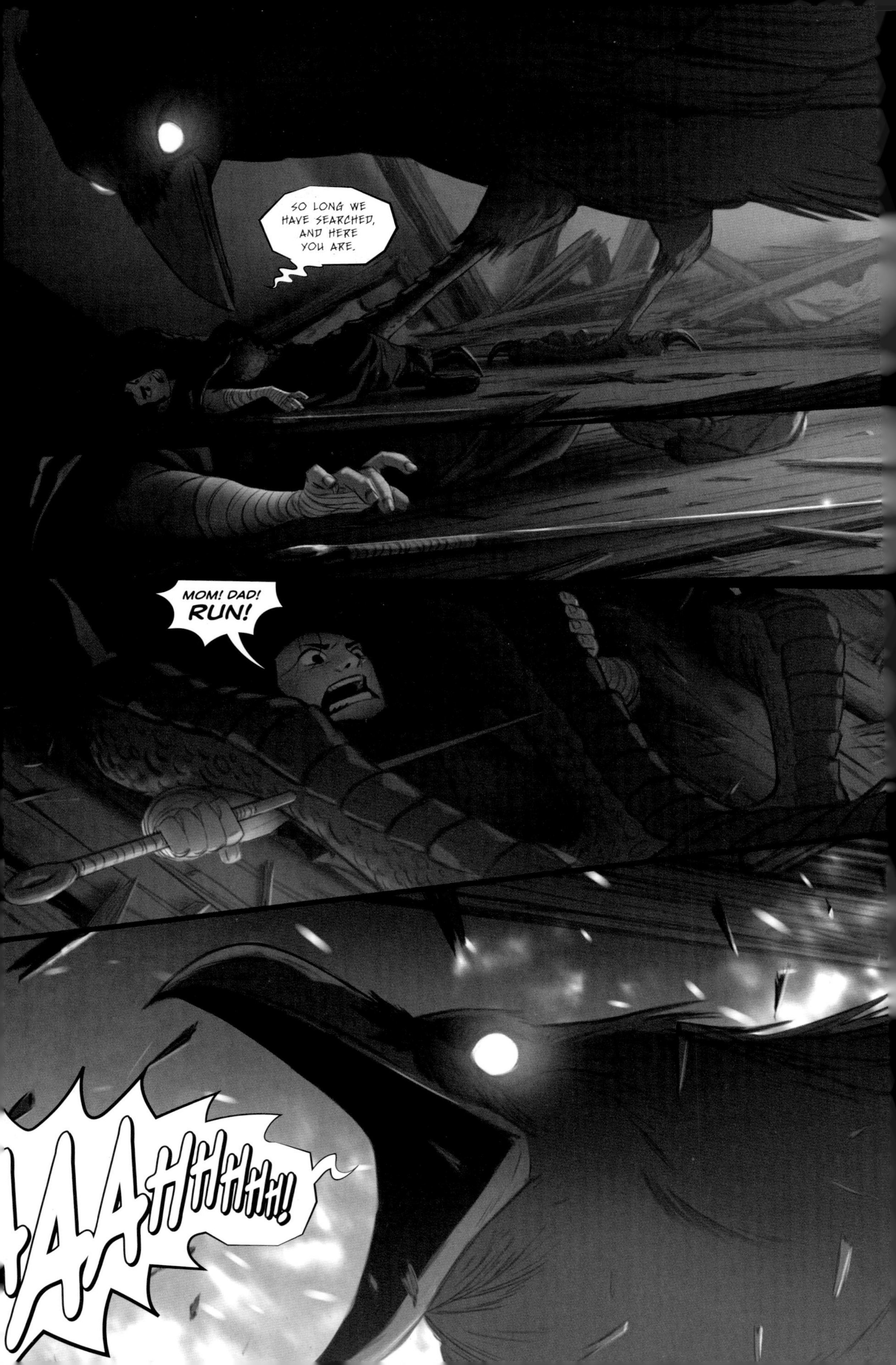
SO LONG WE HAVE SEARCHED, AND HERE YOU ARE.
MOM! DAD! RUN!
AAHHHHHH!

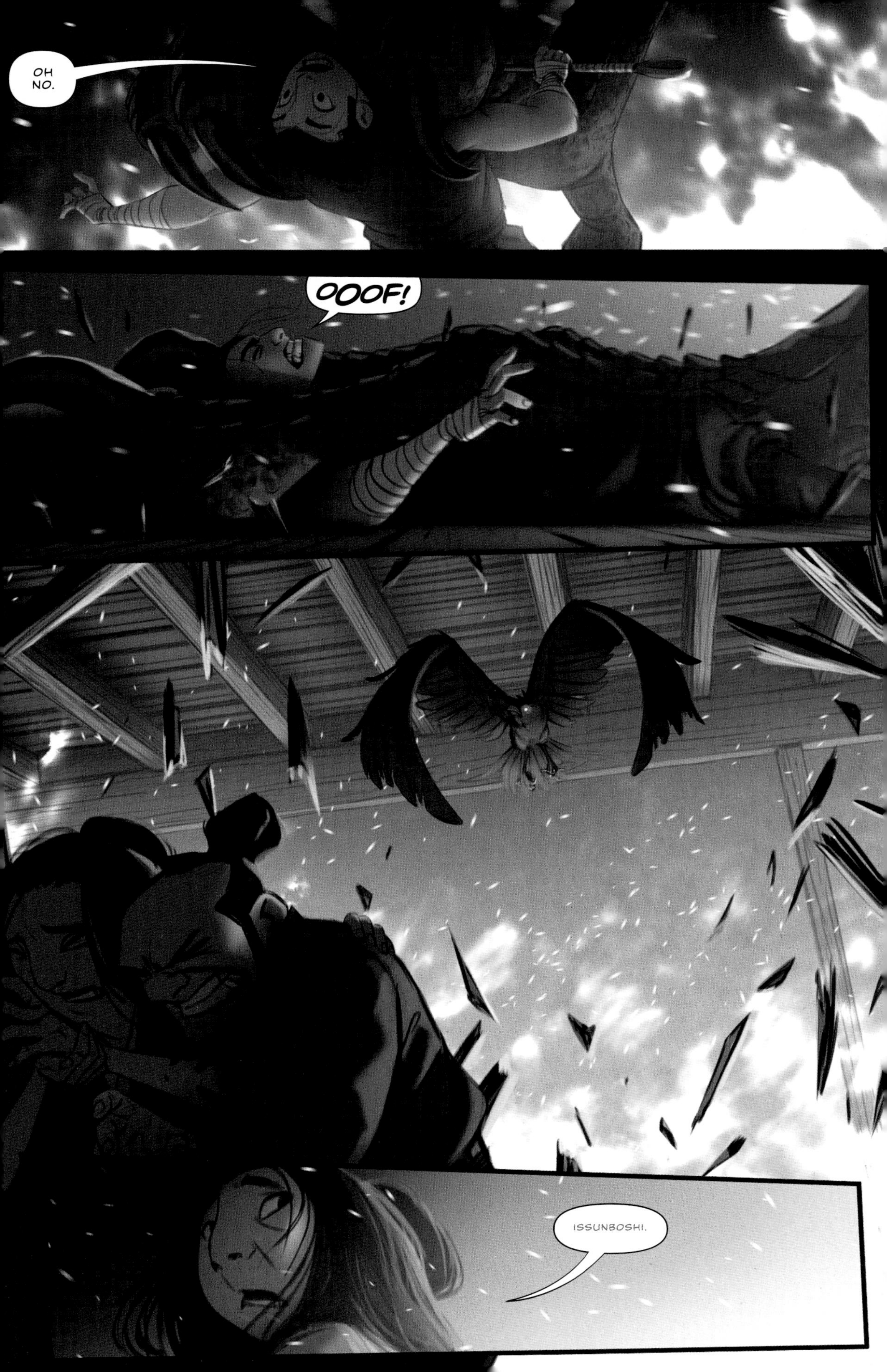
OH NO.
OOOF!
ISSUNBOSHI.

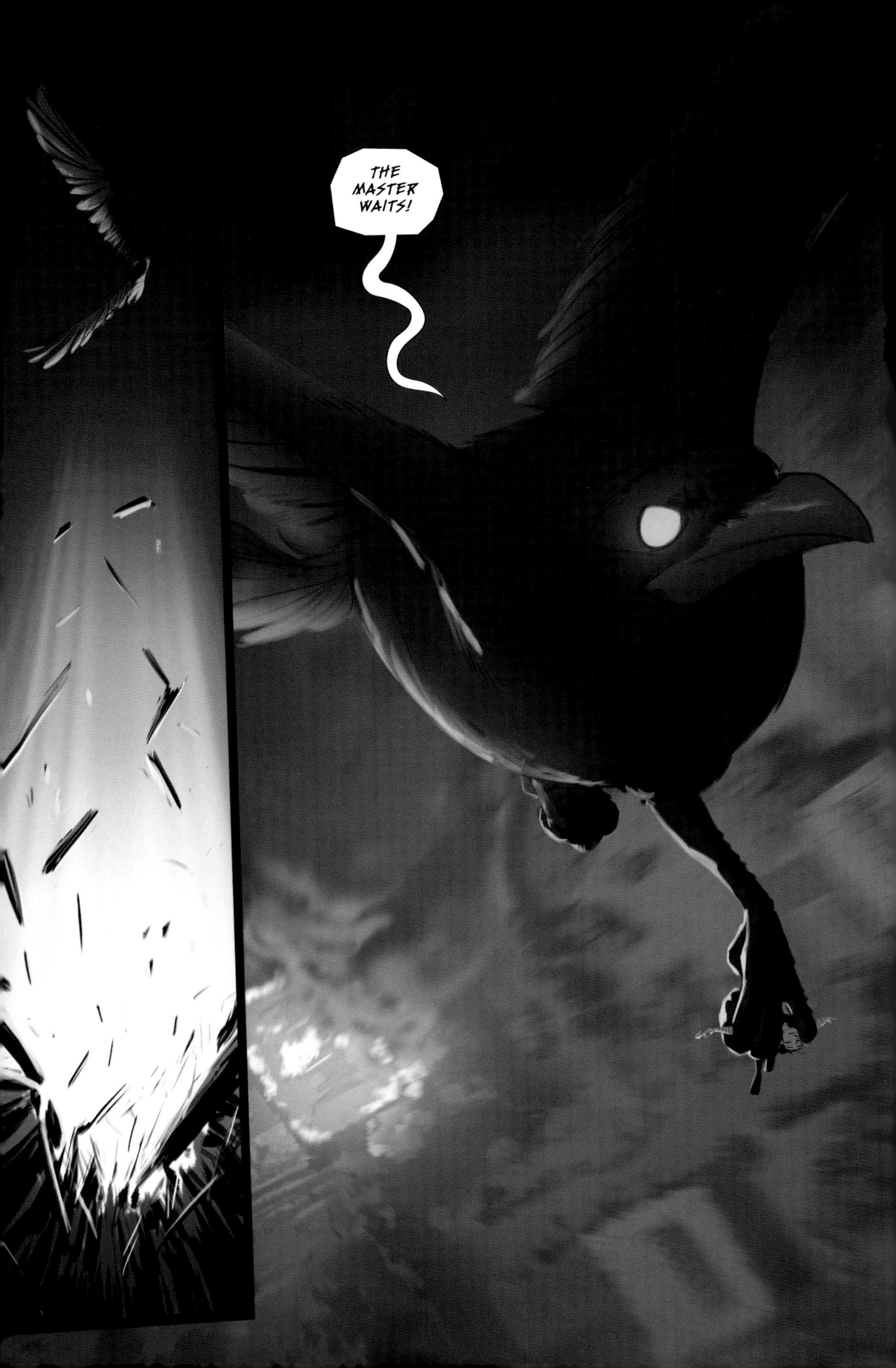
THE MASTER WAITS!

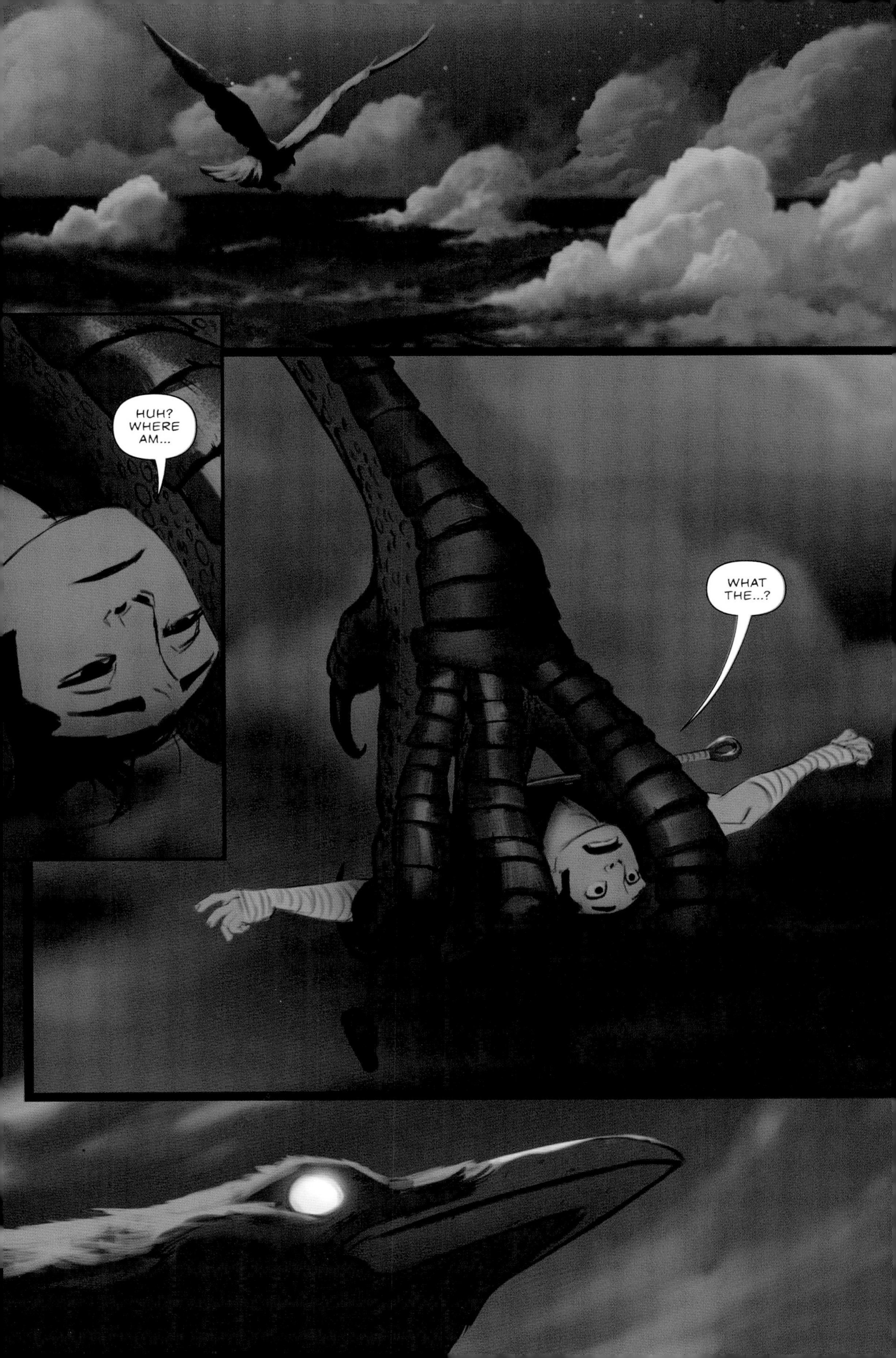
HUH? WHERE AM...
WHAT THE...?

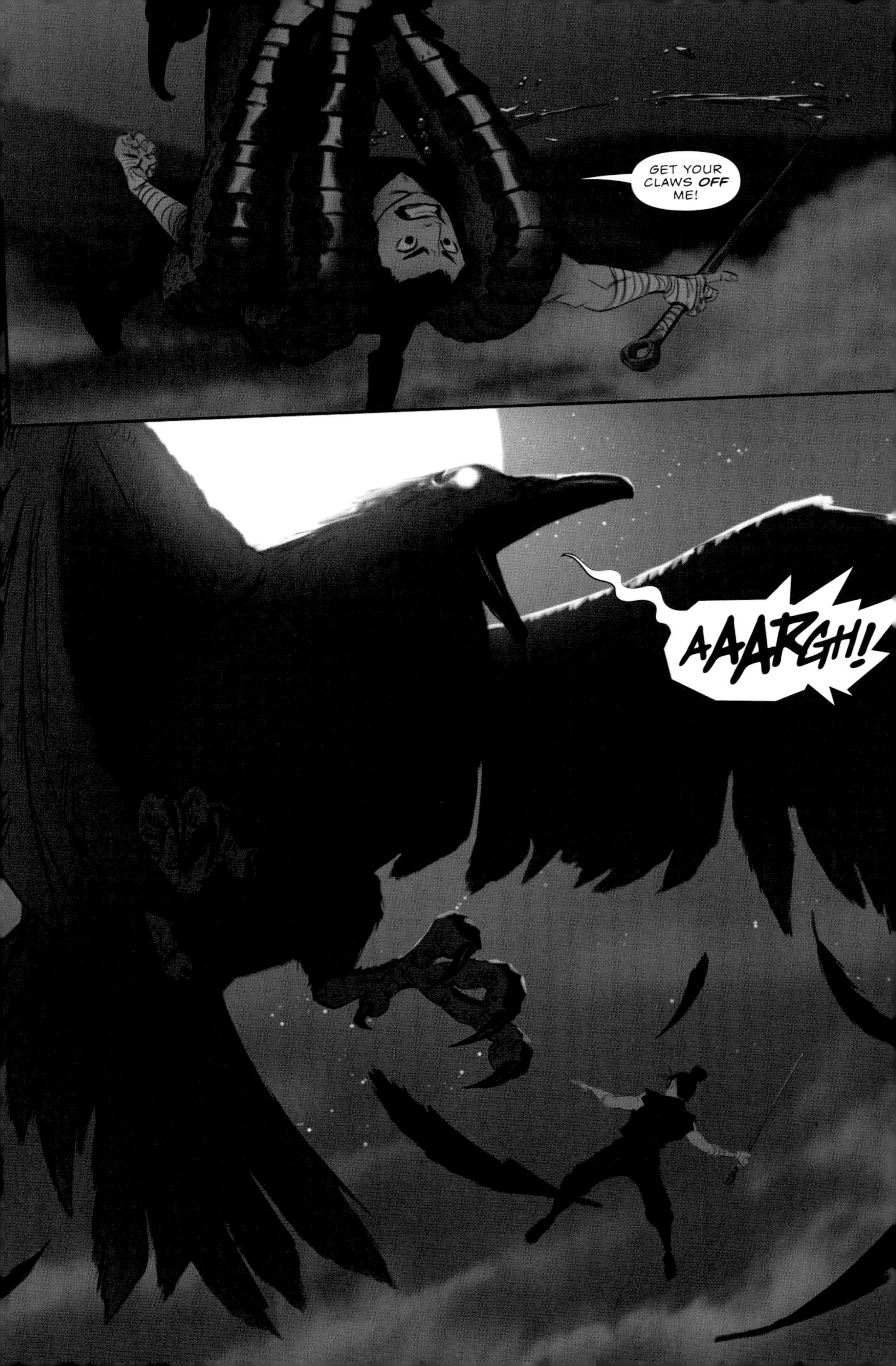
GET YOUR CLAWS OFF ME!
AAARGH!

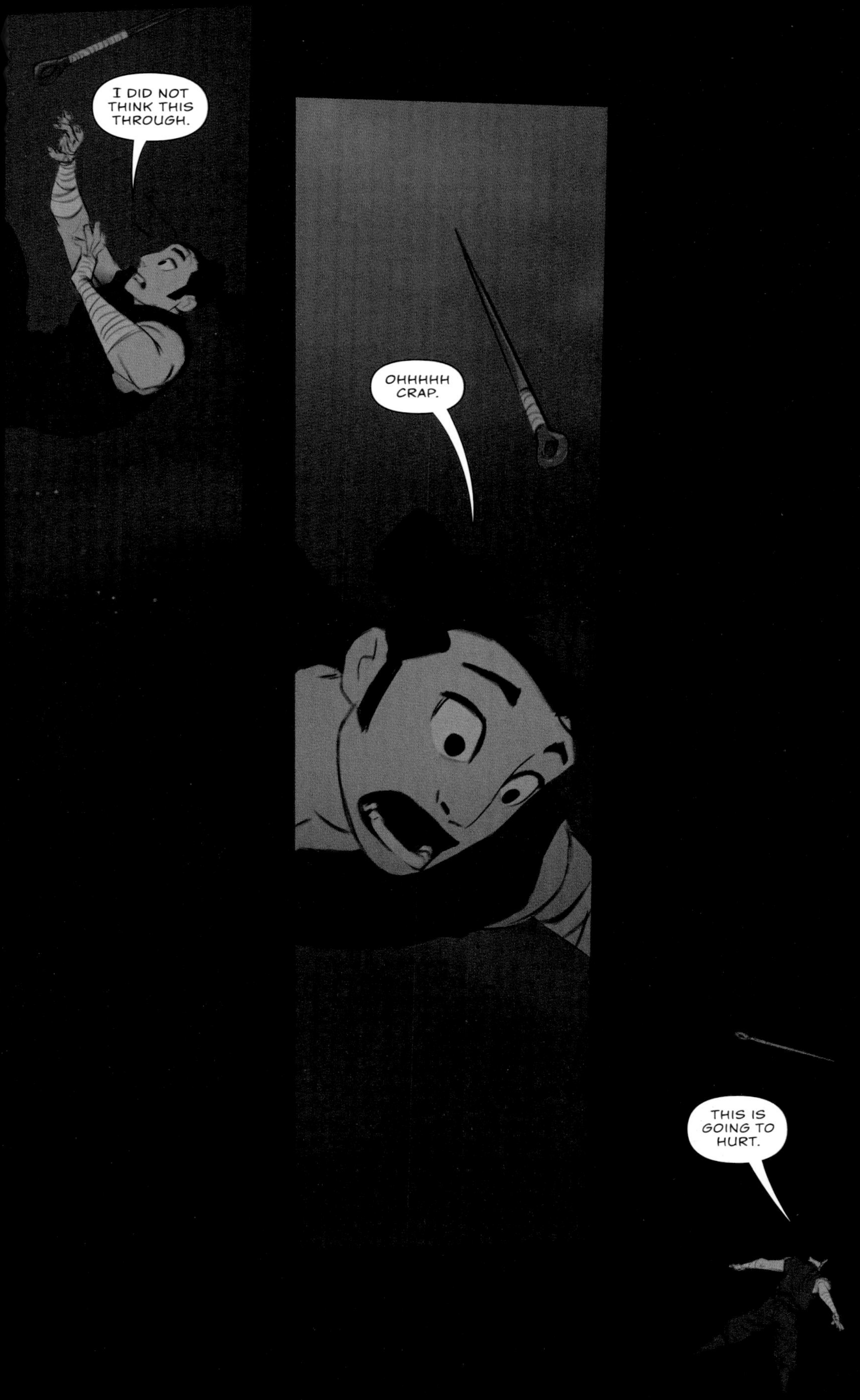
I DID NOT THINK THIS THROUGH.
OHHHHH CRAP.
THIS IS GOING TO HURT.

TWO

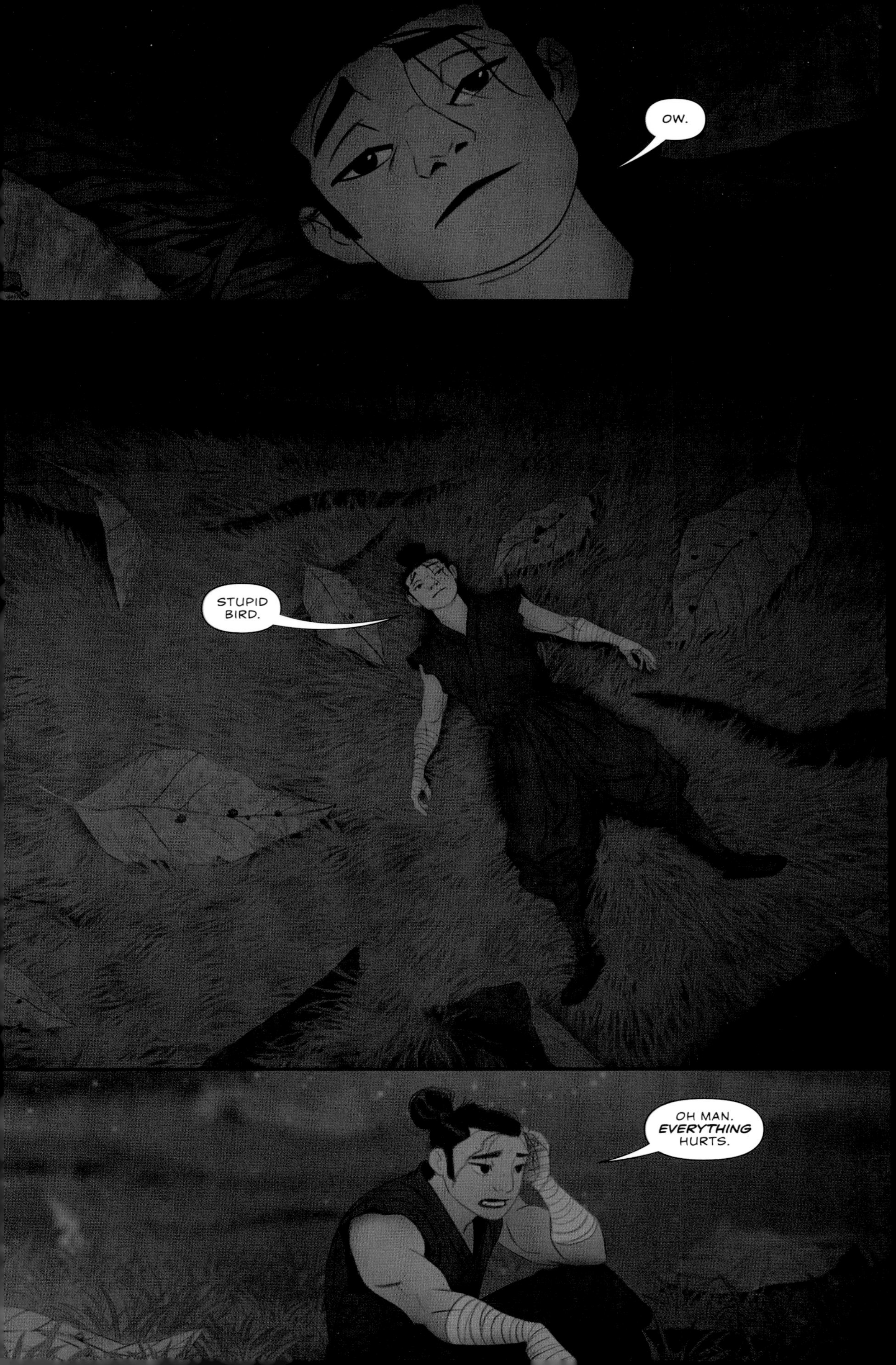
OW.
STUPID BIRD.
OH MAN. *EVERYTHING* HURTS.

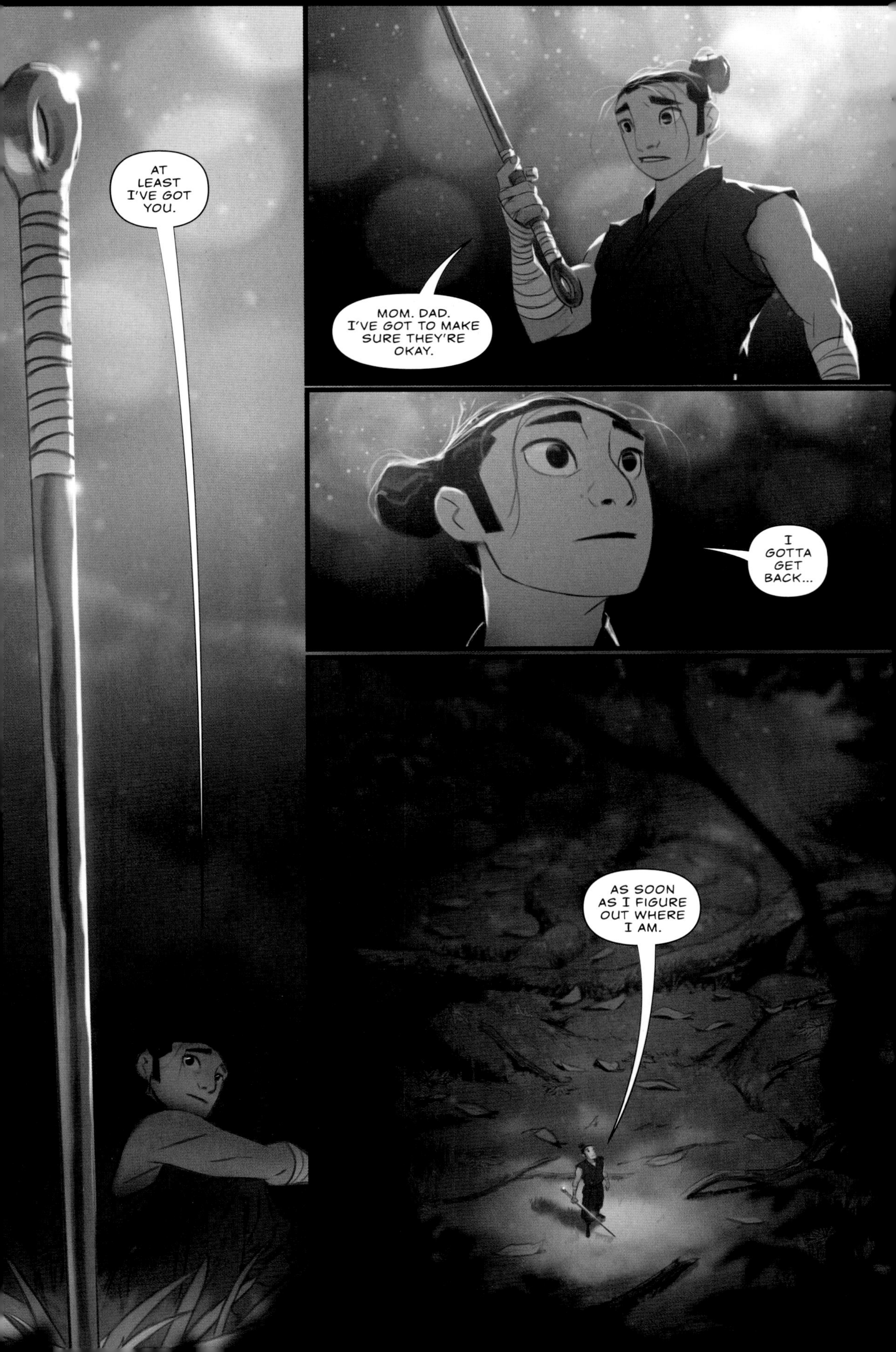
AT LEAST I'VE GOT YOU.
MOM. DAD. I'VE GOT TO MAKE SURE THEY'RE OKAY.
I GOTTA GET BACK...
AS SOON AS I FIGURE OUT WHERE I AM.

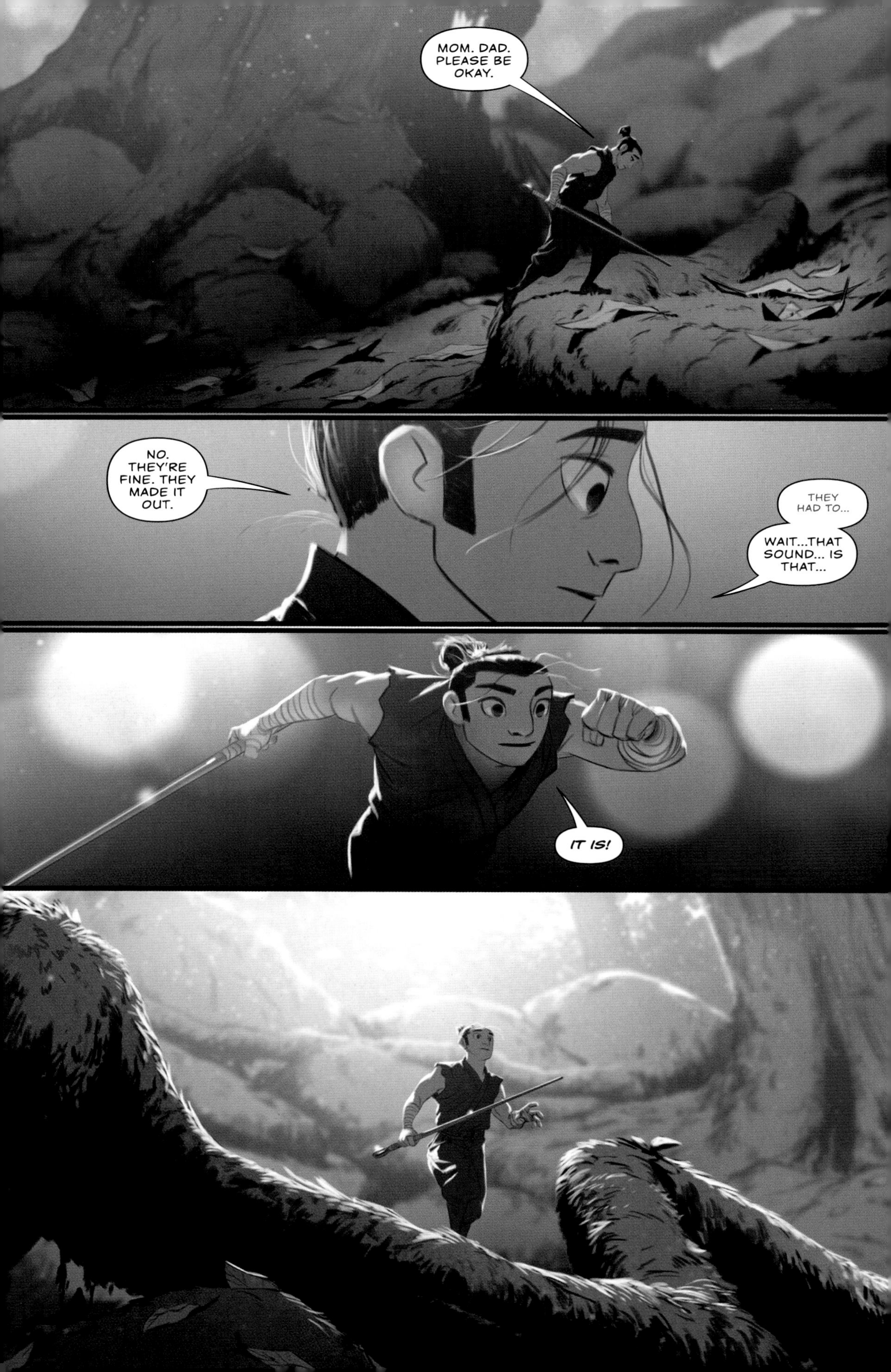
MOM. DAD. PLEASE BE OKAY.
NO. THEY'RE FINE. THEY MADE IT OUT.
THEY HAD TO...
WAIT...THAT SOUND... IS THAT...
IT IS!

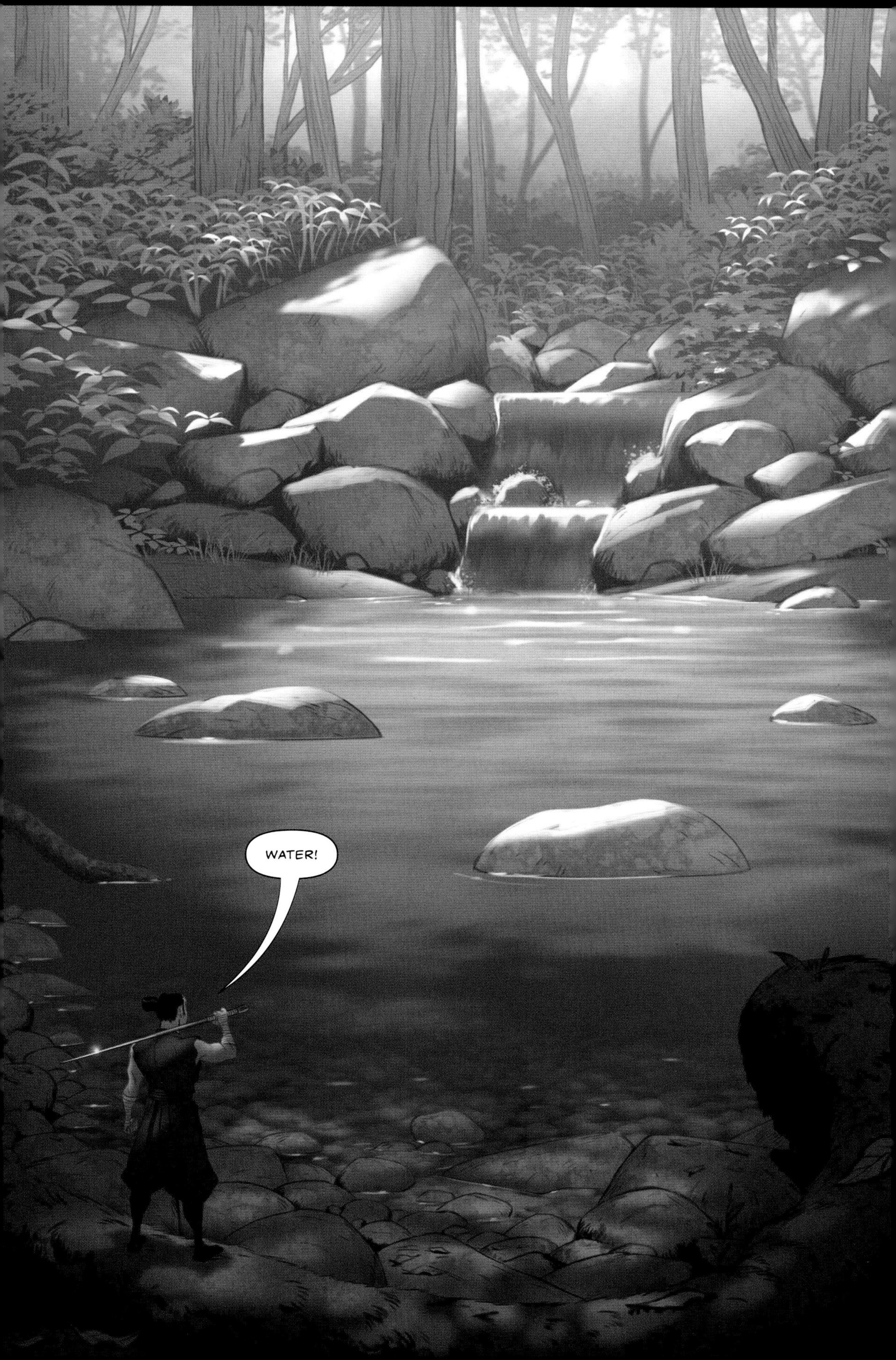
WATER!

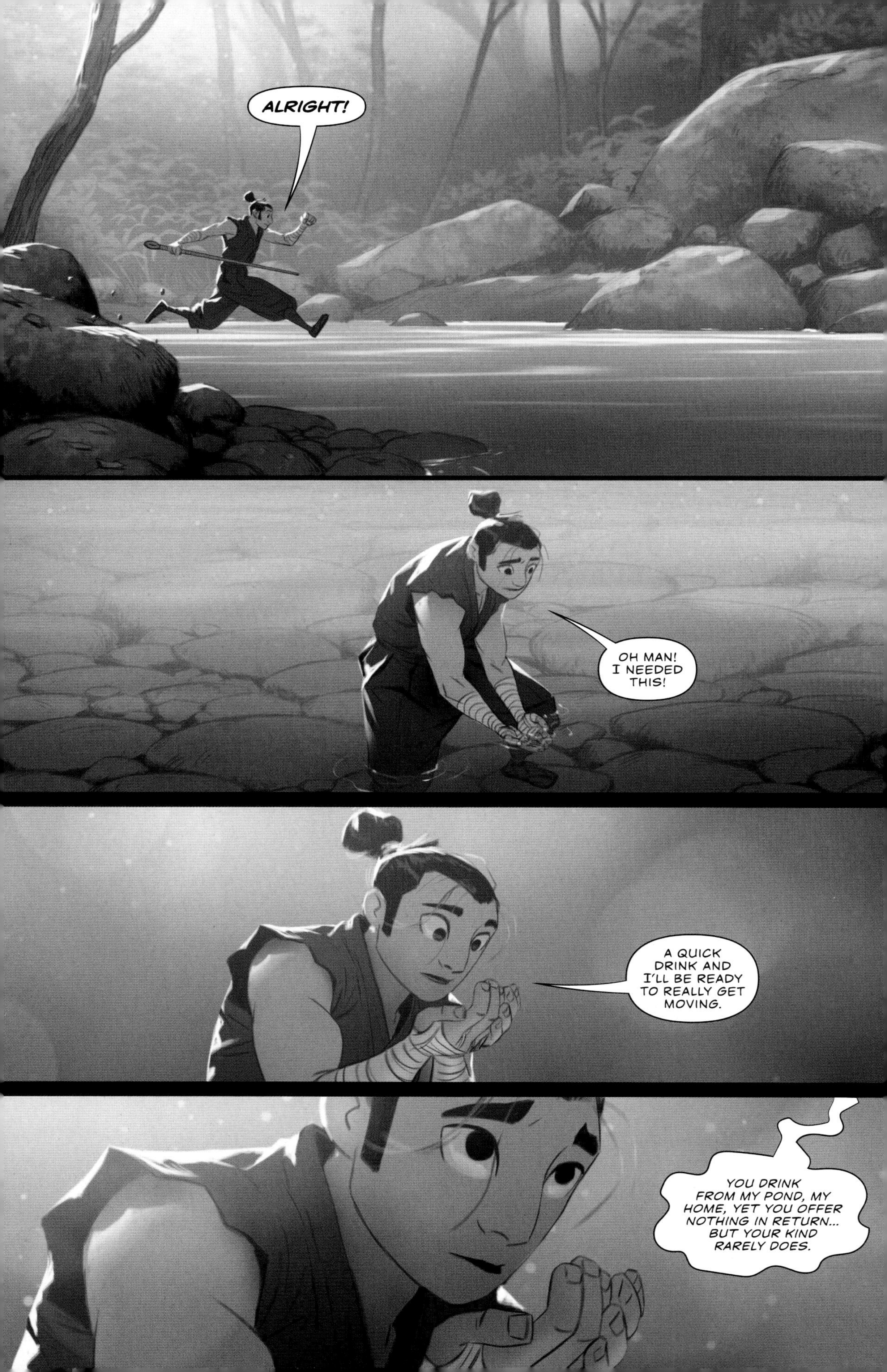
ALRIGHT!
OH MAN! I NEEDED THIS!
A QUICK DRINK AND I'LL BE READY TO REALLY GET MOVING.
YOU DRINK FROM MY POND, MY HOME, YET YOU OFFER NOTHING IN RETURN... BUT YOUR KIND RARELY DOES.

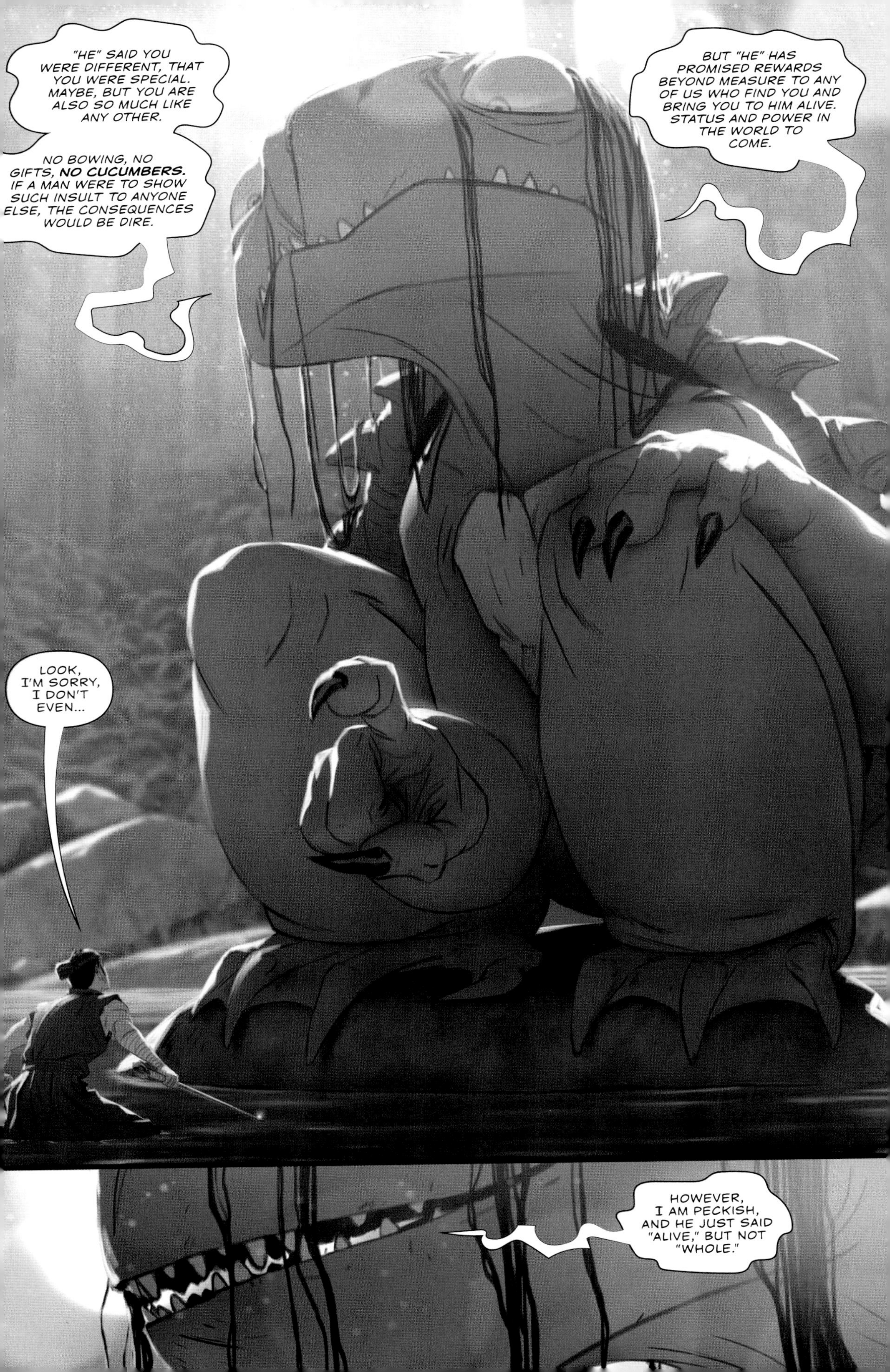
"HE" SAID YOU WERE DIFFERENT, THAT YOU WERE SPECIAL. MAYBE, BUT YOU ARE ALSO SO MUCH LIKE ANY OTHER.
NO BOWING, NO GIFTS, **NO CUCUMBERS.** IF A MAN WERE TO SHOW SUCH INSULT TO ANYONE ELSE, THE CONSEQUENCES WOULD BE DIRE.
BUT "HE" HAS PROMISED REWARDS BEYOND MEASURE TO ANY OF US WHO FIND YOU AND BRING YOU TO HIM ALIVE. STATUS AND POWER IN THE WORLD TO COME.
LOOK, I'M SORRY, I DON'T EVEN...
HOWEVER, I AM PECKISH, AND HE JUST SAID "ALIVE," BUT NOT "WHOLE."

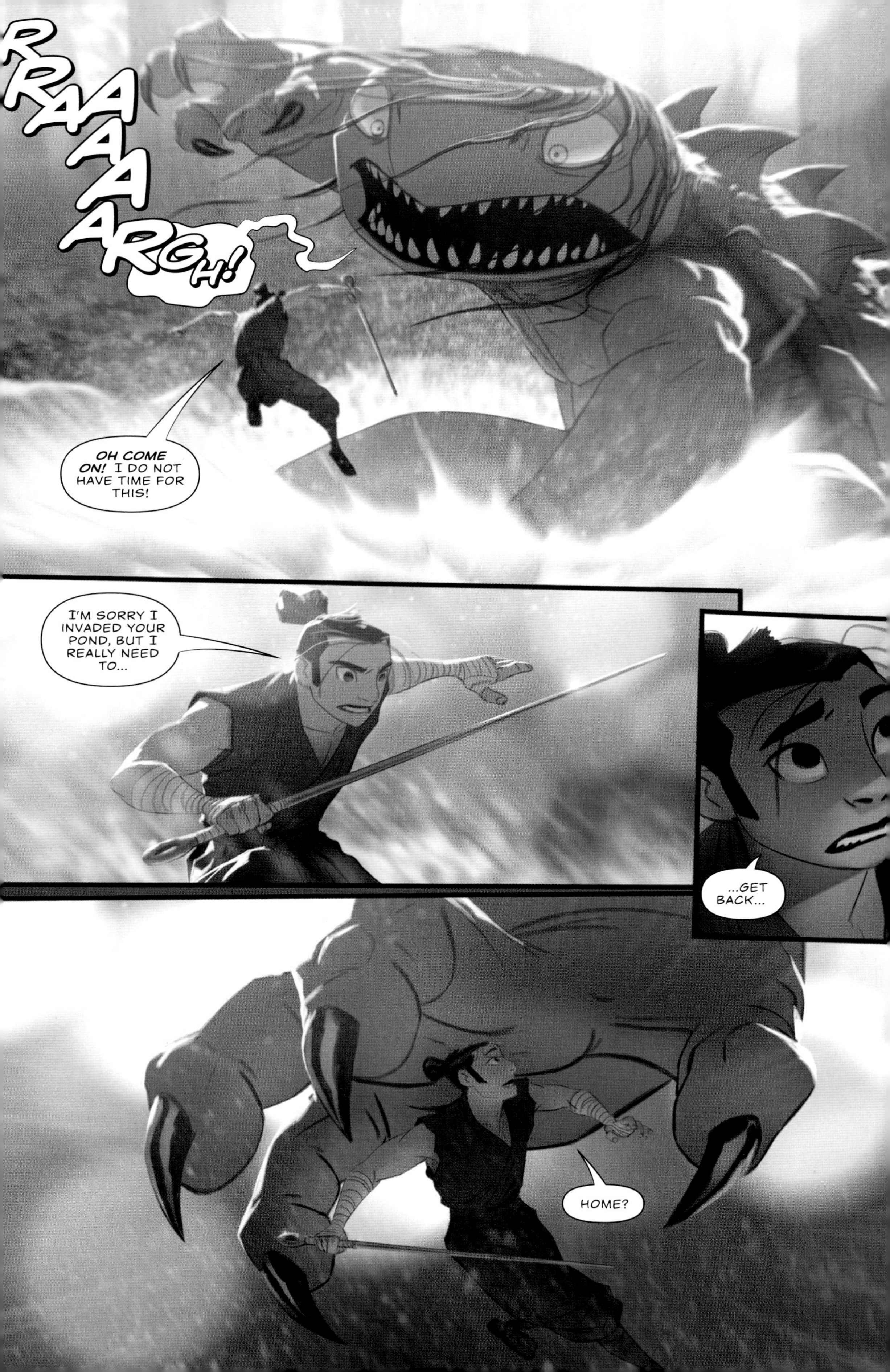
RRAAAAAARGH!
OH COME ON! I DO NOT HAVE TIME FOR THIS!
I'M SORRY I INVADED YOUR POND, BUT I REALLY NEED TO...
...GET BACK...
HOME?

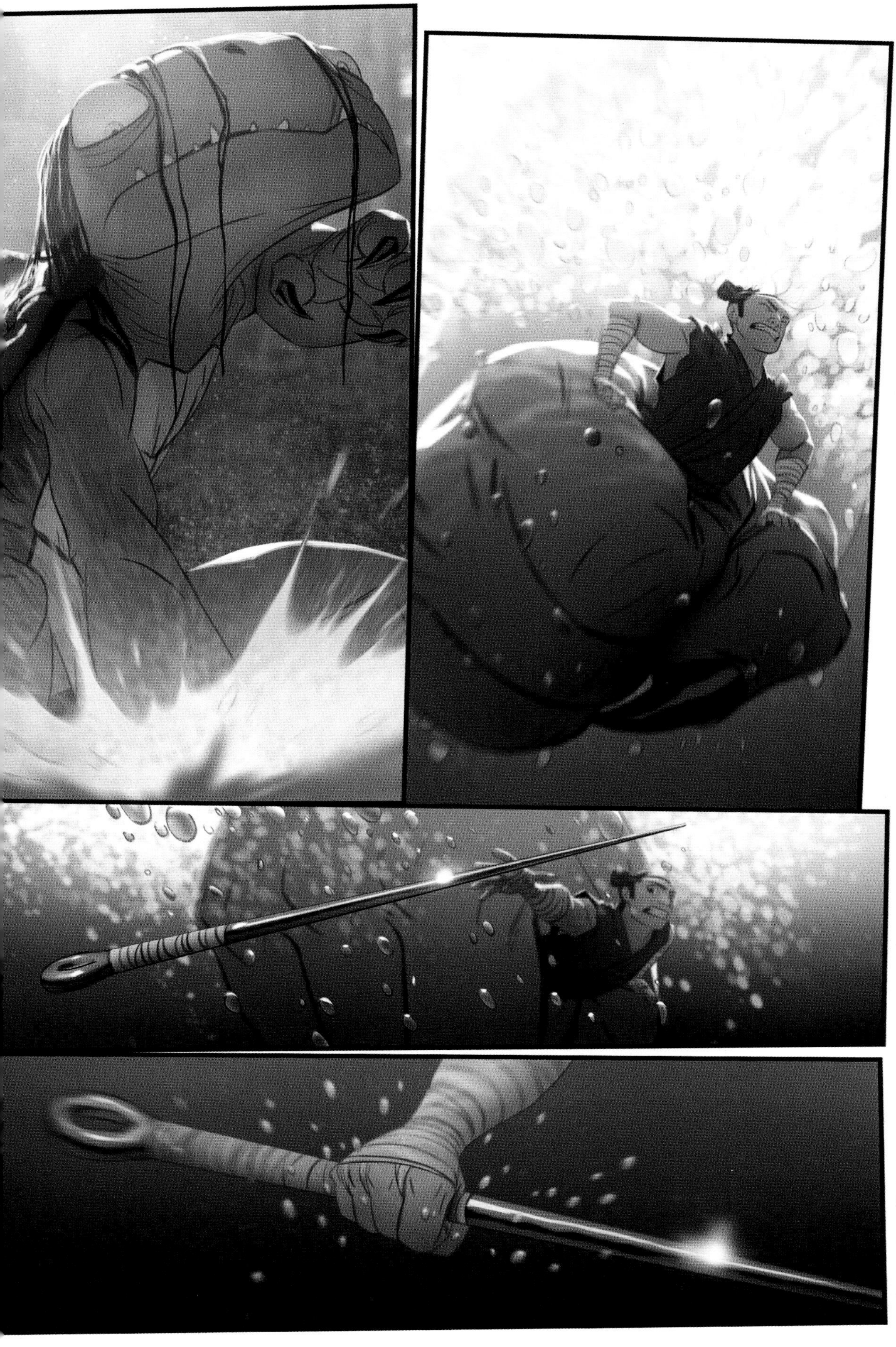

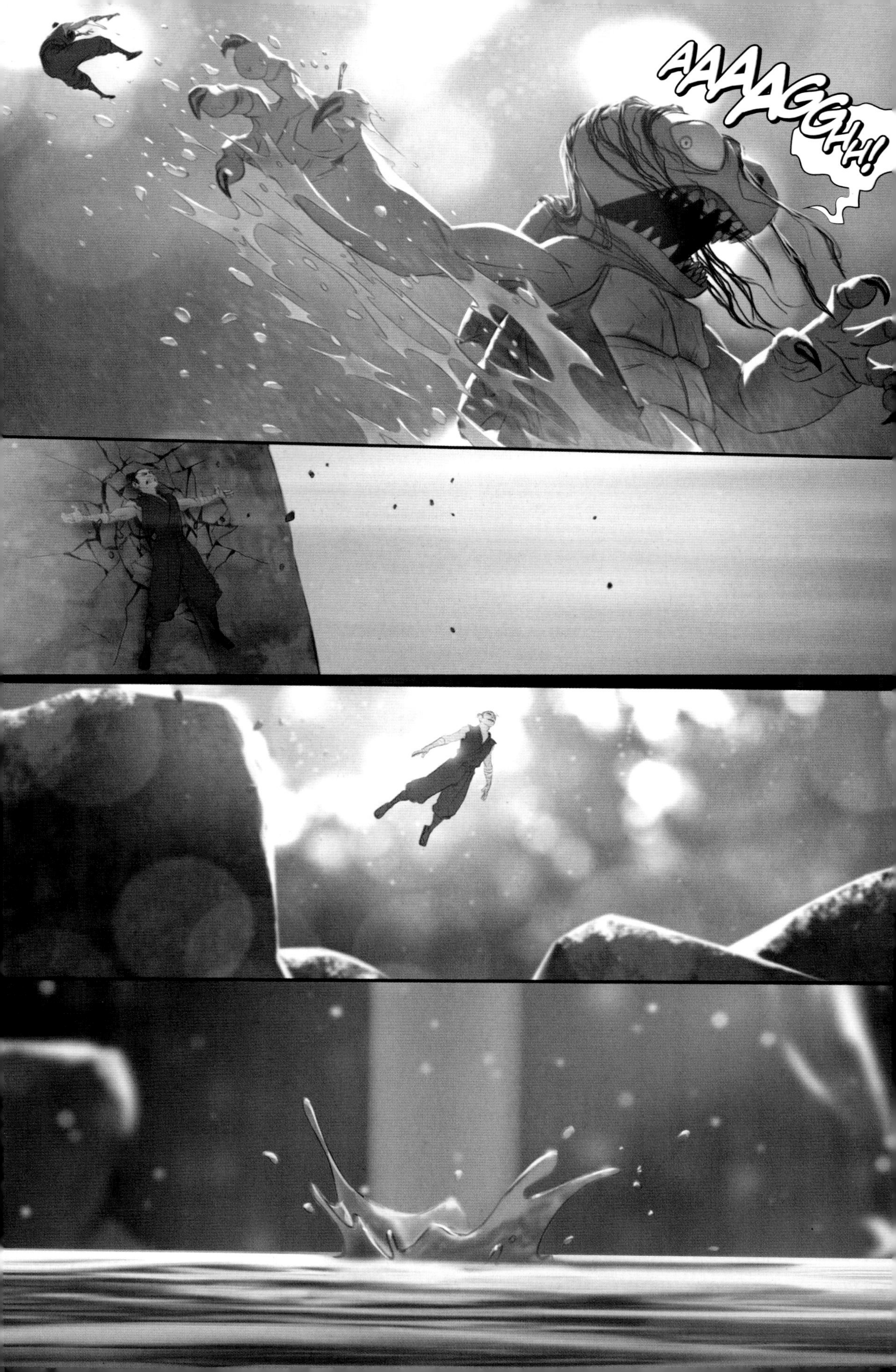
AAAAGGHH!

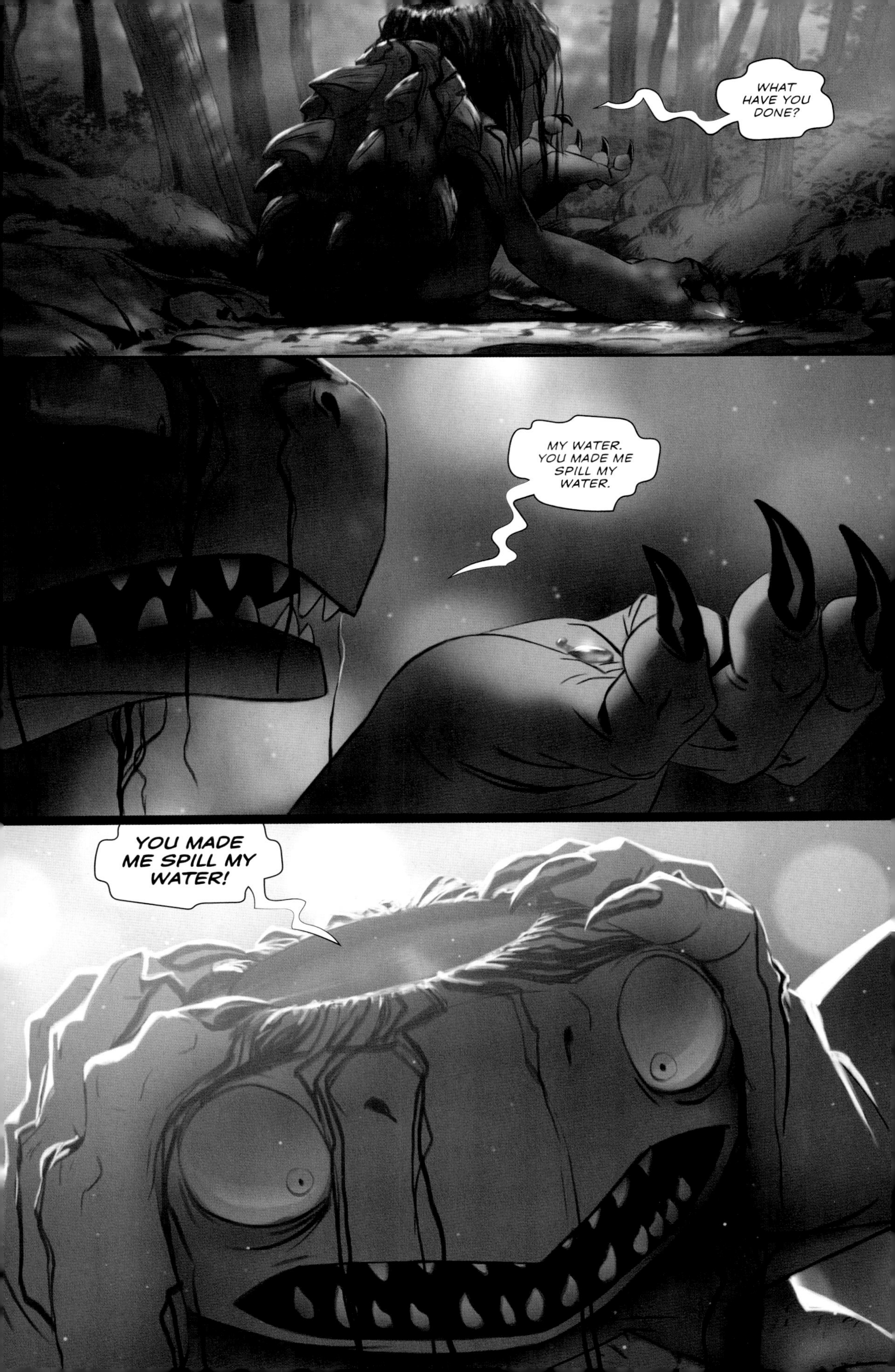
WHAT HAVE YOU DONE?
MY WATER. YOU MADE ME SPILL MY WATER.
YOU MADE ME SPILL MY WATER!

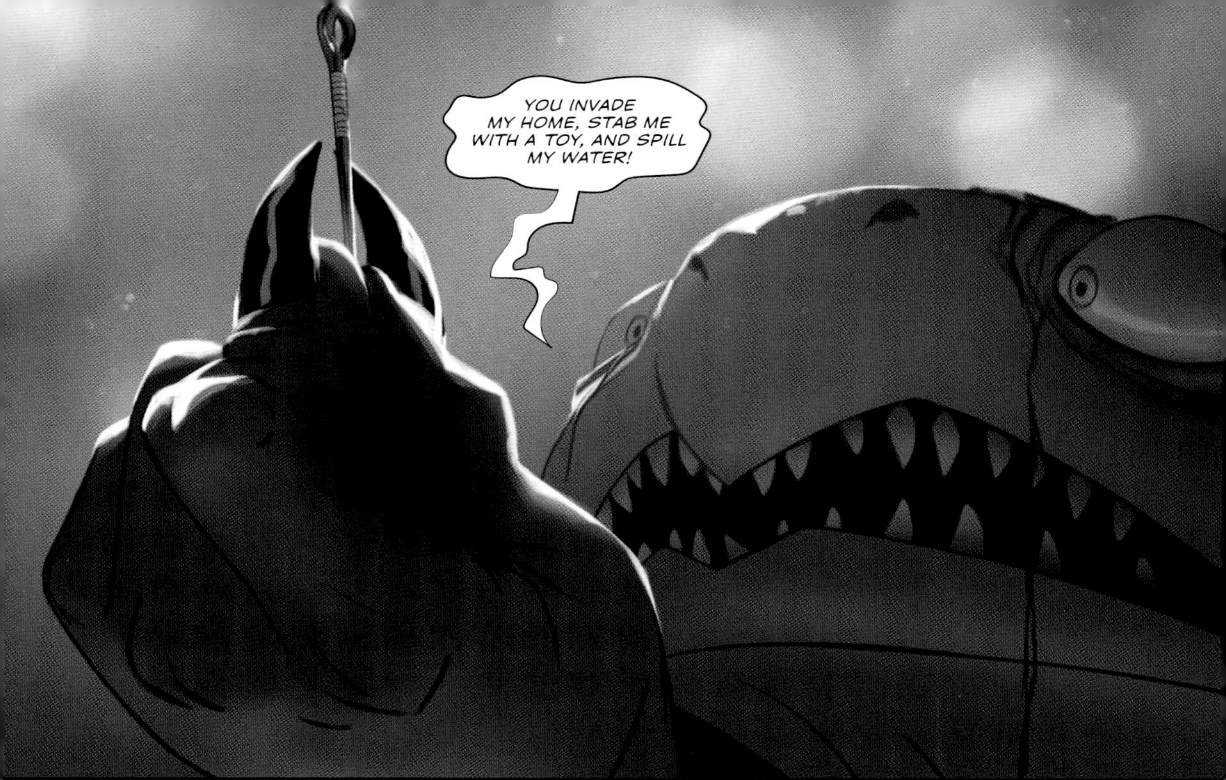
YOU INVADE MY HOME, STAB ME WITH A TOY, AND SPILL MY WATER!

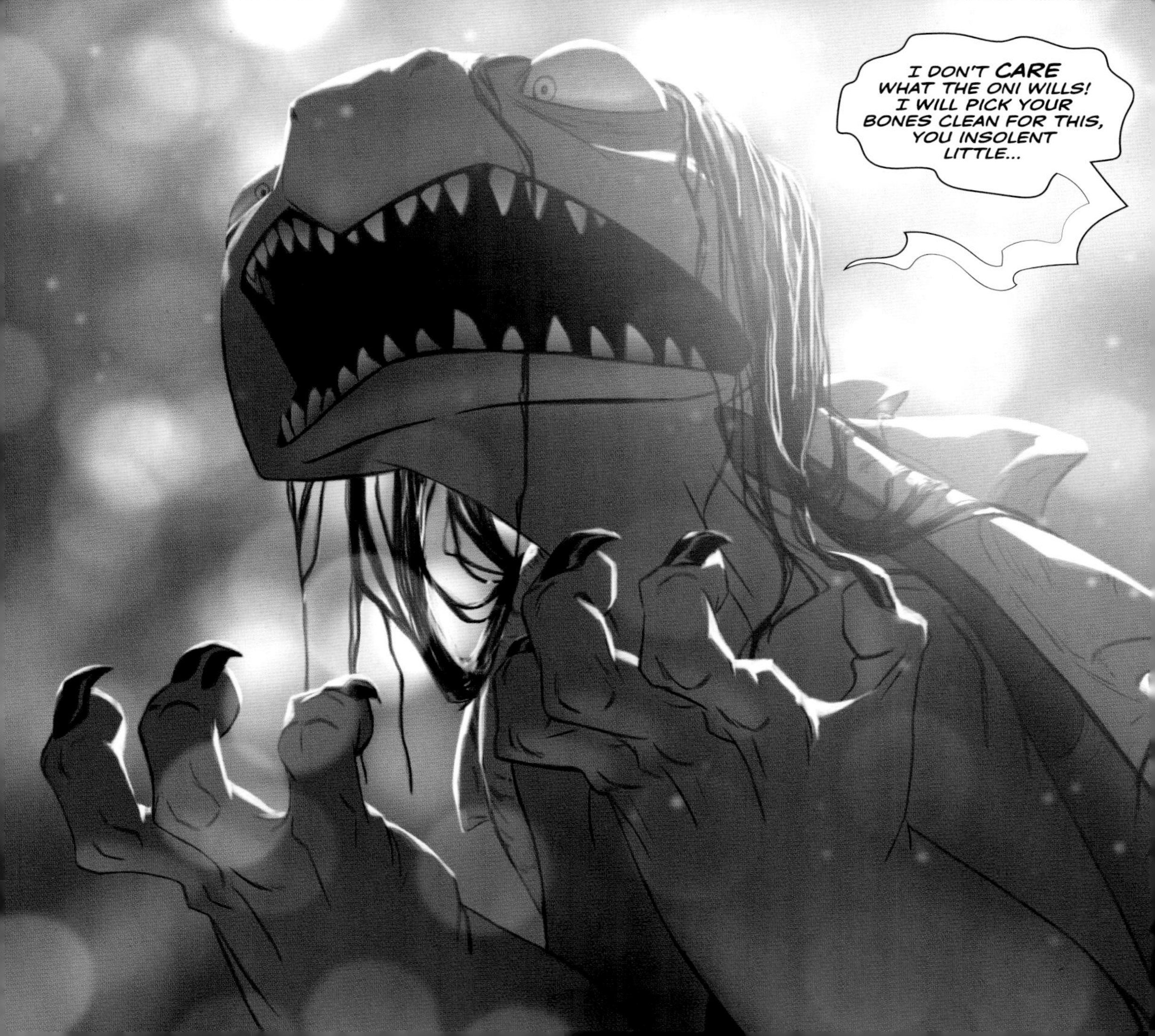
I DON'T CARE WHAT THE ONI WILLS! I WILL PICK YOUR BONES CLEAN FOR THIS, YOU INSOLENT LITTLE...

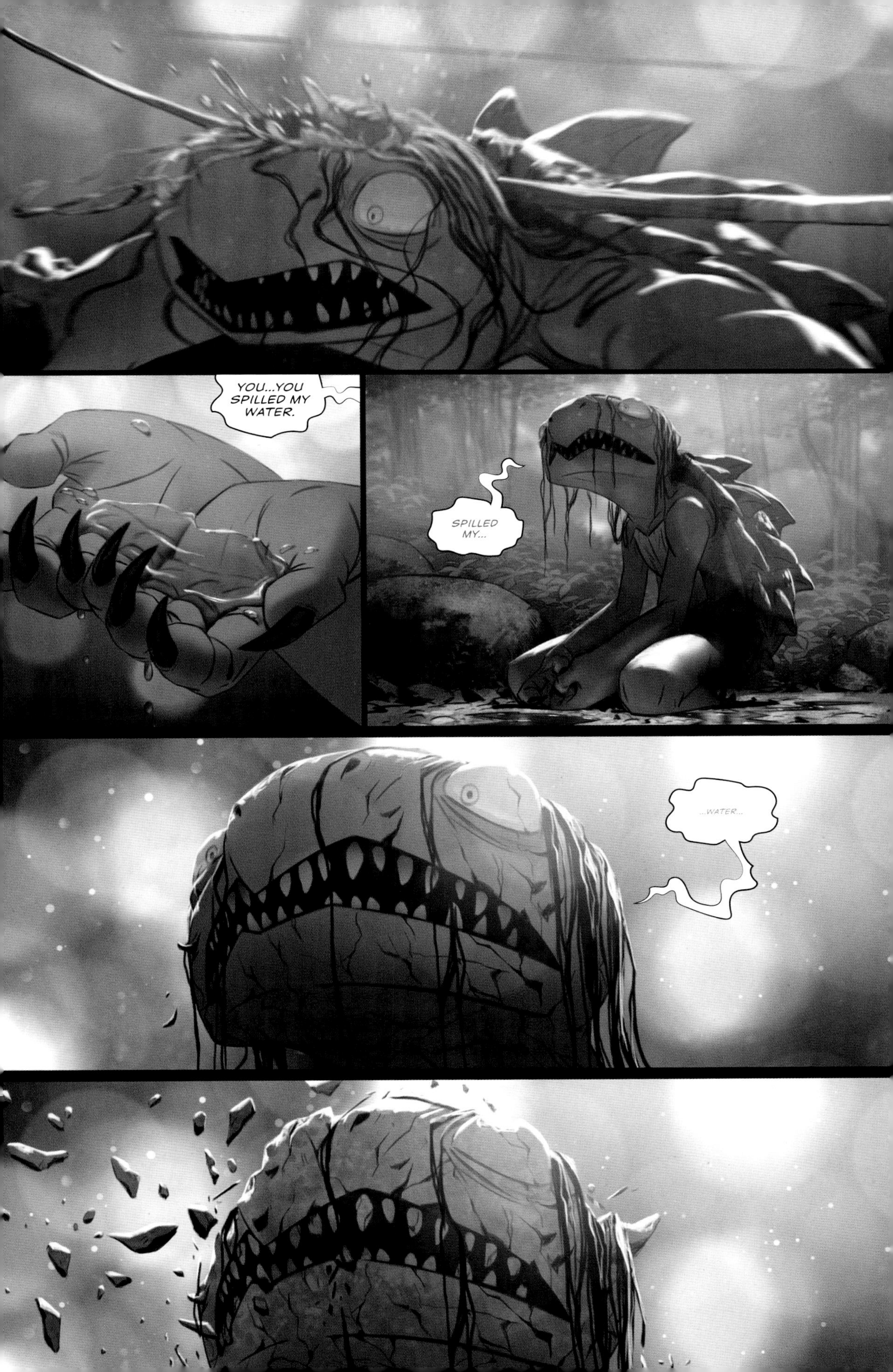
YOU...YOU SPILLED MY WATER.
SPILLED MY...
...WATER...

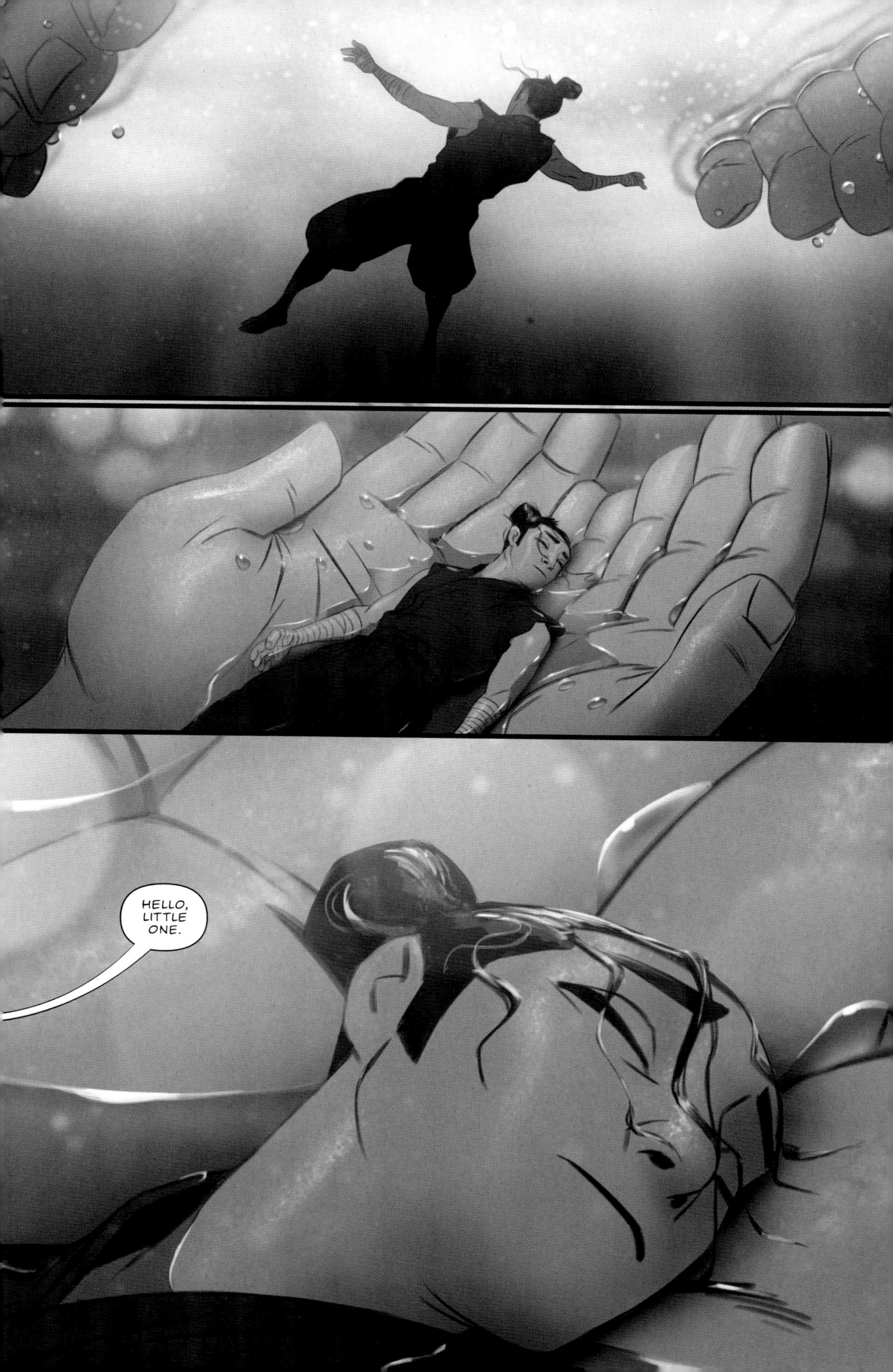
HELLO, LITTLE ONE.

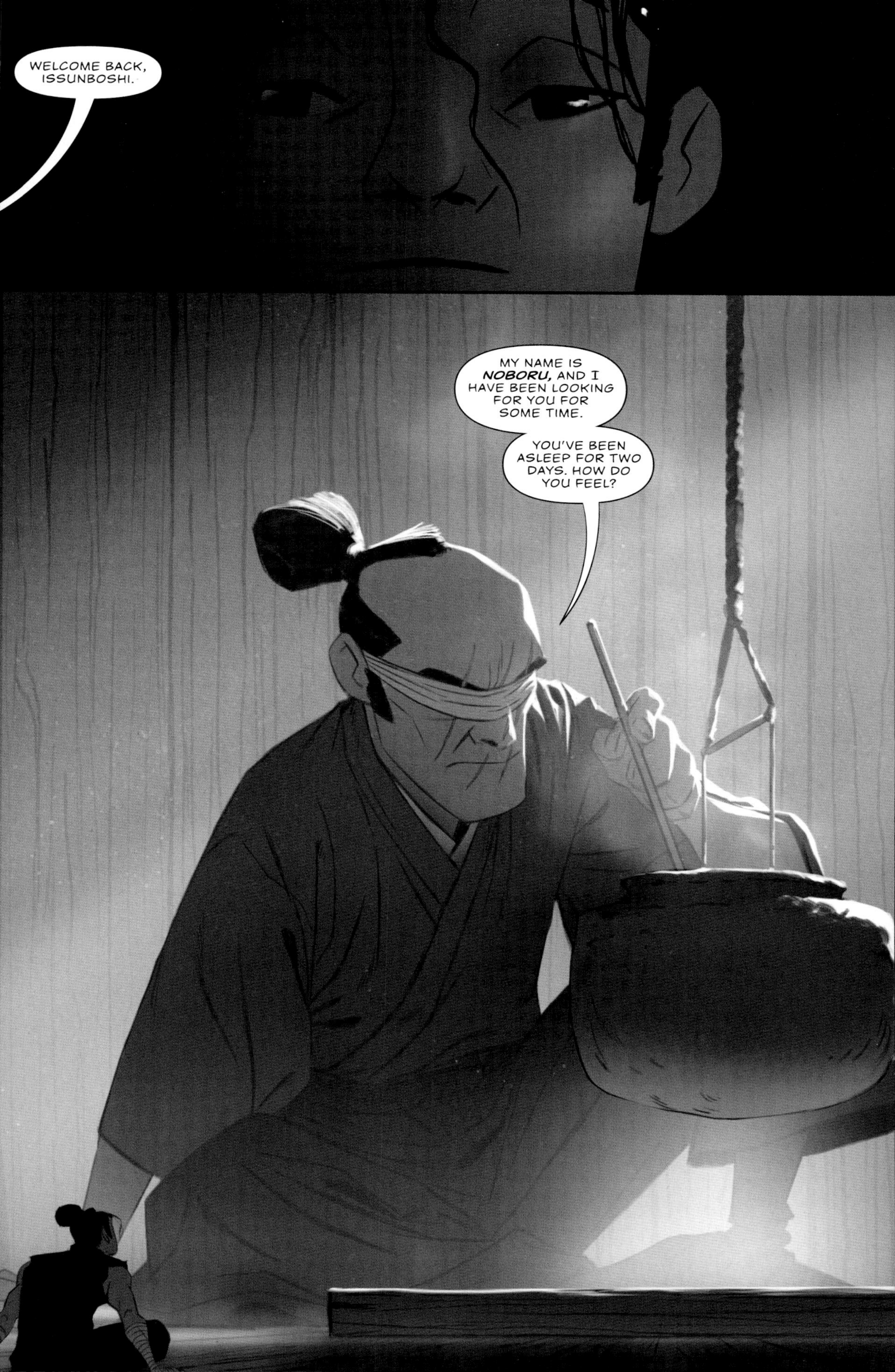
WELCOME BACK, ISSUNBOSHI.
MY NAME IS NOBORU, AND I HAVE BEEN LOOKING FOR YOU FOR SOME TIME.
YOU'VE BEEN ASLEEP FOR TWO DAYS. HOW DO YOU FEEL?

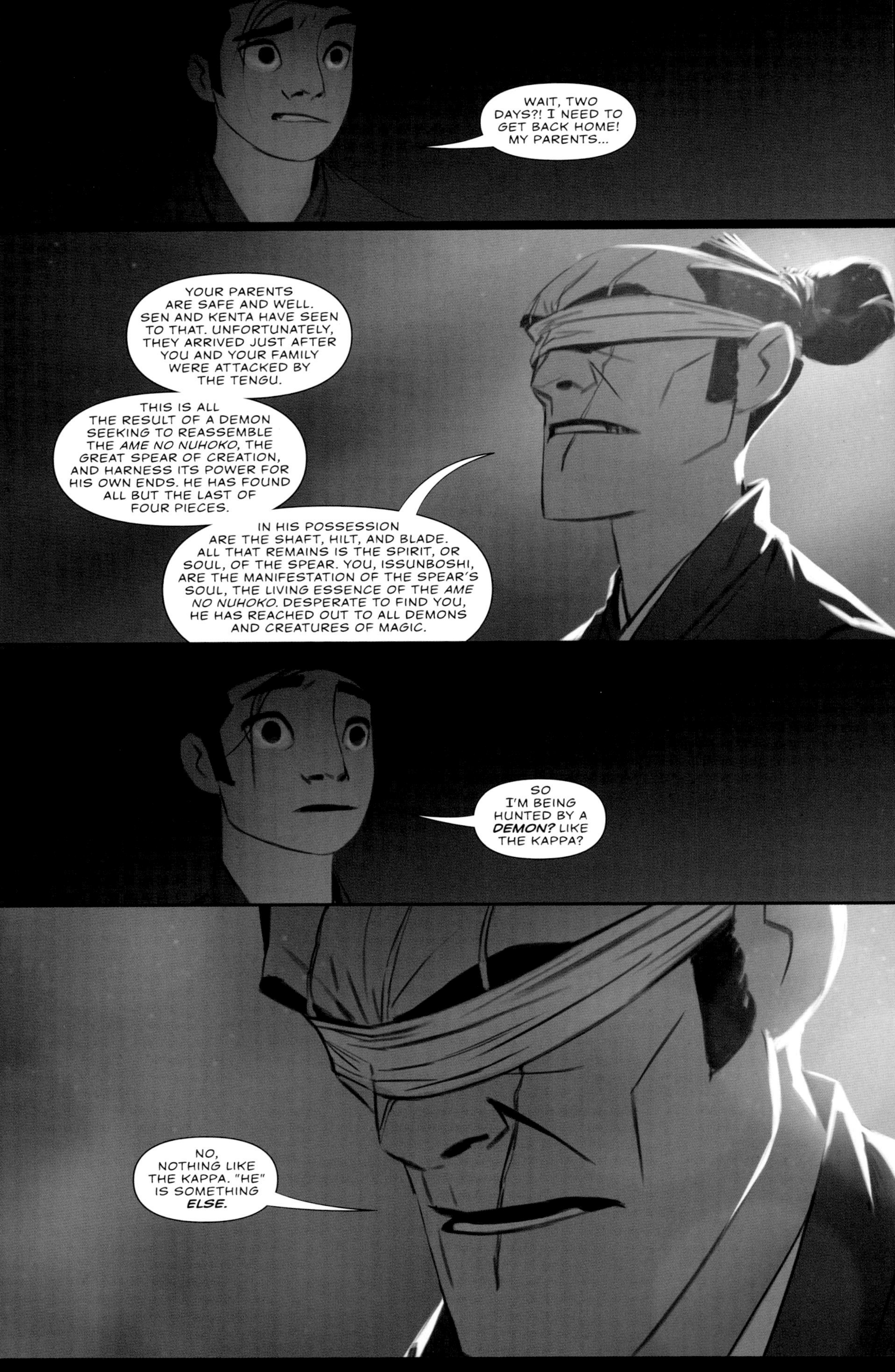
WAIT, TWO DAYS?! I NEED TO GET BACK HOME! MY PARENTS...
YOUR PARENTS ARE SAFE AND WELL. SEN AND KENTA HAVE SEEN TO THAT. UNFORTUNATELY, THEY ARRIVED JUST AFTER YOU AND YOUR FAMILY WERE ATTACKED BY THE TENGU.
THIS IS ALL THE RESULT OF A DEMON SEEKING TO REASSEMBLE THE *AME NO NUHOKO*, THE GREAT SPEAR OF CREATION, AND HARNESS ITS POWER FOR HIS OWN ENDS. HE HAS FOUND ALL BUT THE LAST OF FOUR PIECES.
IN HIS POSSESSION ARE THE SHAFT, HILT, AND BLADE. ALL THAT REMAINS IS THE SPIRIT, OR SOUL, OF THE SPEAR. YOU, ISSUNBOSHI, ARE THE MANIFESTATION OF THE SPEAR'S SOUL, THE LIVING ESSENCE OF THE *AME NO NUHOKO*. DESPERATE TO FIND YOU, HE HAS REACHED OUT TO ALL DEMONS AND CREATURES OF MAGIC.
SO I'M BEING HUNTED BY A ***DEMON?*** LIKE THE KAPPA?
NO, NOTHING LIKE THE KAPPA. "HE" IS SOMETHING ***ELSE.***

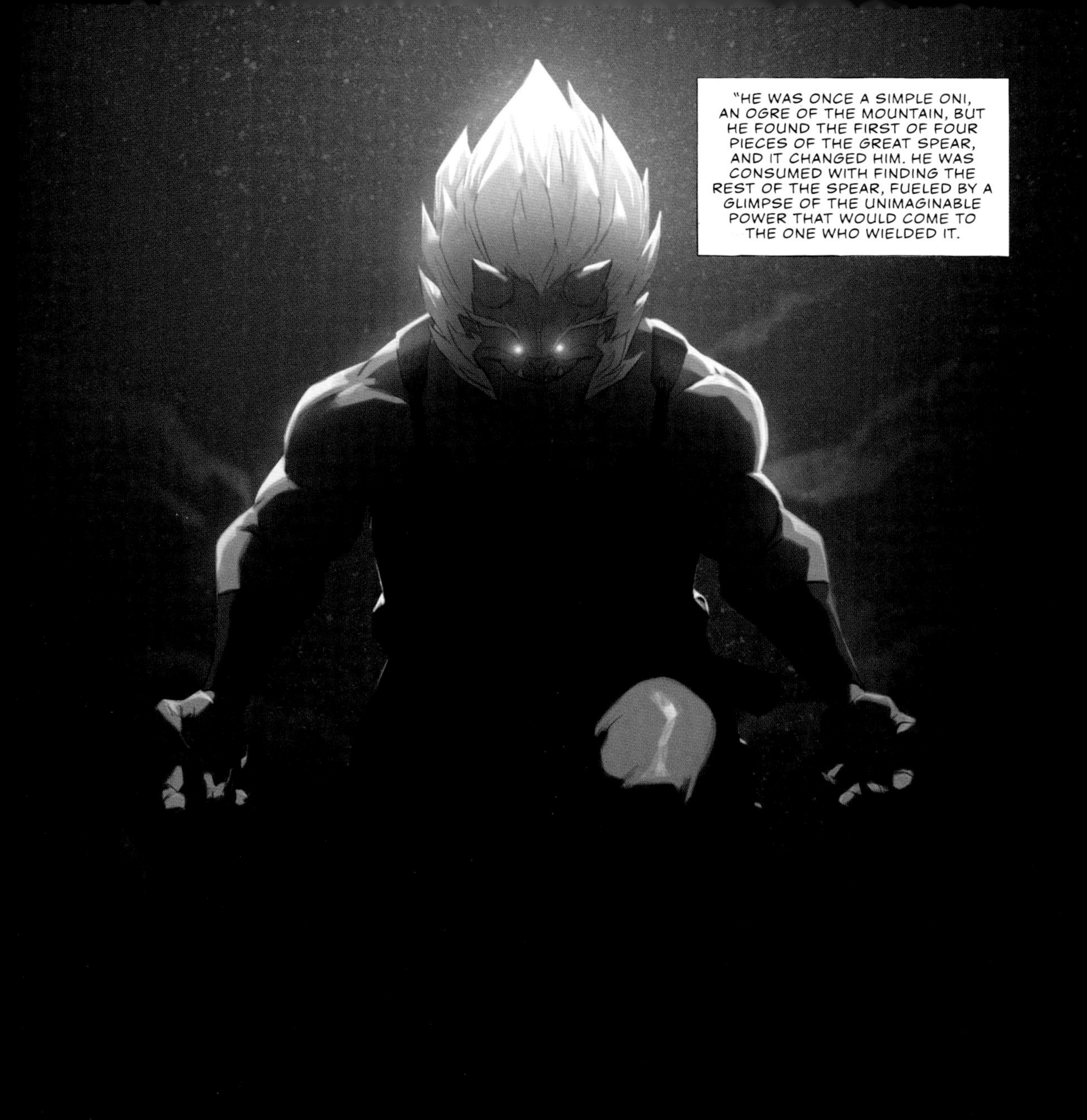
"HE WAS ONCE A SIMPLE ONI, AN *OGRE* OF THE MOUNTAIN, BUT HE FOUND THE FIRST OF FOUR PIECES OF THE GREAT SPEAR, AND IT CHANGED HIM. HE WAS CONSUMED WITH FINDING THE REST OF THE SPEAR, FUELED BY A GLIMPSE OF THE UNIMAGINABLE POWER THAT WOULD COME TO THE ONE WHO WIELDED IT.

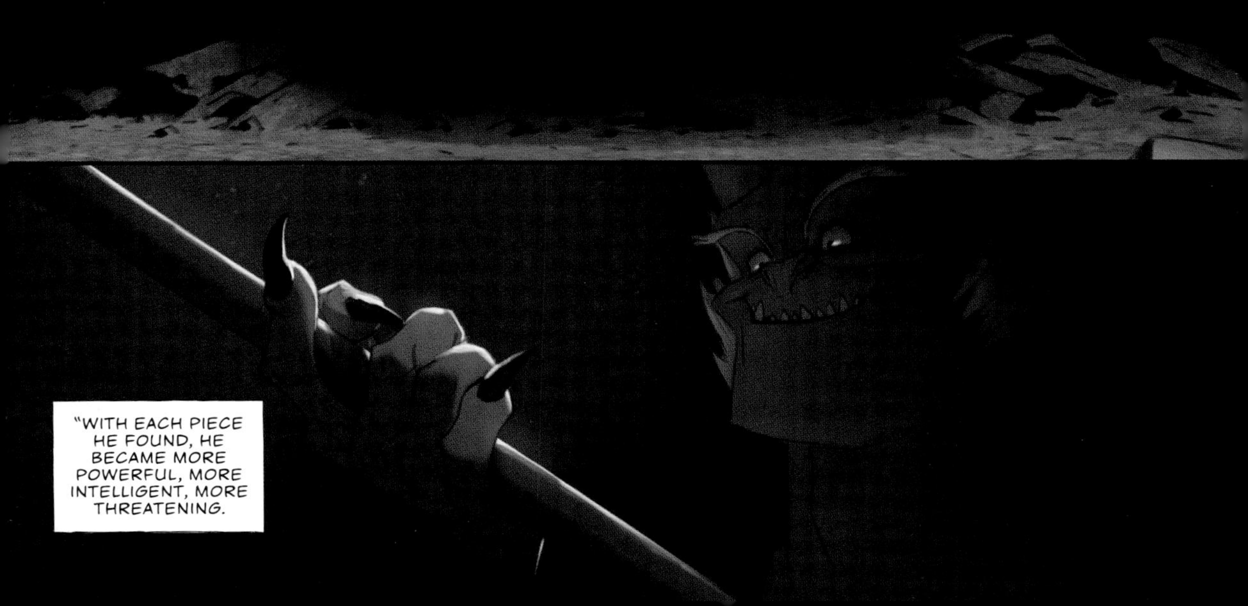
"WITH EACH PIECE HE FOUND, HE BECAME MORE POWERFUL, MORE INTELLIGENT, MORE THREATENING.

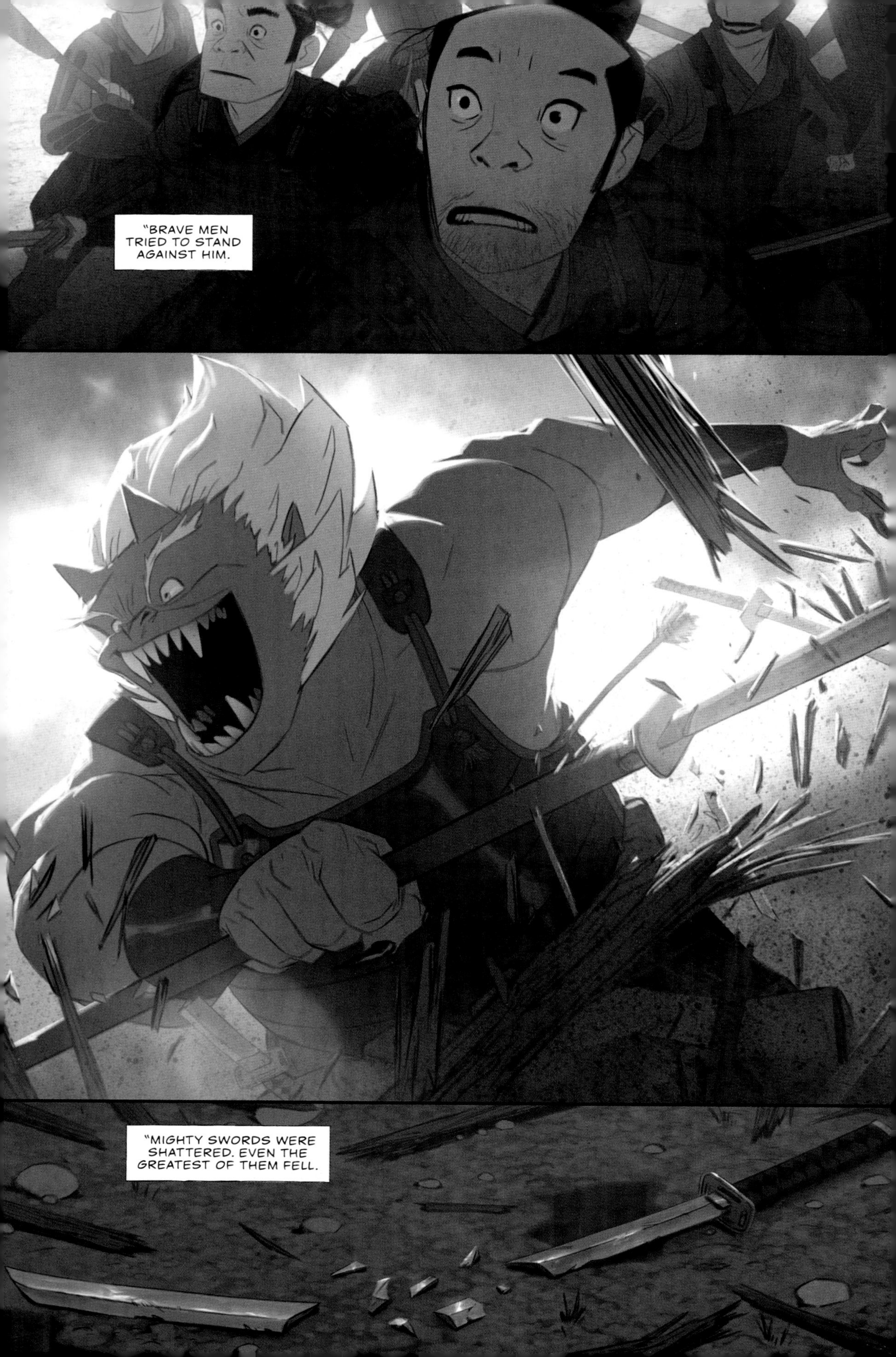
"BRAVE MEN TRIED TO STAND AGAINST HIM.
"MIGHTY SWORDS WERE SHATTERED. EVEN THE GREATEST OF THEM FELL.

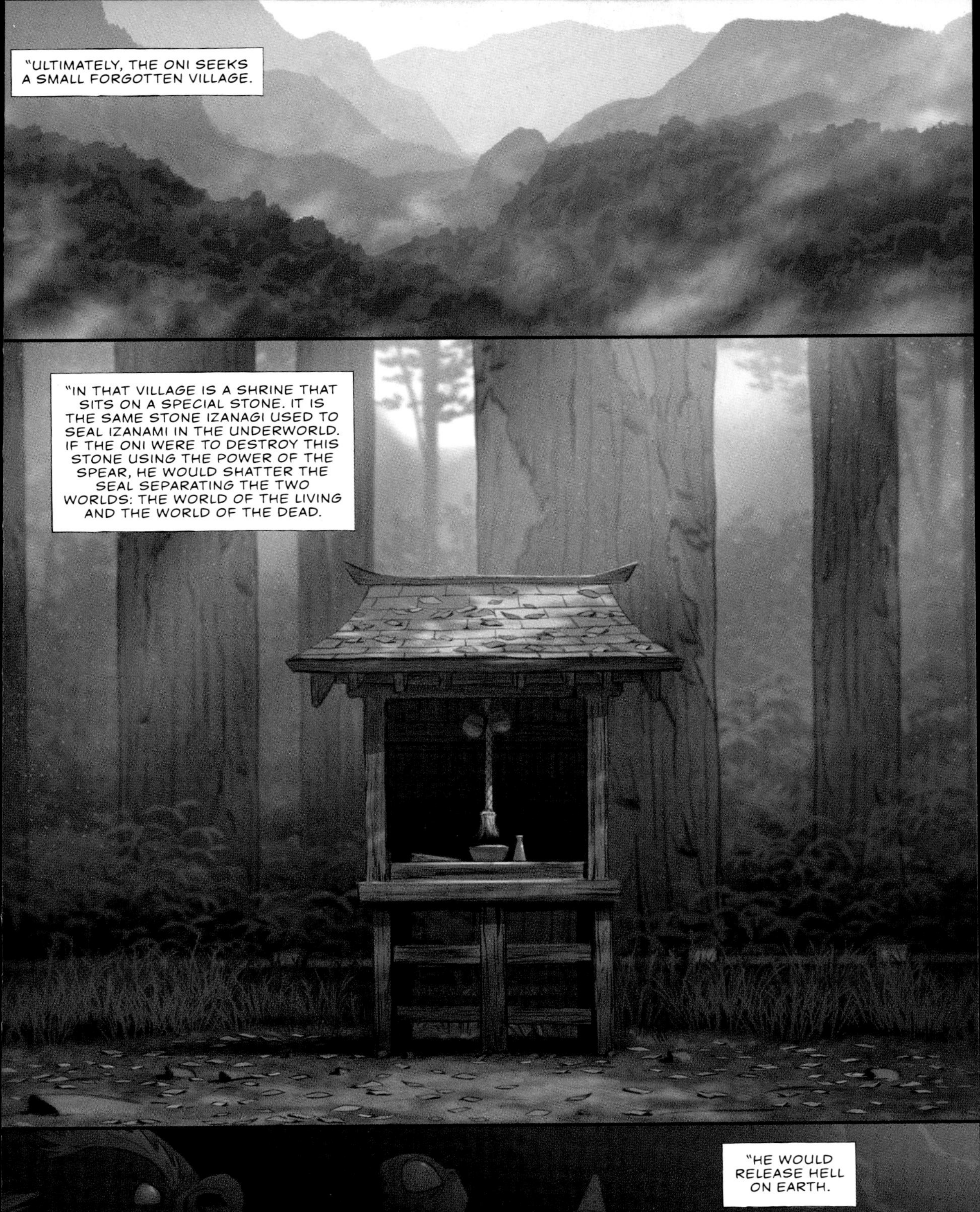
"ULTIMATELY, THE ONI SEEKS A SMALL FORGOTTEN VILLAGE.
"IN THAT VILLAGE IS A SHRINE THAT SITS ON A SPECIAL STONE. IT IS THE SAME STONE IZANAGI USED TO SEAL IZANAMI IN THE UNDERWORLD. IF THE ONI WERE TO DESTROY THIS STONE USING THE POWER OF THE SPEAR, HE WOULD SHATTER THE SEAL SEPARATING THE TWO WORLDS: THE WORLD OF THE LIVING AND THE WORLD OF THE DEAD.
"HE WOULD RELEASE HELL ON EARTH.

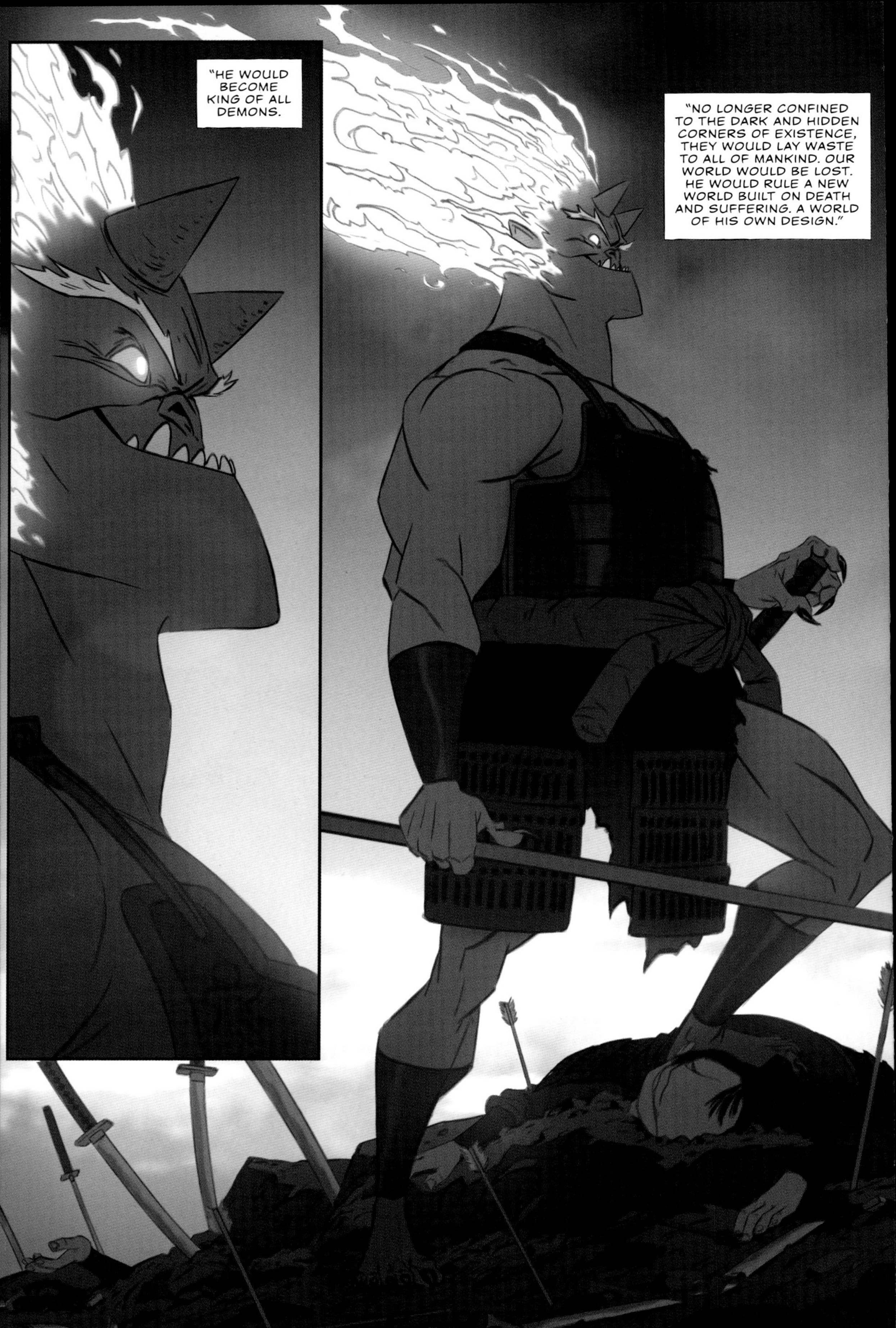
"HE WOULD BECOME KING OF ALL DEMONS.
"NO LONGER CONFINED TO THE DARK AND HIDDEN CORNERS OF EXISTENCE, THEY WOULD LAY WASTE TO ALL OF MANKIND. OUR WORLD WOULD BE LOST. HE WOULD RULE A NEW WORLD BUILT ON DEATH AND SUFFERING. A WORLD OF HIS OWN DESIGN."

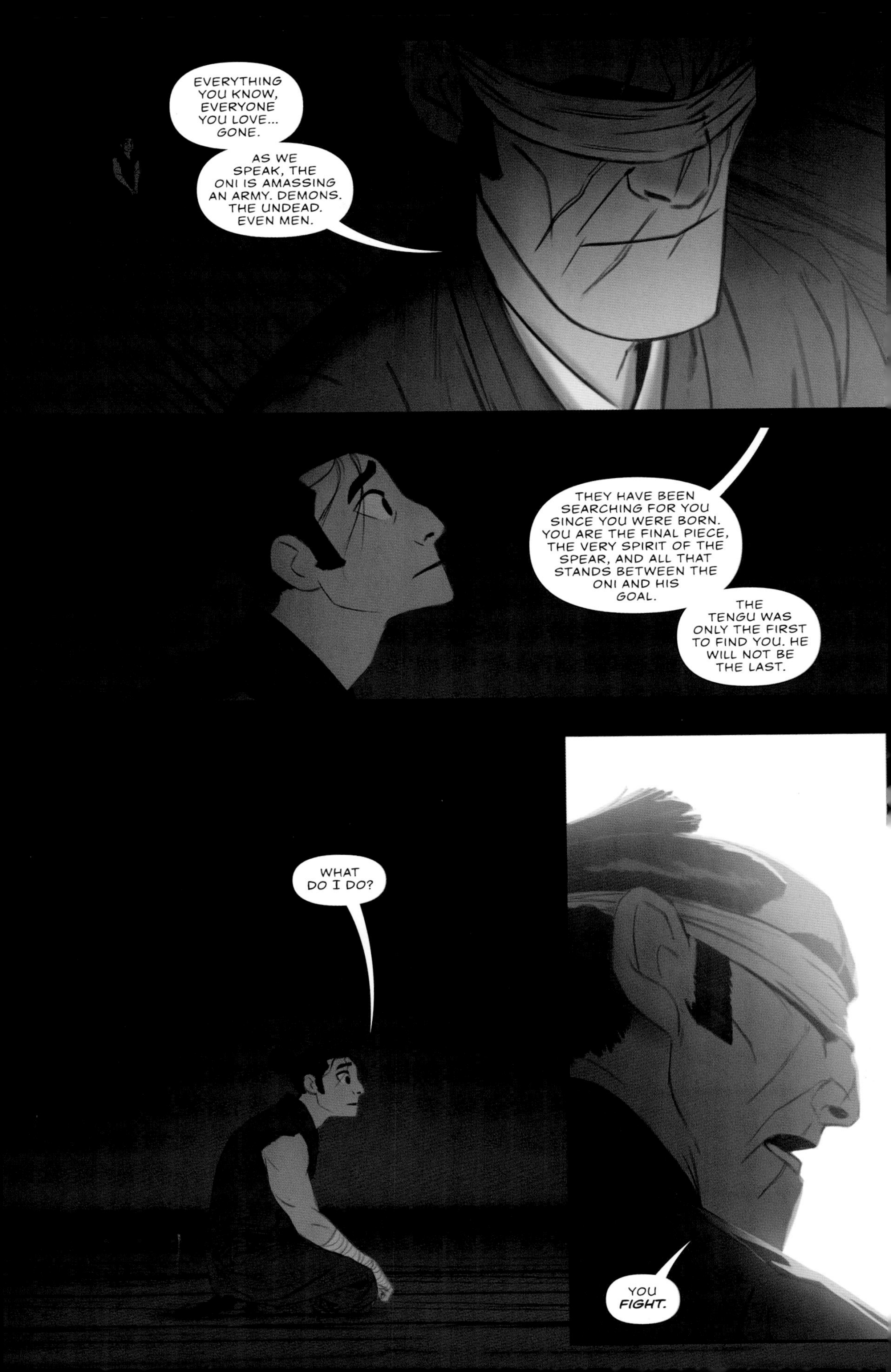

EVERYTHING YOU KNOW, EVERYONE YOU LOVE... GONE.
AS WE SPEAK, THE ONI IS AMASSING AN ARMY. DEMONS. THE UNDEAD. EVEN MEN.
THEY HAVE BEEN SEARCHING FOR YOU SINCE YOU WERE BORN. YOU ARE THE FINAL PIECE, THE VERY SPIRIT OF THE SPEAR, AND ALL THAT STANDS BETWEEN THE ONI AND HIS GOAL.
THE TENGU WAS ONLY THE FIRST TO FIND YOU. HE WILL NOT BE THE LAST.
WHAT DO I DO?
YOU *FIGHT.*

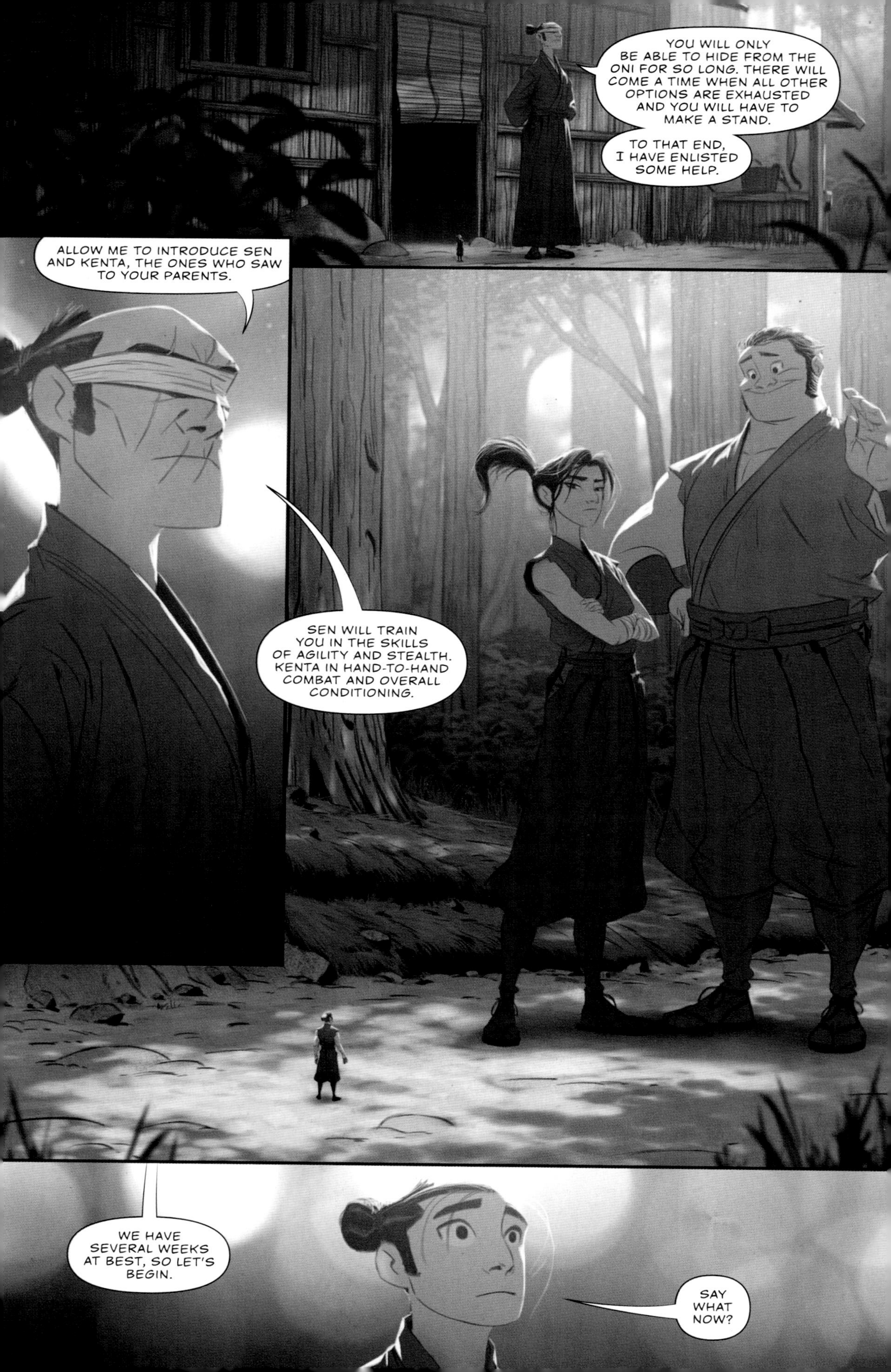
YOU WILL ONLY BE ABLE TO HIDE FROM THE ONI FOR SO LONG. THERE WILL COME A TIME WHEN ALL OTHER OPTIONS ARE EXHAUSTED AND YOU WILL HAVE TO MAKE A STAND.
TO THAT END, I HAVE ENLISTED SOME HELP.
ALLOW ME TO INTRODUCE SEN AND KENTA, THE ONES WHO SAW TO YOUR PARENTS.
SEN WILL TRAIN YOU IN THE SKILLS OF AGILITY AND STEALTH. KENTA IN HAND-TO-HAND COMBAT AND OVERALL CONDITIONING.
WE HAVE SEVERAL WEEKS AT BEST, SO LET'S BEGIN.
SAY WHAT NOW?

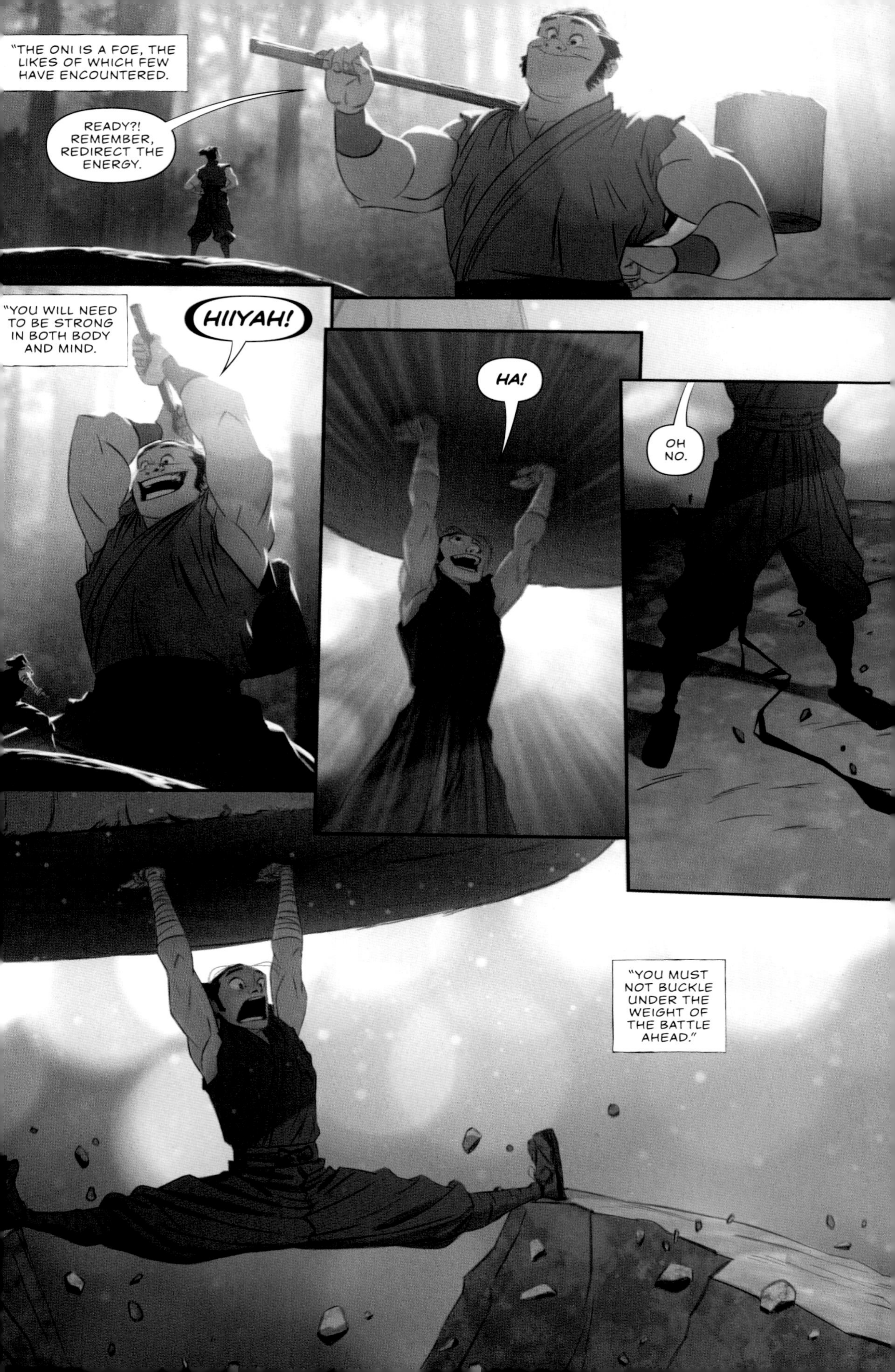
"THE ONI IS A FOE, THE LIKES OF WHICH FEW HAVE ENCOUNTERED.
READY?! REMEMBER, REDIRECT THE ENERGY.
"YOU WILL NEED TO BE STRONG IN BOTH BODY AND MIND.
HIIYAH!
HA!
OH NO.
"YOU MUST NOT BUCKLE UNDER THE WEIGHT OF THE BATTLE AHEAD."

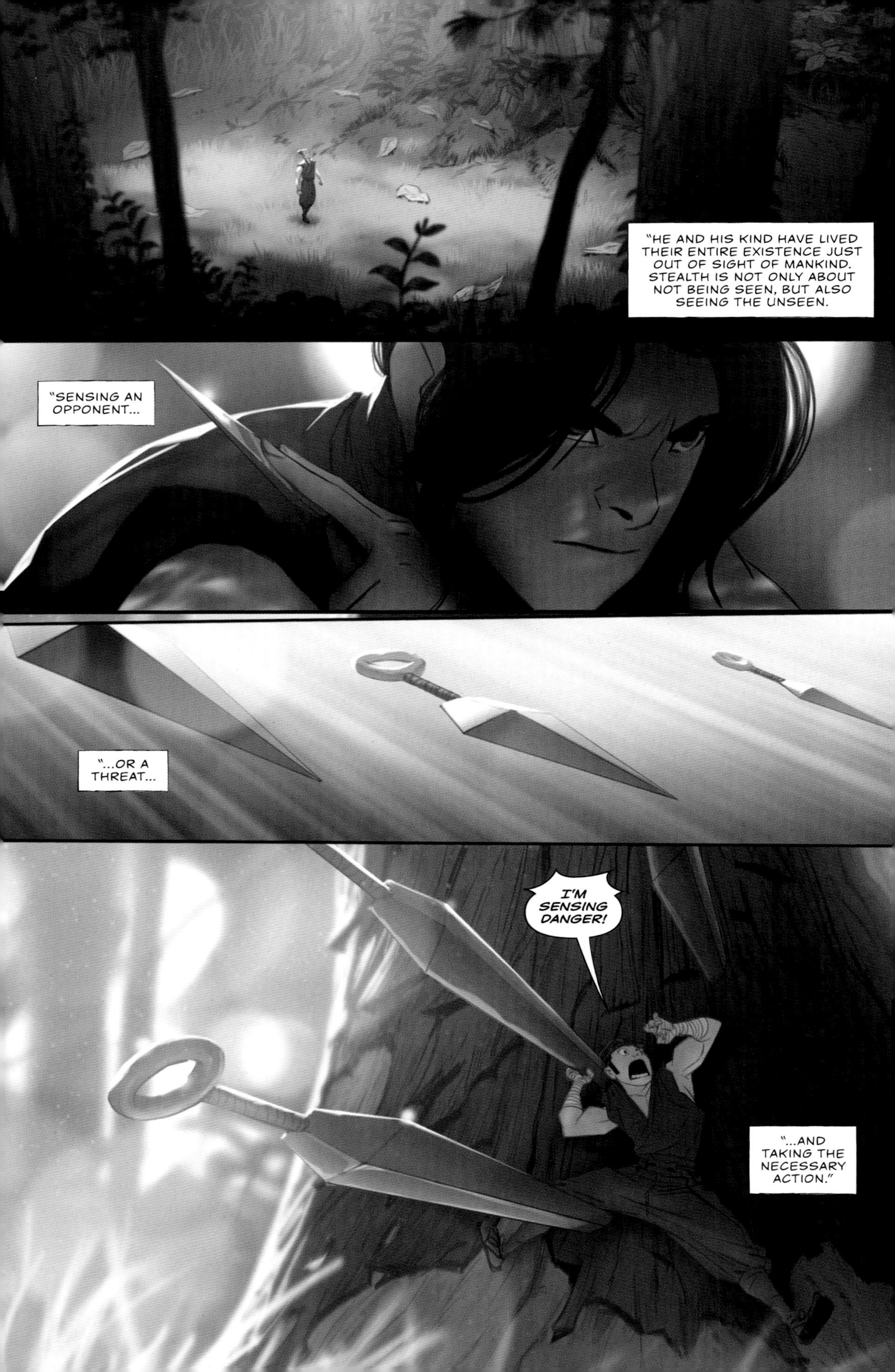
"HE AND HIS KIND HAVE LIVED THEIR ENTIRE EXISTENCE JUST OUT OF SIGHT OF MANKIND. STEALTH IS NOT ONLY ABOUT NOT BEING SEEN, BUT ALSO SEEING THE UNSEEN.
"SENSING AN OPPONENT...
"...OR A THREAT...
I'M SENSING DANGER!
"...AND TAKING THE NECESSARY ACTION."

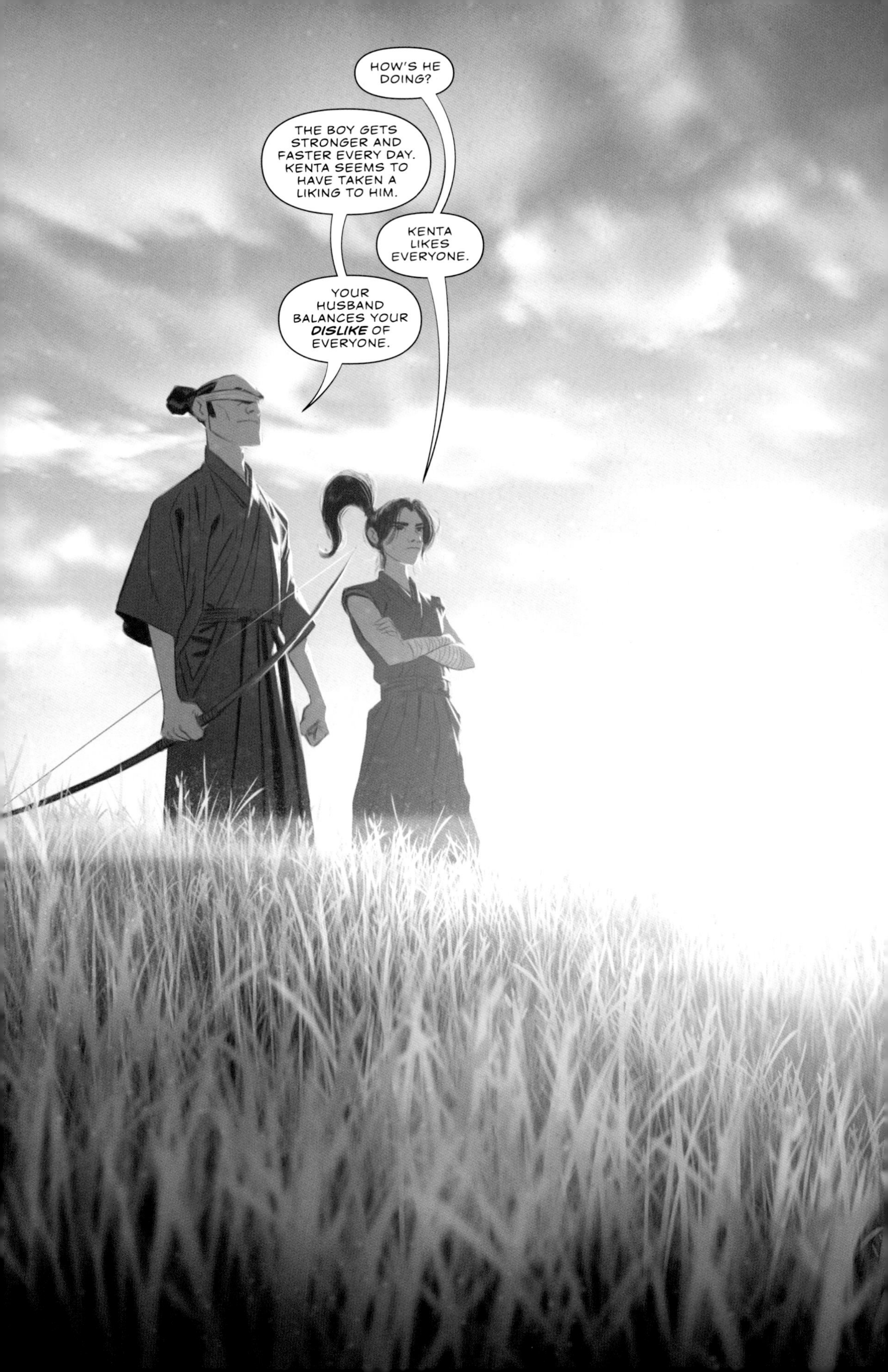
HOW'S HE DOING?
THE BOY GETS STRONGER AND FASTER EVERY DAY. KENTA SEEMS TO HAVE TAKEN A LIKING TO HIM.
KENTA LIKES EVERYONE.
YOUR HUSBAND BALANCES YOUR DISLIKE OF EVERYONE.

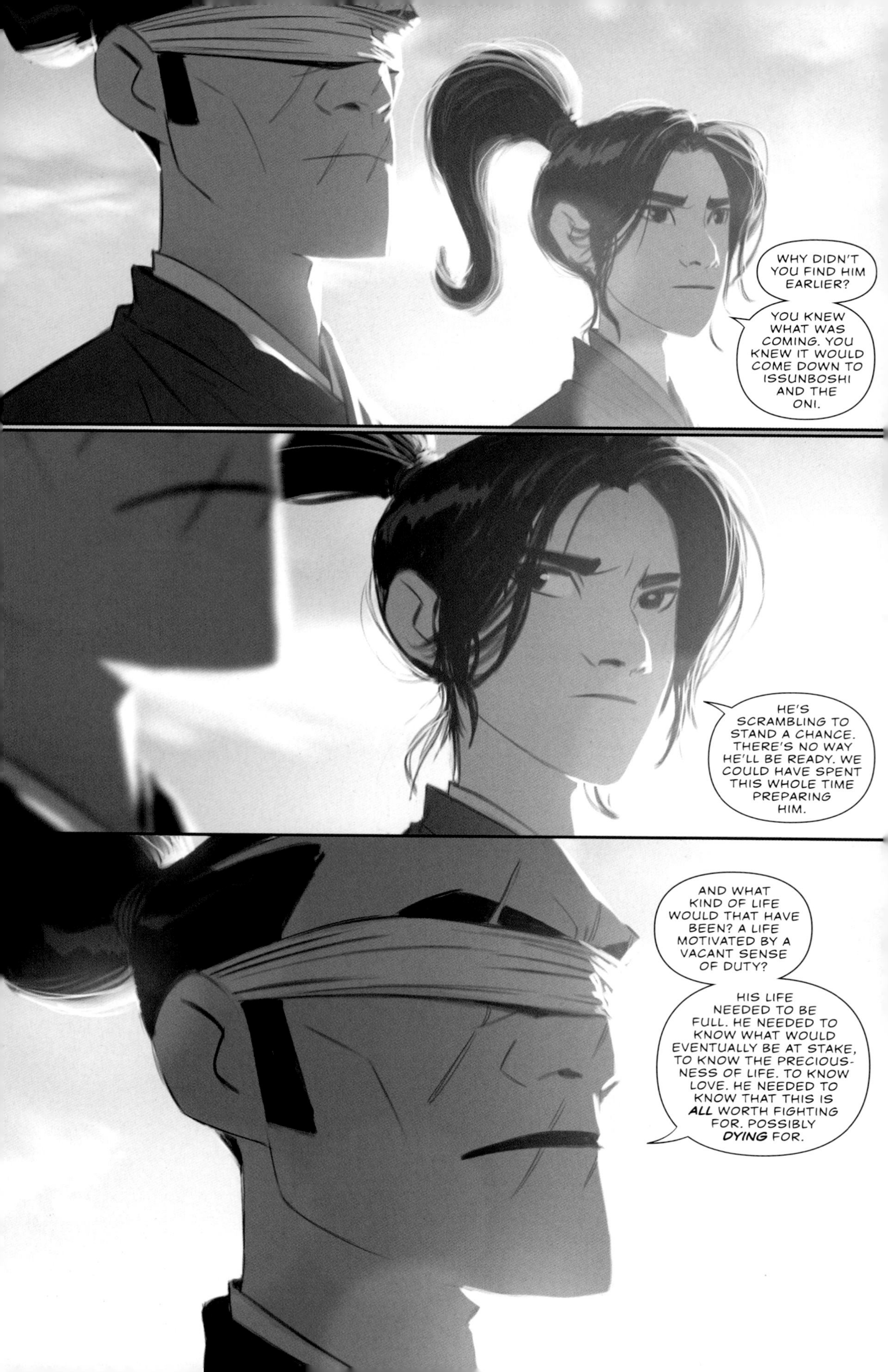
WHY DIDN'T YOU FIND HIM EARLIER?
YOU KNEW WHAT WAS COMING. YOU KNEW IT WOULD COME DOWN TO ISSUNBOSHI AND THE ONI.
HE'S SCRAMBLING TO STAND A CHANCE. THERE'S NO WAY HE'LL BE READY. WE COULD HAVE SPENT THIS WHOLE TIME PREPARING HIM.
AND WHAT KIND OF LIFE WOULD THAT HAVE BEEN? A LIFE MOTIVATED BY A VACANT SENSE OF DUTY?
HIS LIFE NEEDED TO BE FULL. HE NEEDED TO KNOW WHAT WOULD EVENTUALLY BE AT STAKE, TO KNOW THE PRECIOUSNESS OF LIFE. TO KNOW LOVE. HE NEEDED TO KNOW THAT THIS IS ALL WORTH FIGHTING FOR. POSSIBLY DYING FOR.

THREE

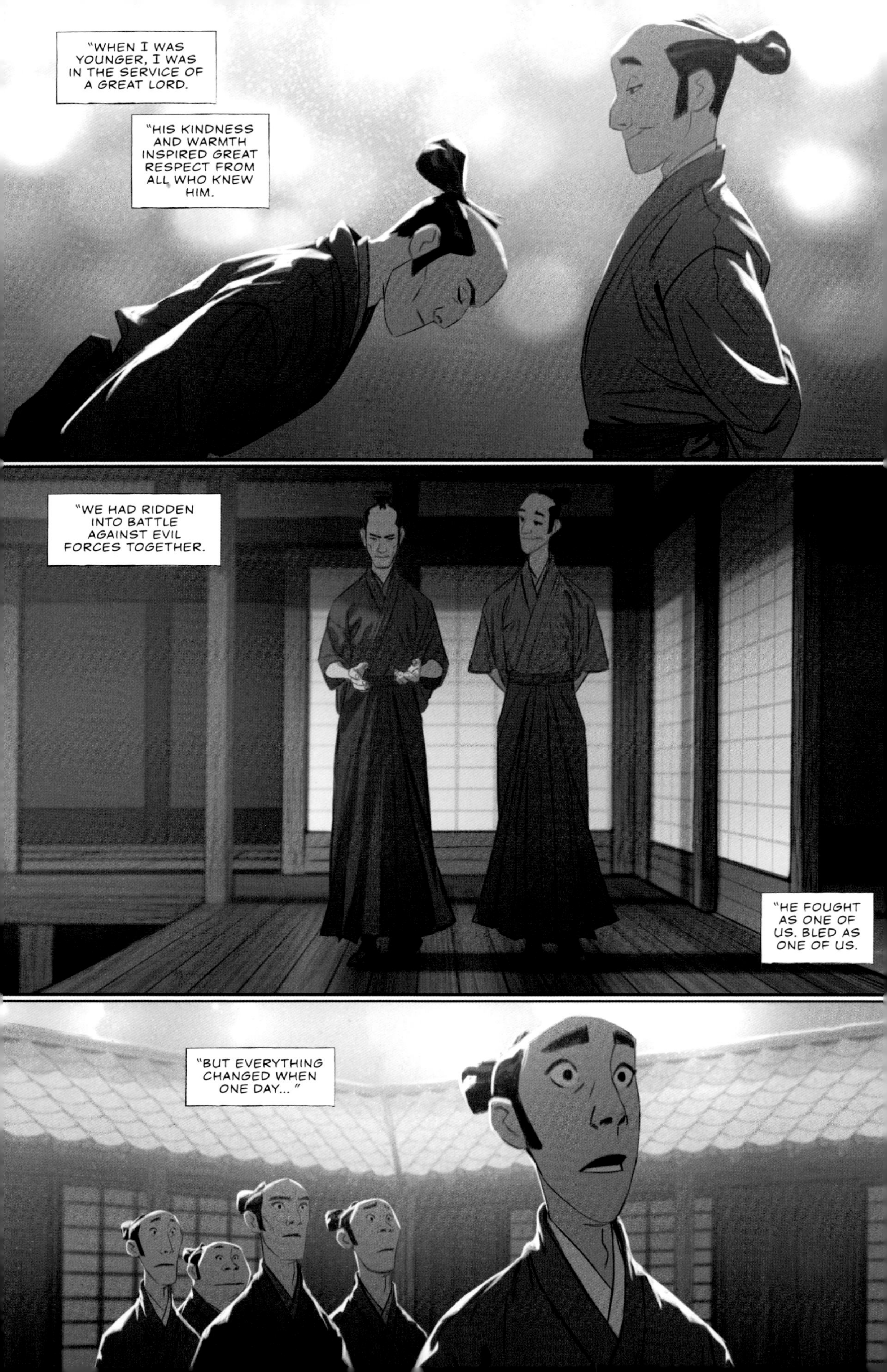
"WHEN I WAS YOUNGER, I WAS IN THE SERVICE OF A GREAT LORD.
"HIS KINDNESS AND WARMTH INSPIRED GREAT RESPECT FROM ALL WHO KNEW HIM.
"WE HAD RIDDEN INTO BATTLE AGAINST EVIL FORCES TOGETHER.
"HE FOUGHT AS ONE OF US. BLED AS ONE OF US.
"BUT EVERYTHING CHANGED WHEN ONE DAY..."

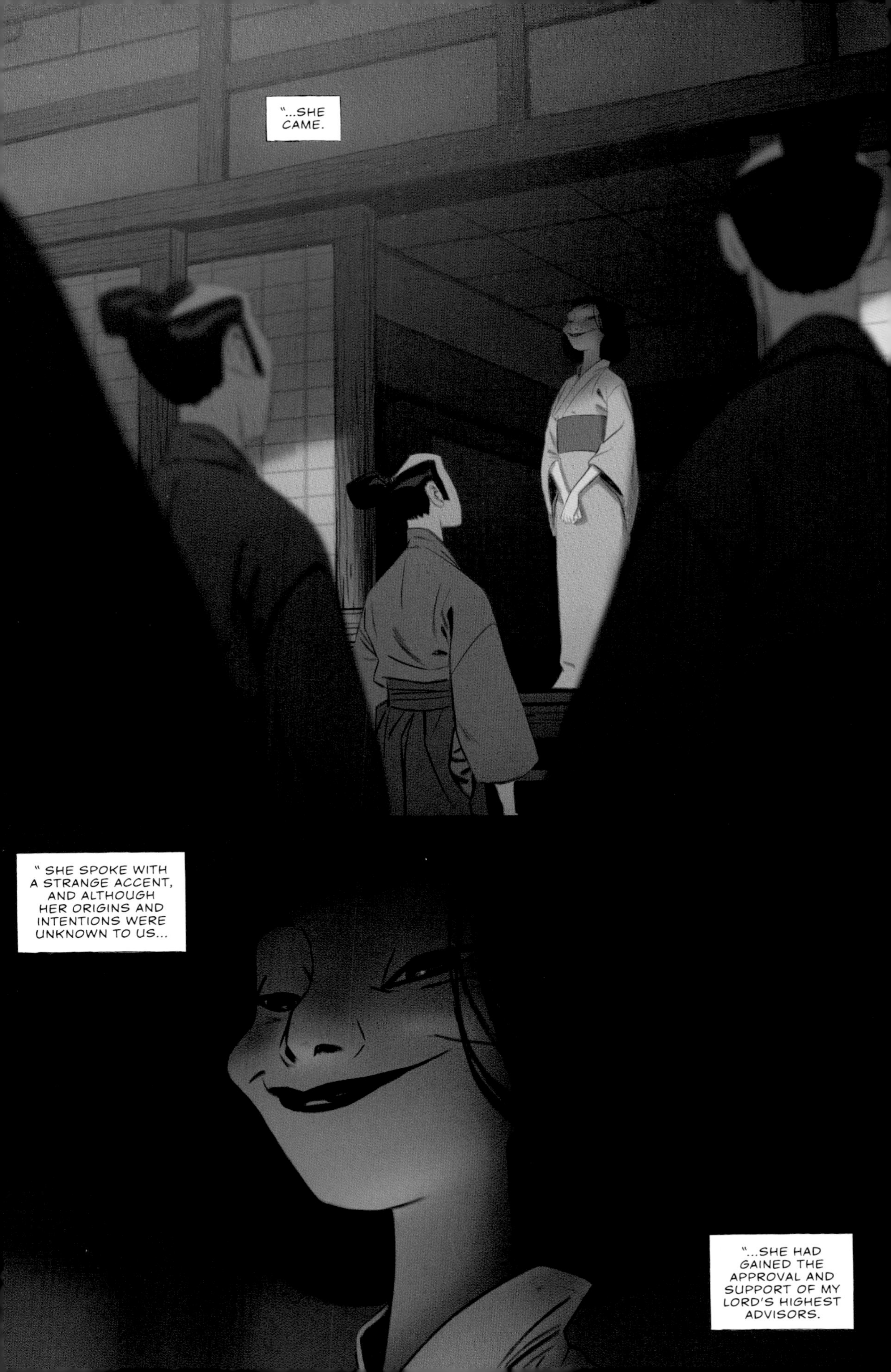
"...SHE CAME.
" SHE SPOKE WITH A STRANGE ACCENT, AND ALTHOUGH HER ORIGINS AND INTENTIONS WERE UNKNOWN TO US...
"...SHE HAD GAINED THE APPROVAL AND SUPPORT OF MY LORD'S HIGHEST ADVISORS.

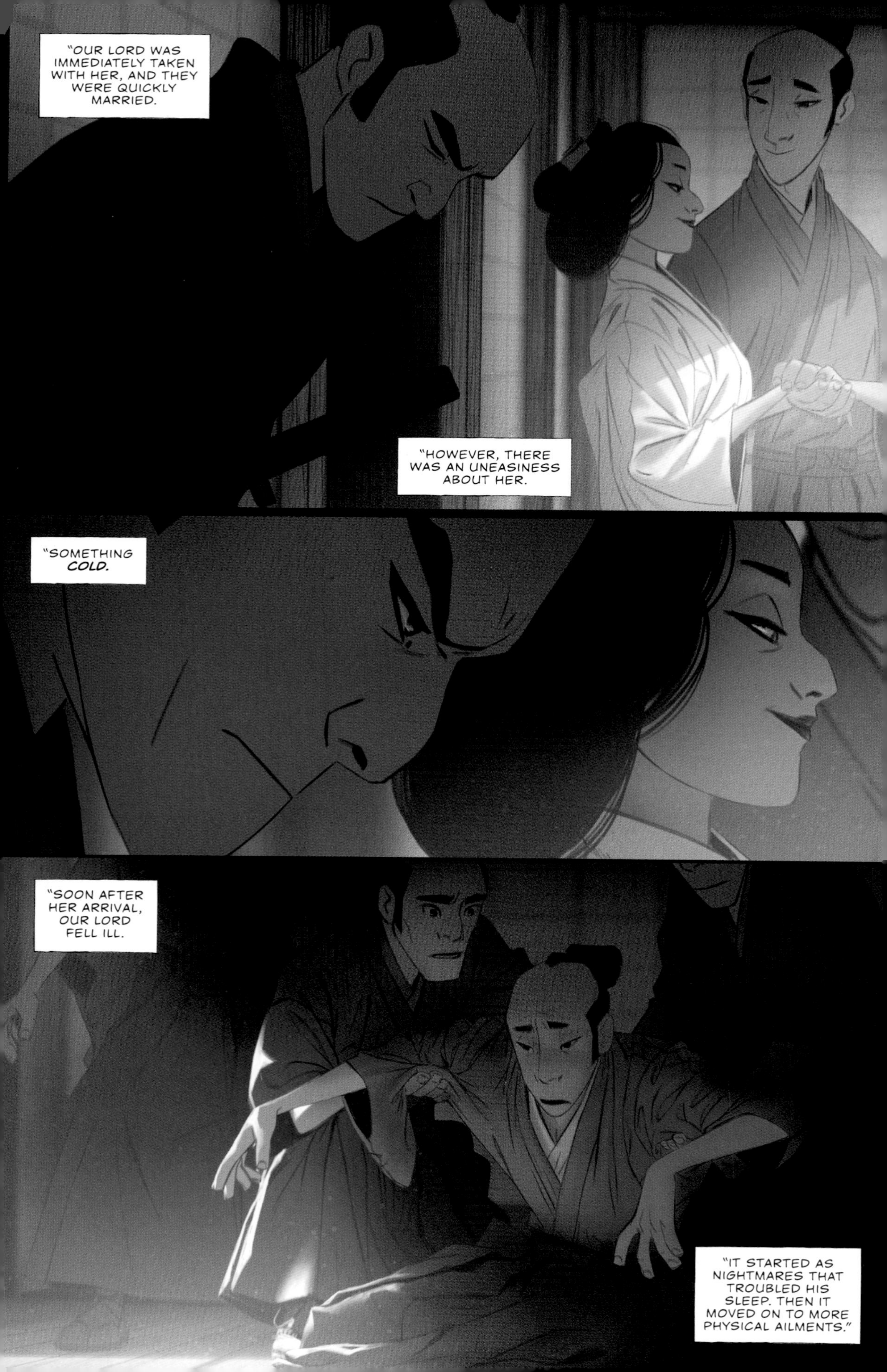
"OUR LORD WAS IMMEDIATELY TAKEN WITH HER, AND THEY WERE QUICKLY MARRIED.
"HOWEVER, THERE WAS AN UNEASINESS ABOUT HER.
"SOMETHING *COLD.*
"SOON AFTER HER ARRIVAL, OUR LORD FELL ILL.
"IT STARTED AS NIGHTMARES THAT TROUBLED HIS SLEEP. THEN IT MOVED ON TO MORE PHYSICAL AILMENTS."

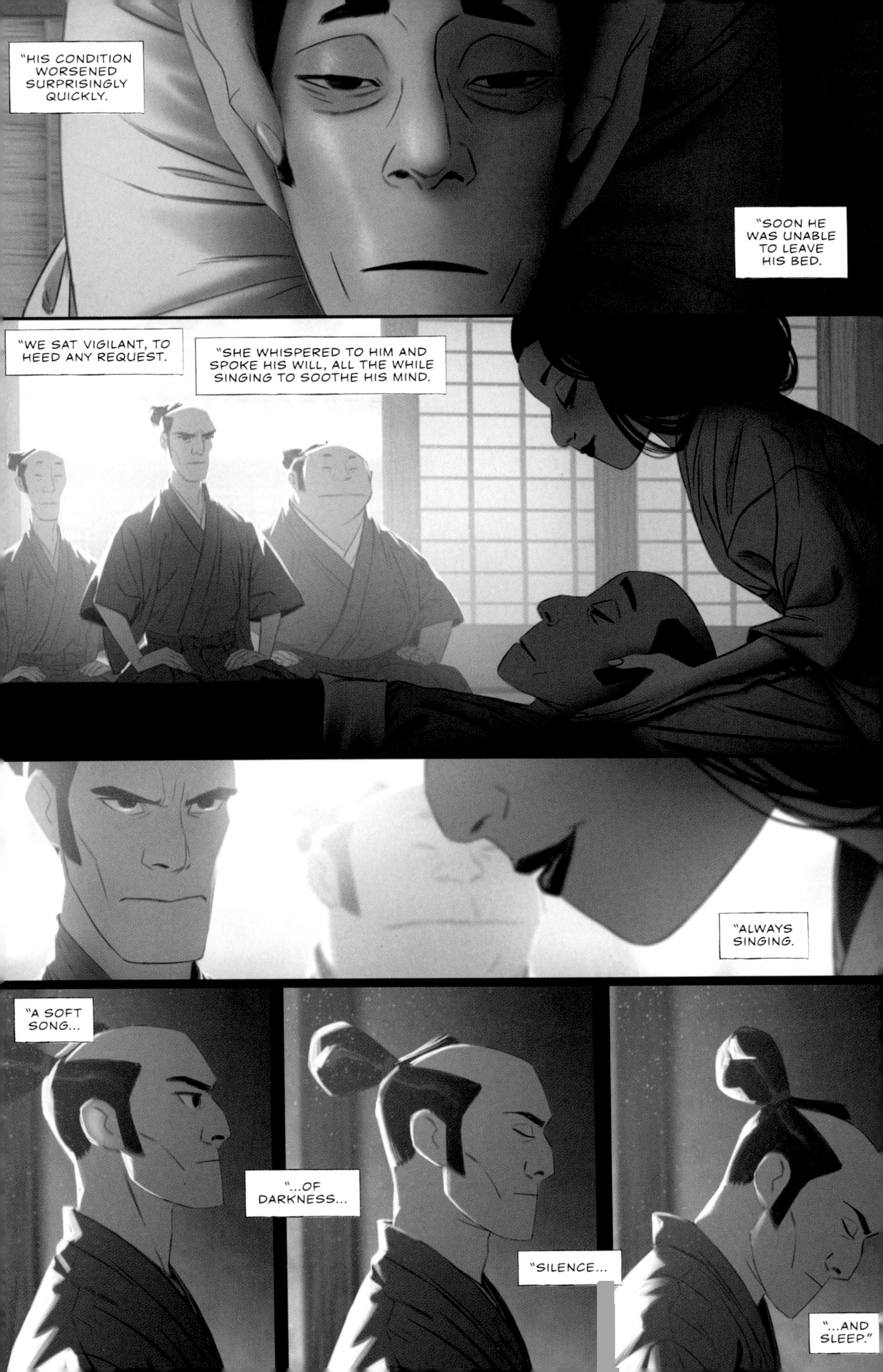
"HIS CONDITION WORSENED SURPRISINGLY QUICKLY.
"SOON HE WAS UNABLE TO LEAVE HIS BED.
"WE SAT VIGILANT, TO HEED ANY REQUEST.
"SHE WHISPERED TO HIM AND SPOKE HIS WILL, ALL THE WHILE SINGING TO SOOTHE HIS MIND.
"ALWAYS SINGING.
"A SOFT SONG...
"...OF DARKNESS...
"SILENCE...
"...AND SLEEP."

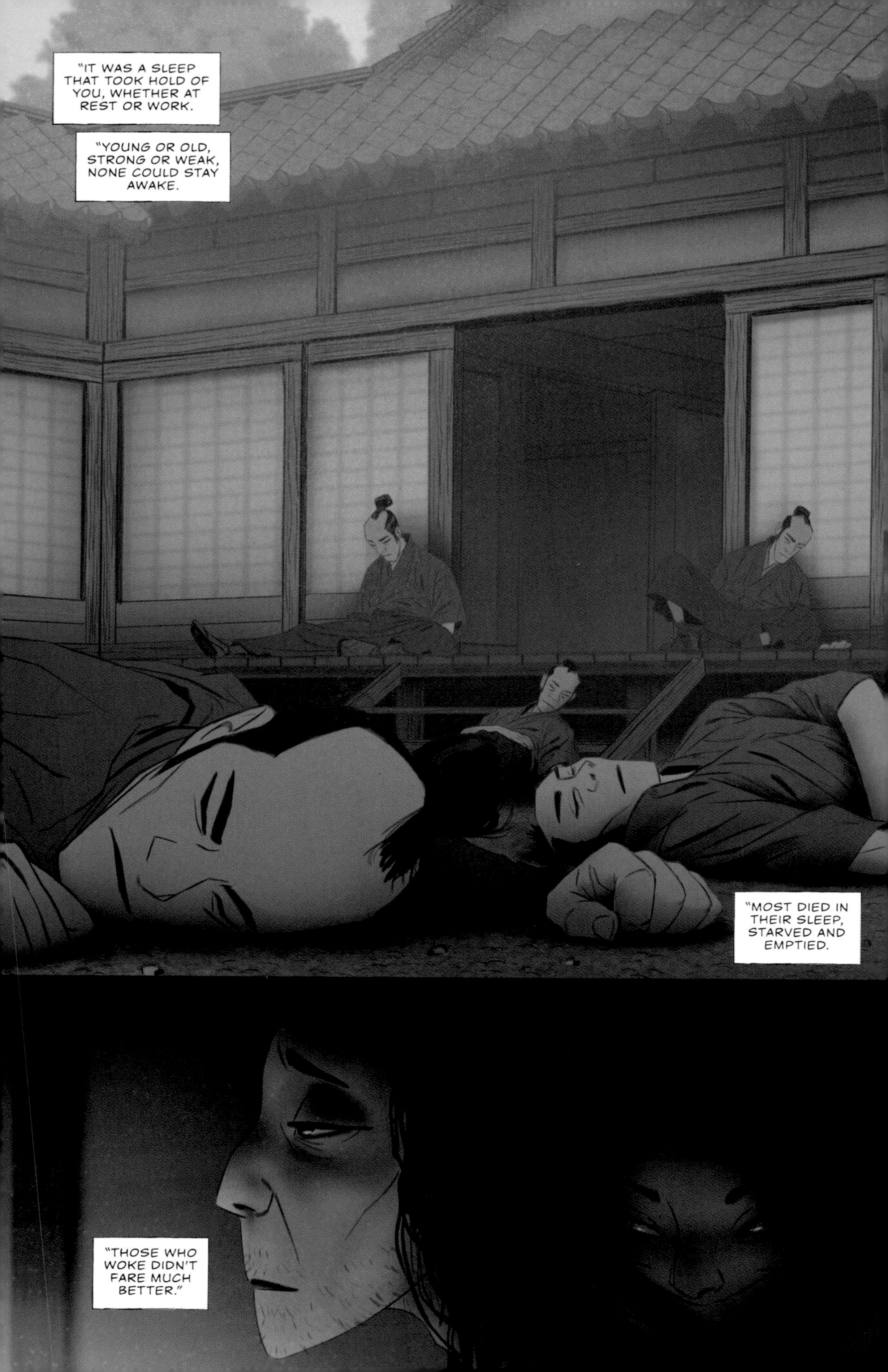
"IT WAS A SLEEP THAT TOOK HOLD OF YOU, WHETHER AT REST OR WORK.
"YOUNG OR OLD, STRONG OR WEAK, NONE COULD STAY AWAKE.
"MOST DIED IN THEIR SLEEP, STARVED AND EMPTIED.
"THOSE WHO WOKE DIDN'T FARE MUCH BETTER."

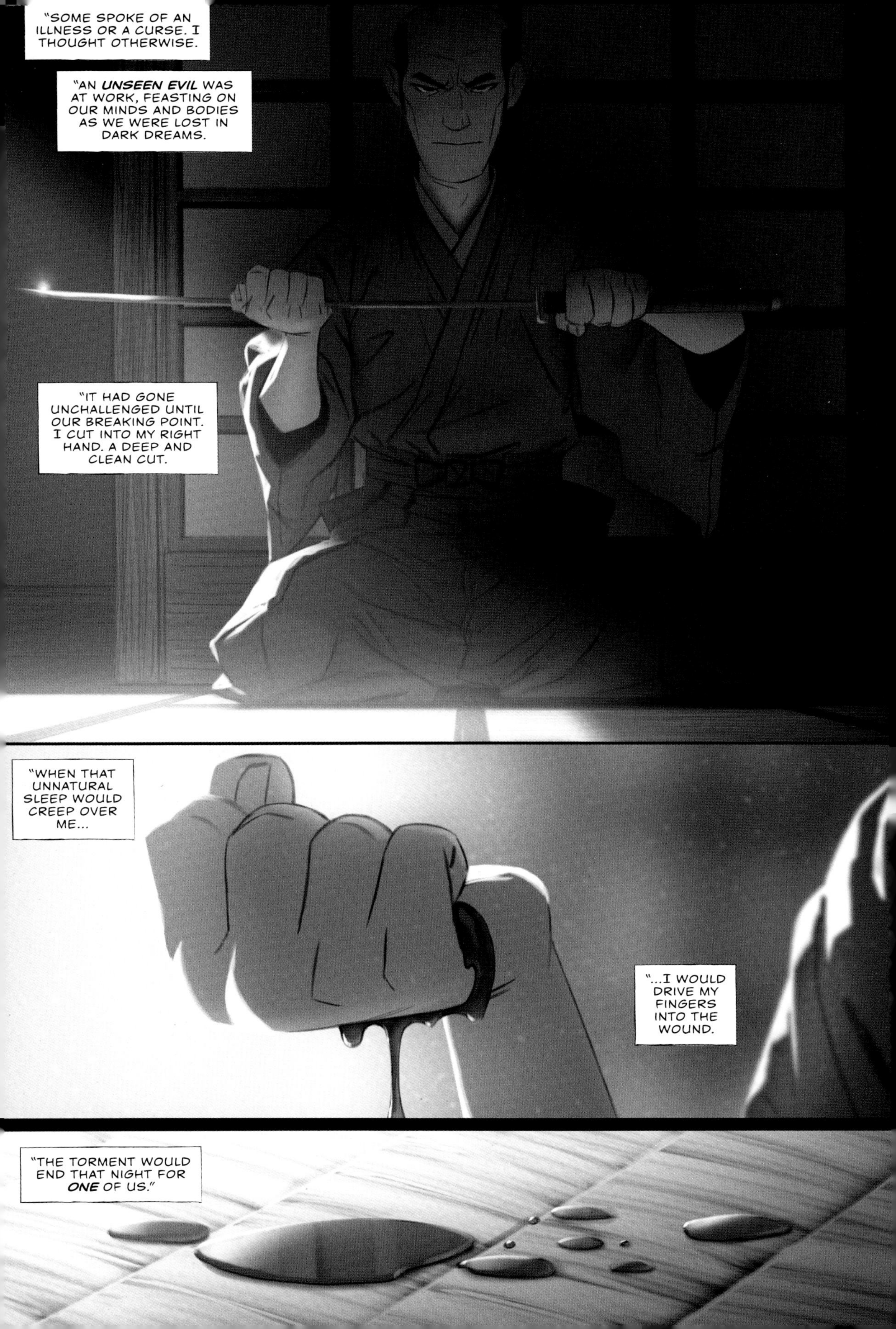
"SOME SPOKE OF AN ILLNESS OR A CURSE. I THOUGHT OTHERWISE.
"AN ***UNSEEN EVIL*** WAS AT WORK, FEASTING ON OUR MINDS AND BODIES AS WE WERE LOST IN DARK DREAMS.
"IT HAD GONE UNCHALLENGED UNTIL OUR BREAKING POINT. I CUT INTO MY RIGHT HAND. A DEEP AND CLEAN CUT.
"WHEN THAT UNNATURAL SLEEP WOULD CREEP OVER ME...
"...I WOULD DRIVE MY FINGERS INTO THE WOUND.
"THE TORMENT WOULD END THAT NIGHT FOR ***ONE*** OF US."

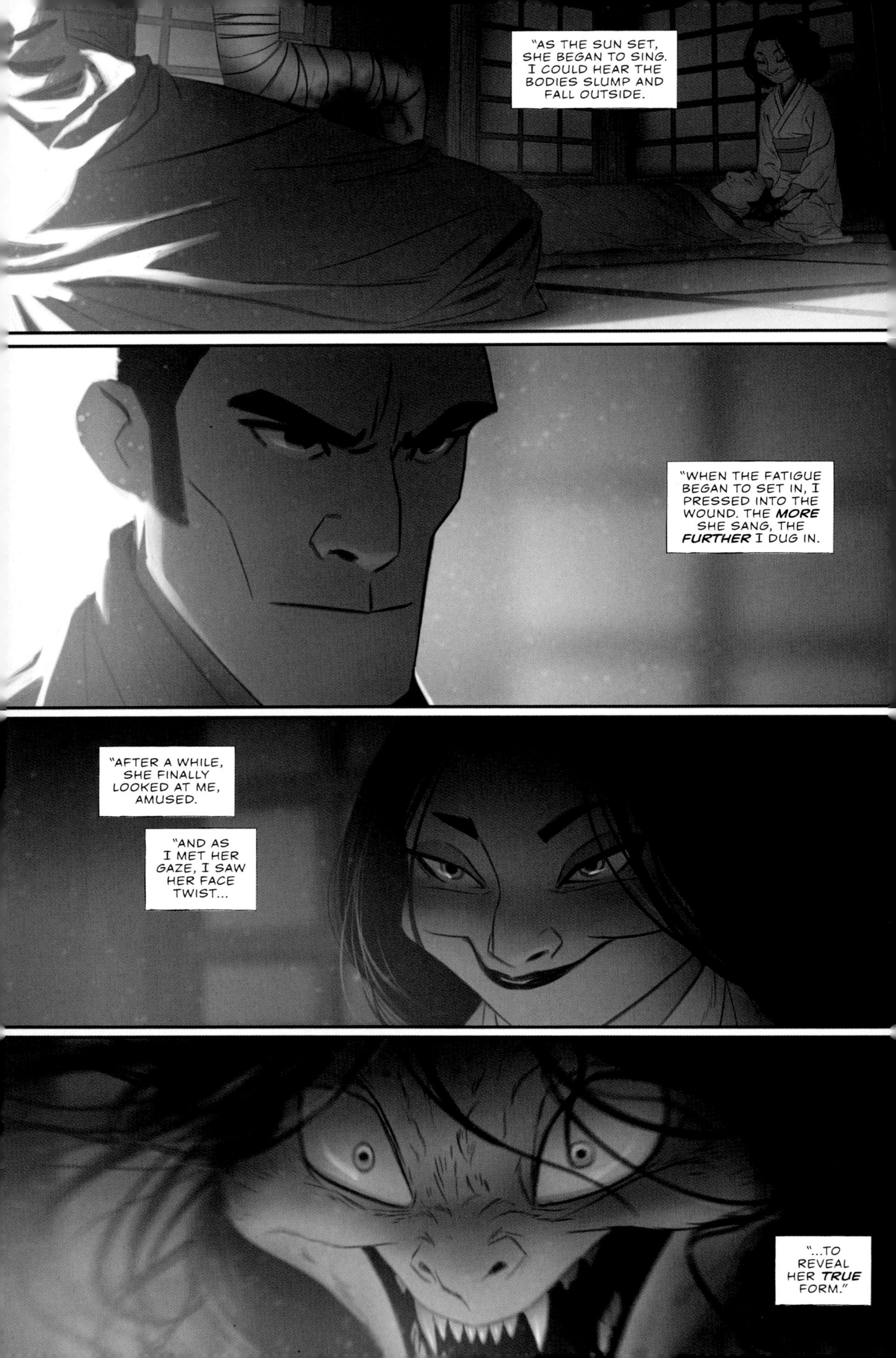
"AS THE SUN SET, SHE BEGAN TO SING. I COULD HEAR THE BODIES SLUMP AND FALL OUTSIDE.
"WHEN THE FATIGUE BEGAN TO SET IN, I PRESSED INTO THE WOUND. THE *MORE* SHE SANG, THE *FURTHER* I DUG IN.
"AFTER A WHILE, SHE FINALLY LOOKED AT ME, AMUSED.
"AND AS I MET HER GAZE, I SAW HER FACE TWIST...
"...TO REVEAL HER *TRUE* FORM."

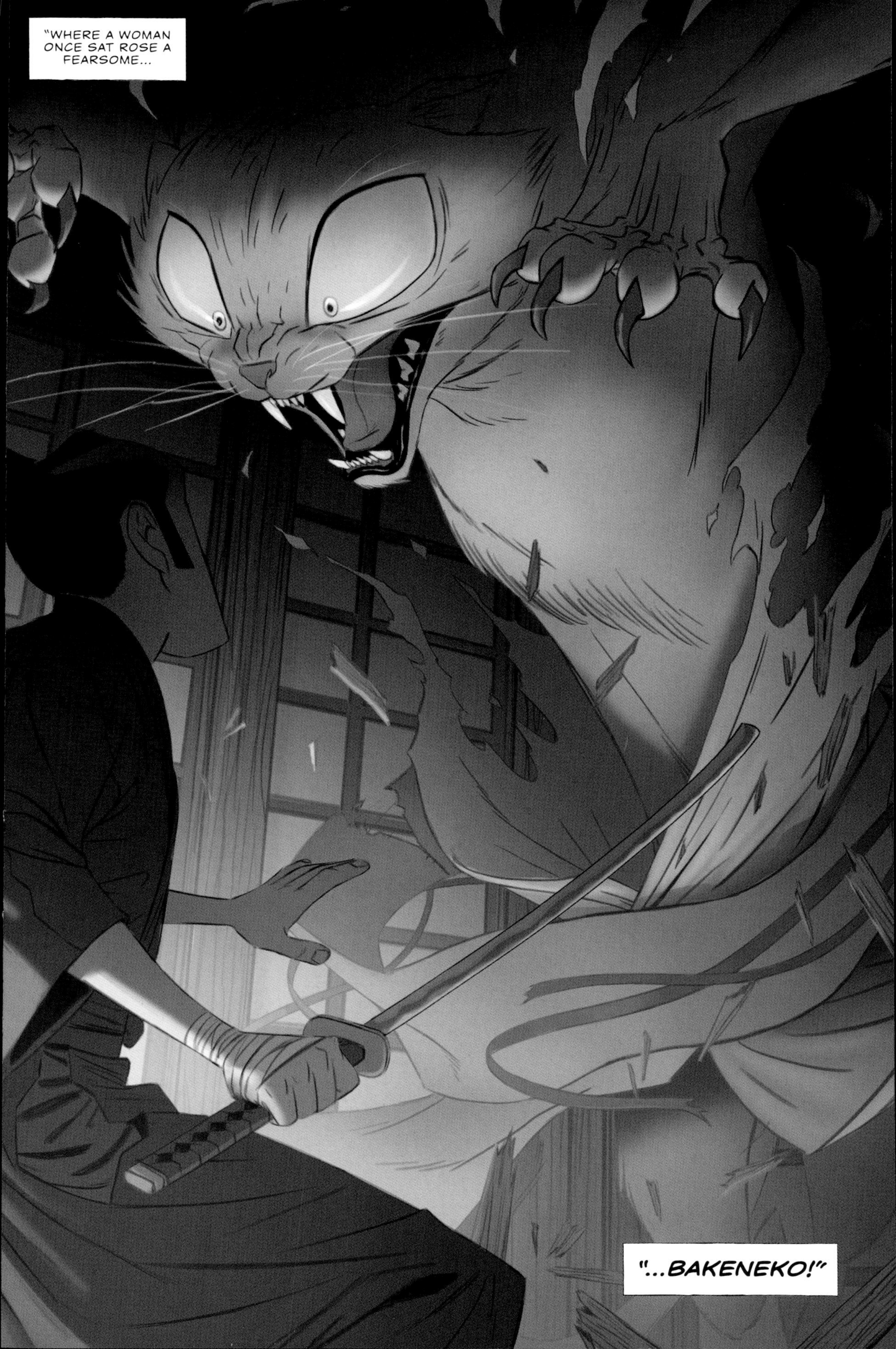
"WHERE A WOMAN ONCE SAT ROSE A FEARSOME...
"...BAKENEKO!"

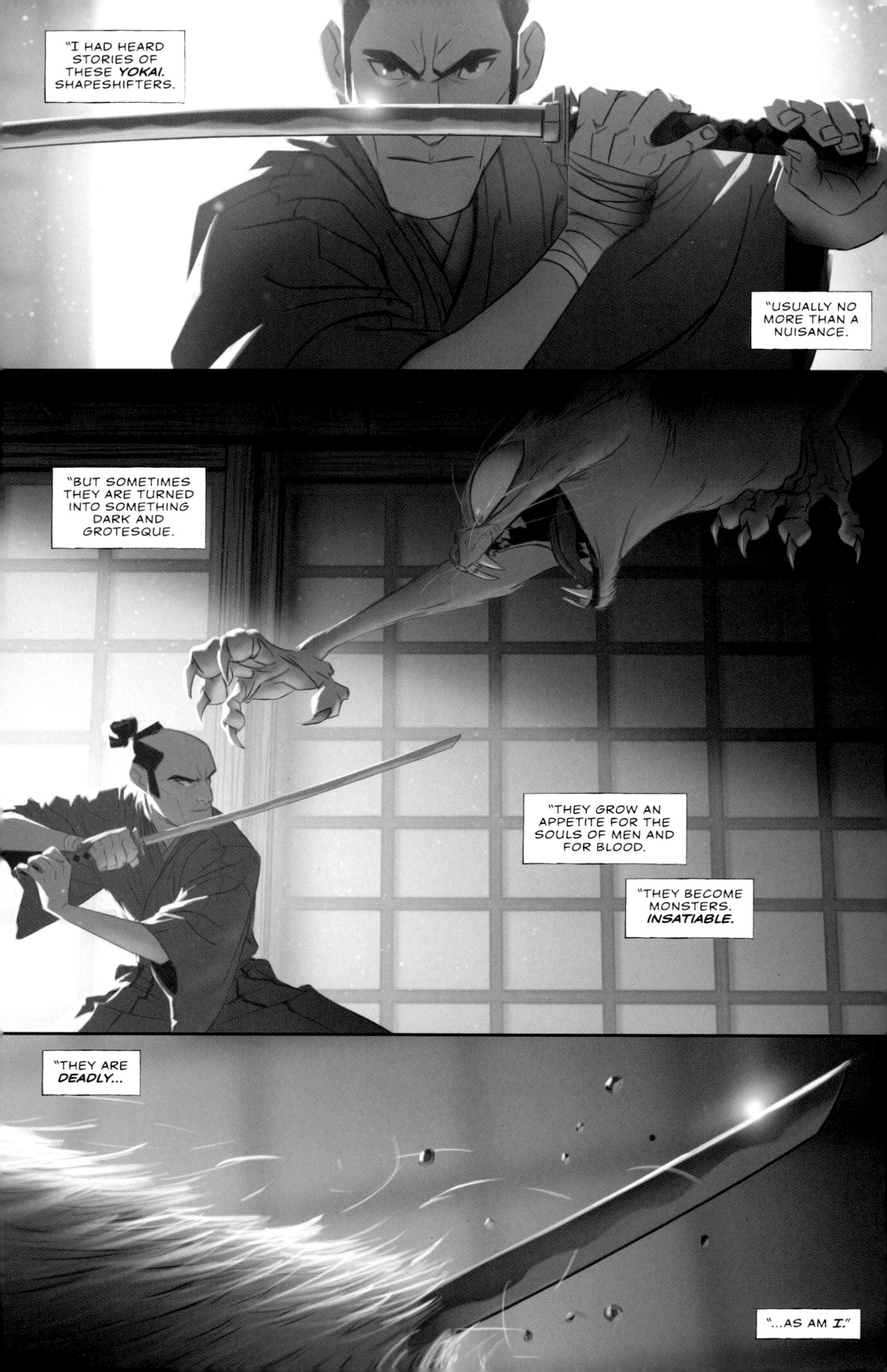
"I HAD HEARD STORIES OF THESE ***YOKAI.*** SHAPESHIFTERS.
"USUALLY NO MORE THAN A NUISANCE.
"BUT SOMETIMES THEY ARE TURNED INTO SOMETHING DARK AND GROTESQUE.
"THEY GROW AN APPETITE FOR THE SOULS OF MEN AND FOR BLOOD.
"THEY BECOME MONSTERS. ***INSATIABLE.***
"THEY ARE ***DEADLY...***
"...AS AM ***I.***"

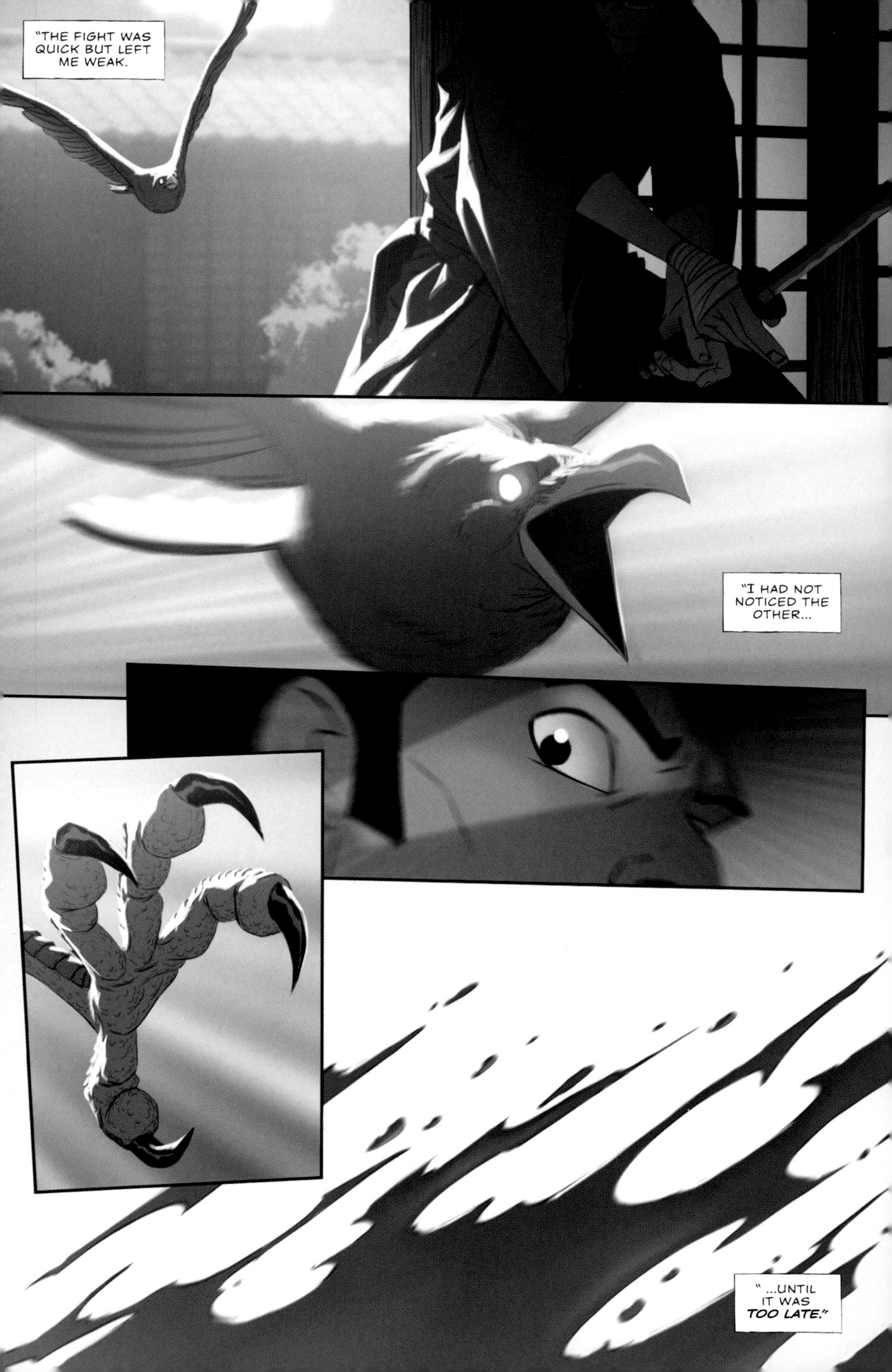
"THE FIGHT WAS QUICK BUT LEFT ME WEAK.
"I HAD NOT NOTICED THE OTHER...
"...UNTIL IT WAS *TOO LATE.*"

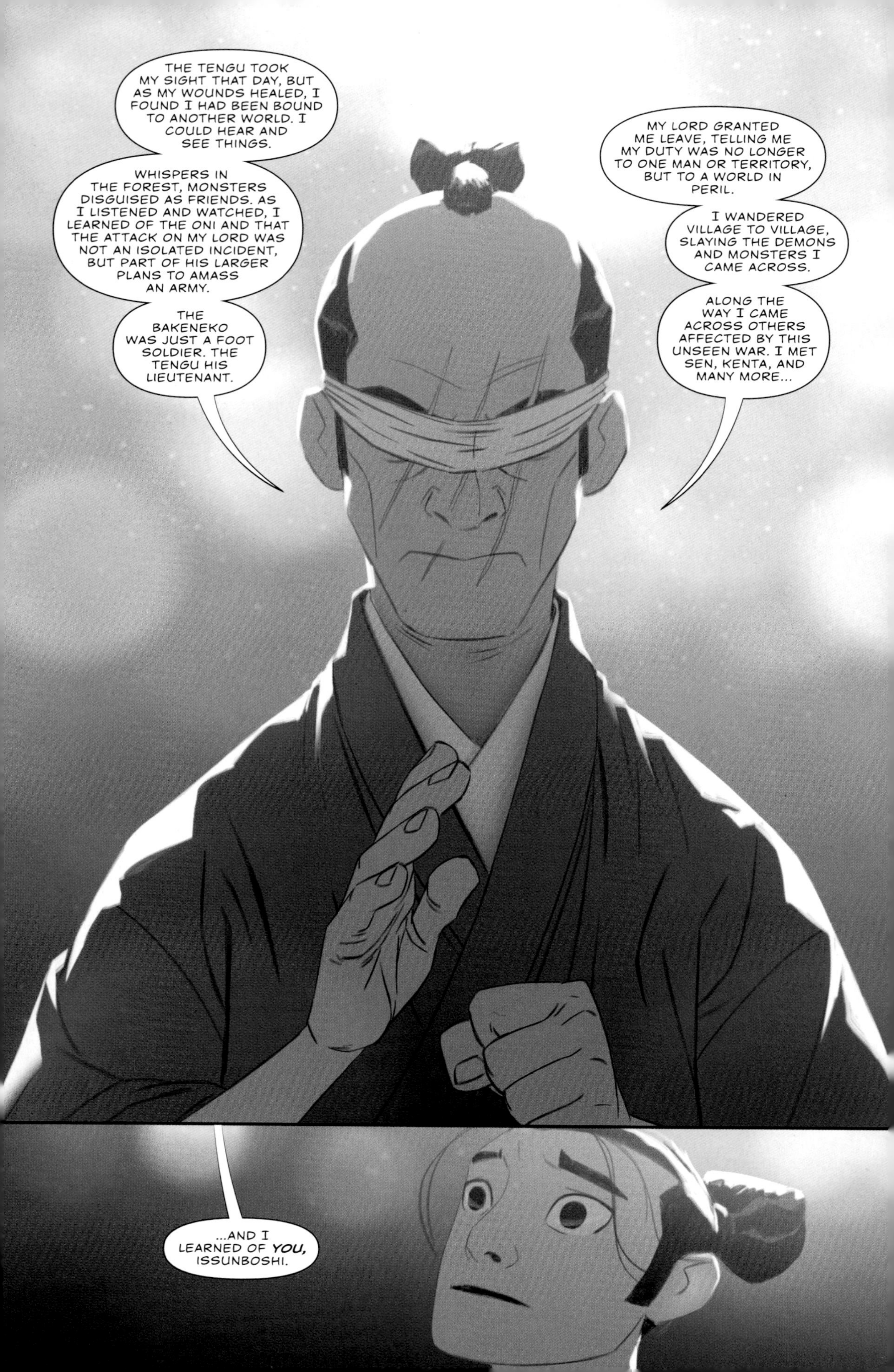
THE TENGU TOOK MY SIGHT THAT DAY, BUT AS MY WOUNDS HEALED, I FOUND I HAD BEEN BOUND TO ANOTHER WORLD. I COULD HEAR AND SEE THINGS.
WHISPERS IN THE FOREST, MONSTERS DISGUISED AS FRIENDS. AS I LISTENED AND WATCHED, I LEARNED OF THE ONI AND THAT THE ATTACK ON MY LORD WAS NOT AN ISOLATED INCIDENT, BUT PART OF HIS LARGER PLANS TO AMASS AN ARMY.
THE BAKENEKO WAS JUST A FOOT SOLDIER. THE TENGU HIS LIEUTENANT.
MY LORD GRANTED ME LEAVE, TELLING ME MY DUTY WAS NO LONGER TO ONE MAN OR TERRITORY, BUT TO A WORLD IN PERIL.
I WANDERED VILLAGE TO VILLAGE, SLAYING THE DEMONS AND MONSTERS I CAME ACROSS.
ALONG THE WAY I CAME ACROSS OTHERS AFFECTED BY THIS UNSEEN WAR. I MET SEN, KENTA, AND MANY MORE...
...AND I LEARNED OF ***YOU,*** ISSUNBOSHI.

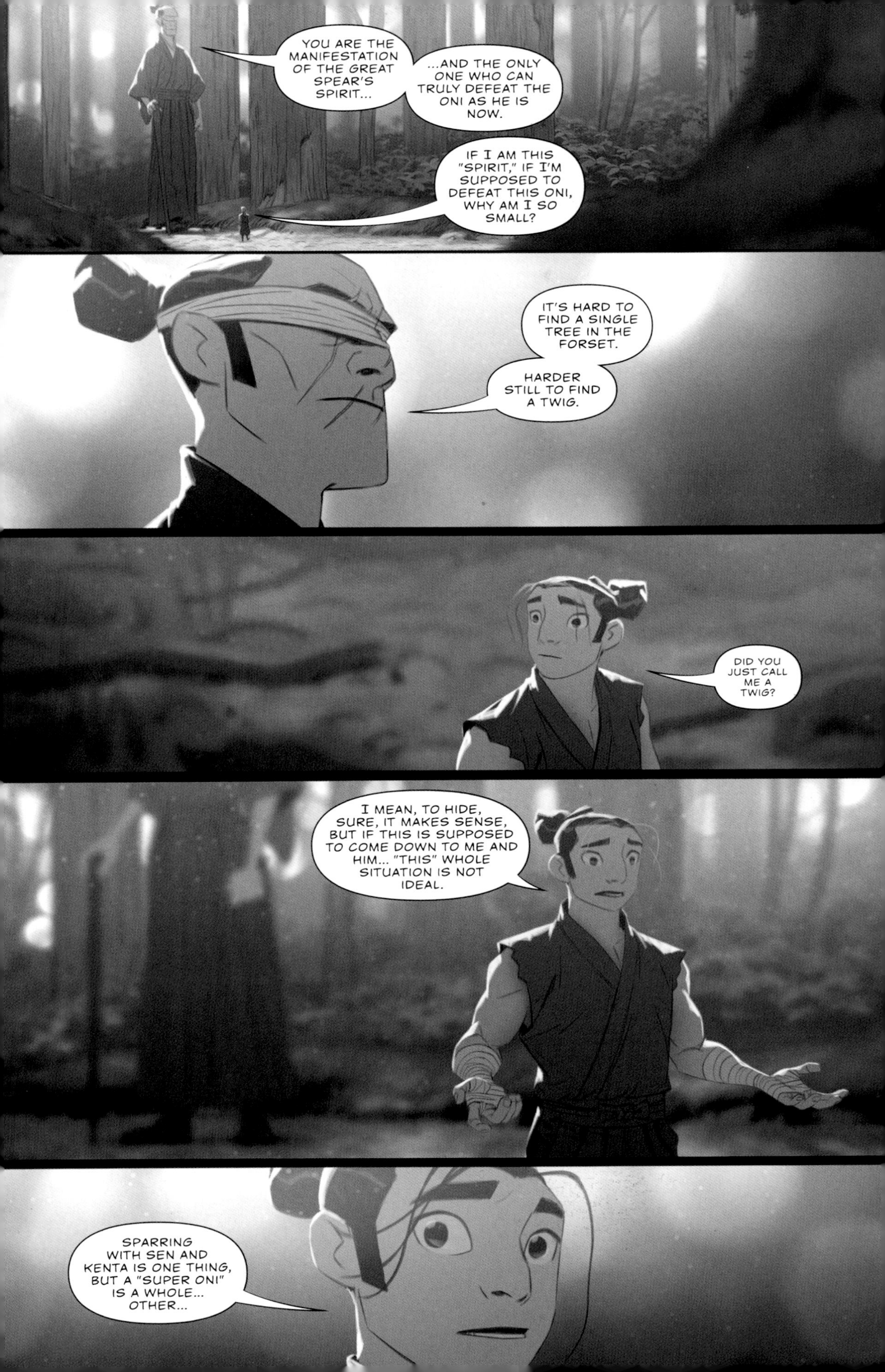
YOU ARE THE MANIFESTATION OF THE GREAT SPEAR'S SPIRIT...
...AND THE ONLY ONE WHO CAN TRULY DEFEAT THE ONI AS HE IS NOW.
IF I AM THIS "SPIRIT," IF I'M SUPPOSED TO DEFEAT THIS ONI, WHY AM I SO SMALL?
IT'S HARD TO FIND A SINGLE TREE IN THE FORSET.
HARDER STILL TO FIND A TWIG.
DID YOU JUST CALL ME A TWIG?
I MEAN, TO HIDE, SURE, IT MAKES SENSE, BUT IF THIS IS SUPPOSED TO COME DOWN TO ME AND HIM... "THIS" WHOLE SITUATION IS NOT IDEAL.
SPARRING WITH SEN AND KENTA IS ONE THING, BUT A "SUPER ONI" IS A WHOLE... OTHER...

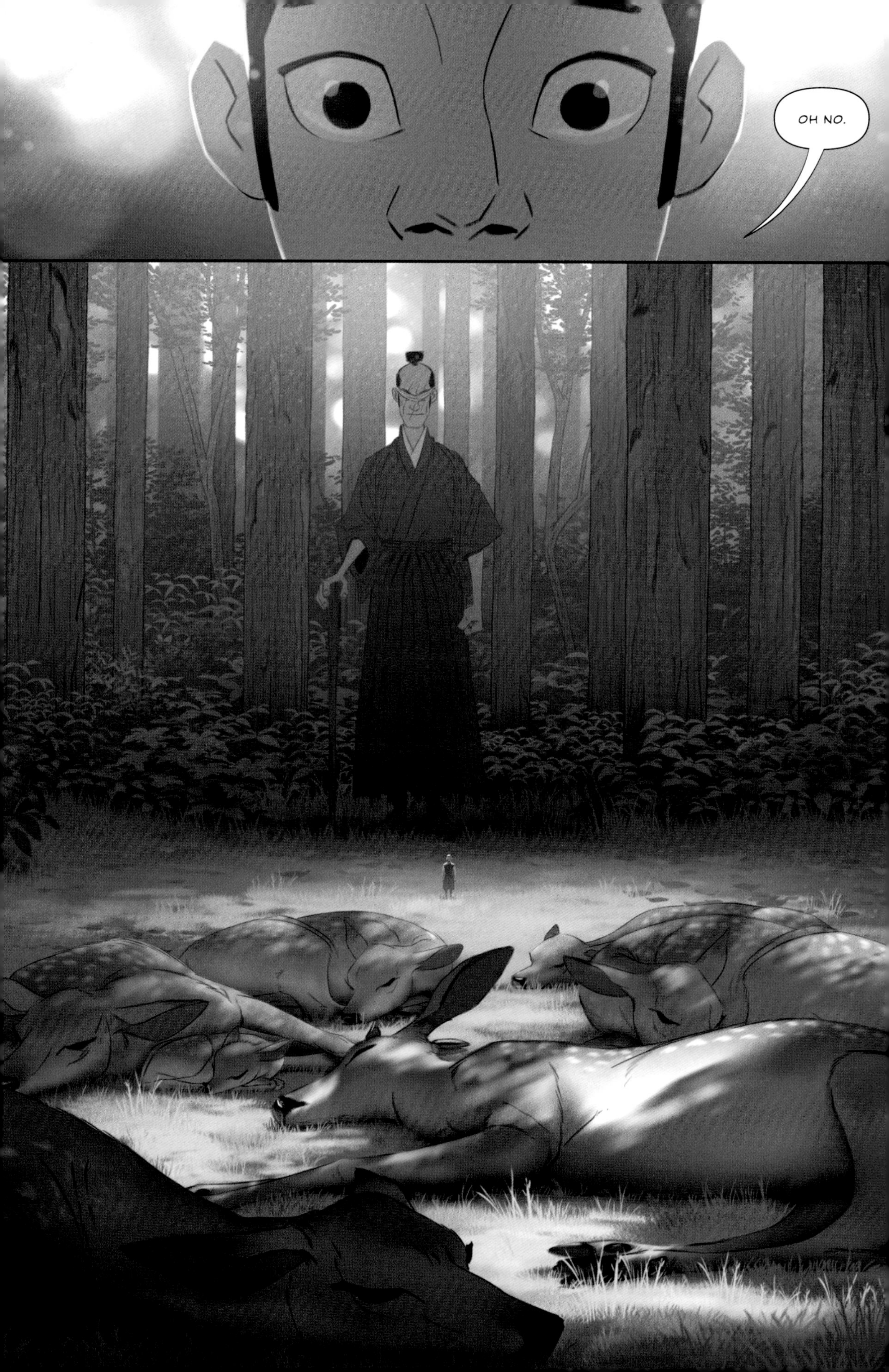
OH NO.

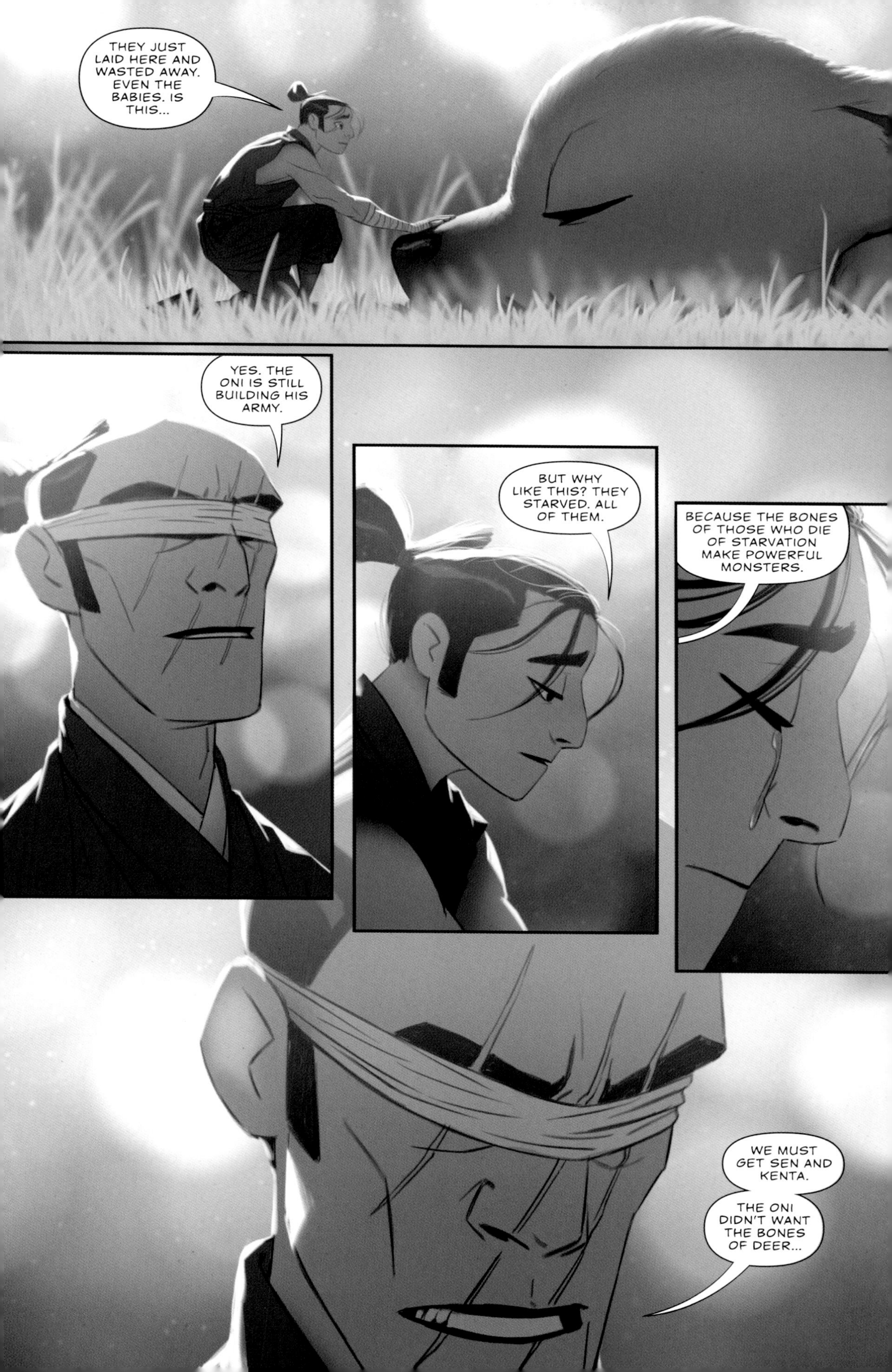
THEY JUST LAID HERE AND WASTED AWAY. EVEN THE BABIES. IS THIS...
YES. THE ONI IS STILL BUILDING HIS ARMY.
BUT WHY LIKE THIS? THEY STARVED. ALL OF THEM.
BECAUSE THE BONES OF THOSE WHO DIE OF STARVATION MAKE POWERFUL MONSTERS.
WE MUST GET SEN AND KENTA.
THE ONI DIDN'T WANT THE BONES OF DEER...

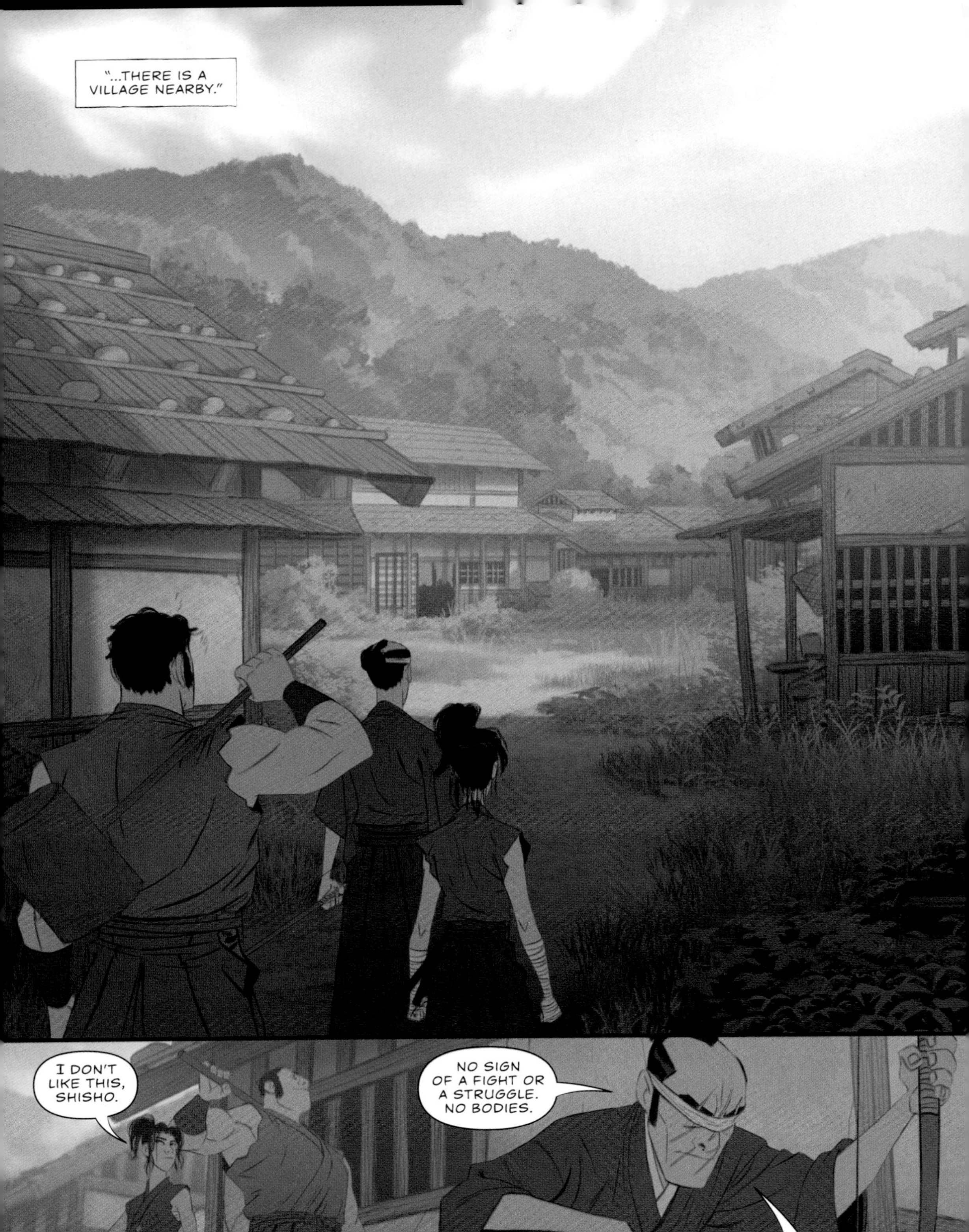
"...THERE IS A VILLAGE NEARBY."

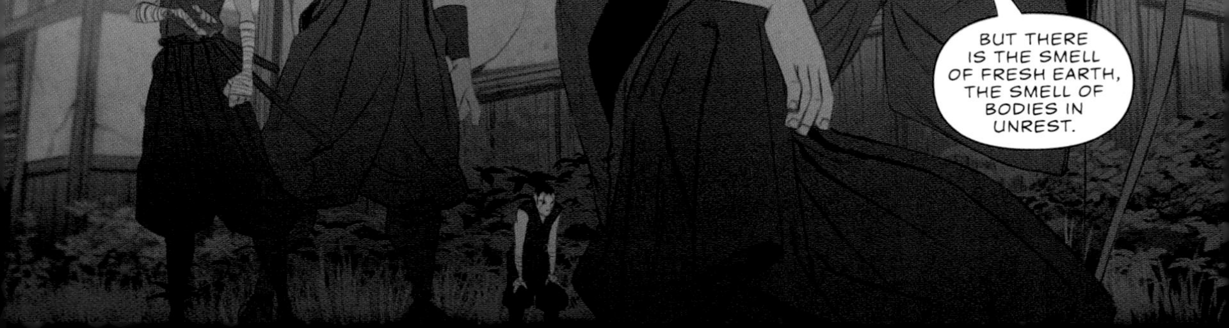
I DON'T LIKE THIS, SHISHO.
NO SIGN OF A FIGHT OR A STRUGGLE. NO BODIES.
BUT THERE IS THE SMELL OF FRESH EARTH, THE SMELL OF BODIES IN UNREST.

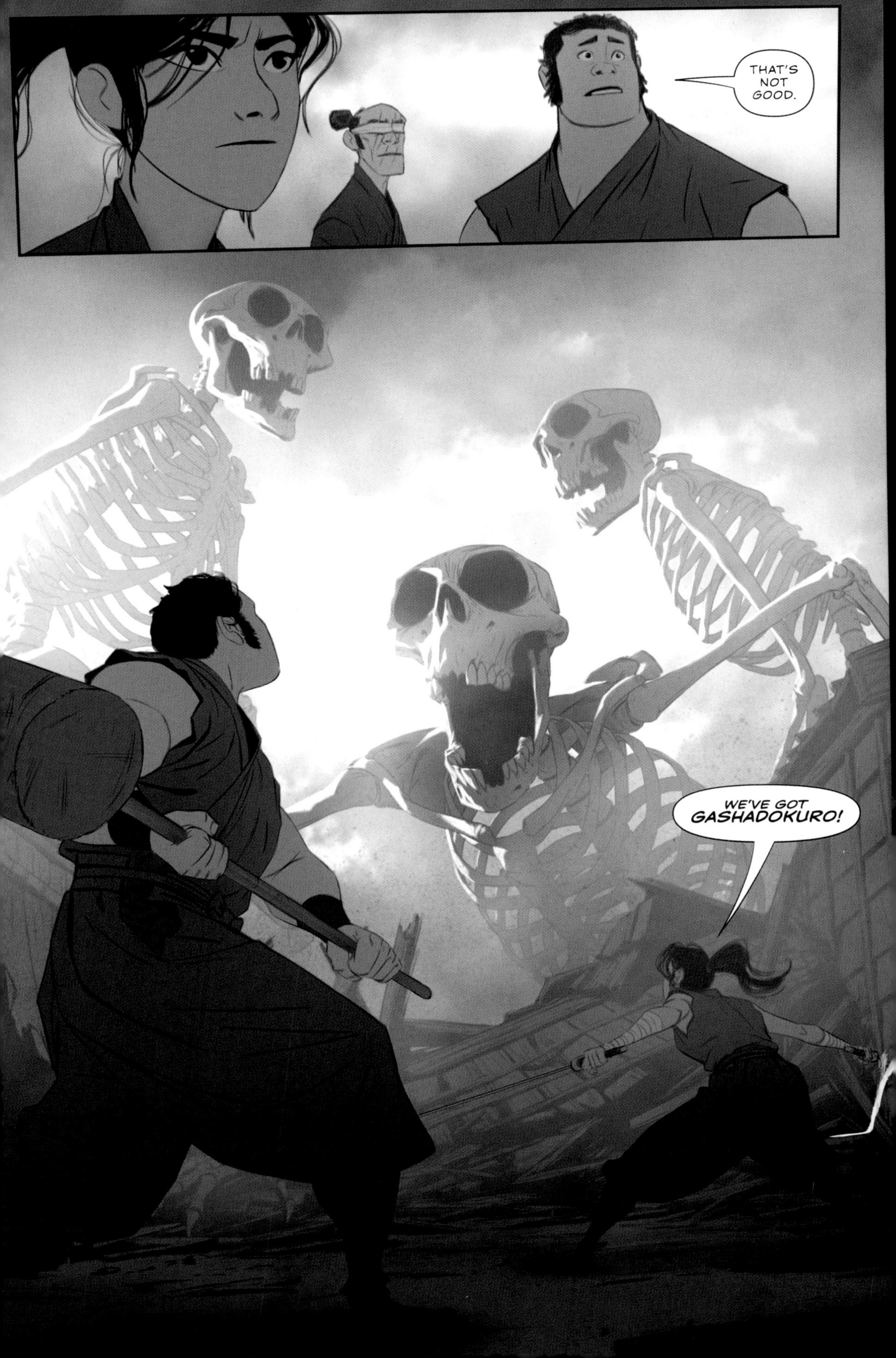
THAT'S NOT GOOD.
WE'VE GOT GASHADOKURO!

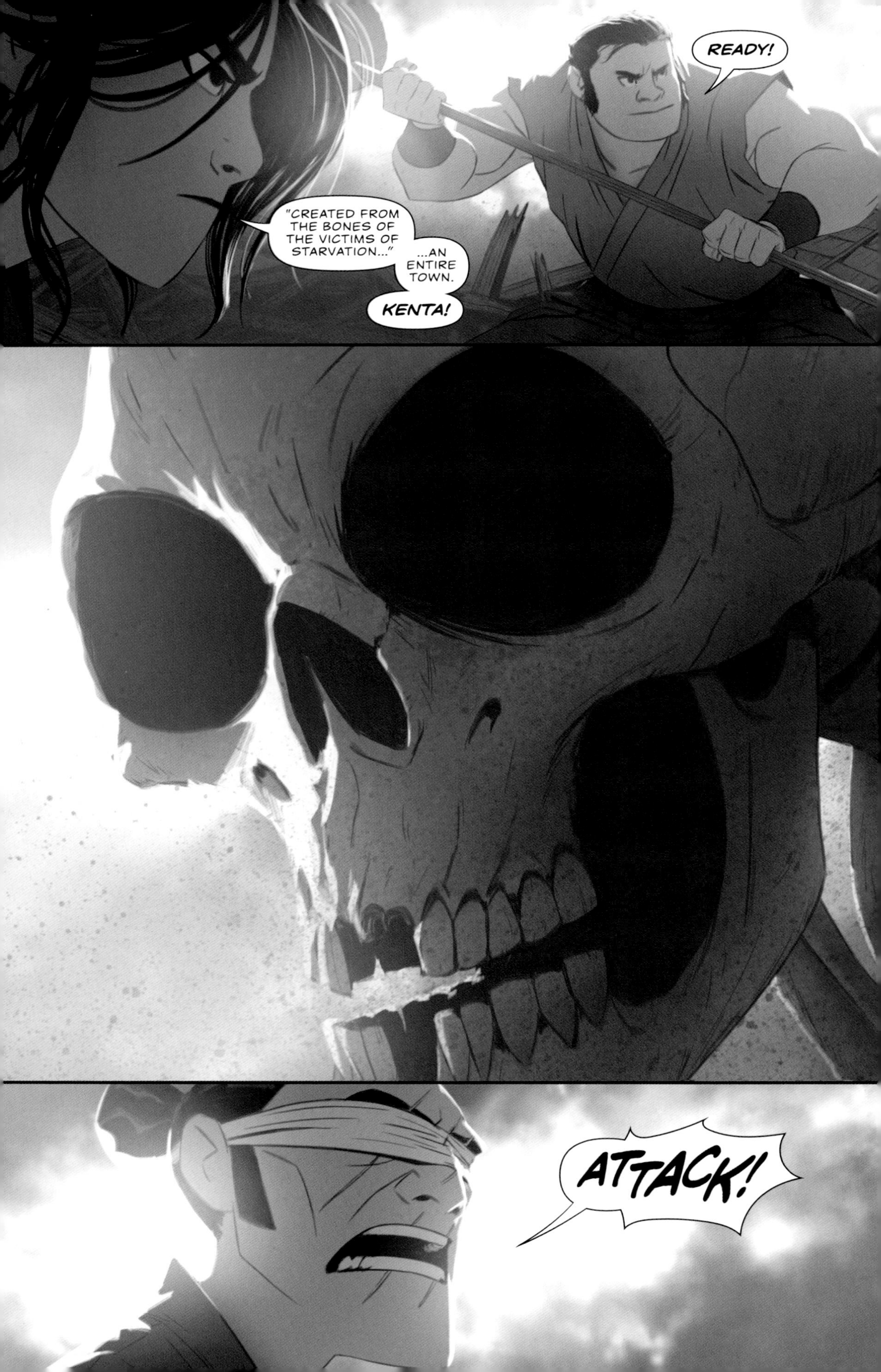
READY!
"CREATED FROM THE BONES OF THE VICTIMS OF STARVATION..."
...AN ENTIRE TOWN.
KENTA!
ATTACK!

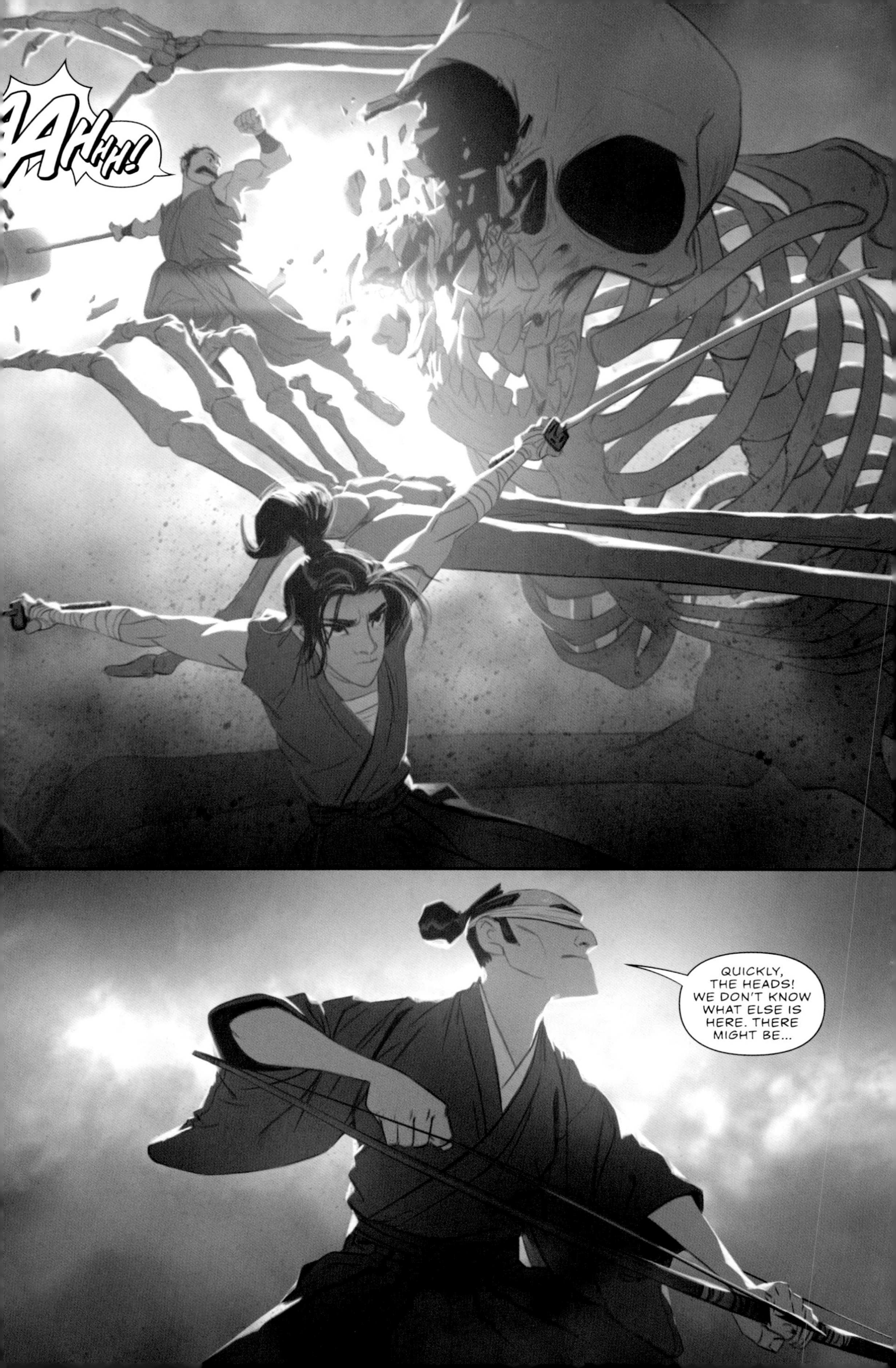
AHHH!
QUICKLY, THE HEADS! WE DON'T KNOW WHAT ELSE IS HERE. THERE MIGHT BE...

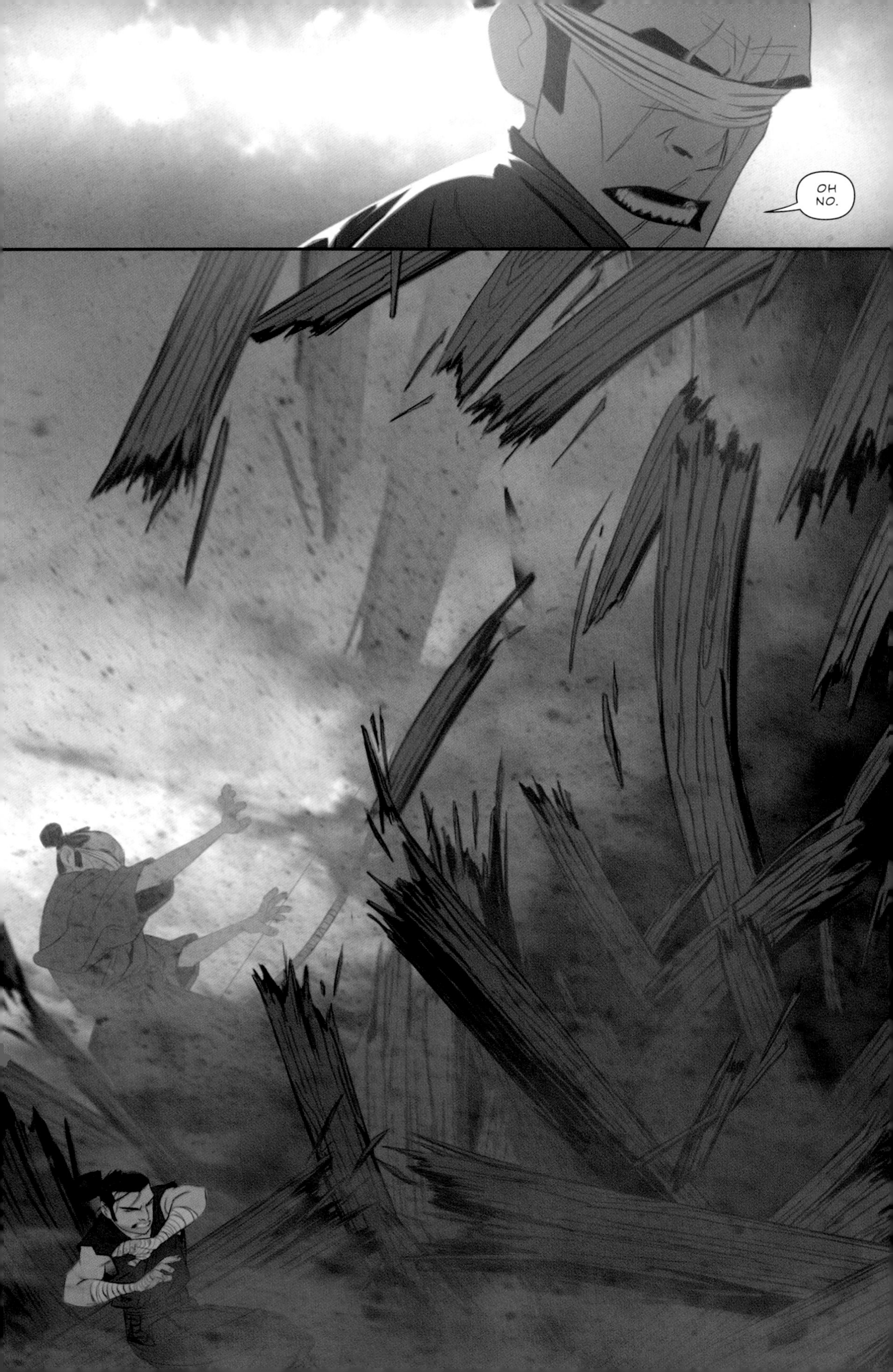
OH NO.

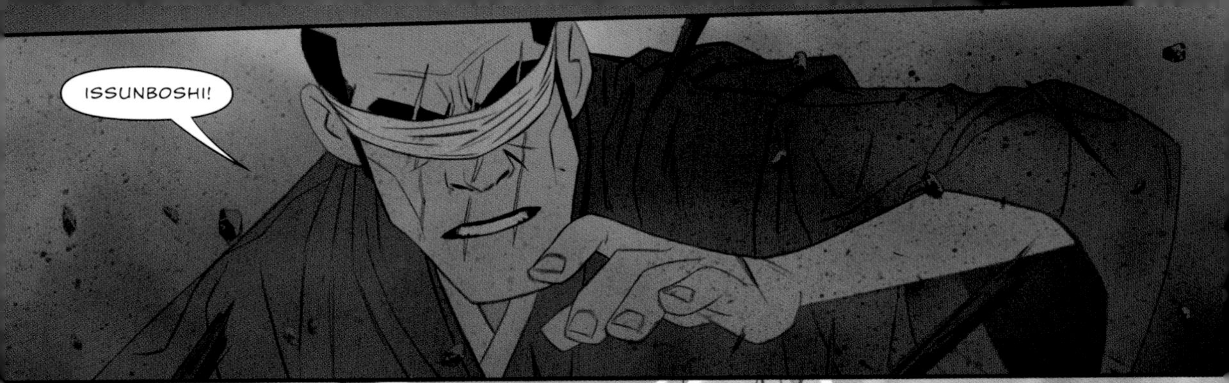
ISSUNBOSHI!

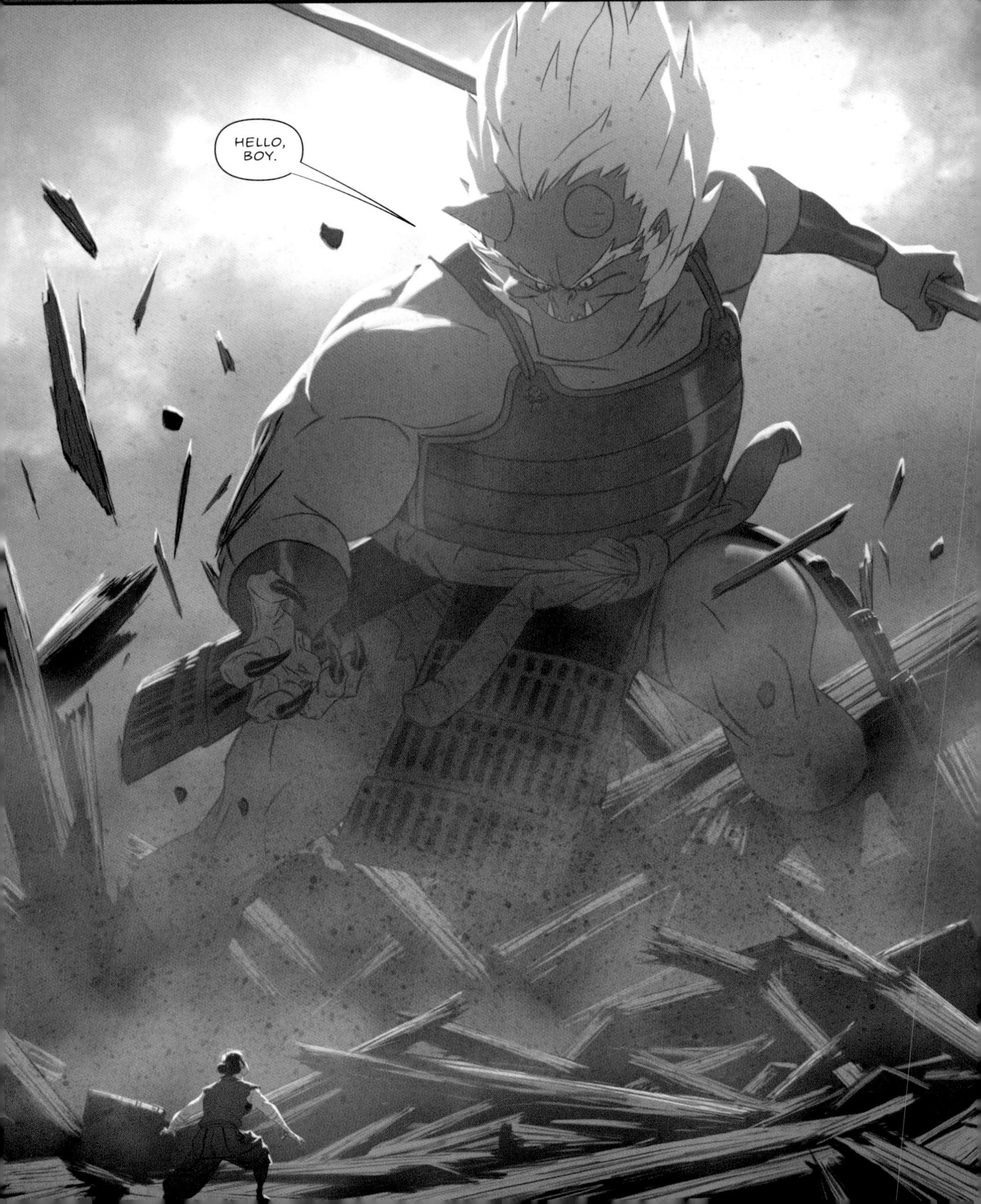
HELLO, BOY.

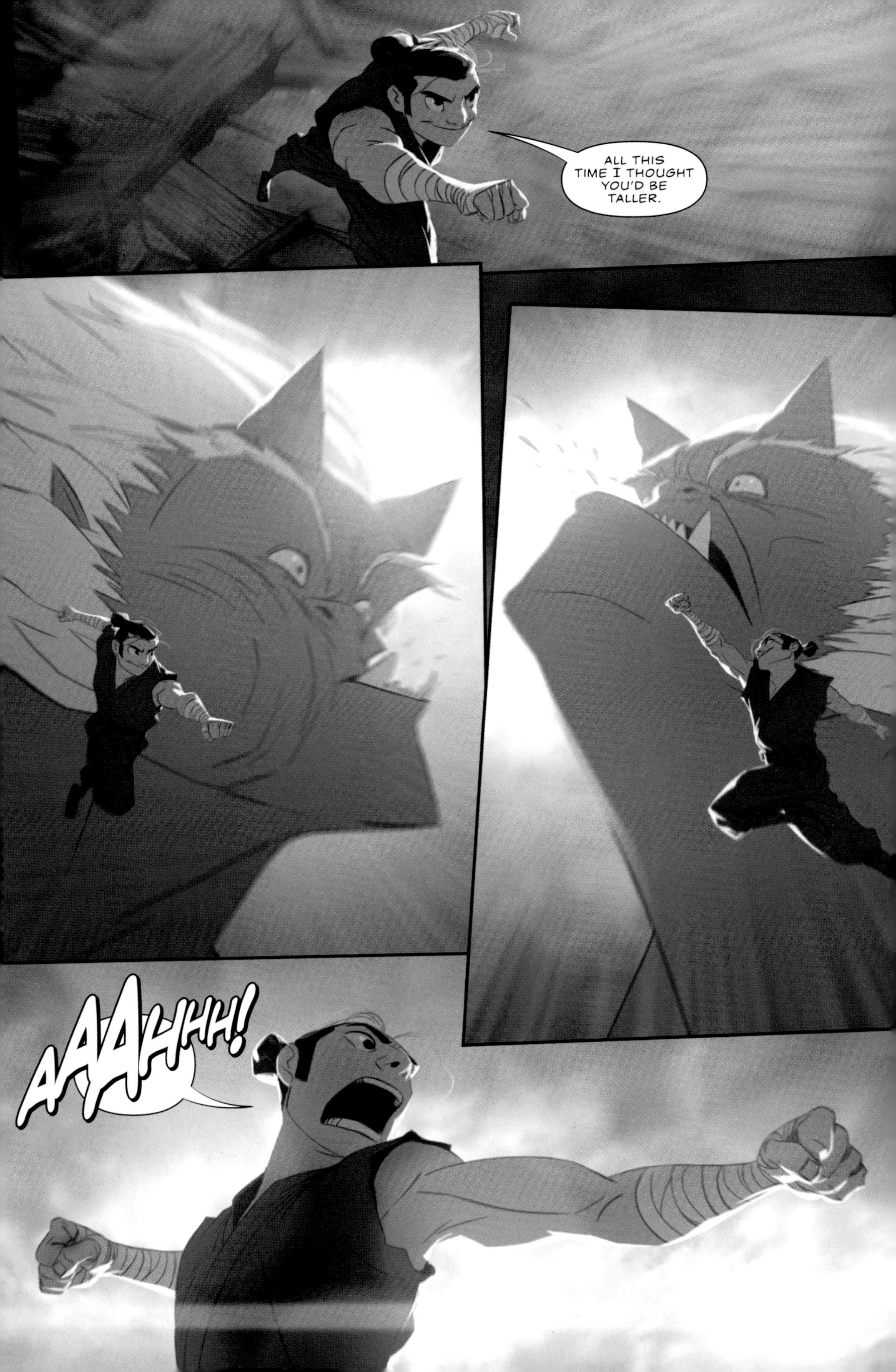
ALL THIS TIME I THOUGHT YOU'D BE TALLER.
AAAHHH!

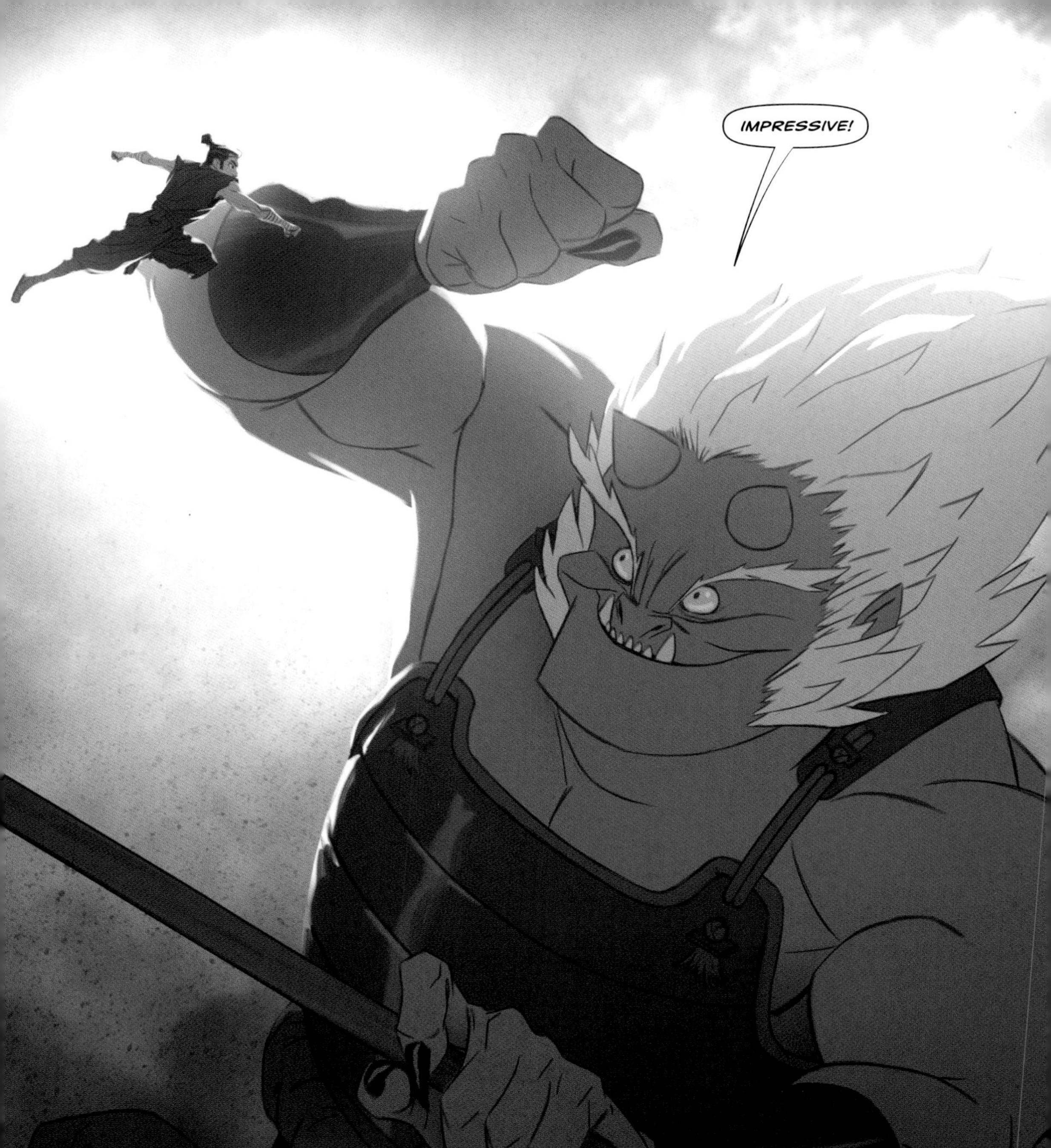
IMPRESSIVE!
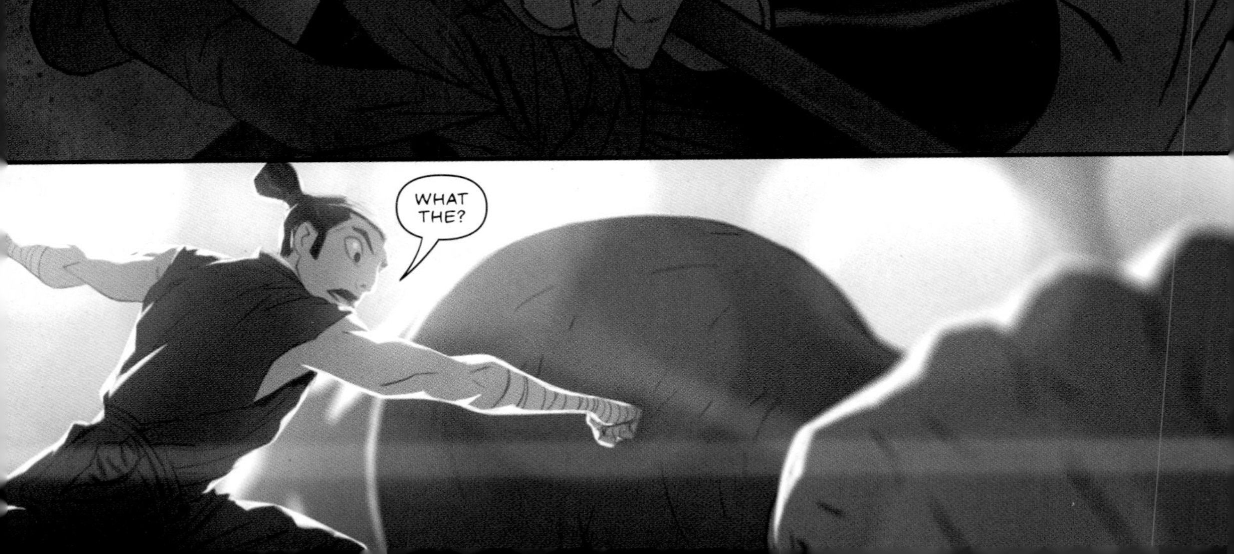
WHAT THE?

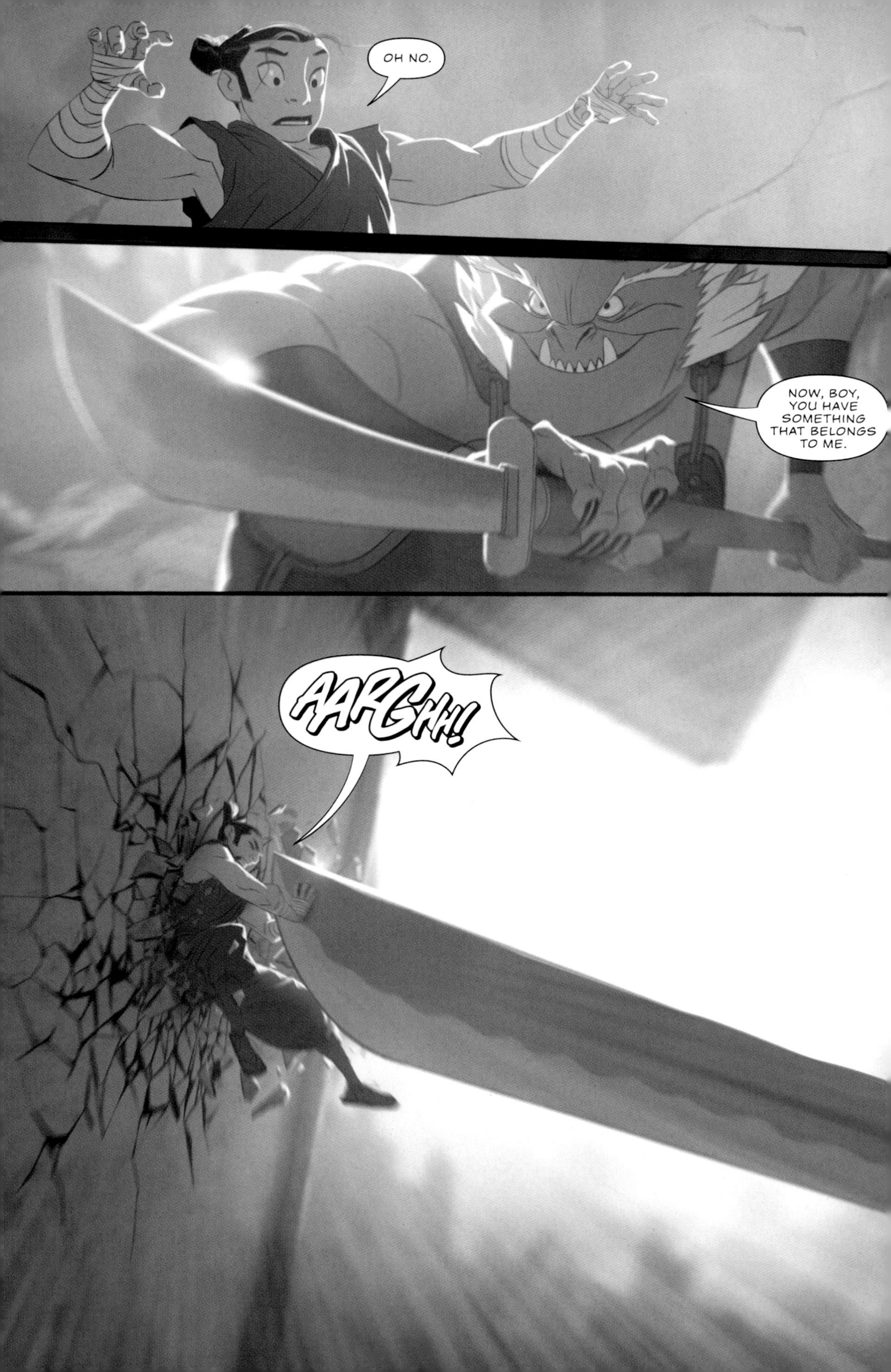
OH NO.
NOW, BOY, YOU HAVE SOMETHING THAT BELONGS TO ME.
AARGHH!

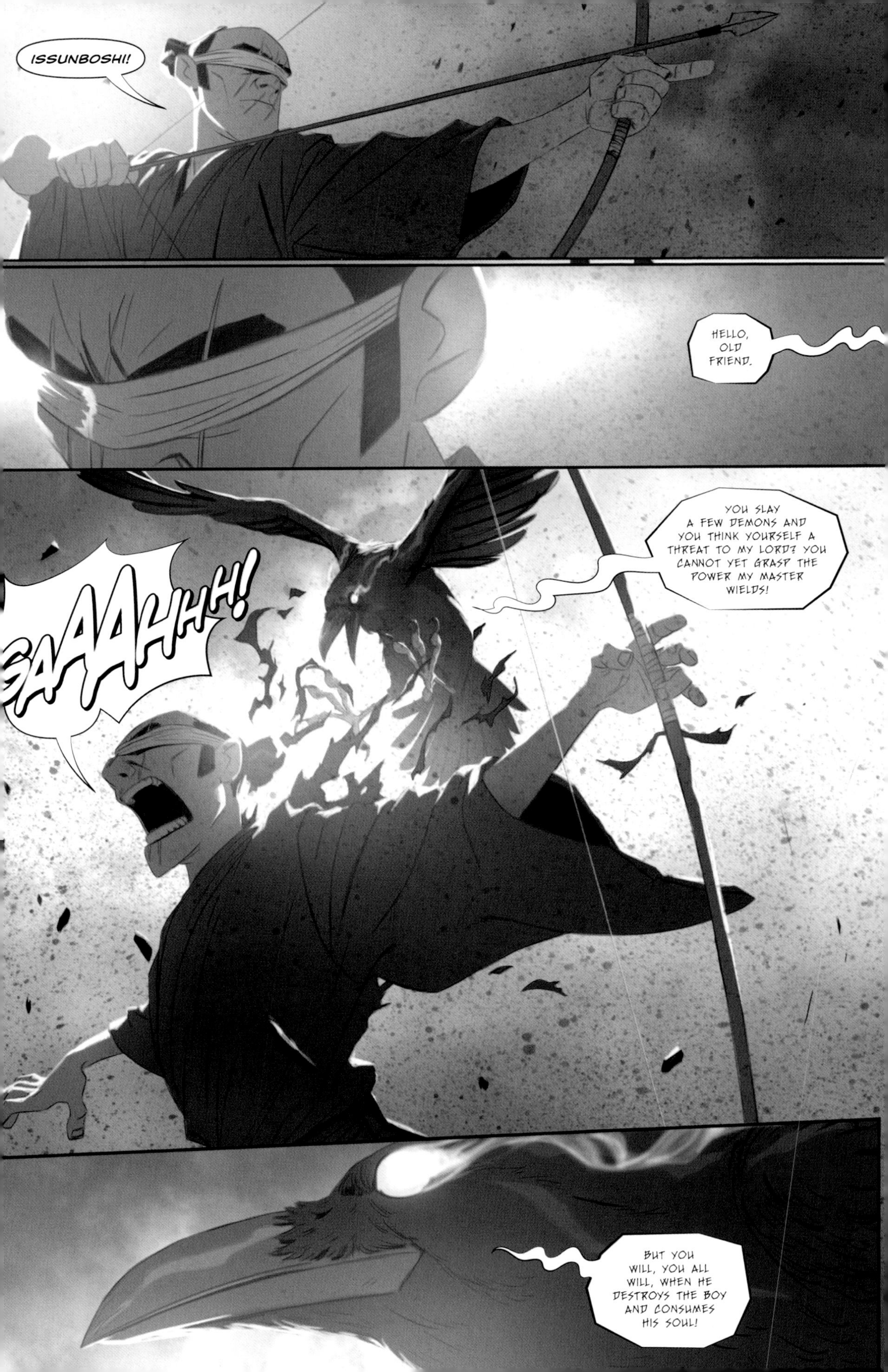
ISSUNBOSHI!
HELLO, OLD FRIEND.
GAAAHHH!
YOU SLAY A FEW DEMONS AND YOU THINK YOURSELF A THREAT TO MY LORD? YOU CANNOT YET GRASP THE POWER MY MASTER WIELDS!
BUT YOU WILL, YOU ALL WILL, WHEN HE DESTROYS THE BOY AND CONSUMES HIS SOUL!

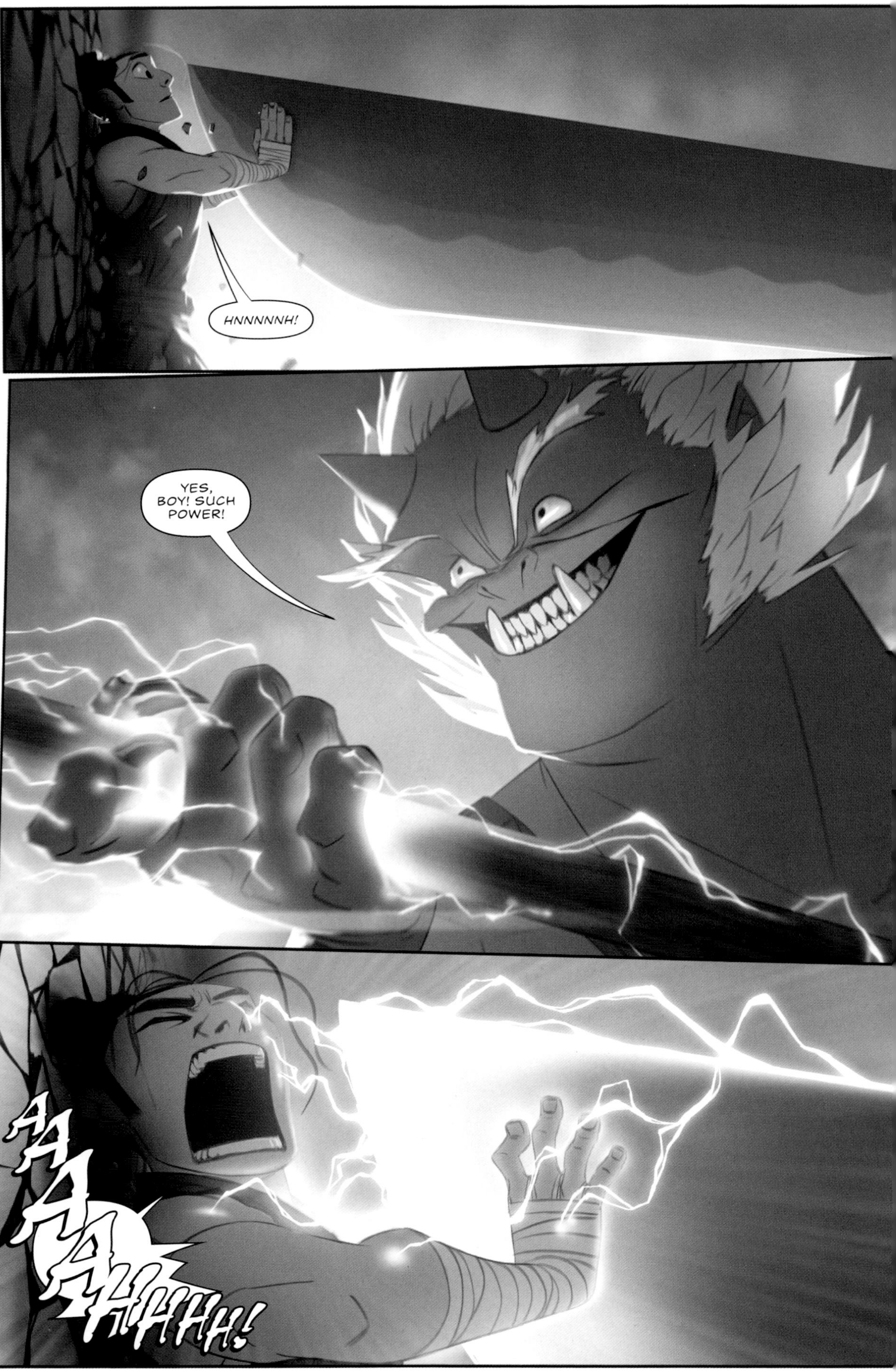
HNNNNNH!
YES, BOY! SUCH POWER!
AAAAHHHHH!

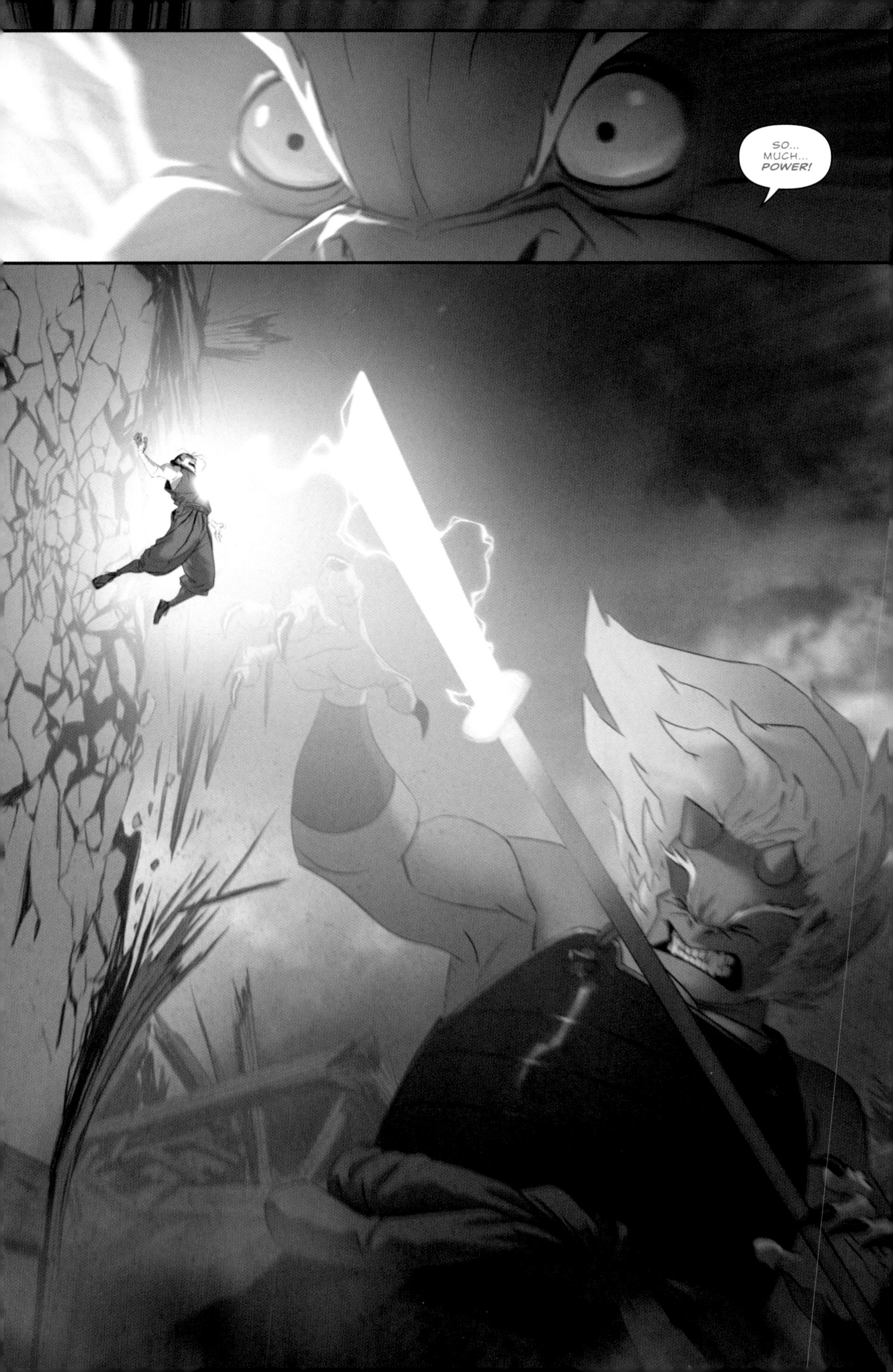
SO... MUCH... POWER!

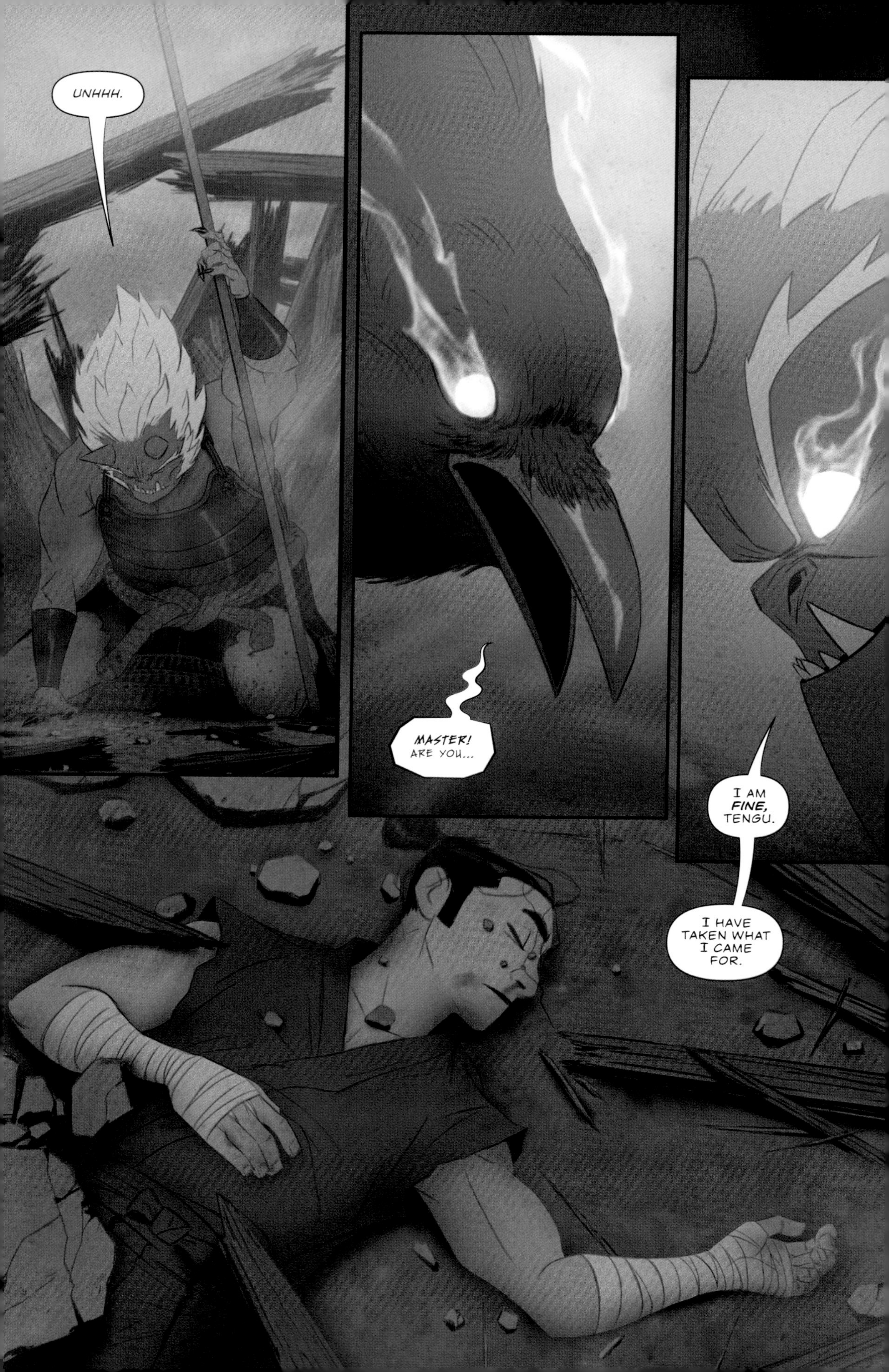
UNHHH.
MASTER! ARE YOU...
I AM FINE, TENGU.
I HAVE TAKEN WHAT I CAME FOR.

FOUR

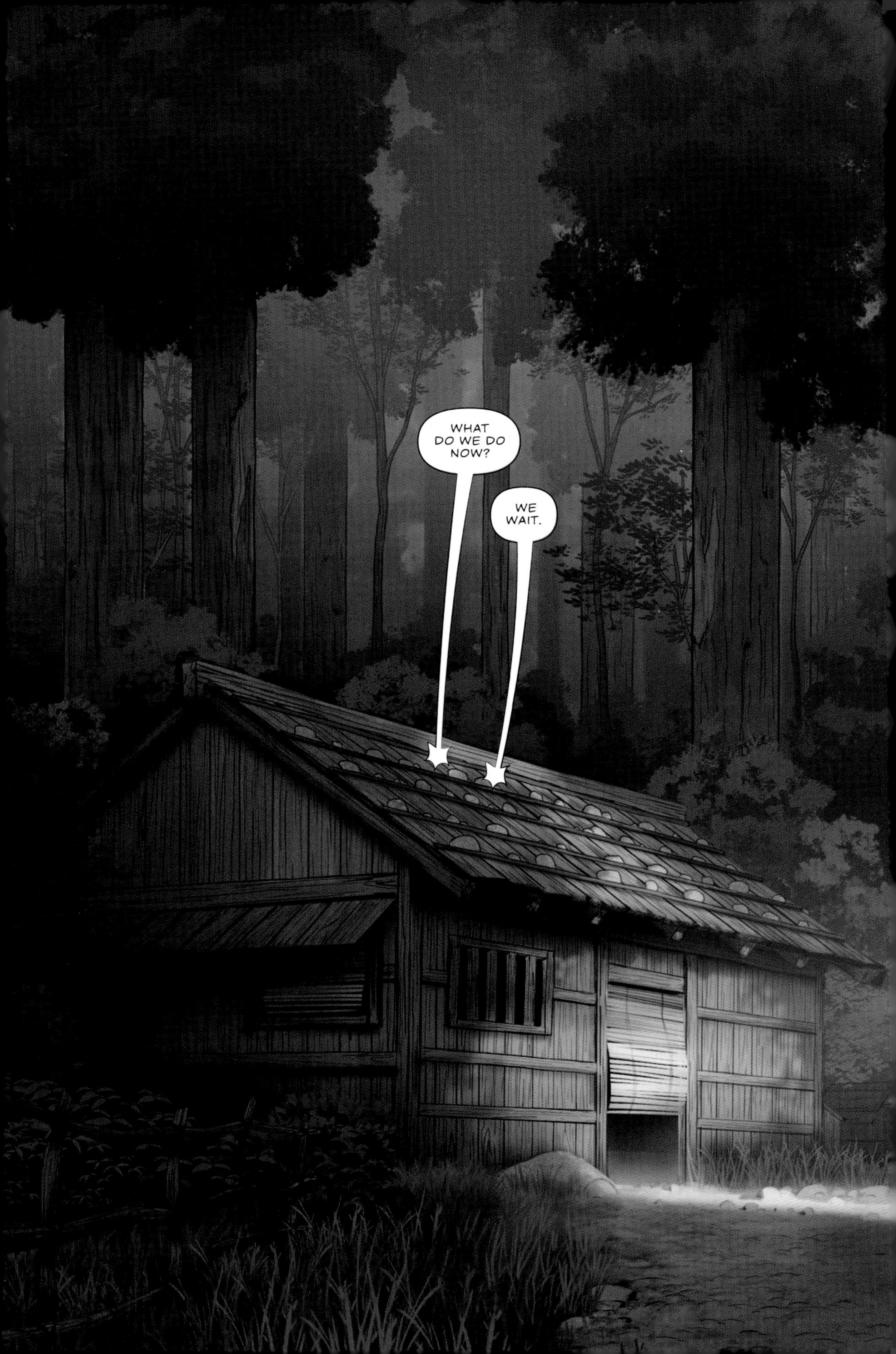
WHAT DO WE DO NOW?
WE WAIT.

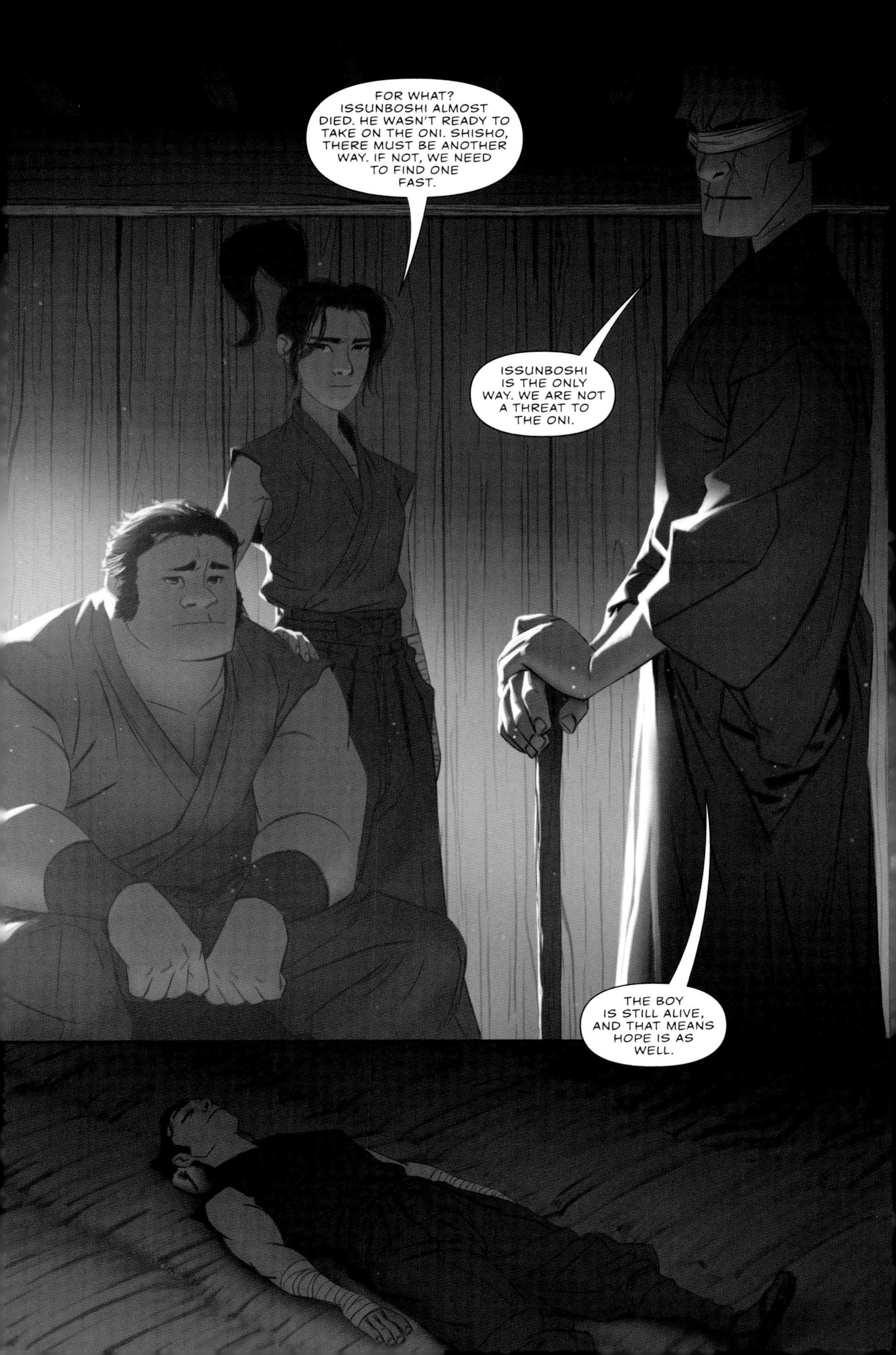
FOR WHAT? ISSUNBOSHI ALMOST DIED. HE WASN'T READY TO TAKE ON THE ONI. SHISHO, THERE MUST BE ANOTHER WAY. IF NOT, WE NEED TO FIND ONE FAST.
ISSUNBOSHI IS THE ONLY WAY. WE ARE NOT A THREAT TO THE ONI.
THE BOY IS STILL ALIVE, AND THAT MEANS HOPE IS AS WELL.

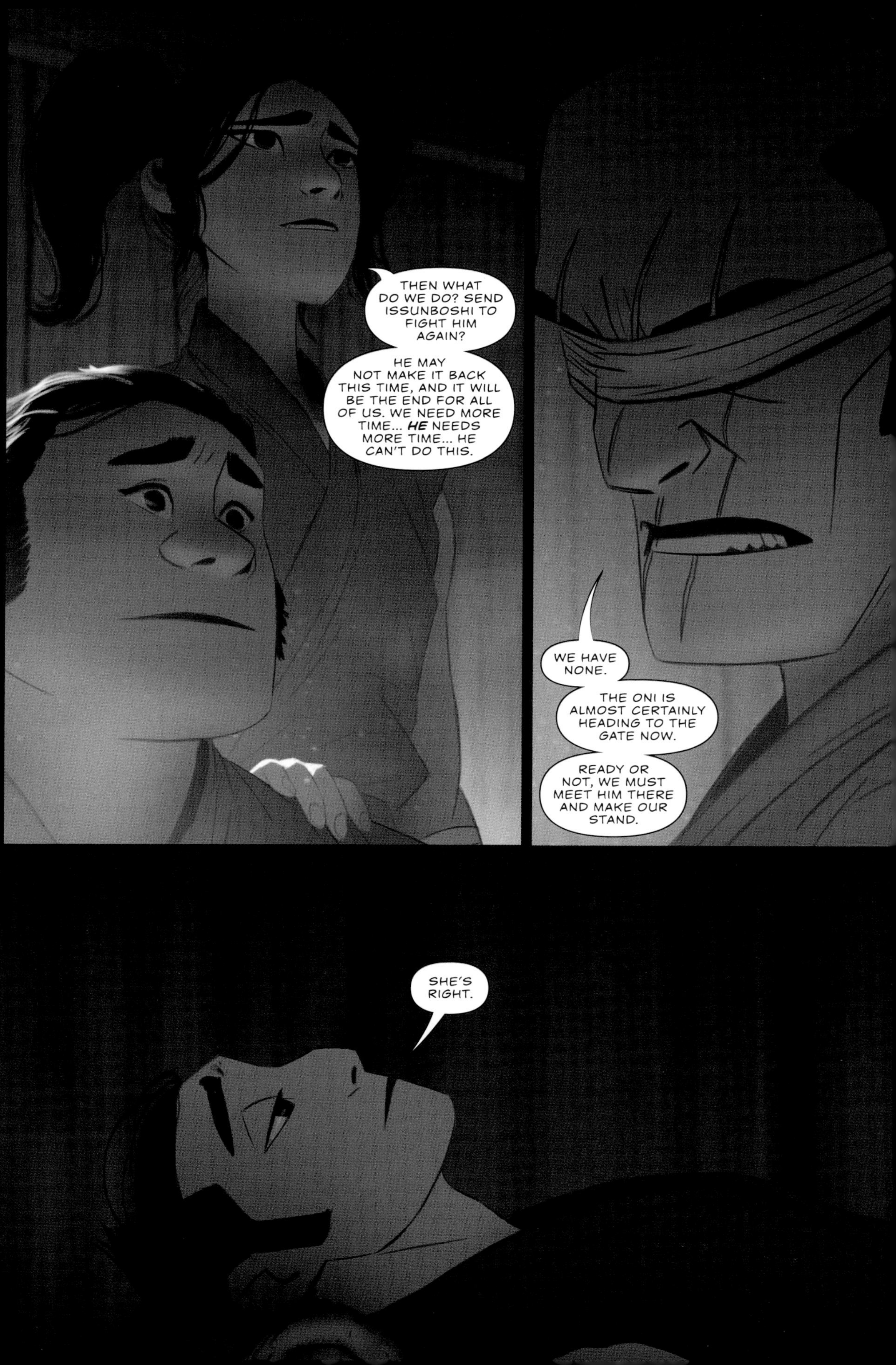
THEN WHAT DO WE DO? SEND ISSUNBOSHI TO FIGHT HIM AGAIN?
HE MAY NOT MAKE IT BACK THIS TIME, AND IT WILL BE THE END FOR ALL OF US. WE NEED MORE TIME... ***HE*** NEEDS MORE TIME... HE CAN'T DO THIS.
WE HAVE NONE.
THE ONI IS ALMOST CERTAINLY HEADING TO THE GATE NOW.
READY OR NOT, WE MUST MEET HIM THERE AND MAKE OUR STAND.
SHE'S RIGHT.

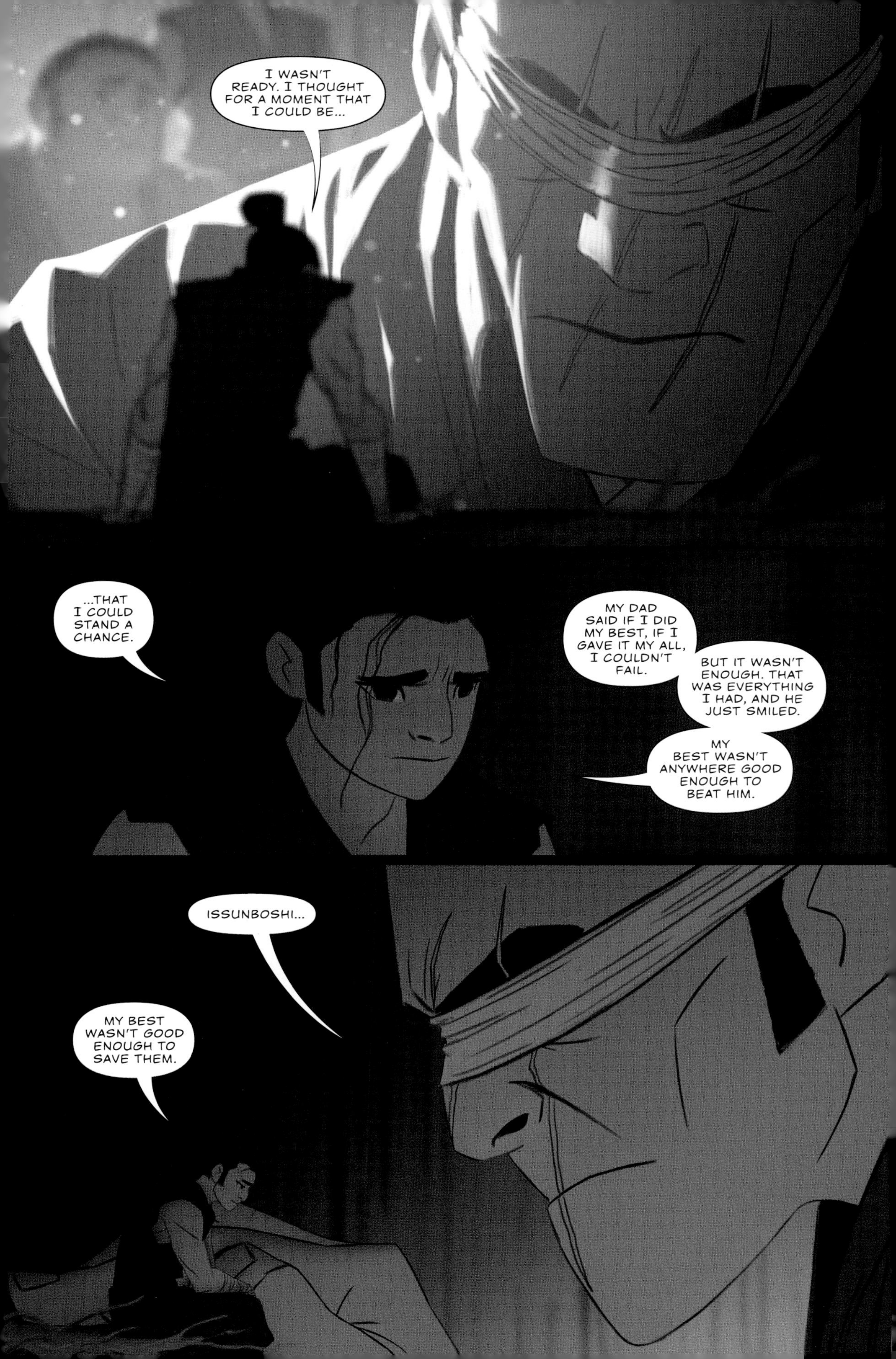
I WASN'T READY. I THOUGHT FOR A MOMENT THAT I COULD BE...
...THAT I COULD STAND A CHANCE.
MY DAD SAID IF I DID MY BEST, IF I GAVE IT MY ALL, I COULDN'T FAIL.
BUT IT WASN'T ENOUGH. THAT WAS EVERYTHING I HAD, AND HE JUST SMILED.
MY BEST WASN'T ANYWHERE GOOD ENOUGH TO BEAT HIM.
ISSUNBOSHI...
MY BEST WASN'T GOOD ENOUGH TO SAVE THEM.

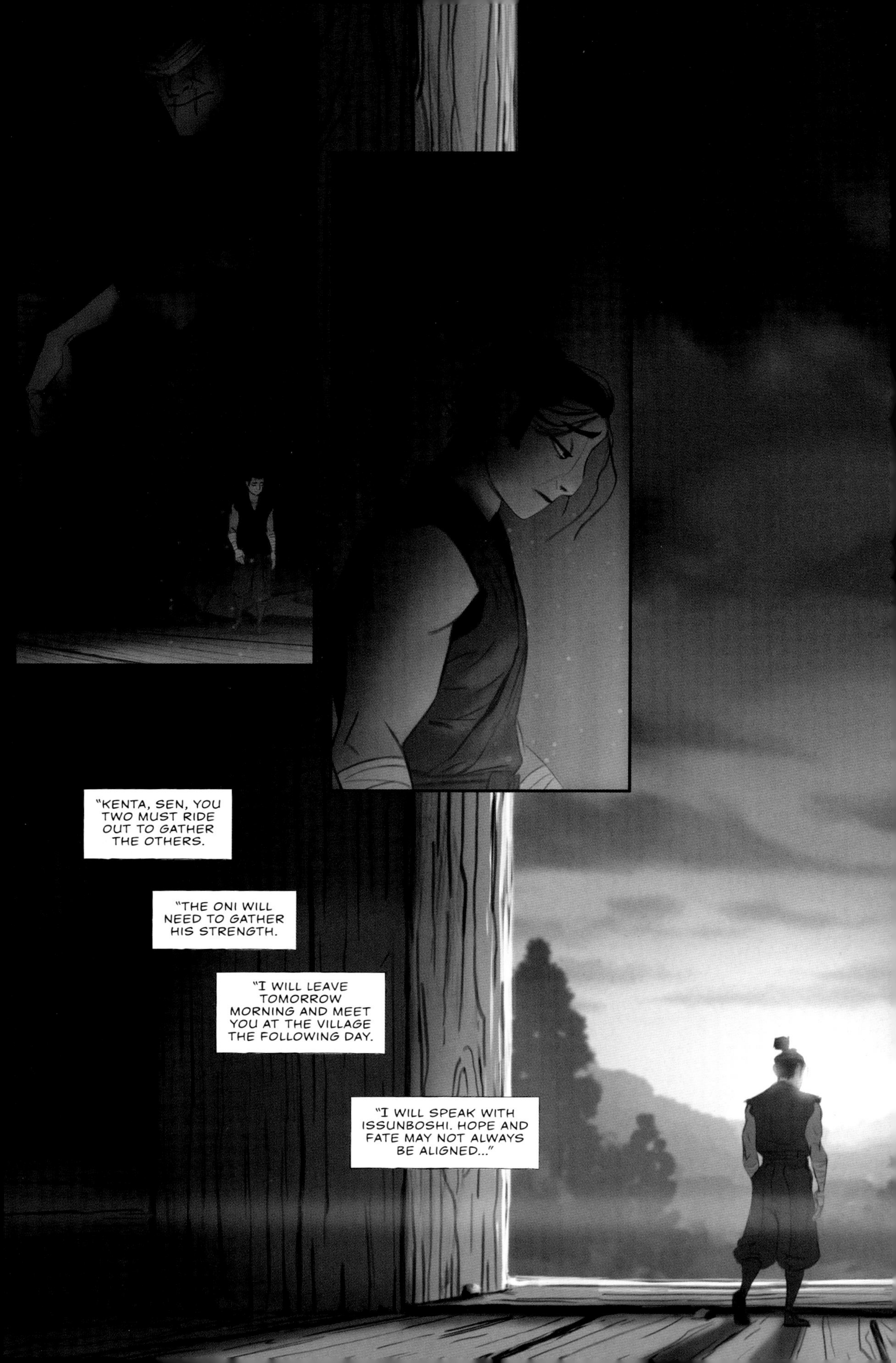
"KENTA, SEN, YOU TWO MUST RIDE OUT TO GATHER THE OTHERS.
"THE ONI WILL NEED TO GATHER HIS STRENGTH.
"I WILL LEAVE TOMORROW MORNING AND MEET YOU AT THE VILLAGE THE FOLLOWING DAY.
"I WILL SPEAK WITH ISSUNBOSHI. HOPE AND FATE MAY NOT ALWAYS BE ALIGNED..."

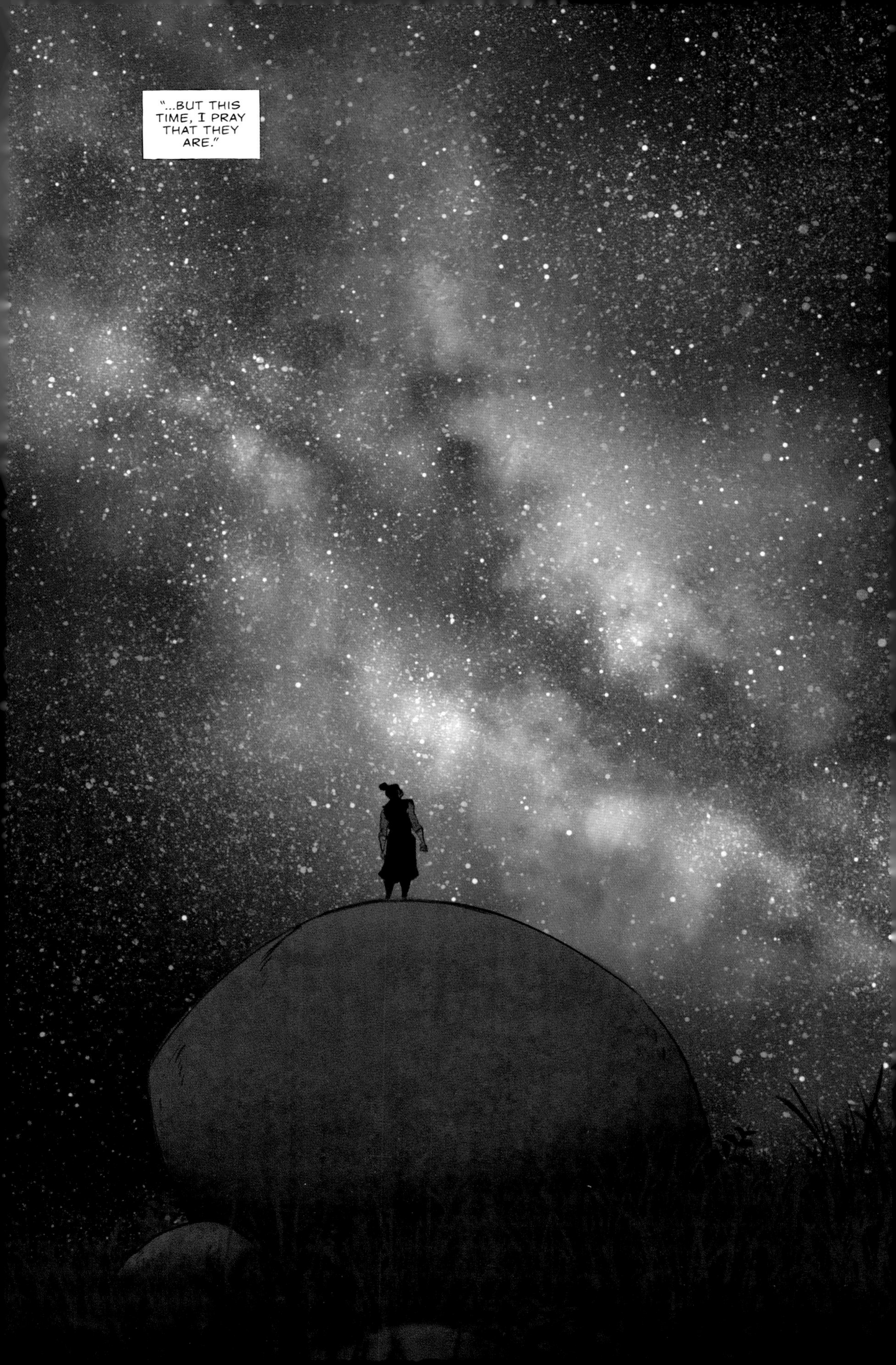
"...BUT THIS TIME, I PRAY THAT THEY ARE."

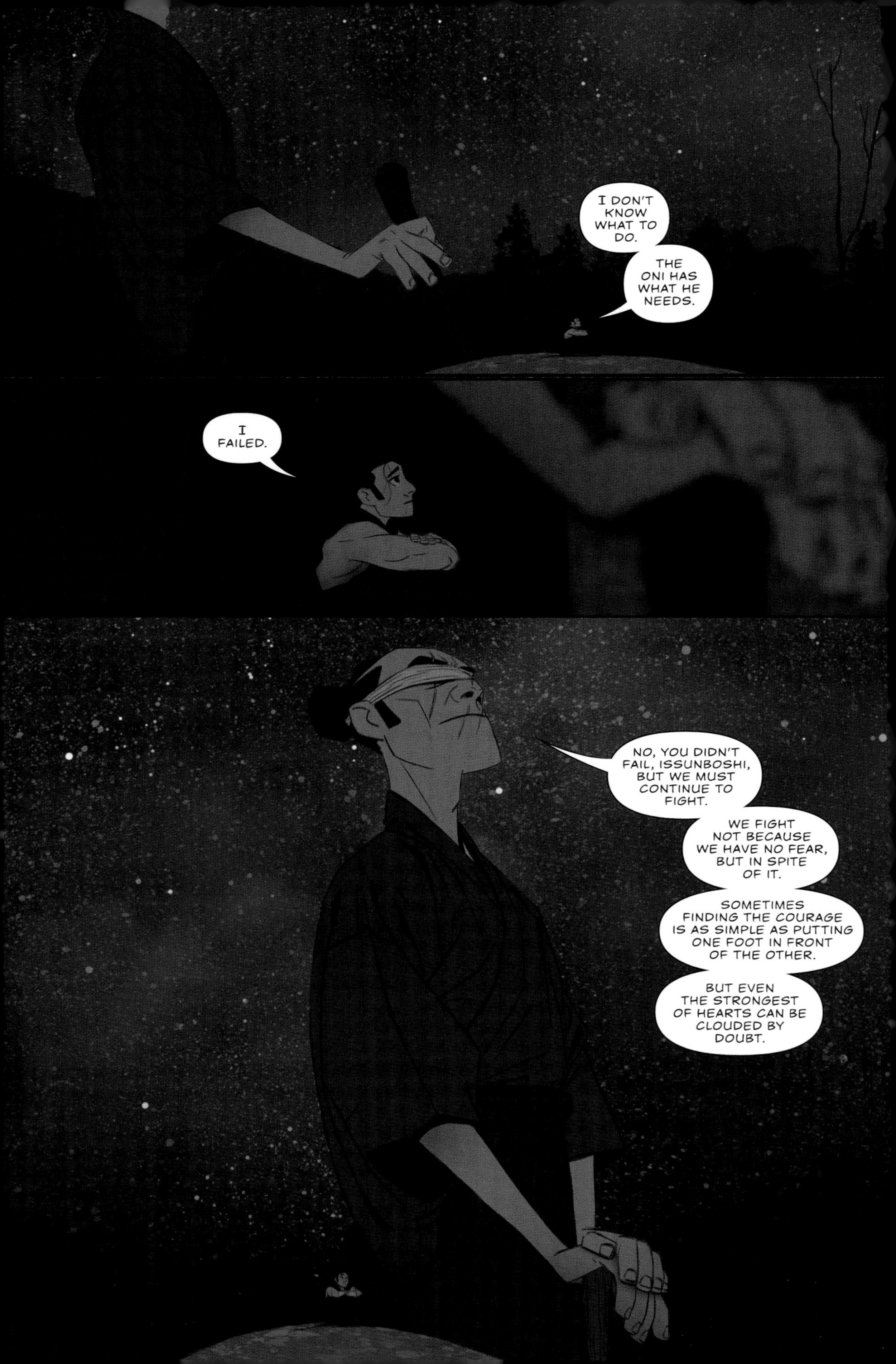
I DON'T KNOW WHAT TO DO.
THE ONI HAS WHAT HE NEEDS.
I FAILED.
NO, YOU DIDN'T FAIL, ISSUNBOSHI, BUT WE MUST CONTINUE TO FIGHT.
WE FIGHT NOT BECAUSE WE HAVE NO FEAR, BUT IN SPITE OF IT.
SOMETIMES FINDING THE COURAGE IS AS SIMPLE AS PUTTING ONE FOOT IN FRONT OF THE OTHER.
BUT EVEN THE STRONGEST OF HEARTS CAN BE CLOUDED BY DOUBT.

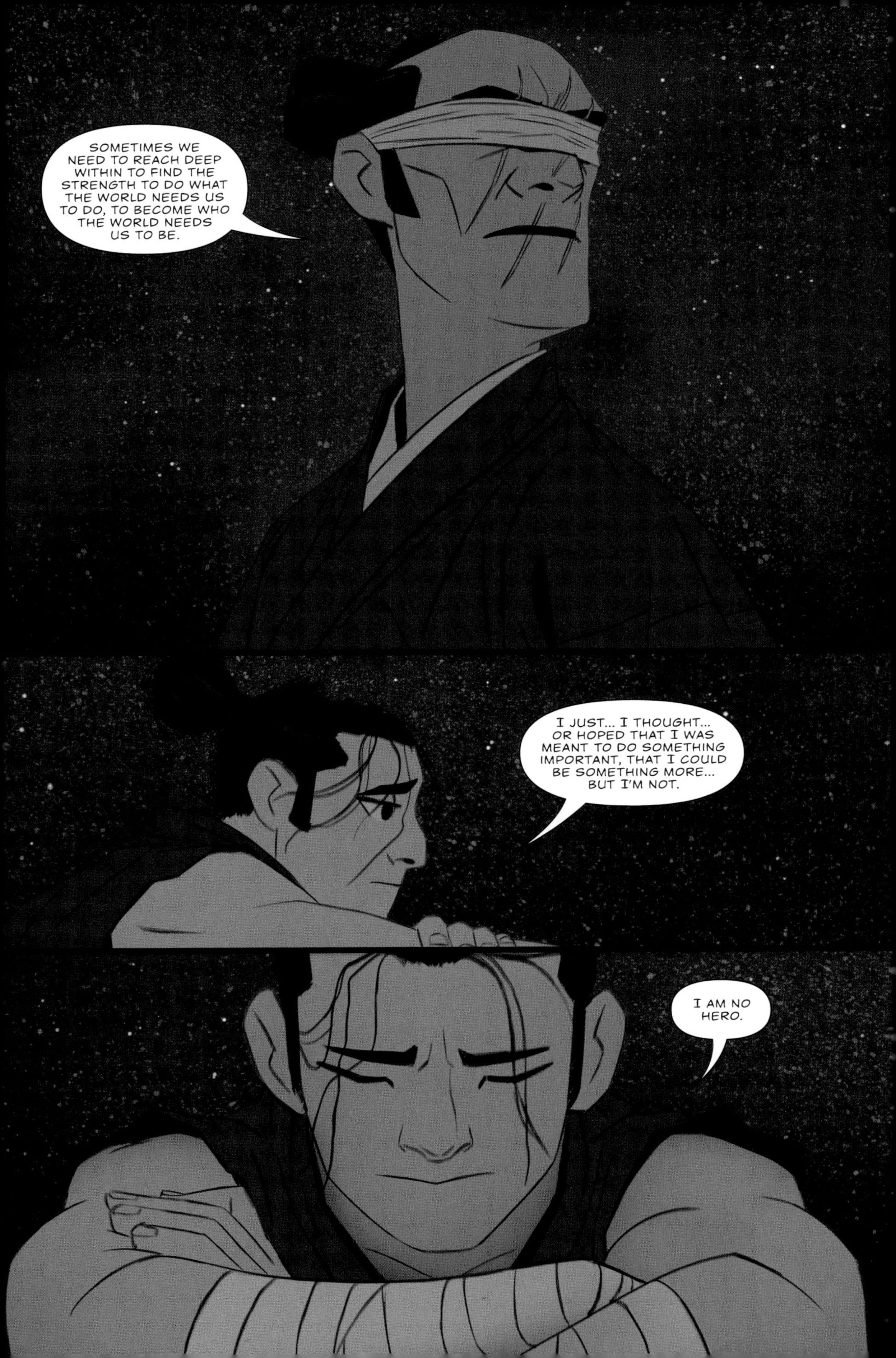
SOMETIMES WE NEED TO REACH DEEP WITHIN TO FIND THE STRENGTH TO DO WHAT THE WORLD NEEDS US TO DO, TO BECOME WHO THE WORLD NEEDS US TO BE.
I JUST... I THOUGHT... OR HOPED THAT I WAS MEANT TO DO SOMETHING IMPORTANT, THAT I COULD BE SOMETHING MORE... BUT I'M NOT.
I AM NO HERO.

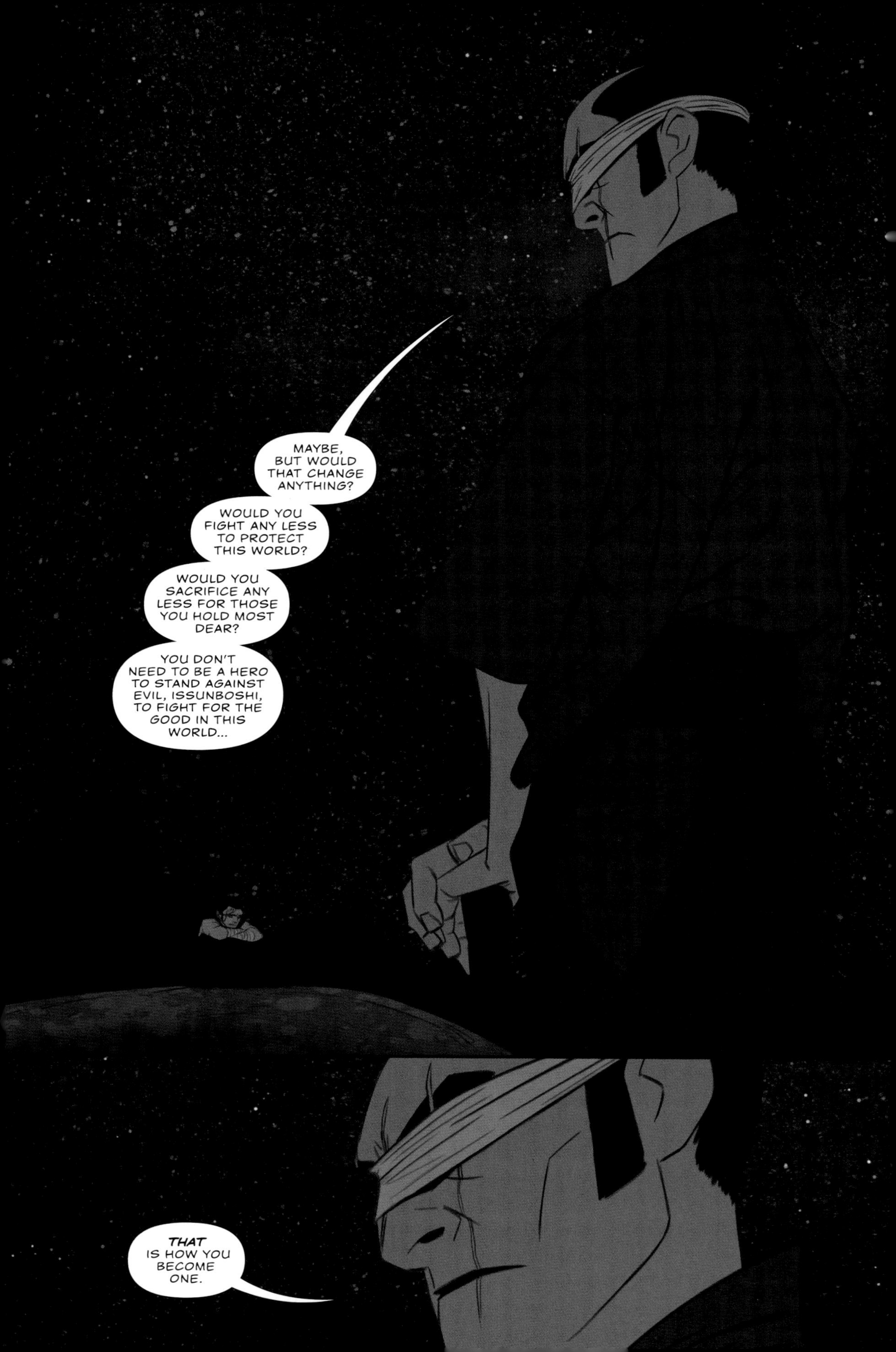
MAYBE, BUT WOULD THAT CHANGE ANYTHING?
WOULD YOU FIGHT ANY LESS TO PROTECT THIS WORLD?
WOULD YOU SACRIFICE ANY LESS FOR THOSE YOU HOLD MOST DEAR?
YOU DON'T NEED TO BE A HERO TO STAND AGAINST EVIL, ISSUNBOSHI, TO FIGHT FOR THE GOOD IN THIS WORLD...
THAT IS HOW YOU BECOME ONE.

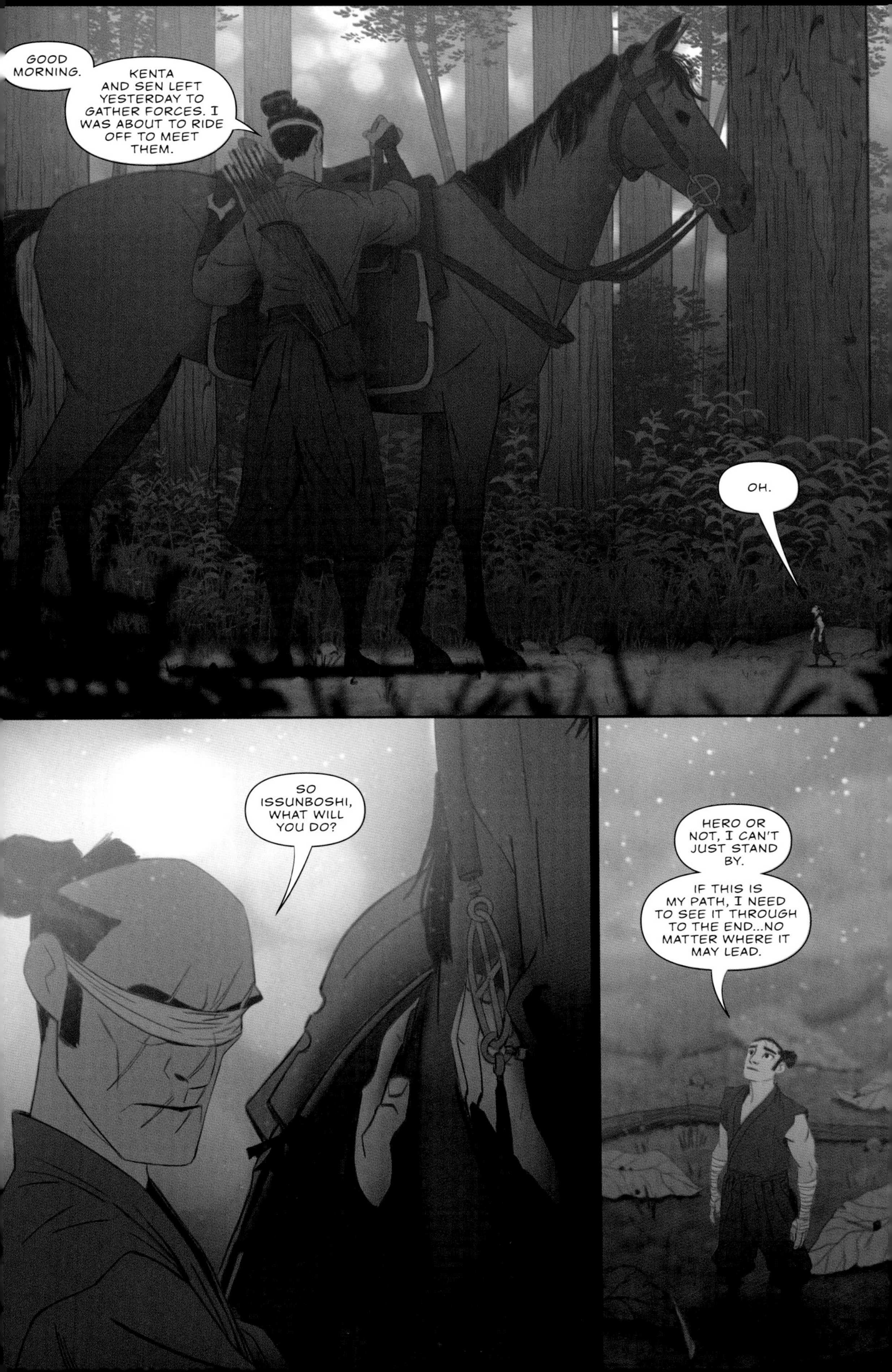
GOOD MORNING.
KENTA AND SEN LEFT YESTERDAY TO GATHER FORCES. I WAS ABOUT TO RIDE OFF TO MEET THEM.
OH.
SO ISSUNBOSHI, WHAT WILL YOU DO?
HERO OR NOT, I CAN'T JUST STAND BY.
IF THIS IS MY PATH, I NEED TO SEE IT THROUGH TO THE END...NO MATTER WHERE IT MAY LEAD.

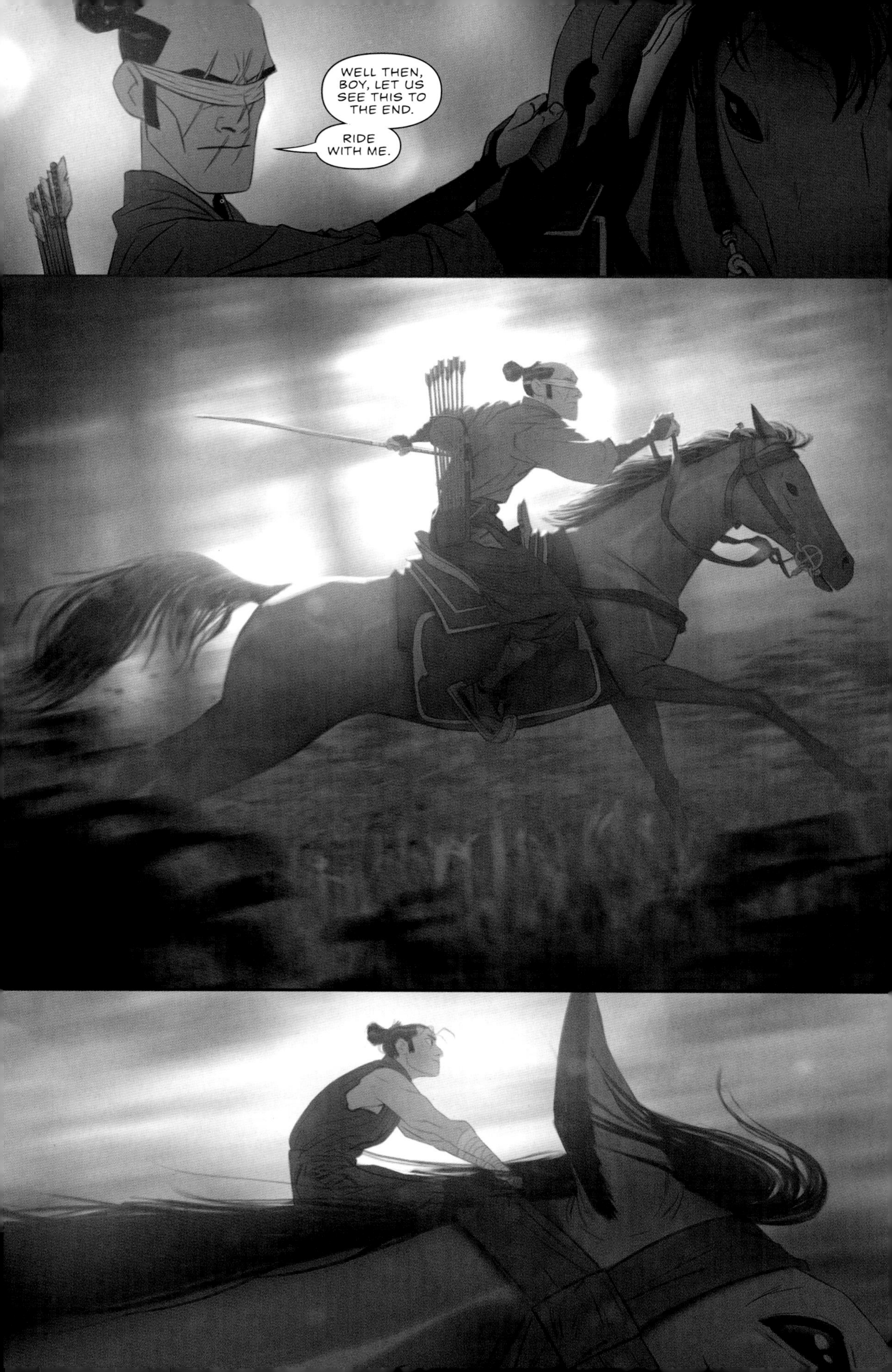
WELL THEN, BOY, LET US SEE THIS TO THE END.
RIDE WITH ME.

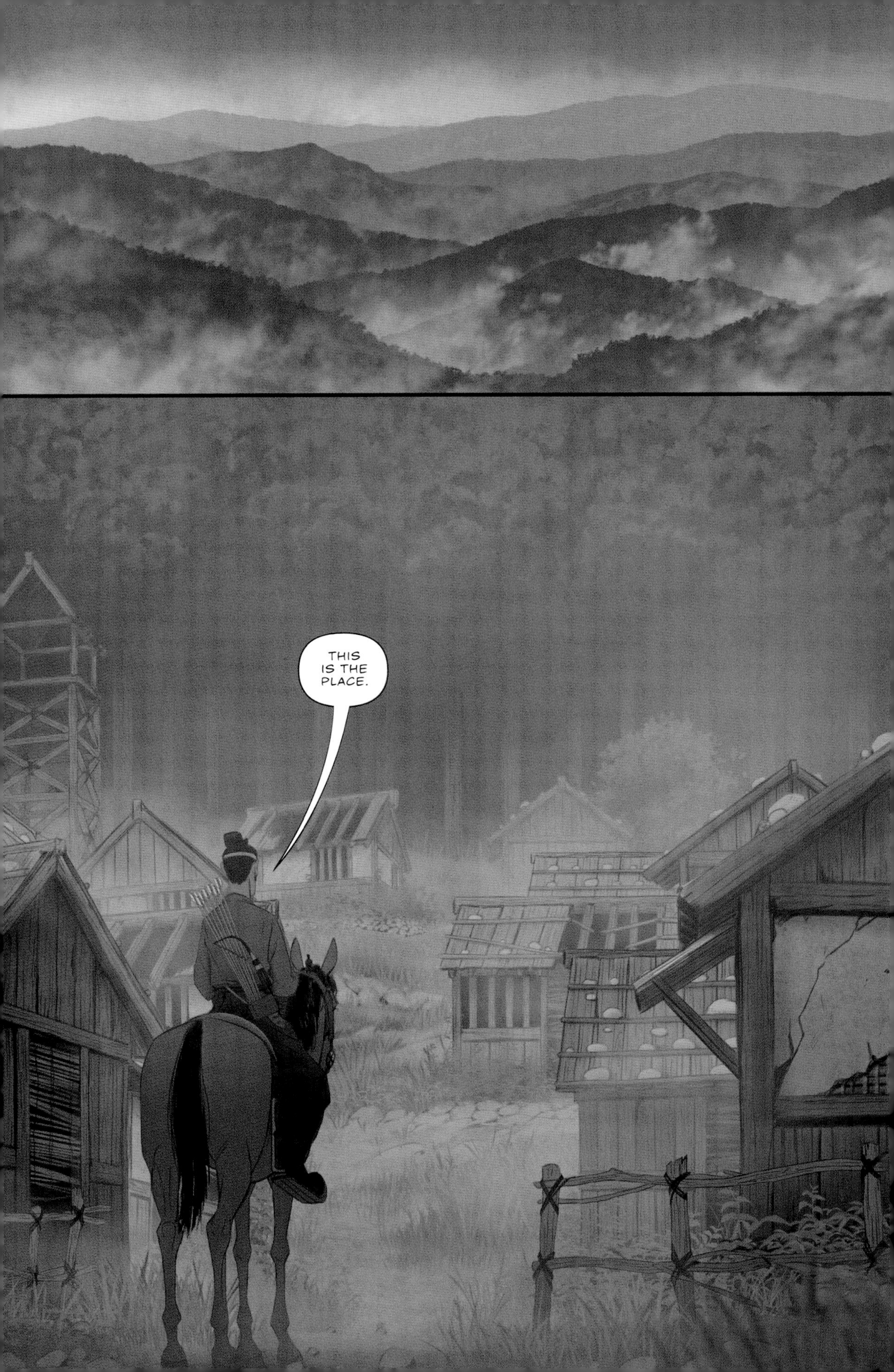
THIS IS THE PLACE.

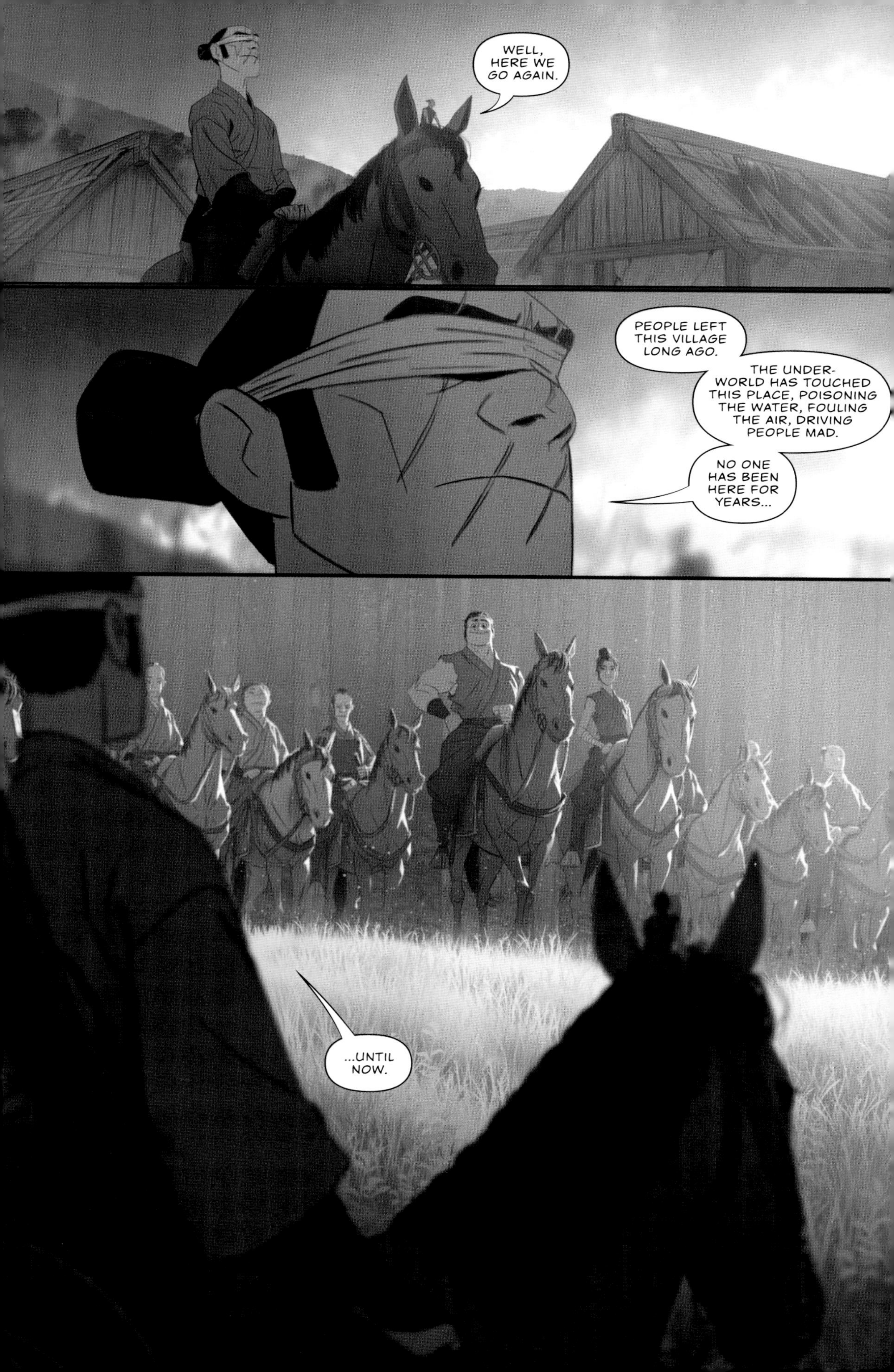
WELL, HERE WE GO AGAIN.
PEOPLE LEFT THIS VILLAGE LONG AGO.
THE UNDER-WORLD HAS TOUCHED THIS PLACE, POISONING THE WATER, FOULING THE AIR, DRIVING PEOPLE MAD.
NO ONE HAS BEEN HERE FOR YEARS...
...UNTIL NOW.

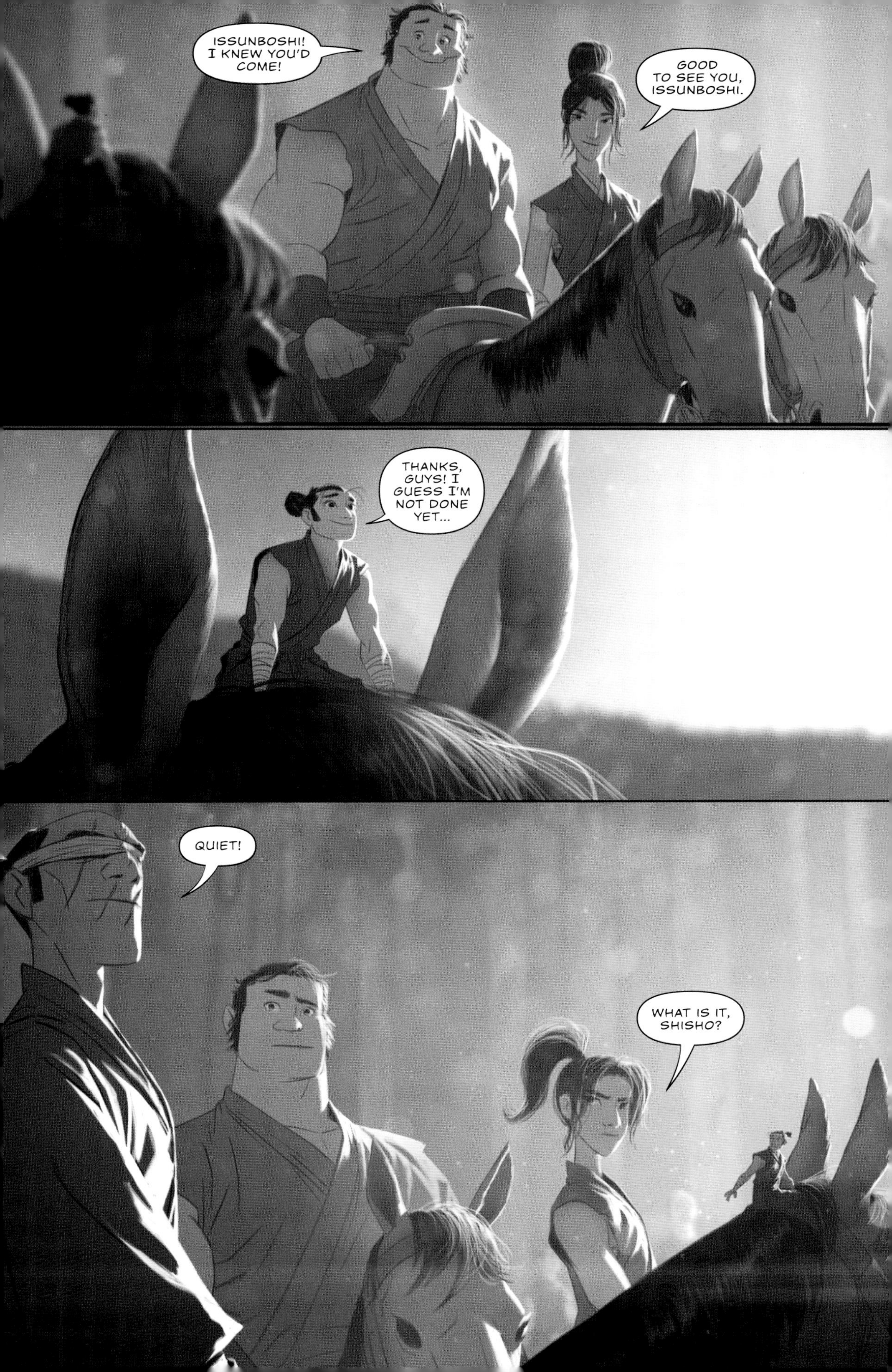
ISSUNBOSHI! I KNEW YOU'D COME!
GOOD TO SEE YOU, ISSUNBOSHI.
THANKS, GUYS! I GUESS I'M NOT DONE YET...
QUIET!
WHAT IS IT, SHISHO?

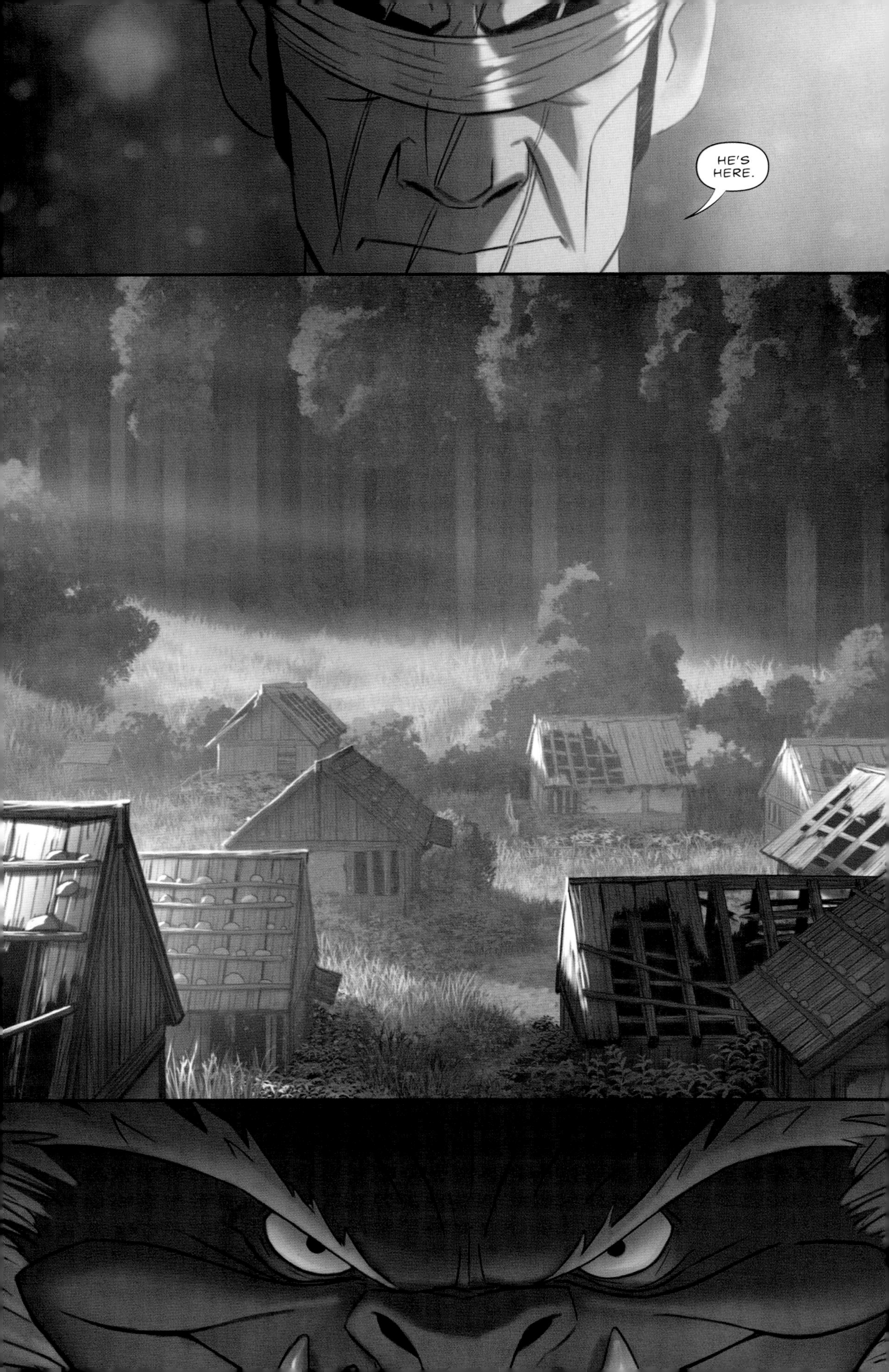
HE'S HERE.

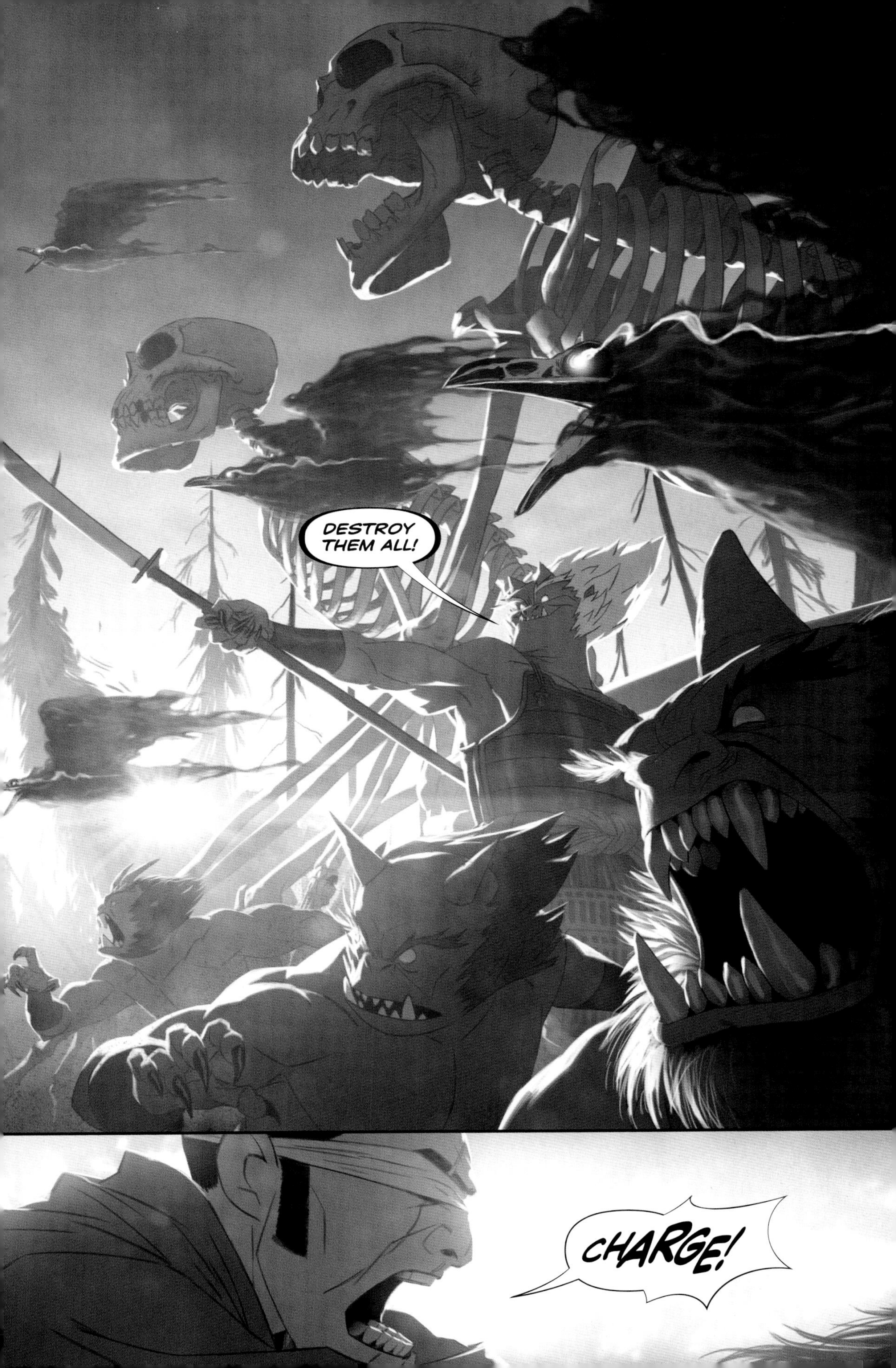
DESTROY THEM ALL!
CHARGE!

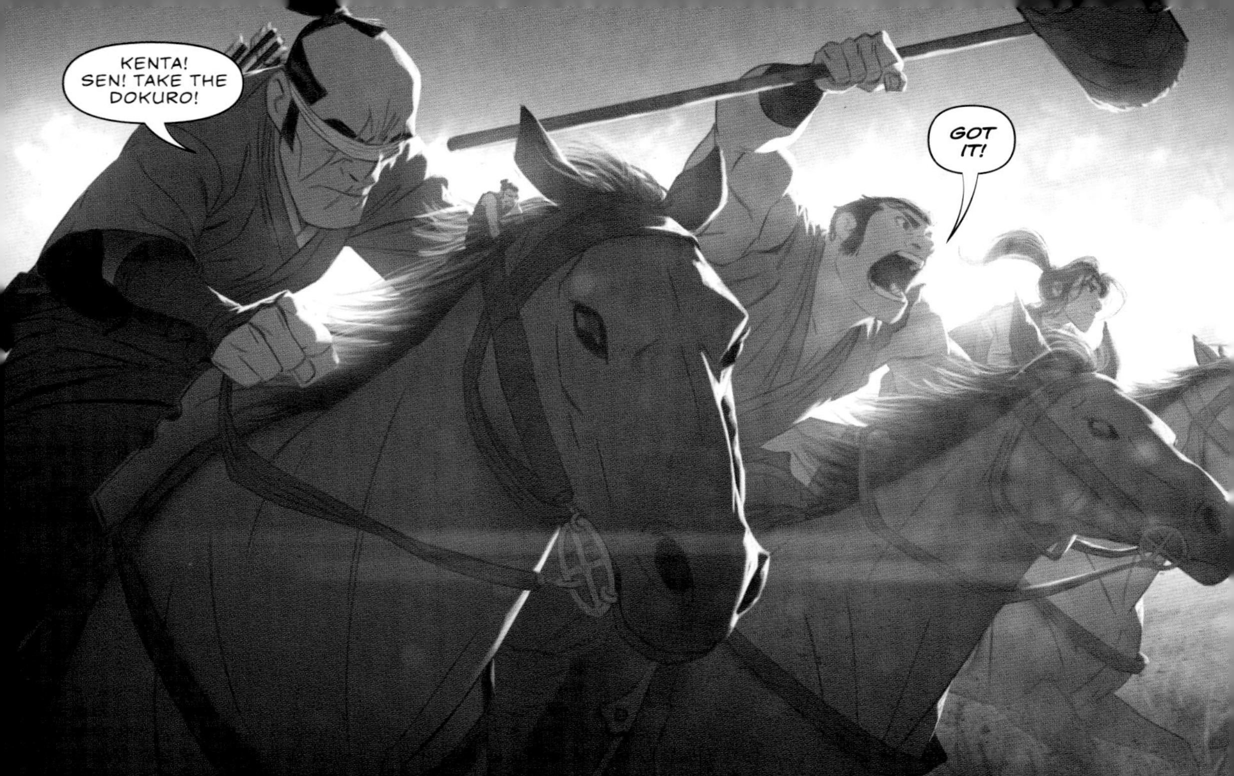
KENTA! SEN! TAKE THE DOKURO!
GOT IT!

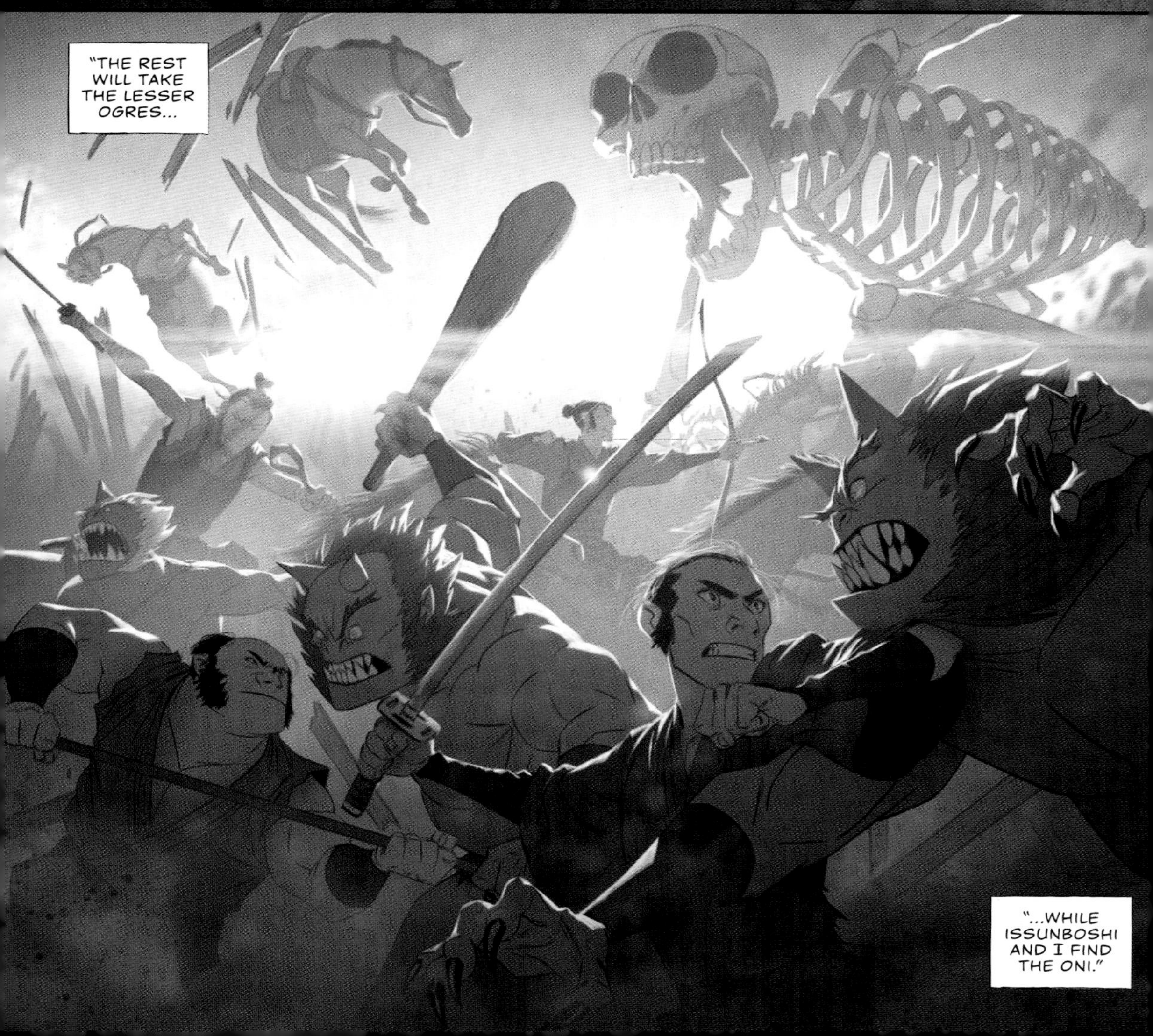
"THE REST WILL TAKE THE LESSER OGRES...
"...WHILE ISSUNBOSHI AND I FIND THE ONI."

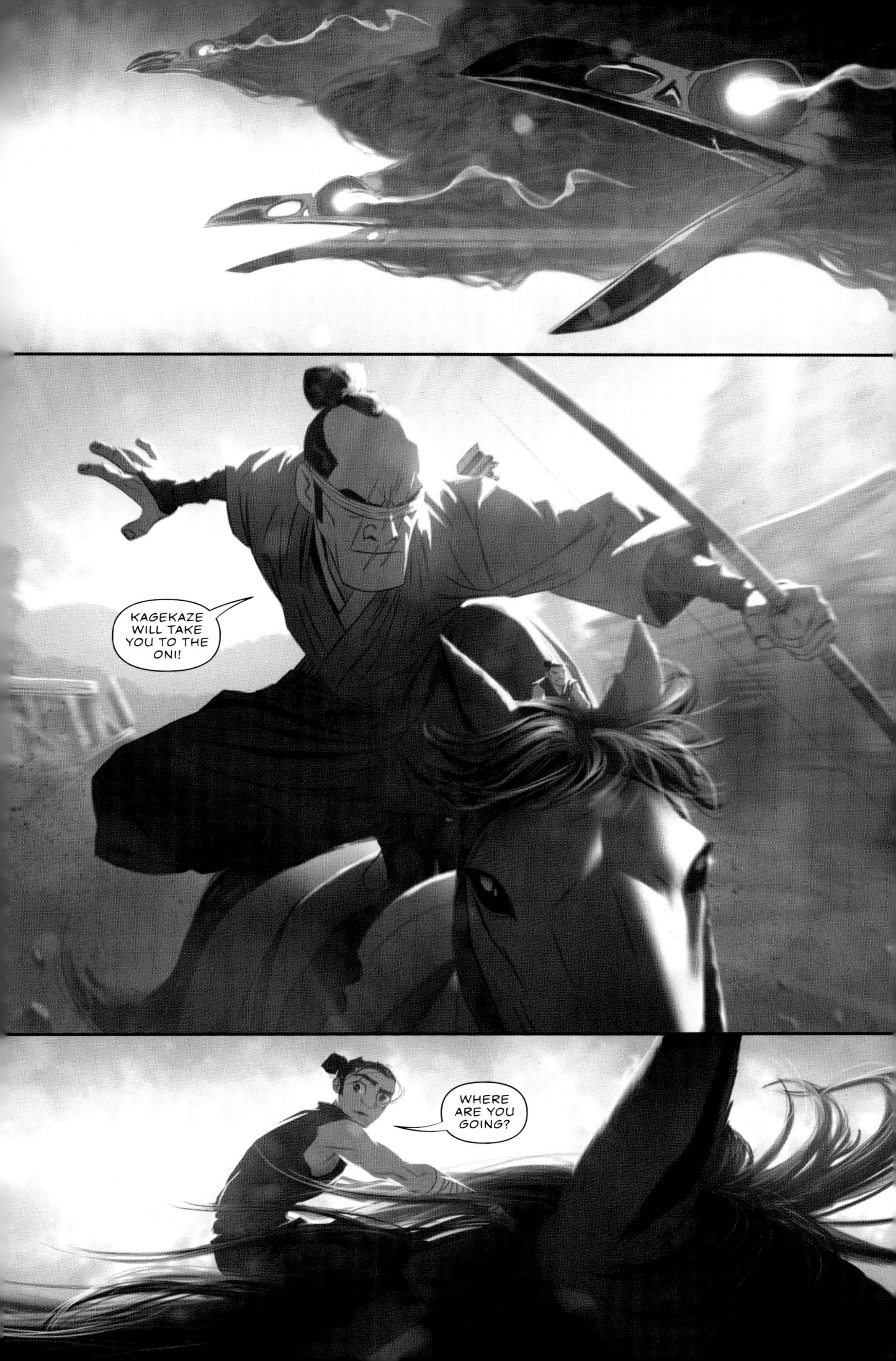
KAGEKAZE WILL TAKE YOU TO THE ONI!
WHERE ARE YOU GOING?

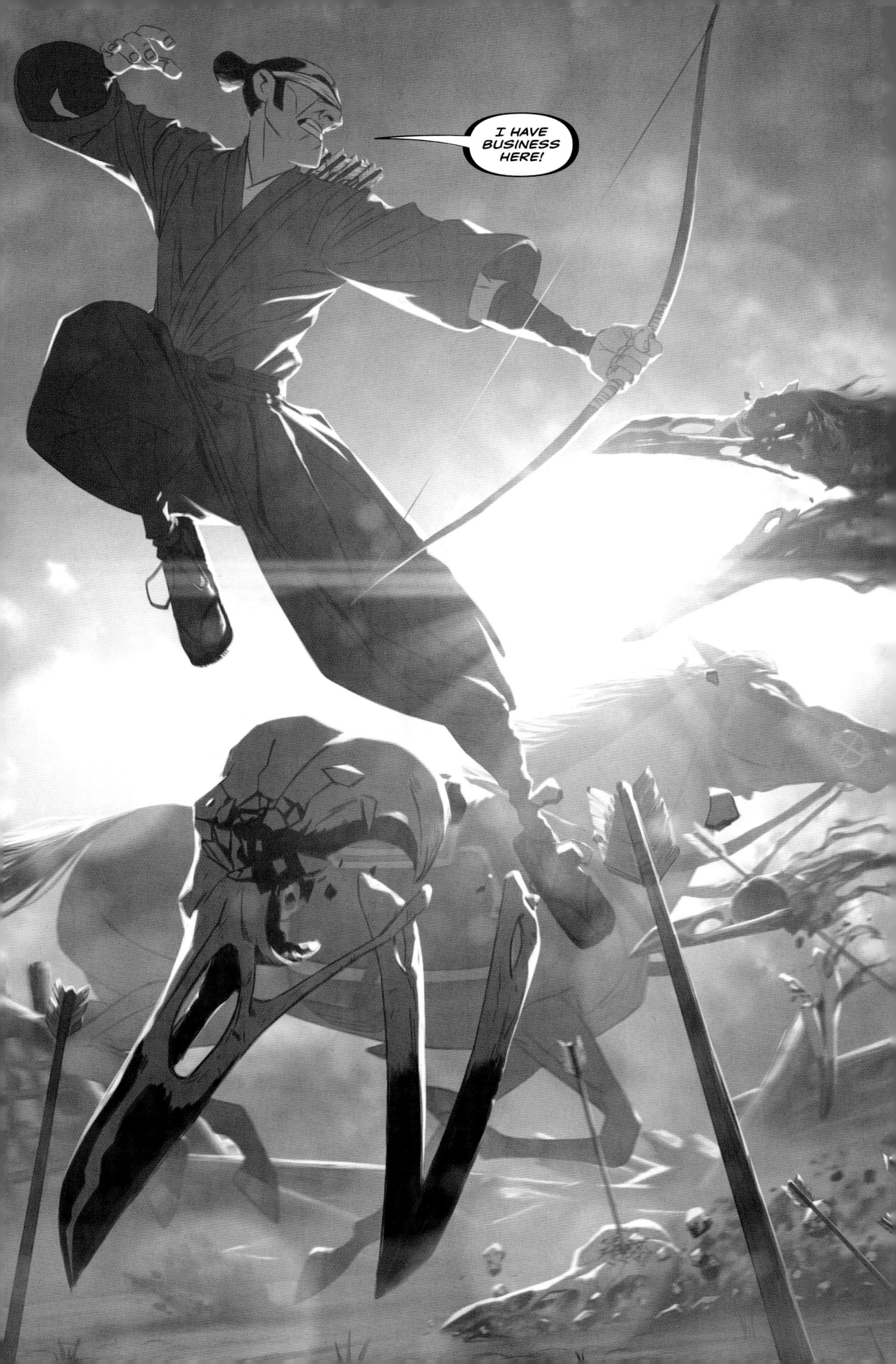
I HAVE BUSINESS HERE!

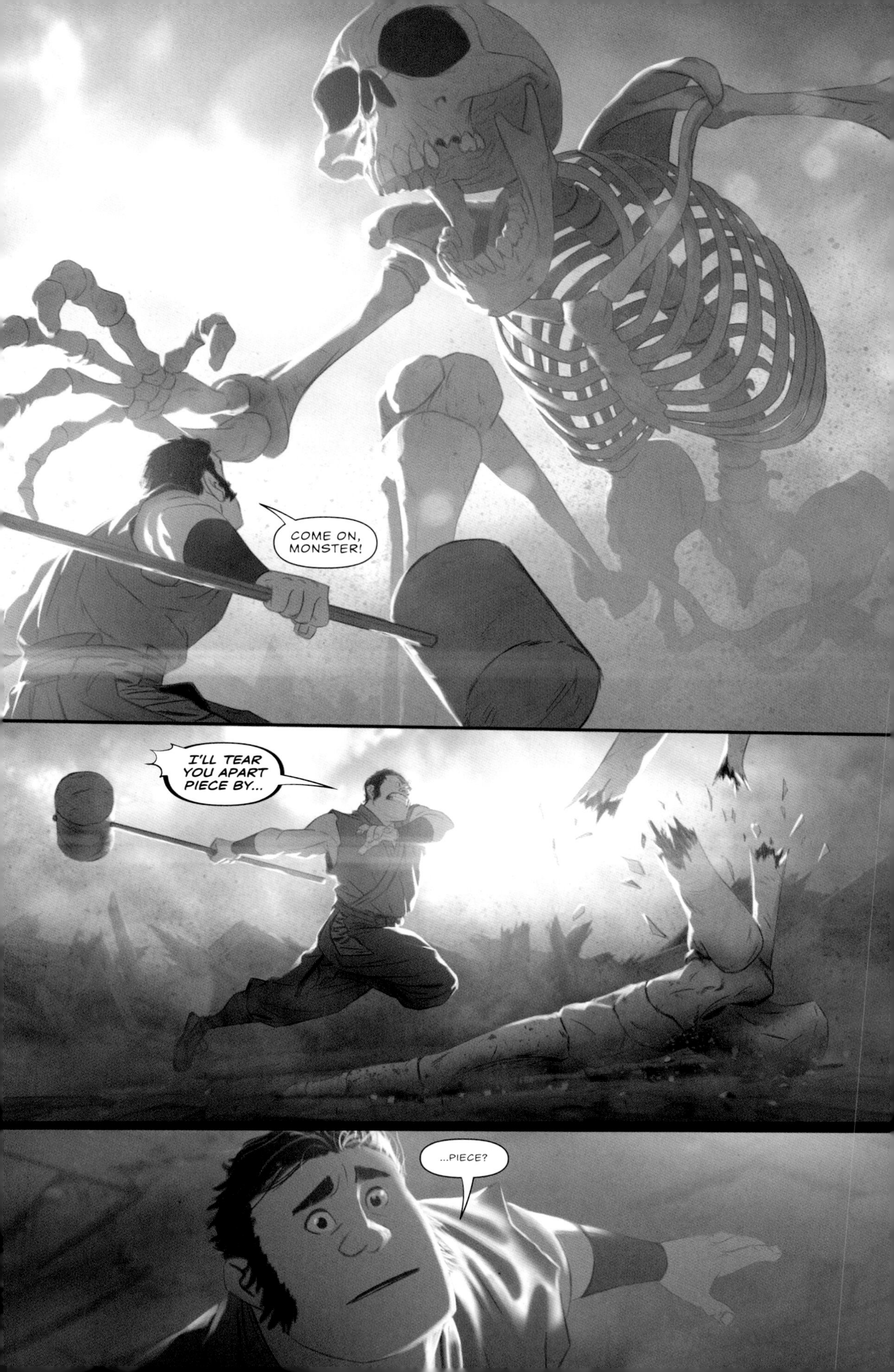
COME ON, MONSTER!
I'LL TEAR YOU APART PIECE BY...
...PIECE?

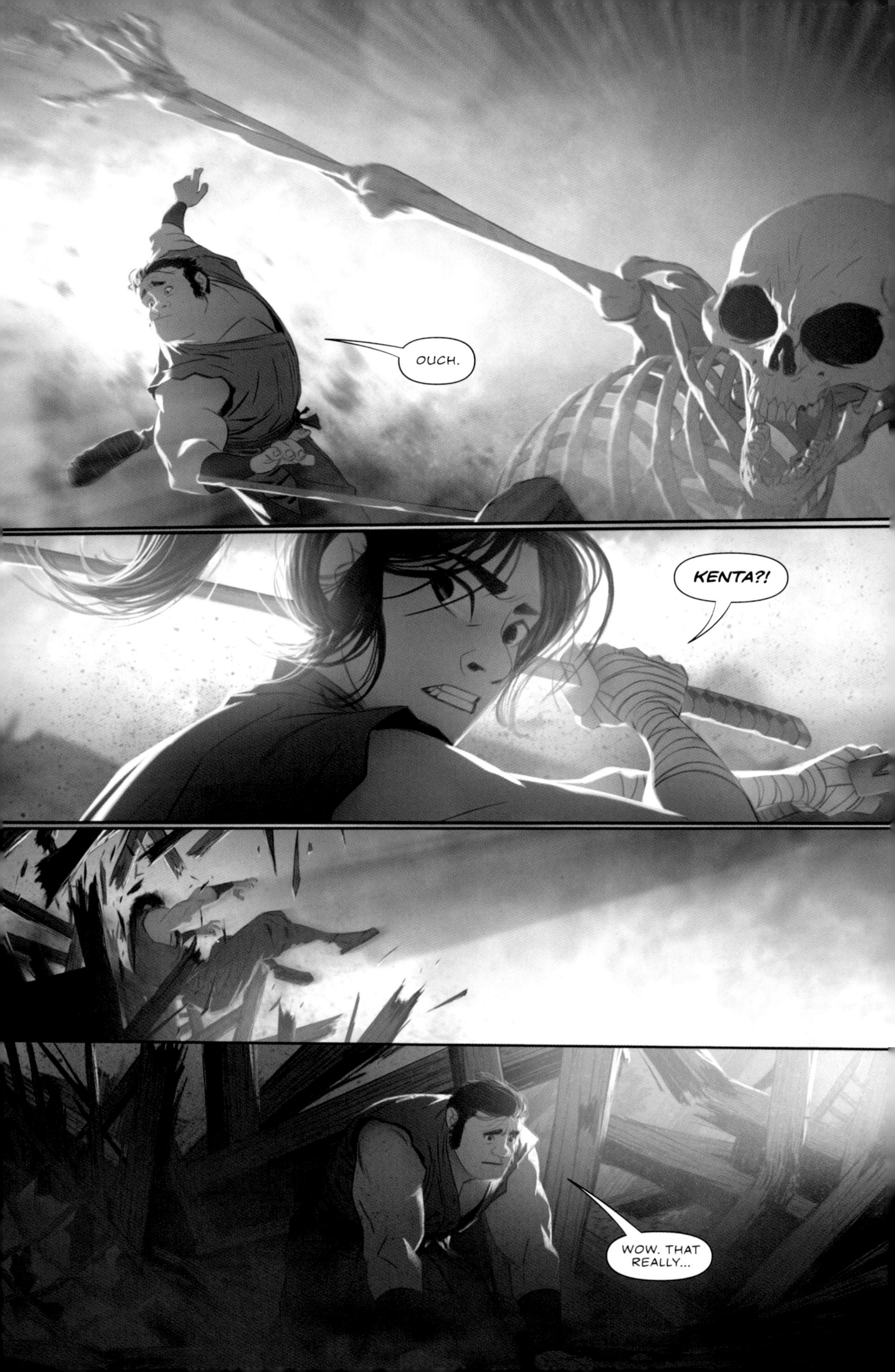
OUCH.
KENTA?!
WOW. THAT REALLY...

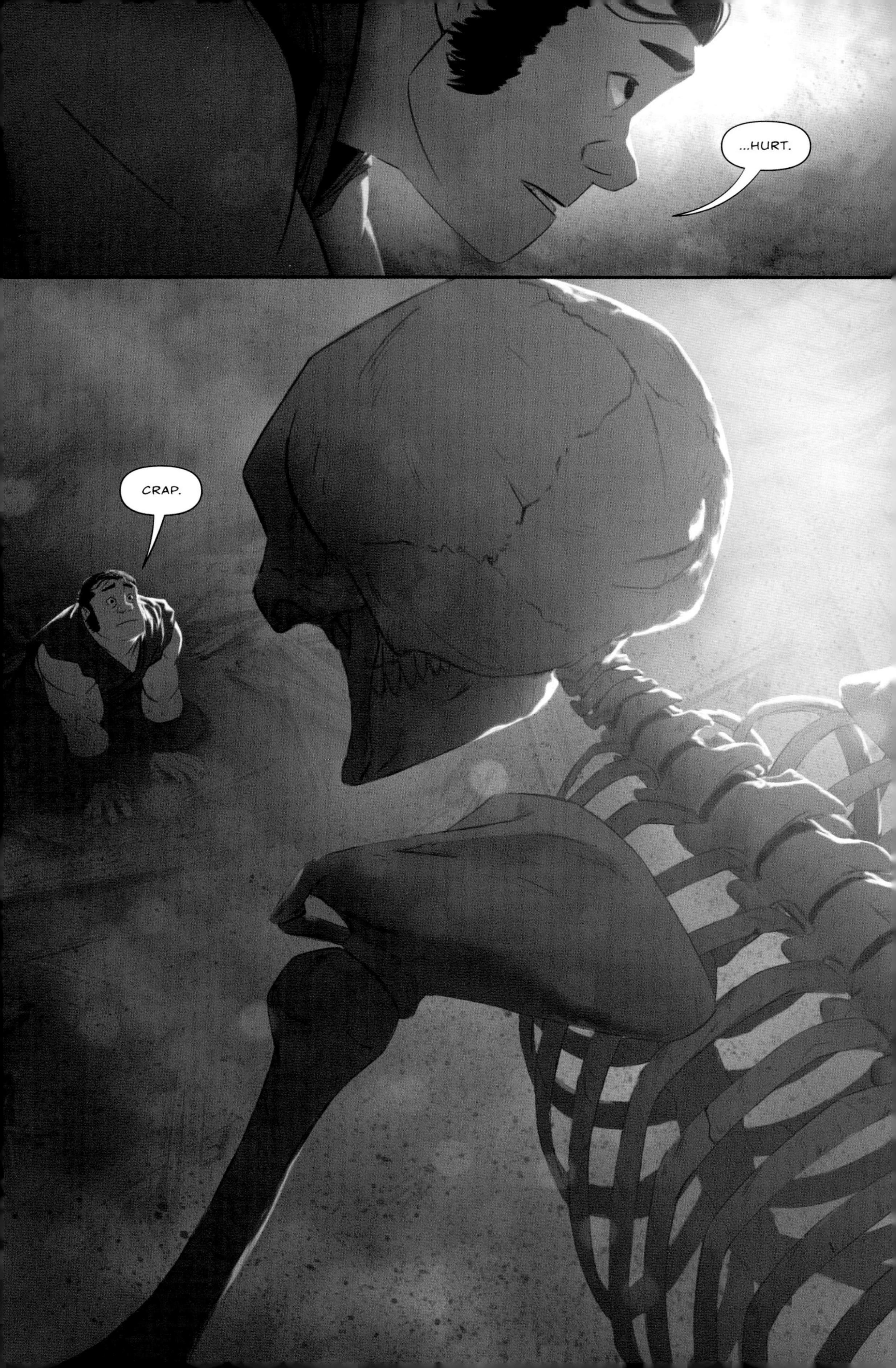
...HURT.
CRAP.

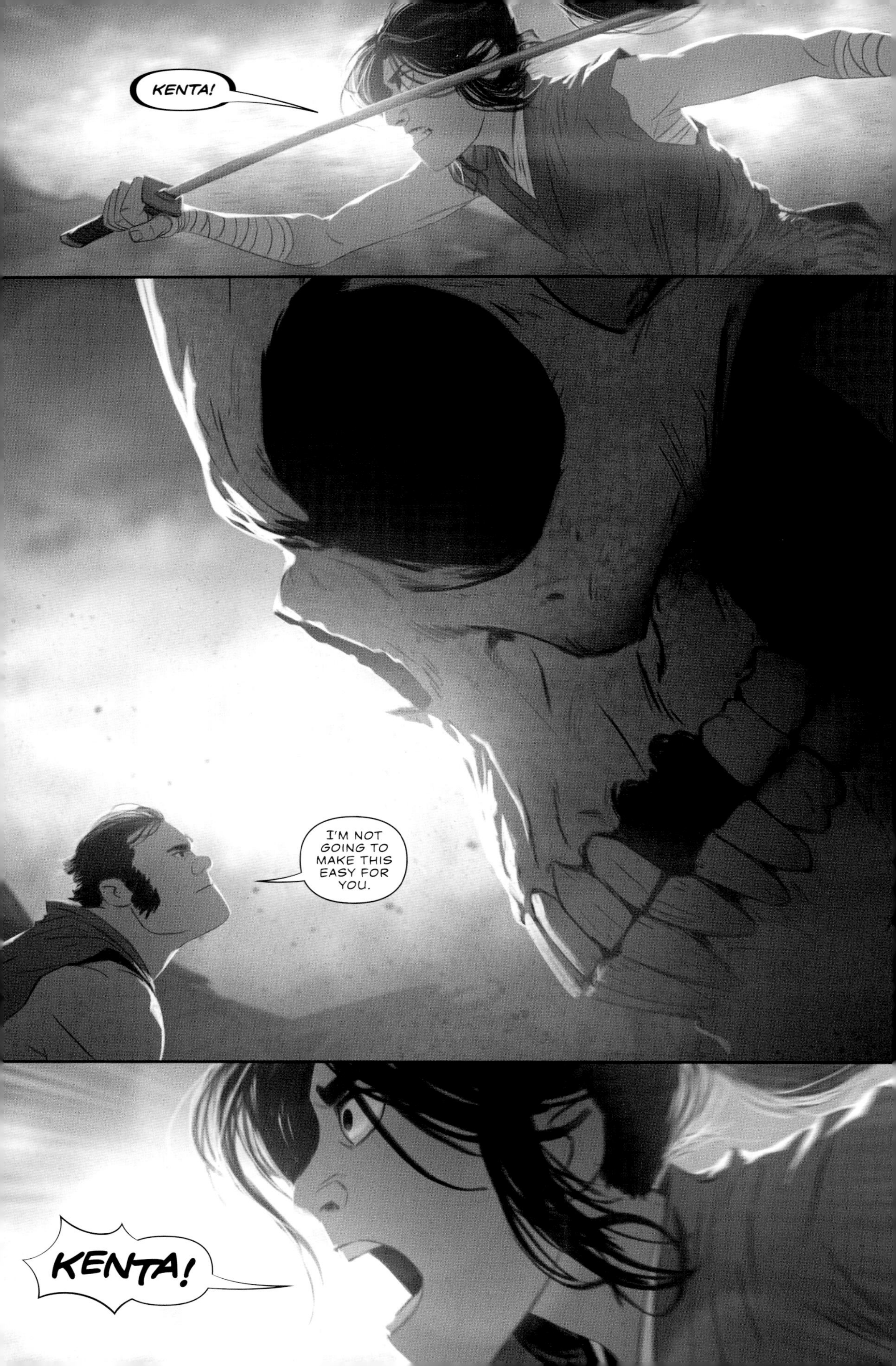
KENTA!
I'M NOT GOING TO MAKE THIS EASY FOR YOU.
KENTA!

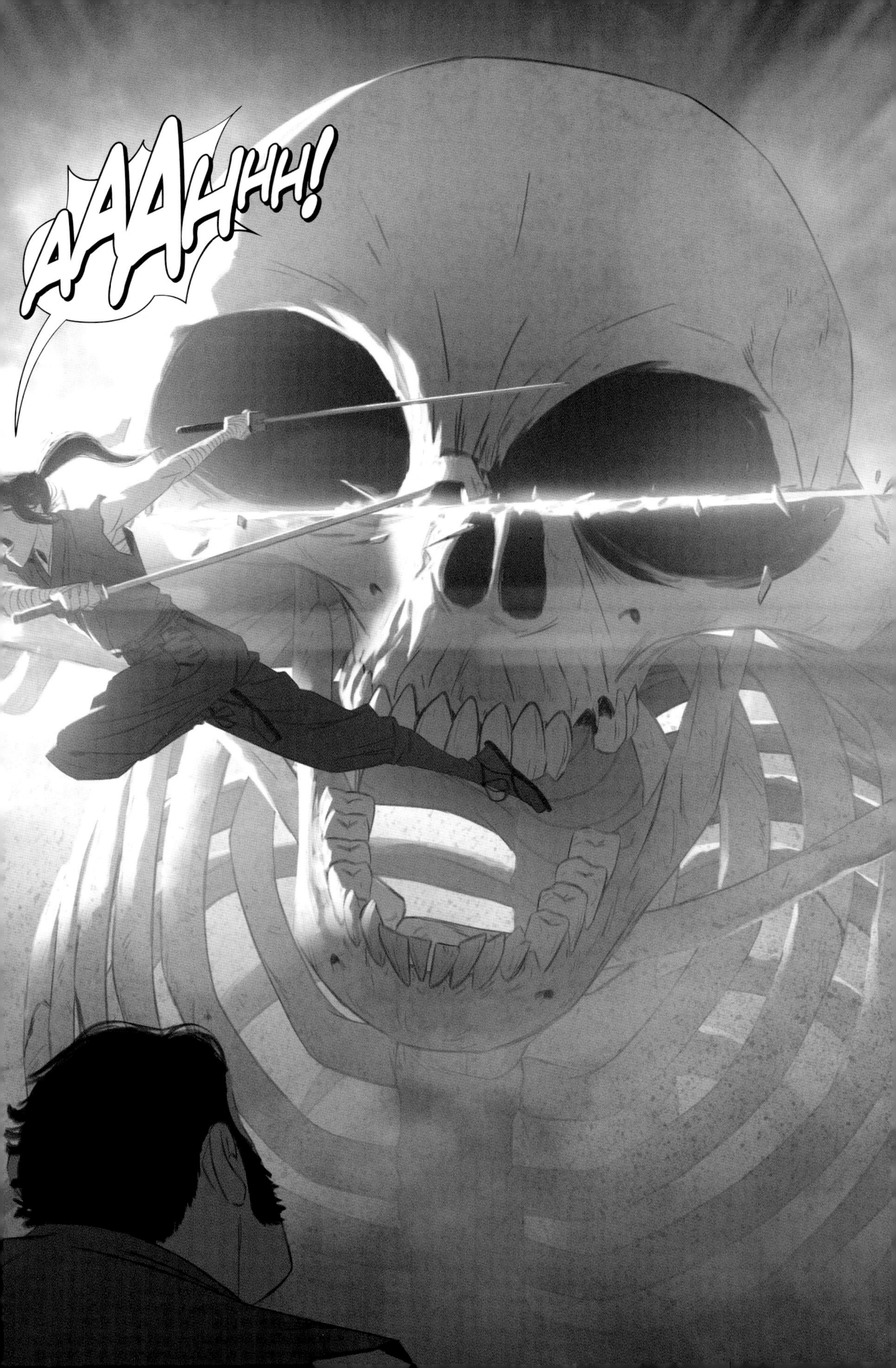
AAAHHH!

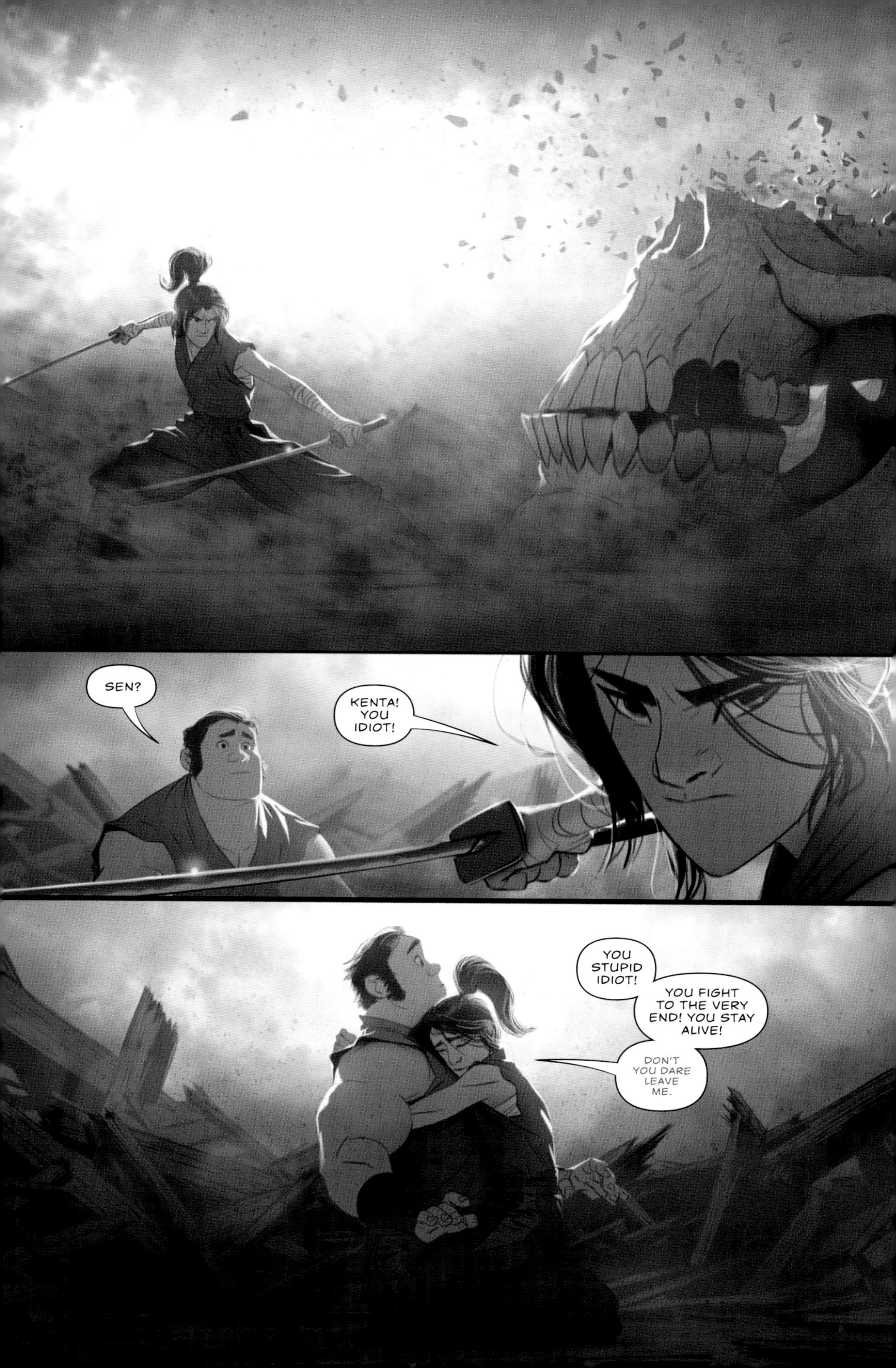
SEN?
KENTA! YOU IDIOT!
YOU STUPID IDIOT!
YOU FIGHT TO THE VERY END! YOU STAY ALIVE!
DON'T YOU DARE LEAVE ME.

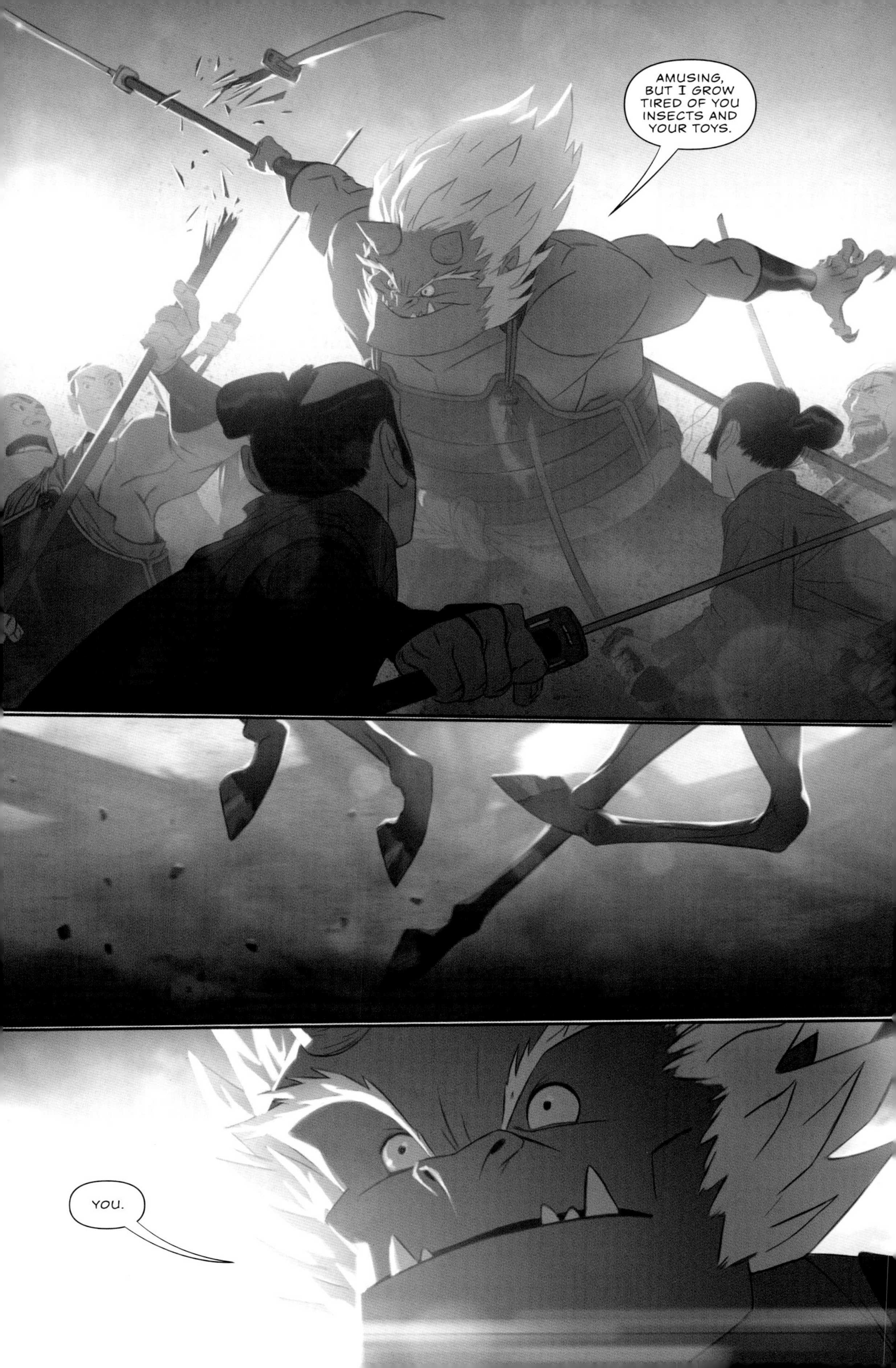
AMUSING, BUT I GROW TIRED OF YOU INSECTS AND YOUR TOYS.
YOU.

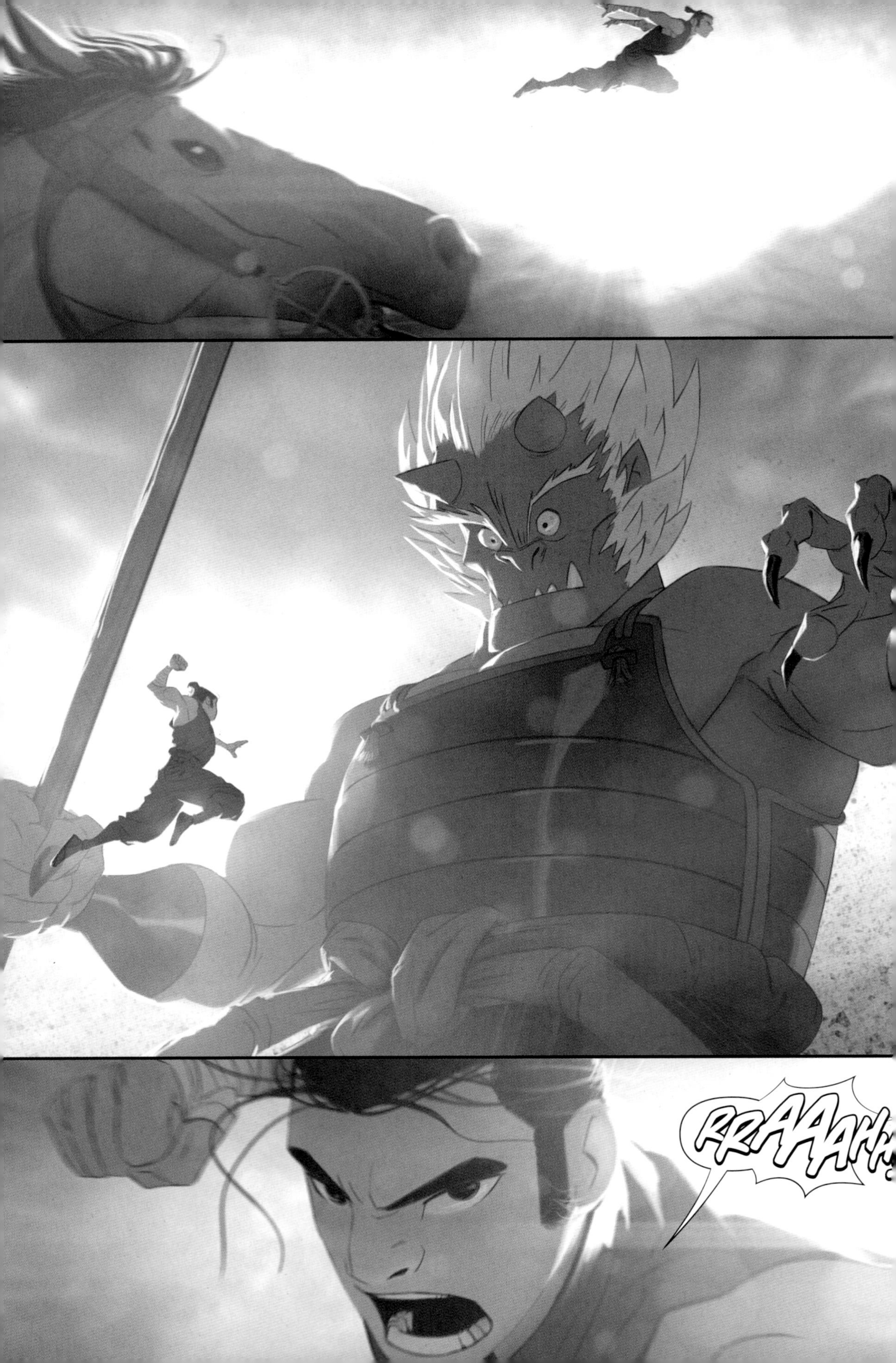
RRAAAHH!

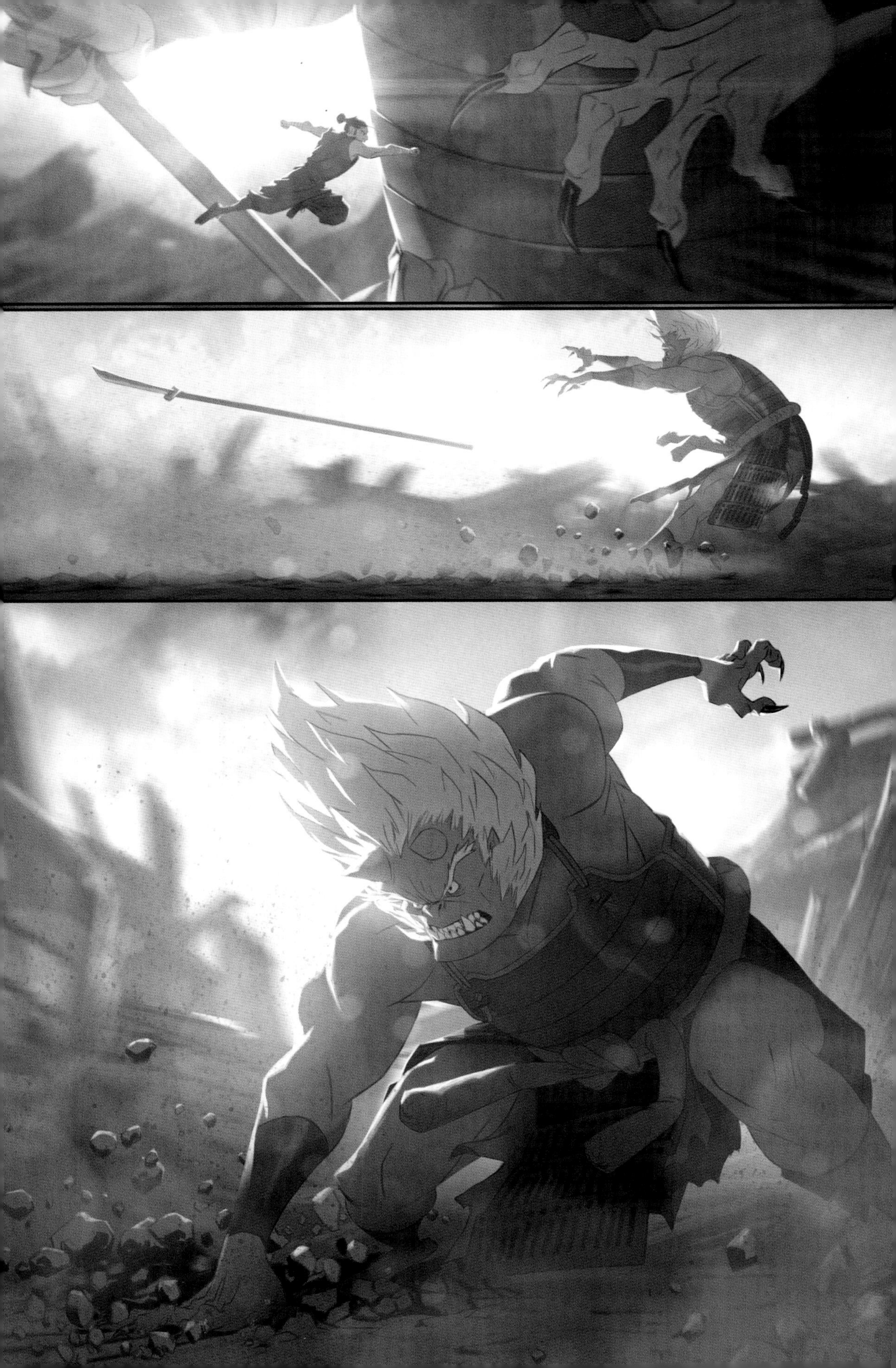

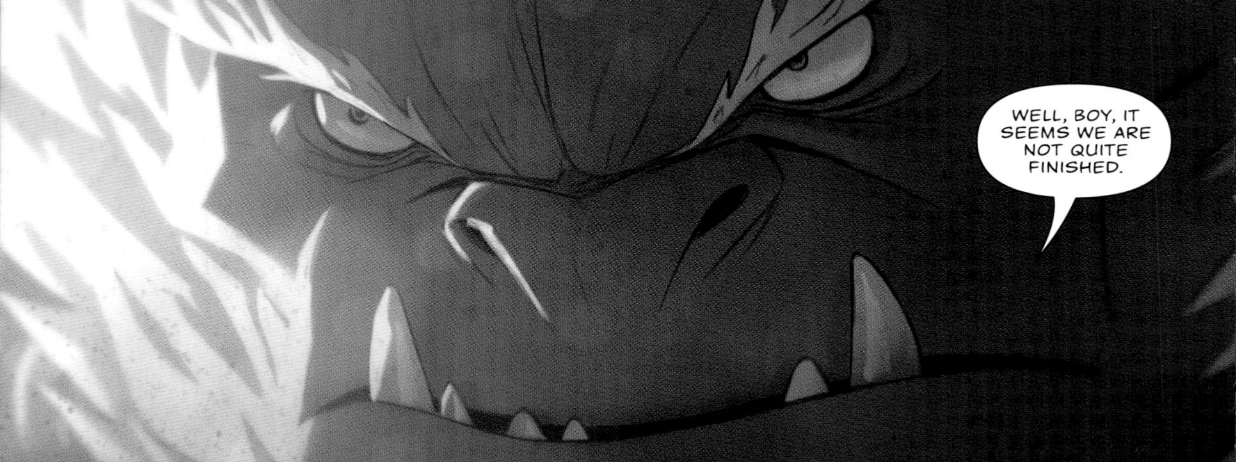
WELL, BOY, IT SEEMS WE ARE NOT QUITE FINISHED.
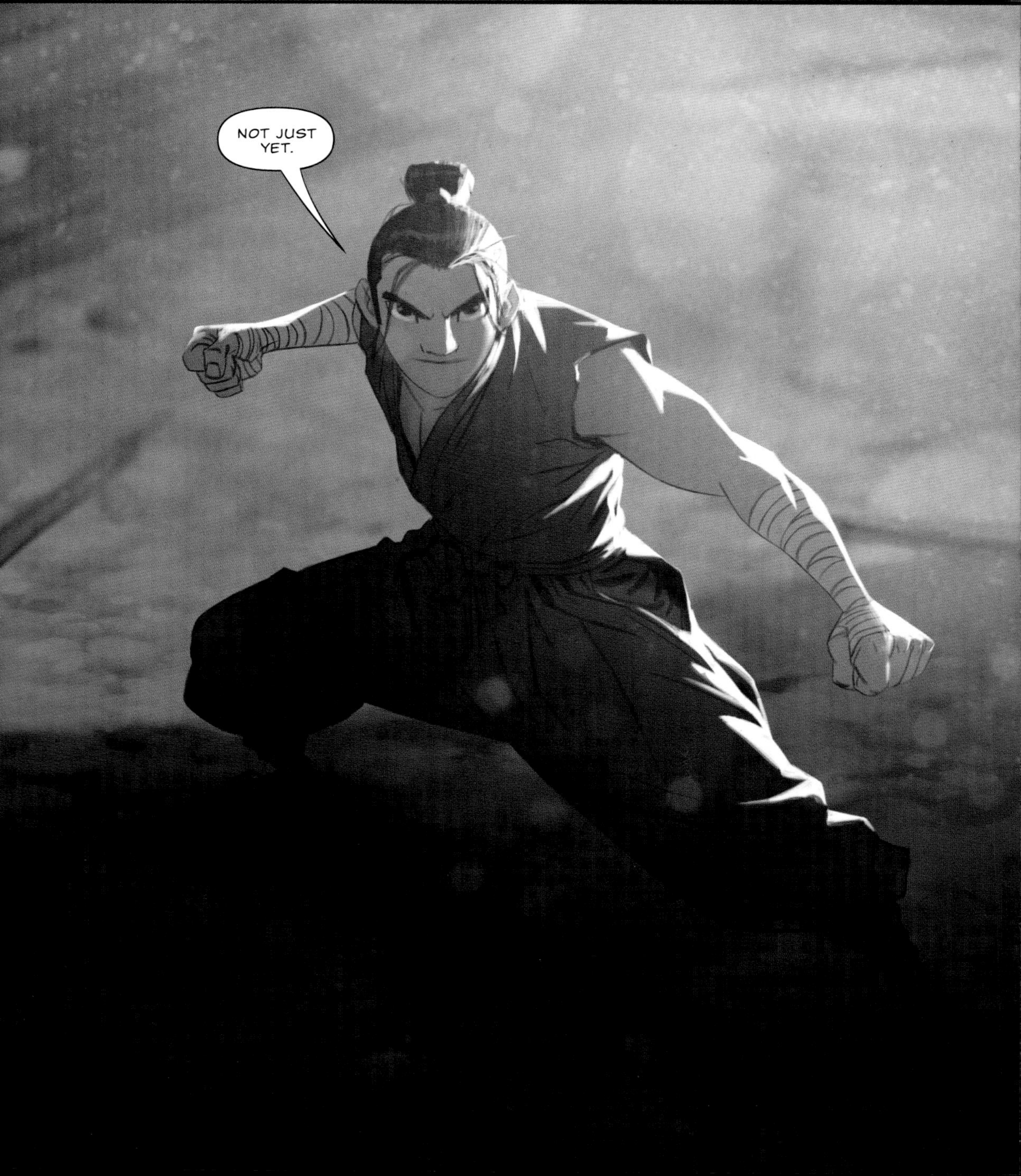
NOT JUST YET.

FIVE

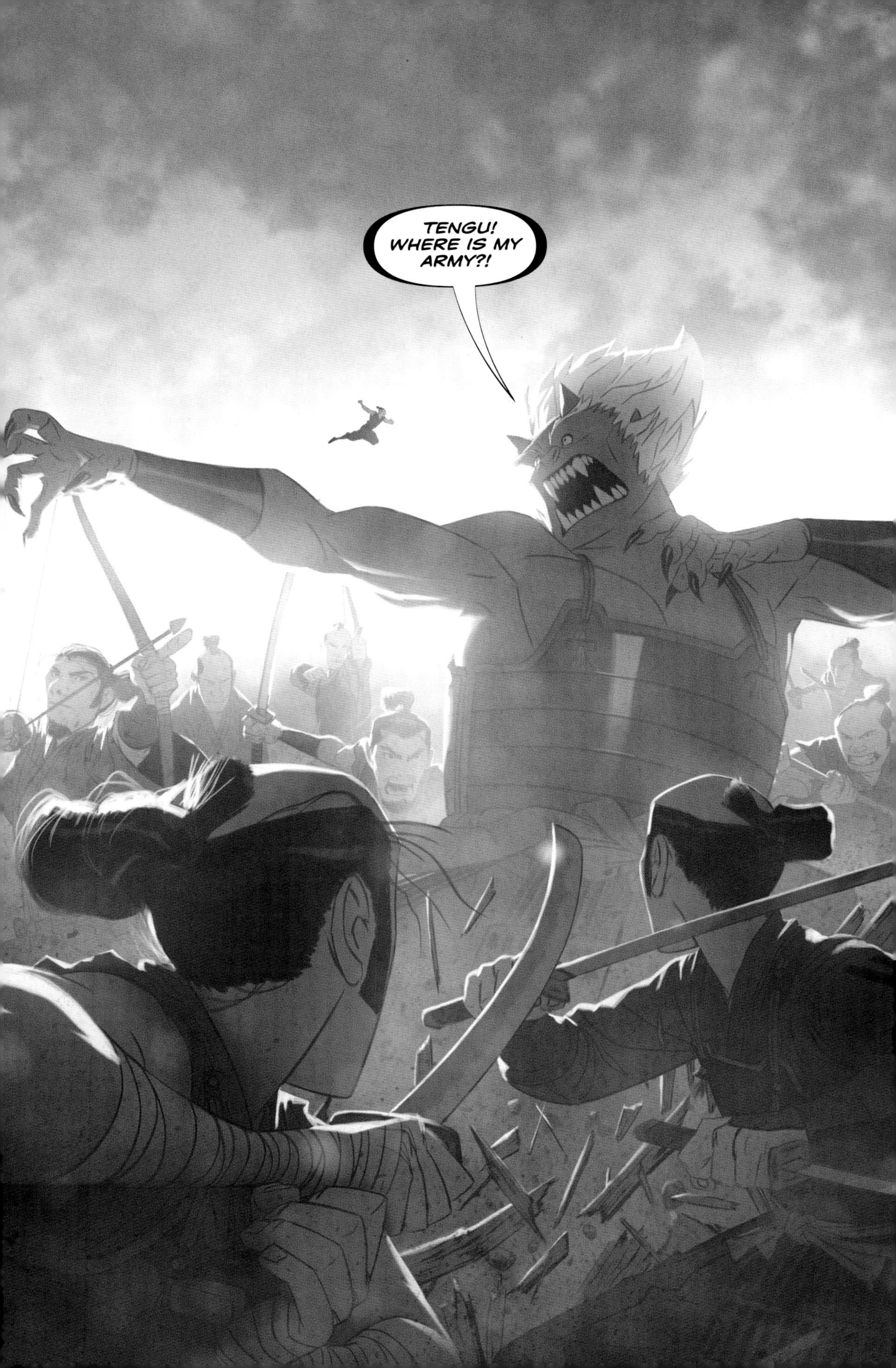
TENGU! WHERE IS MY ARMY?!

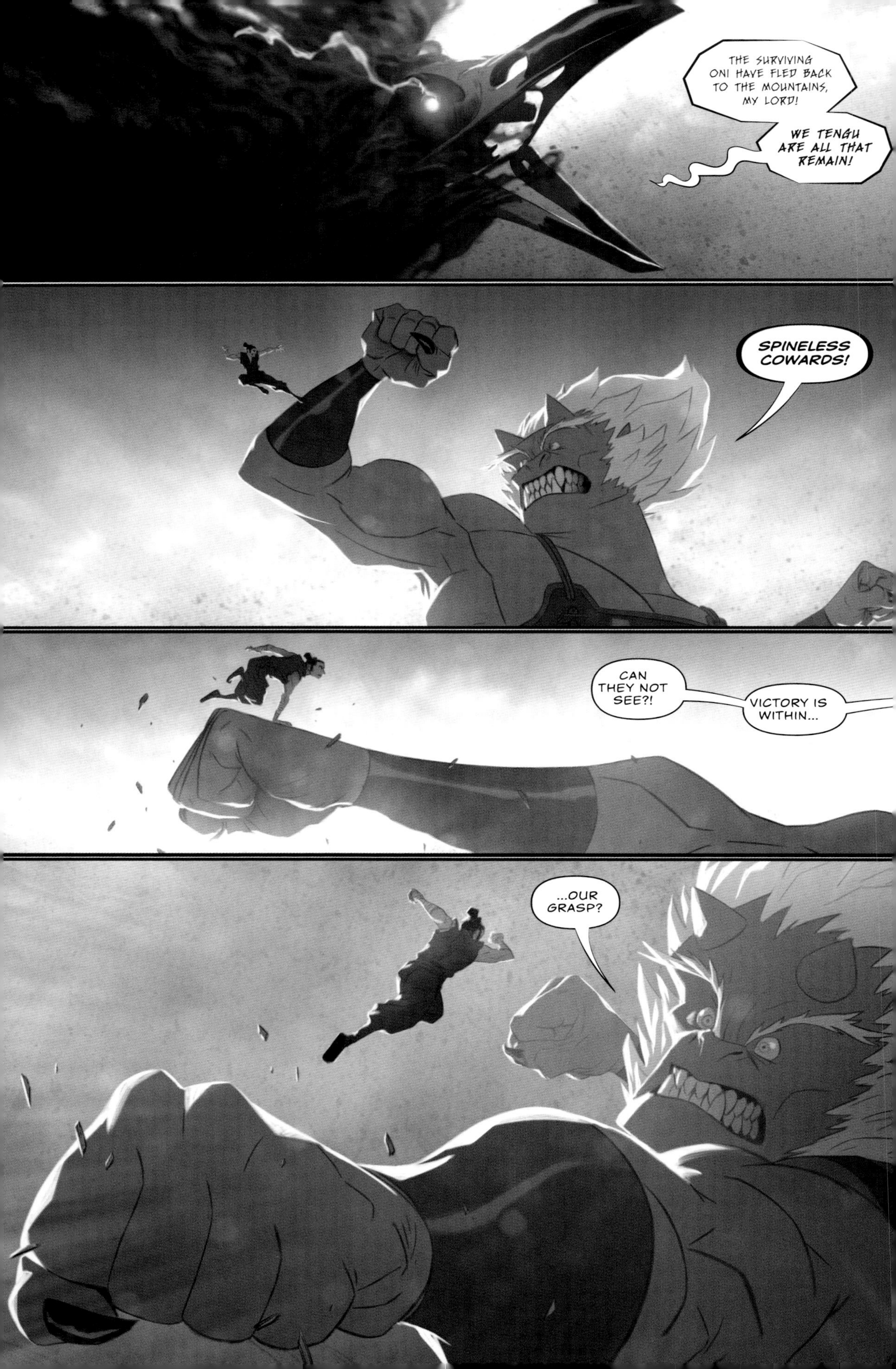
THE SURVIVING ONI HAVE FLED BACK TO THE MOUNTAINS, MY LORD!
WE TENGU ARE ALL THAT REMAIN!
SPINELESS COWARDS!
CAN THEY NOT SEE?!
VICTORY IS WITHIN...
...OUR GRASP?

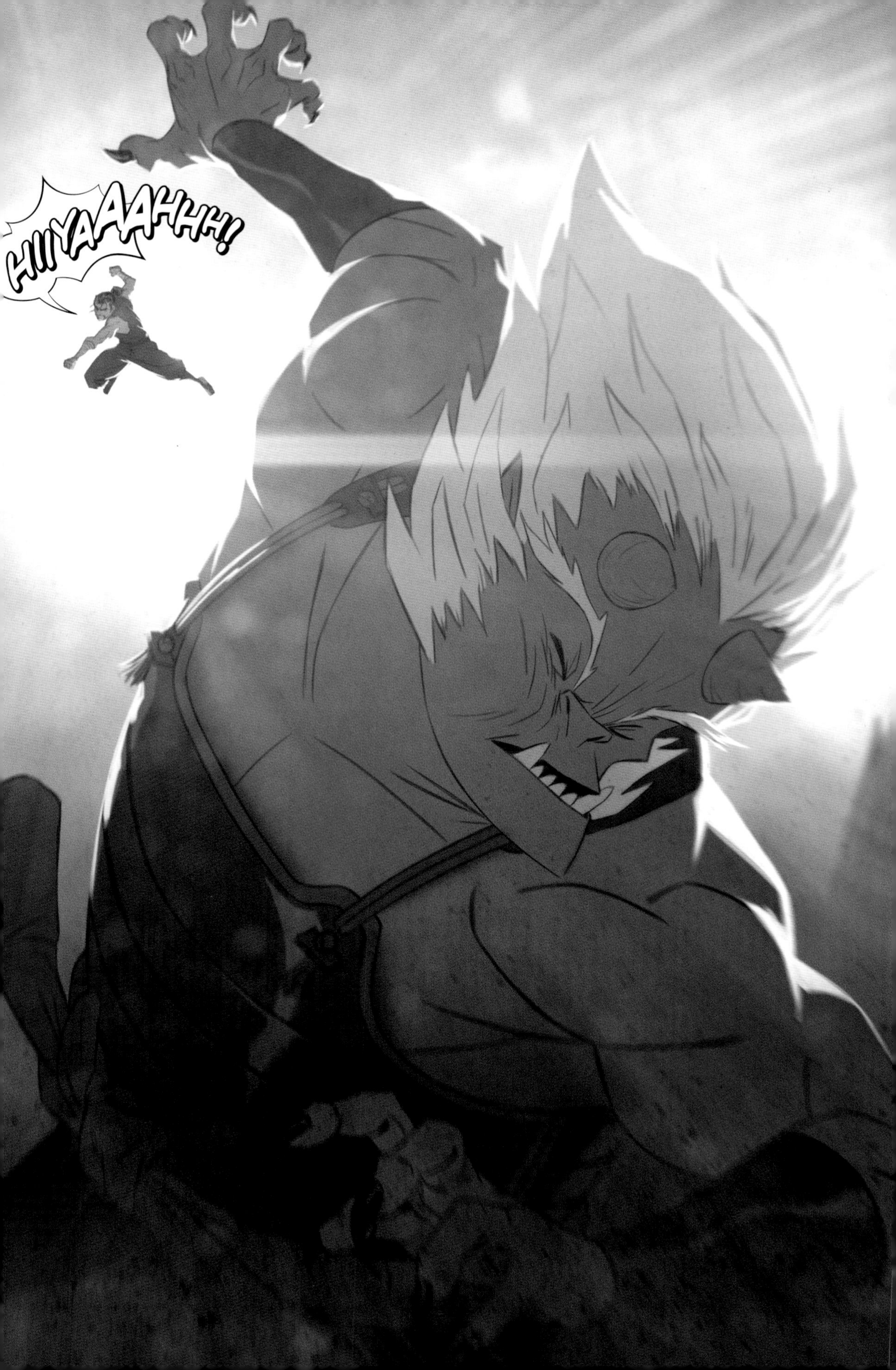
HIIIYAAAHHH!

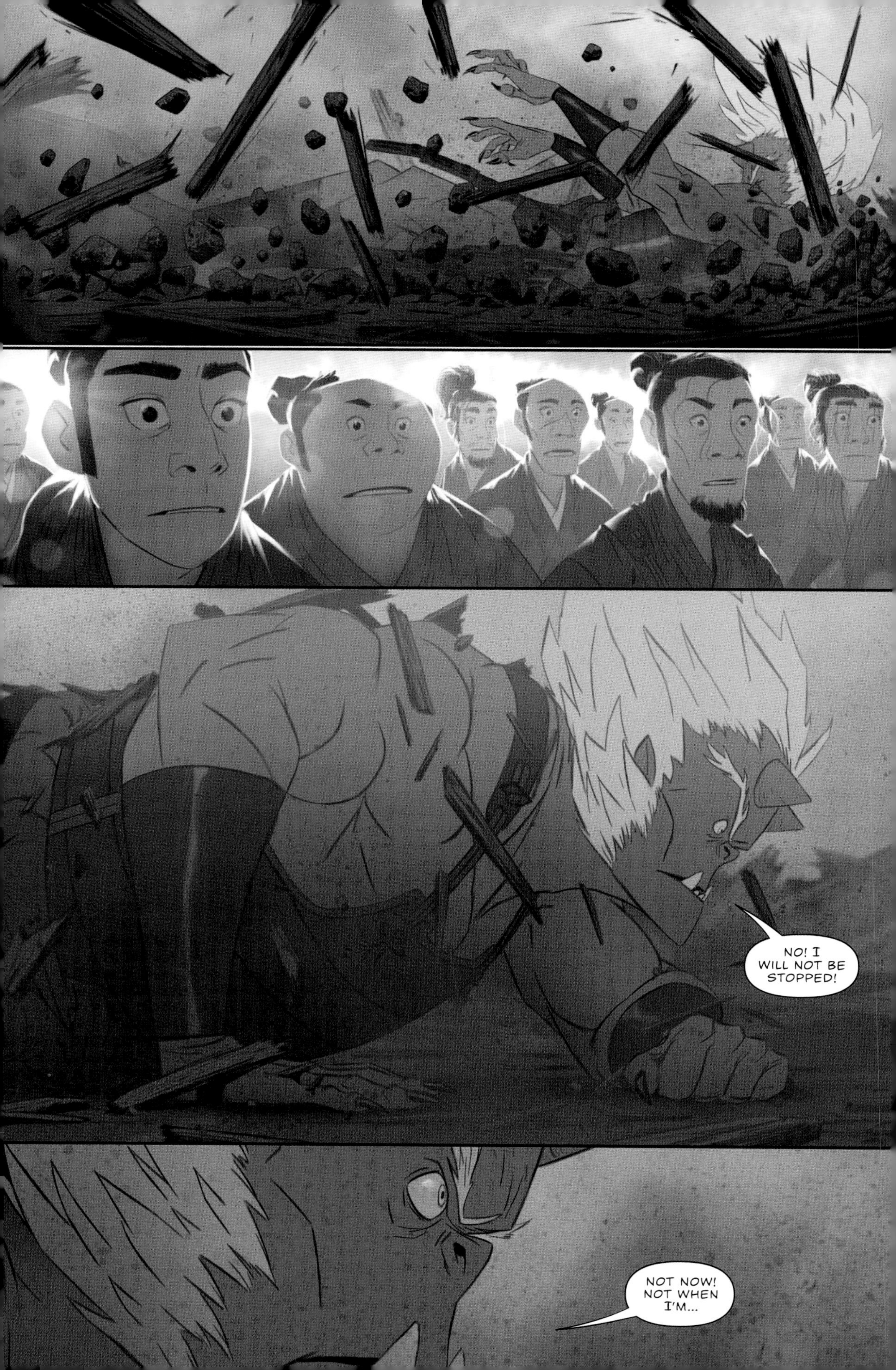
NO! I WILL NOT BE STOPPED!
NOT NOW! NOT WHEN I'M...

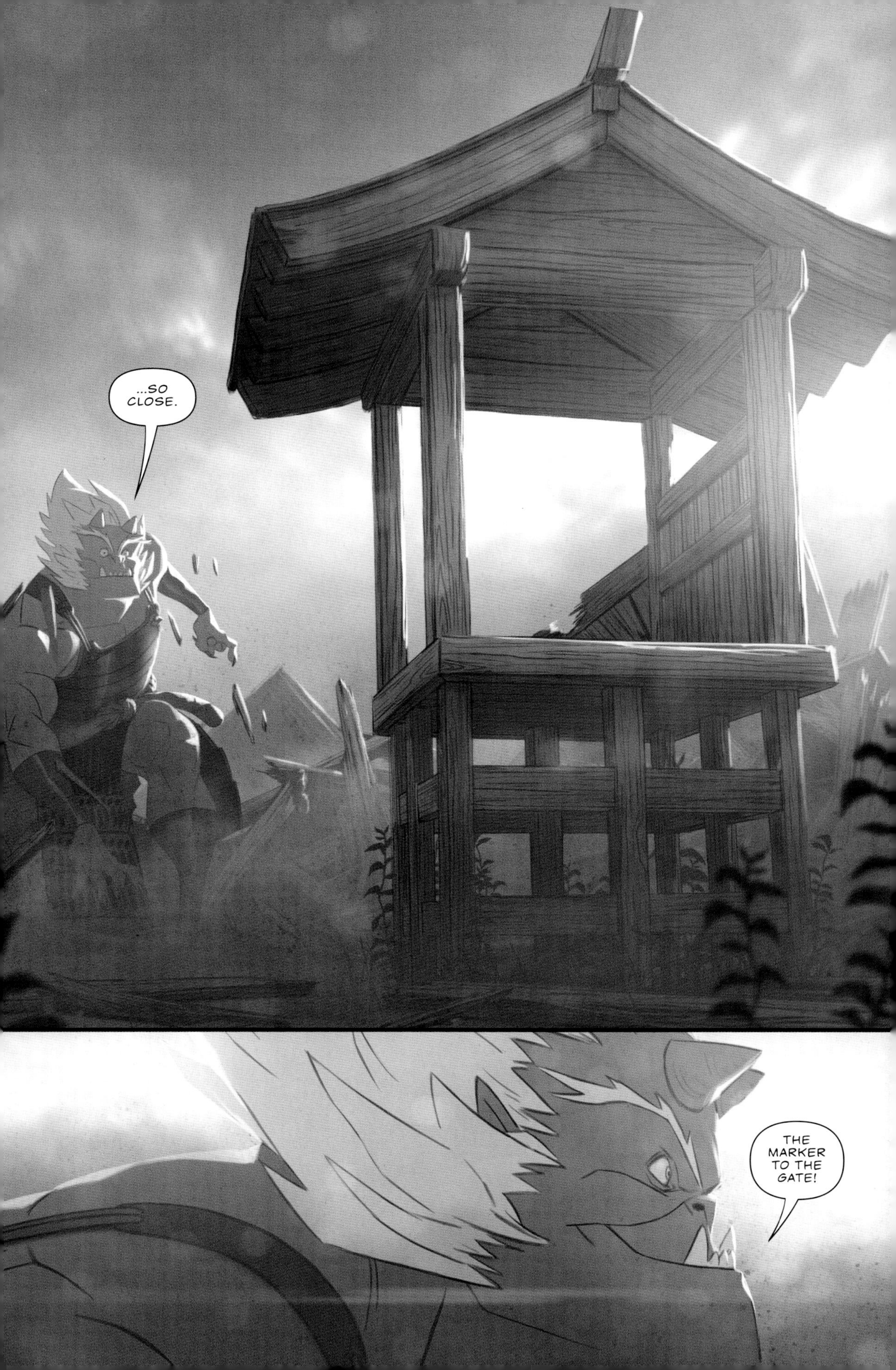
...SO CLOSE.
THE MARKER TO THE GATE!

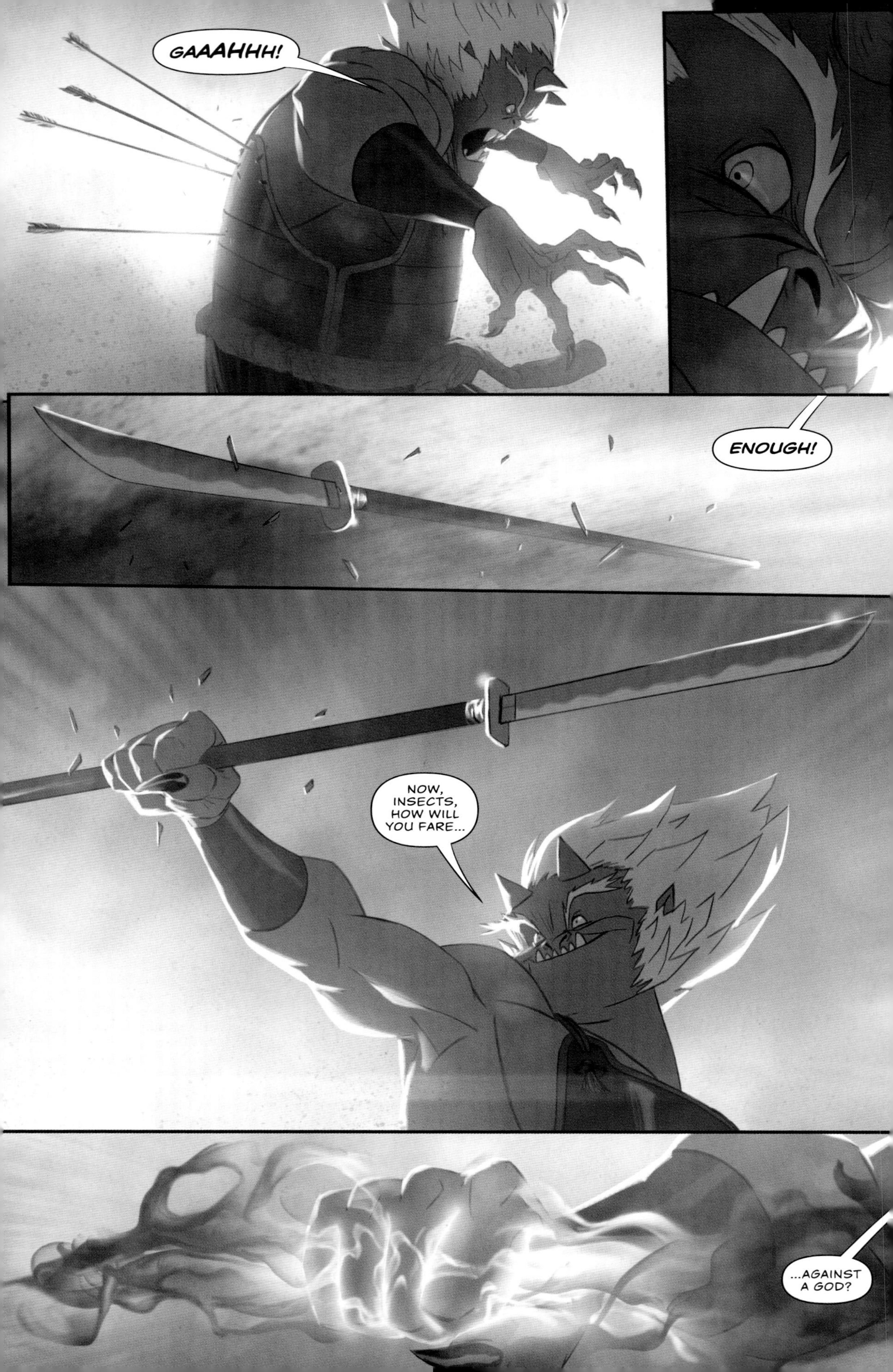
GAAAHHH!
ENOUGH!
NOW, INSECTS, HOW WILL YOU FARE...
...AGAINST A GOD?

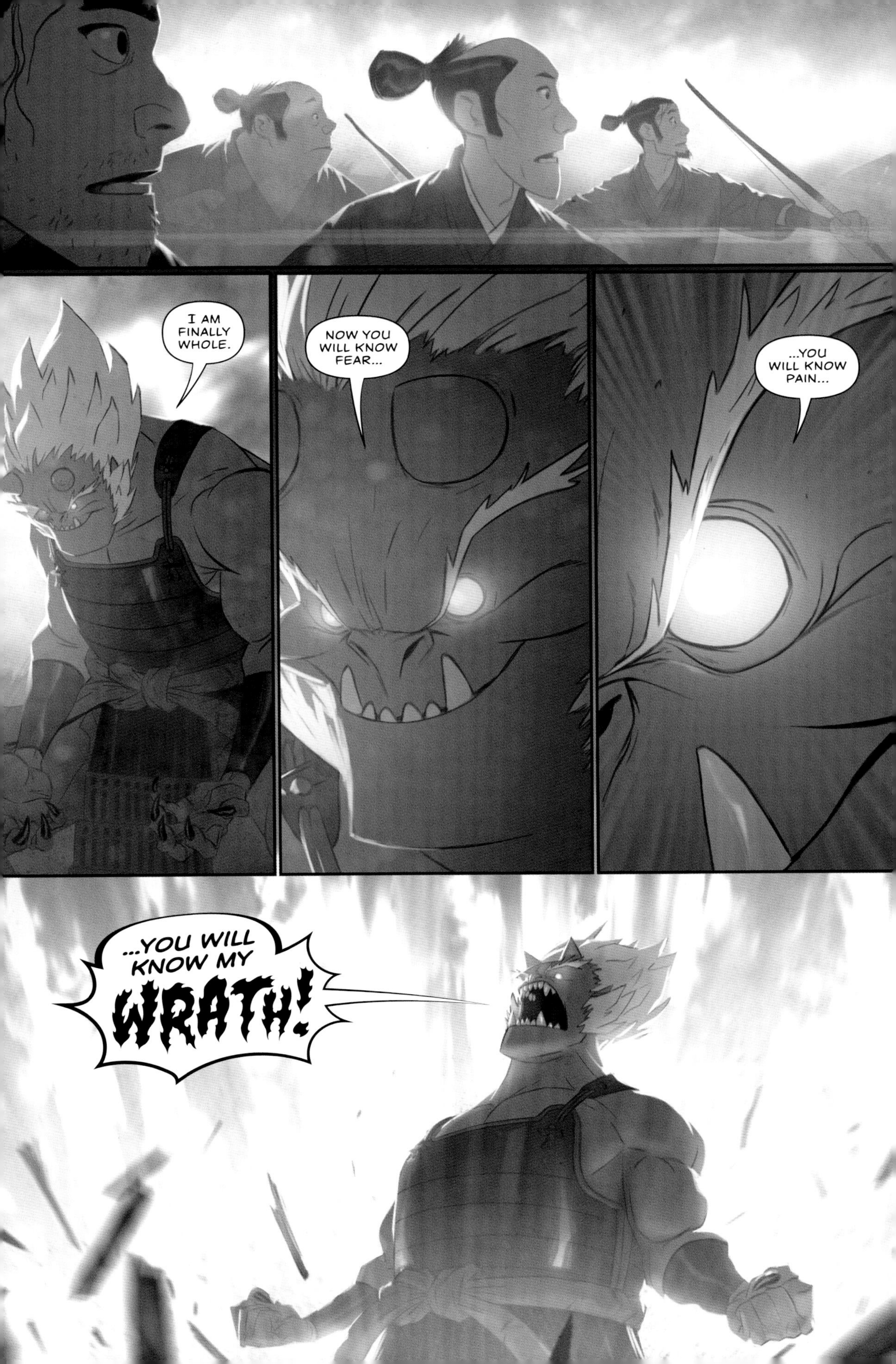
I AM FINALLY WHOLE.
NOW YOU WILL KNOW FEAR...
...YOU WILL KNOW PAIN...
...YOU WILL KNOW MY WRATH!

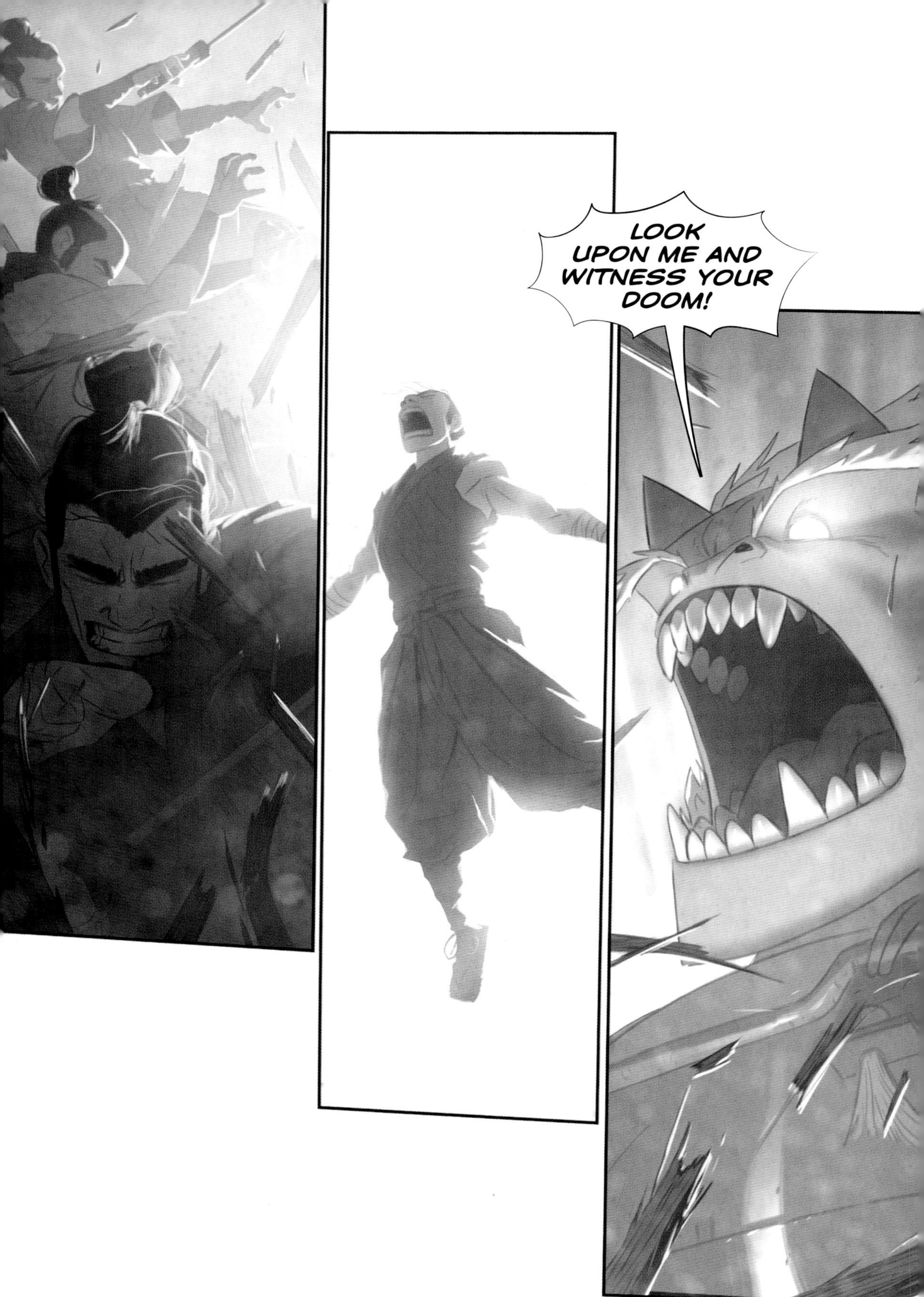
LOOK UPON ME AND WITNESS YOUR DOOM!

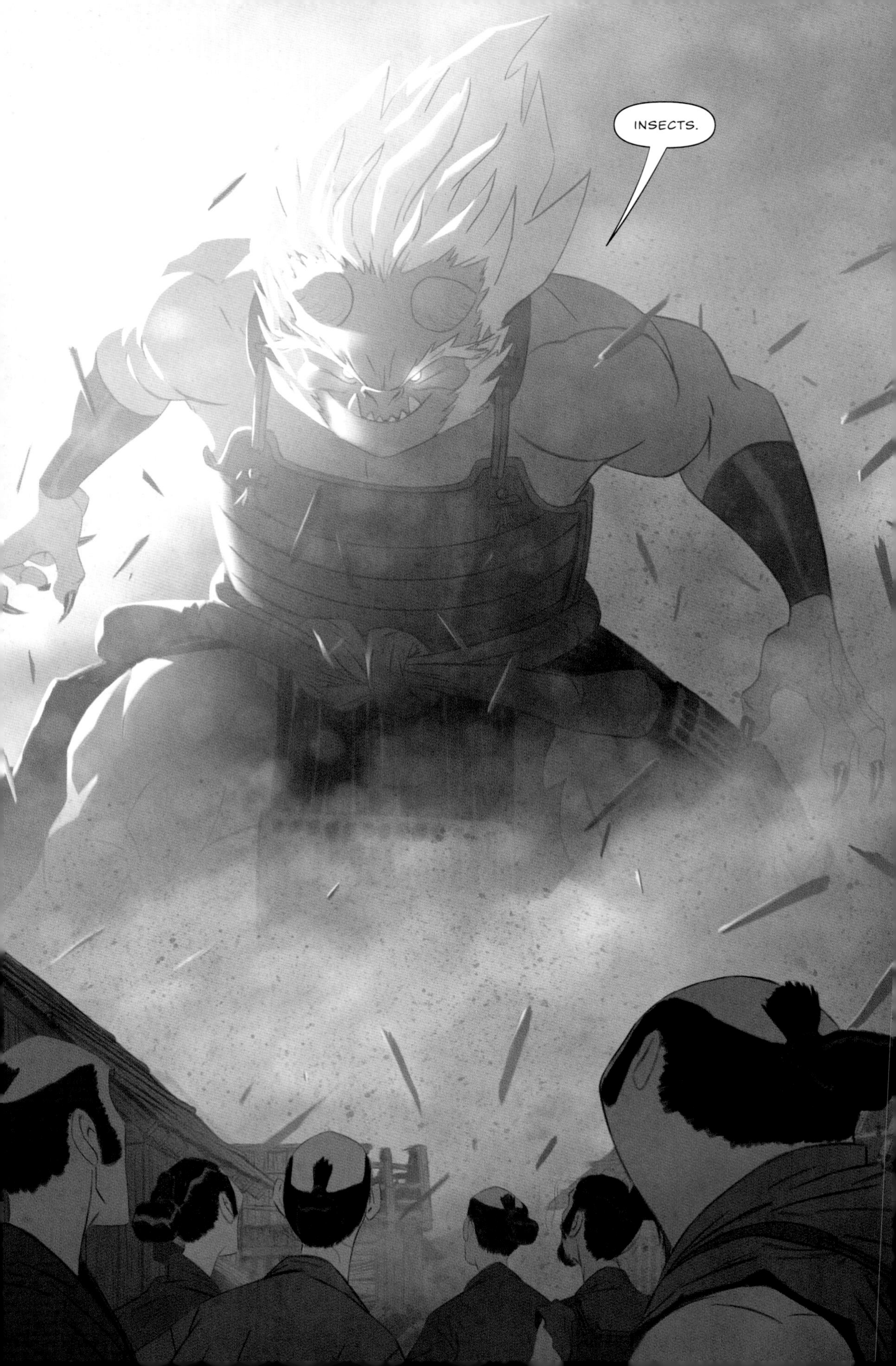
INSECTS.

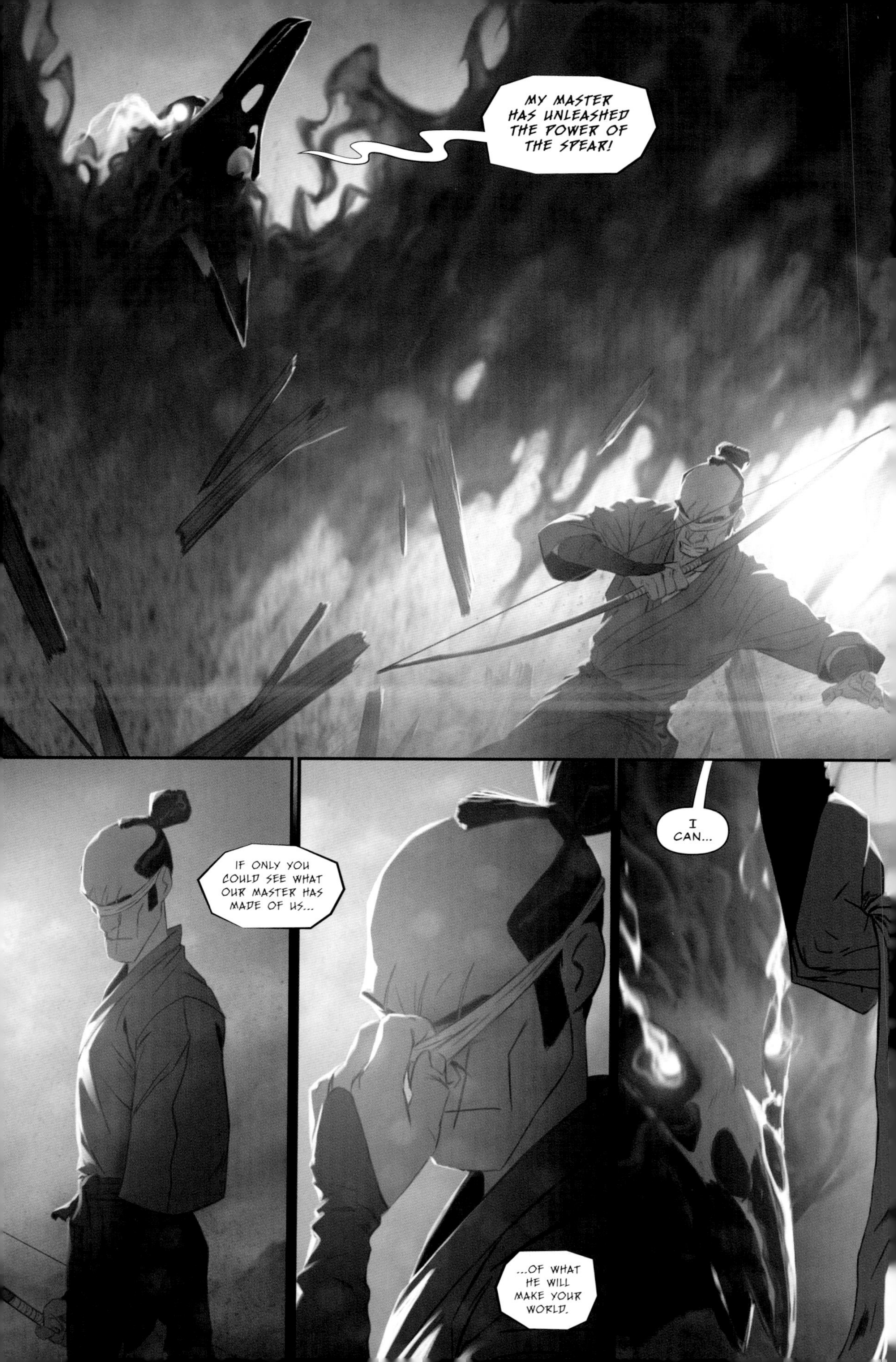
MY MASTER HAS UNLEASHED THE POWER OF THE SPEAR!
IF ONLY YOU COULD SEE WHAT OUR MASTER HAS MADE OF US...
I CAN...
...OF WHAT HE WILL MAKE YOUR WORLD.

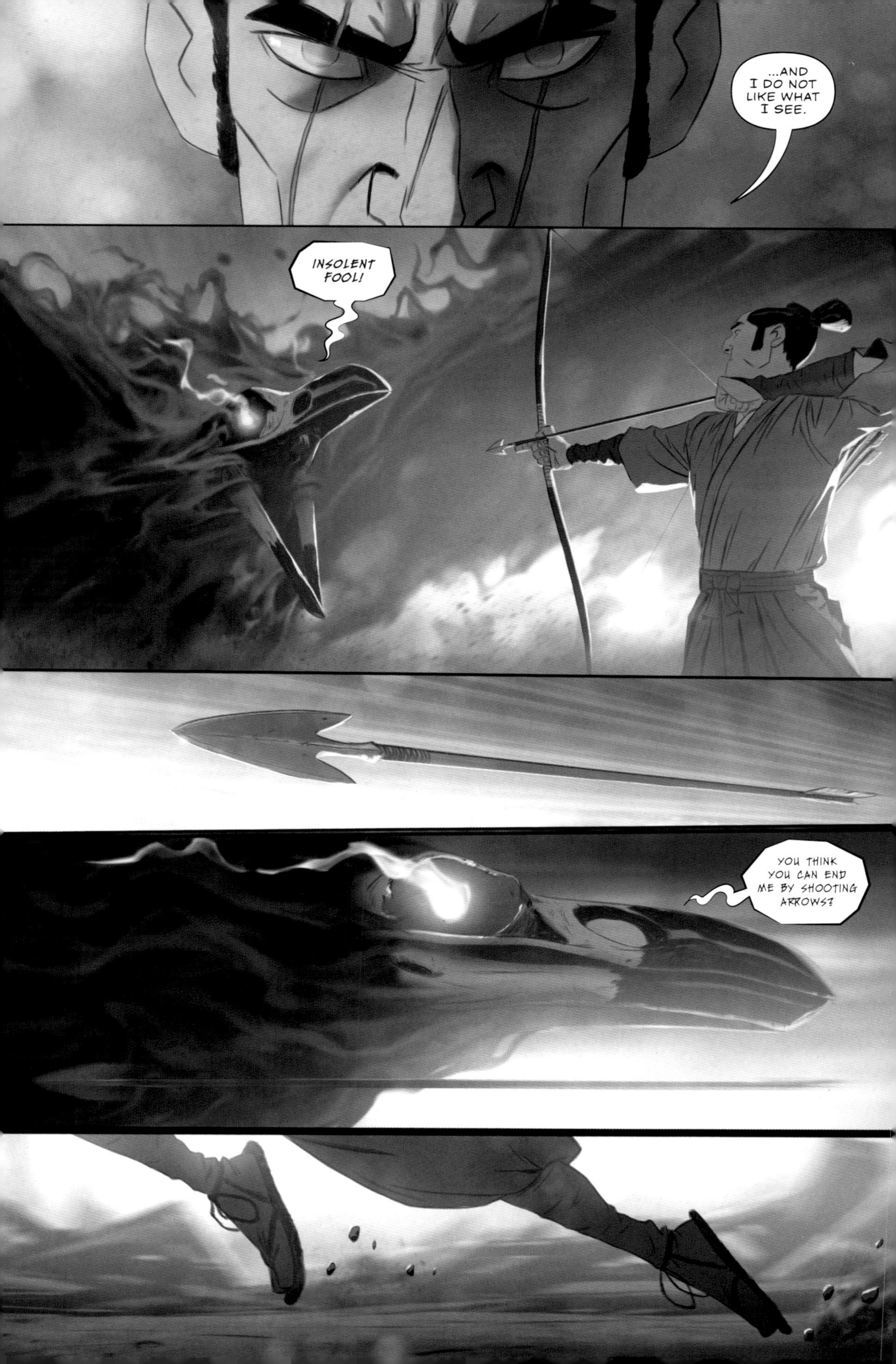
...AND I DO NOT LIKE WHAT I SEE.
INSOLENT FOOL!
YOU THINK YOU CAN END ME BY SHOOTING ARROWS?

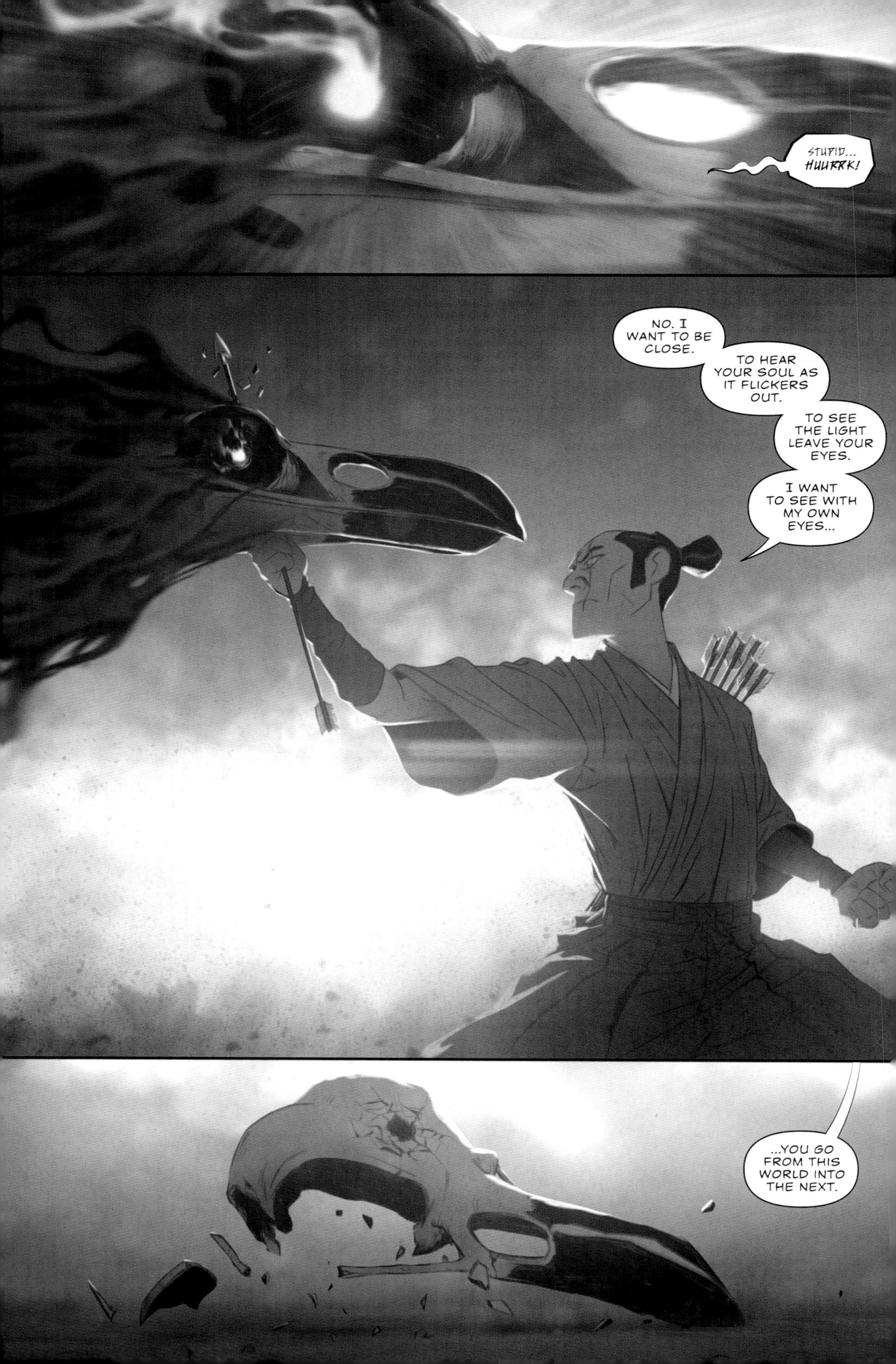
STUPID... HUURRK!
NO. I WANT TO BE CLOSE.
TO HEAR YOUR SOUL AS IT FLICKERS OUT.
TO SEE THE LIGHT LEAVE YOUR EYES.
I WANT TO SEE WITH MY OWN EYES...
...YOU GO FROM THIS WORLD INTO THE NEXT.

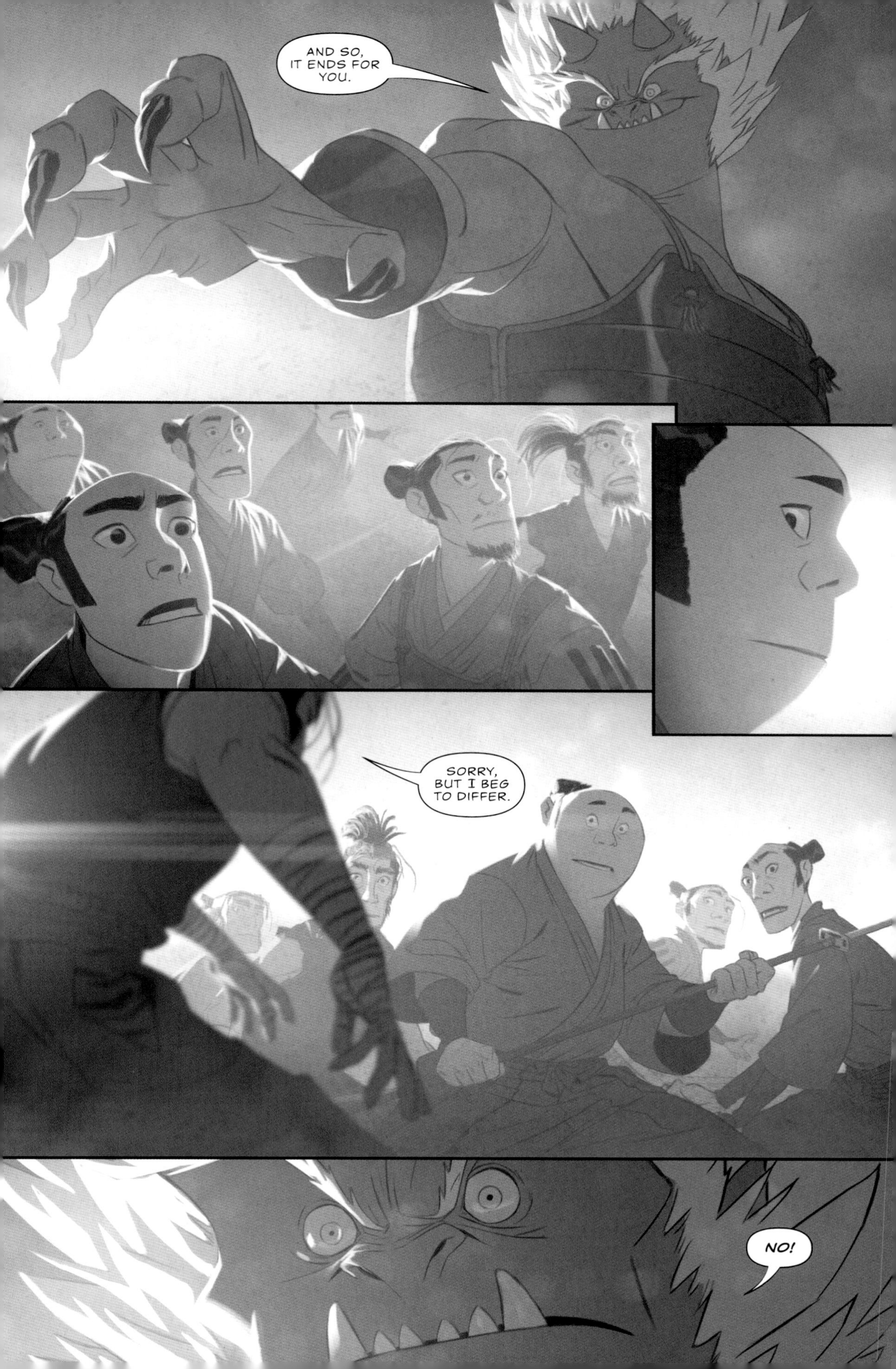
AND SO, IT ENDS FOR YOU.
SORRY, BUT I BEG TO DIFFER.
NO!

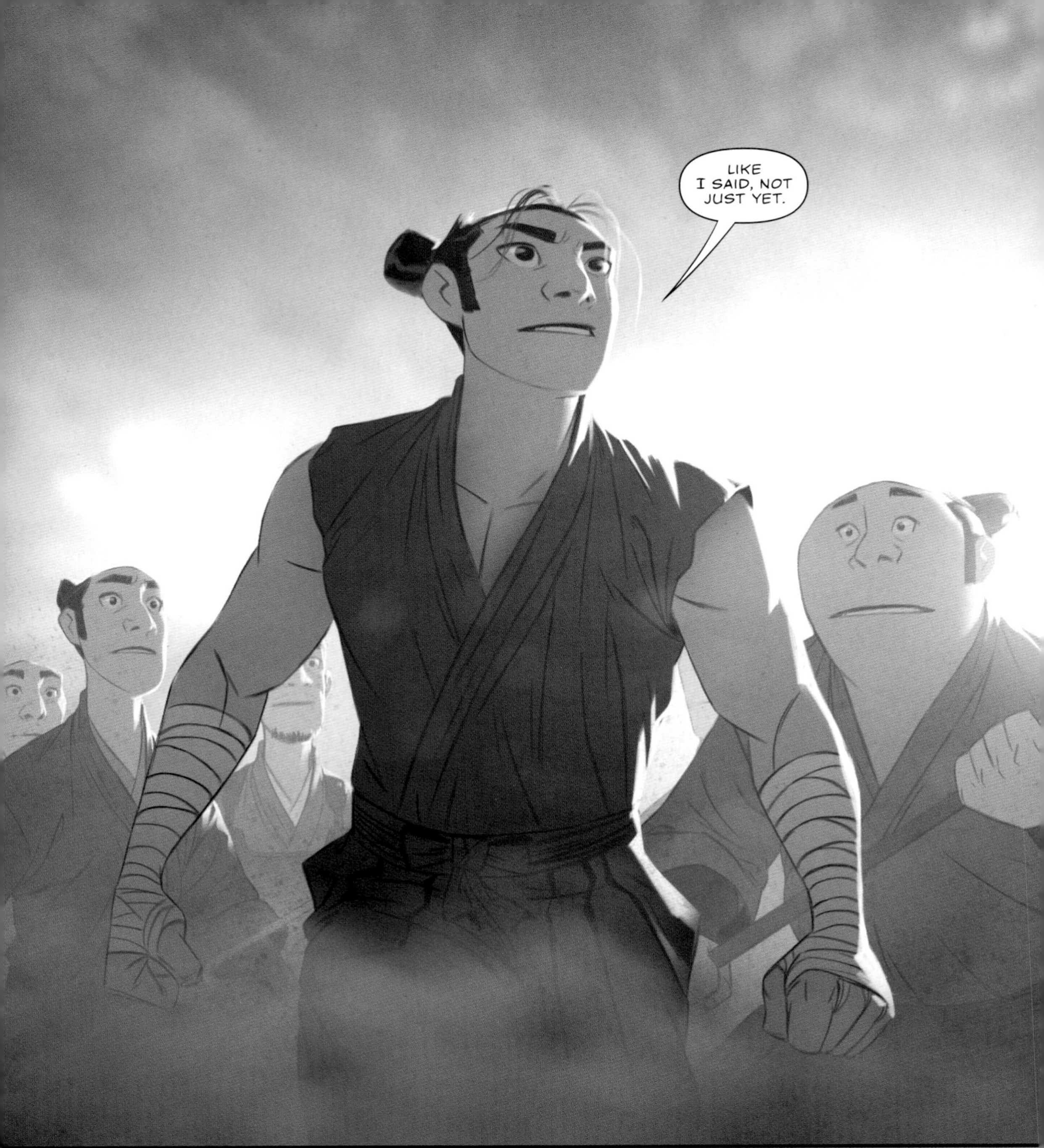
LIKE I SAID, NOT JUST YET.

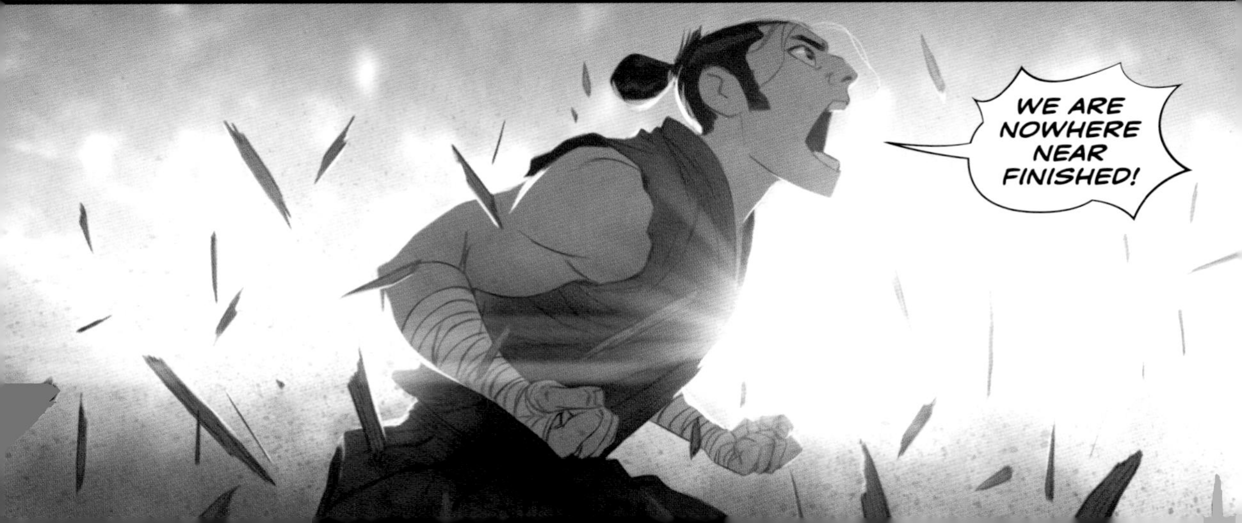
WE ARE NOWHERE NEAR FINISHED!

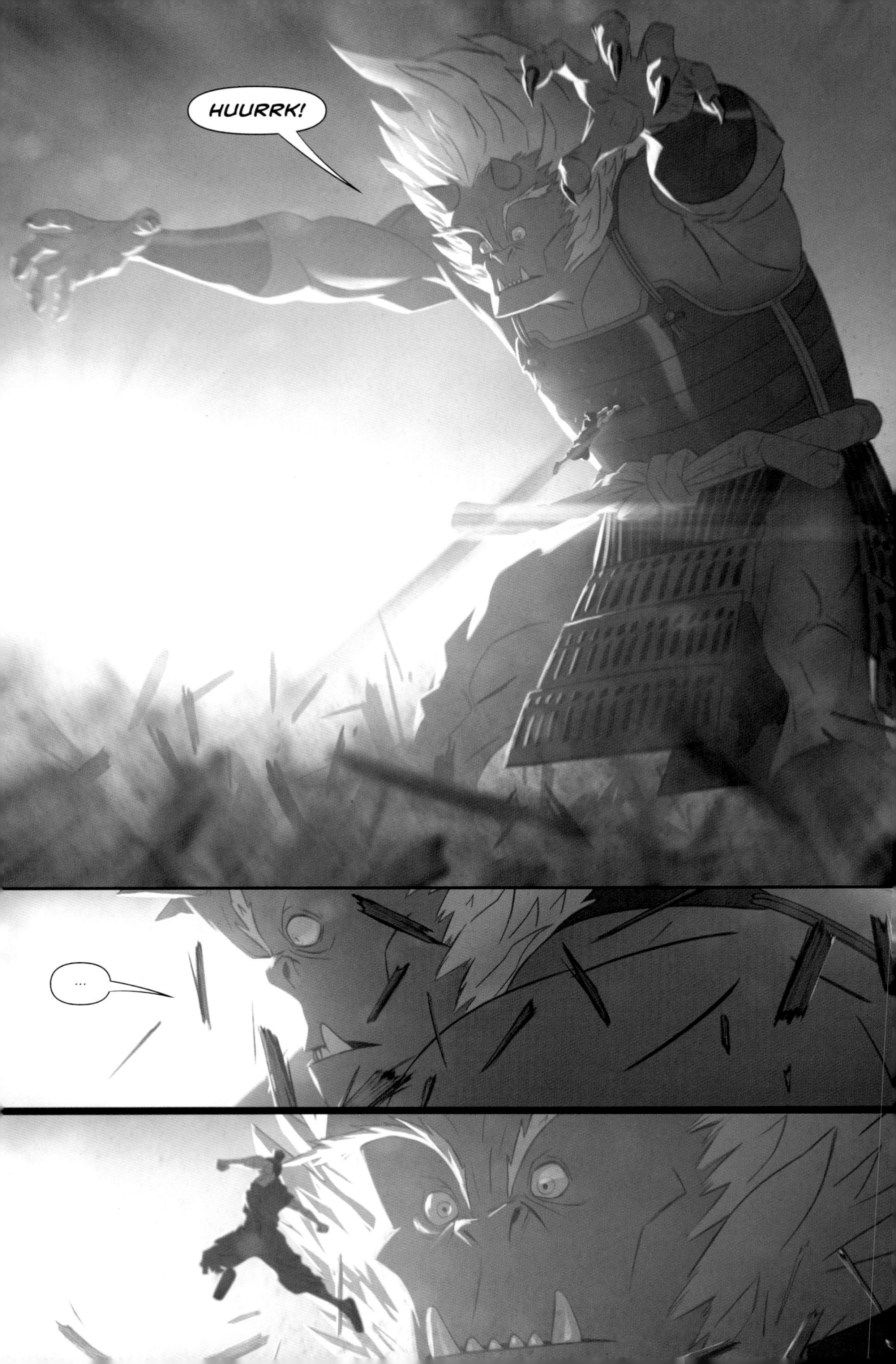
HUURRK!
...

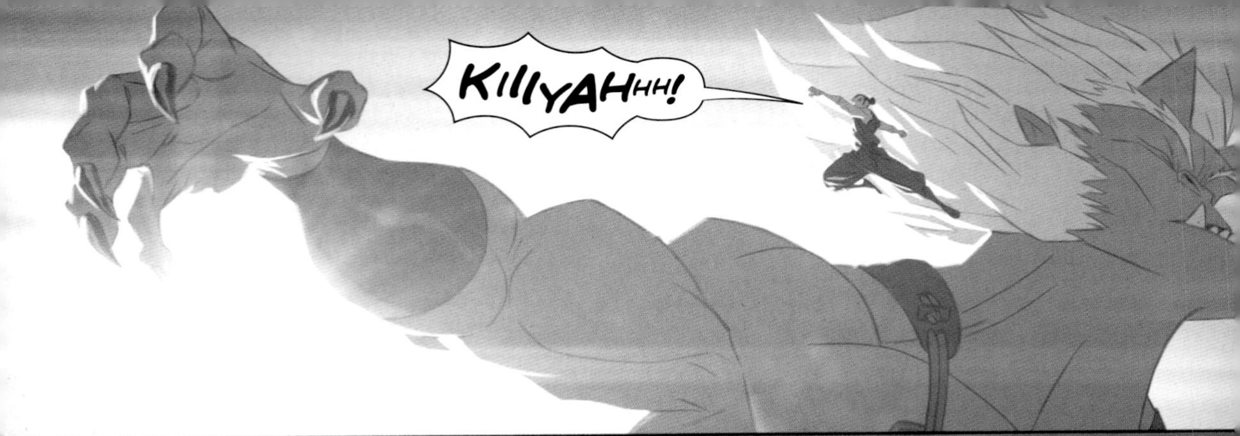
KIIIYAHHH!

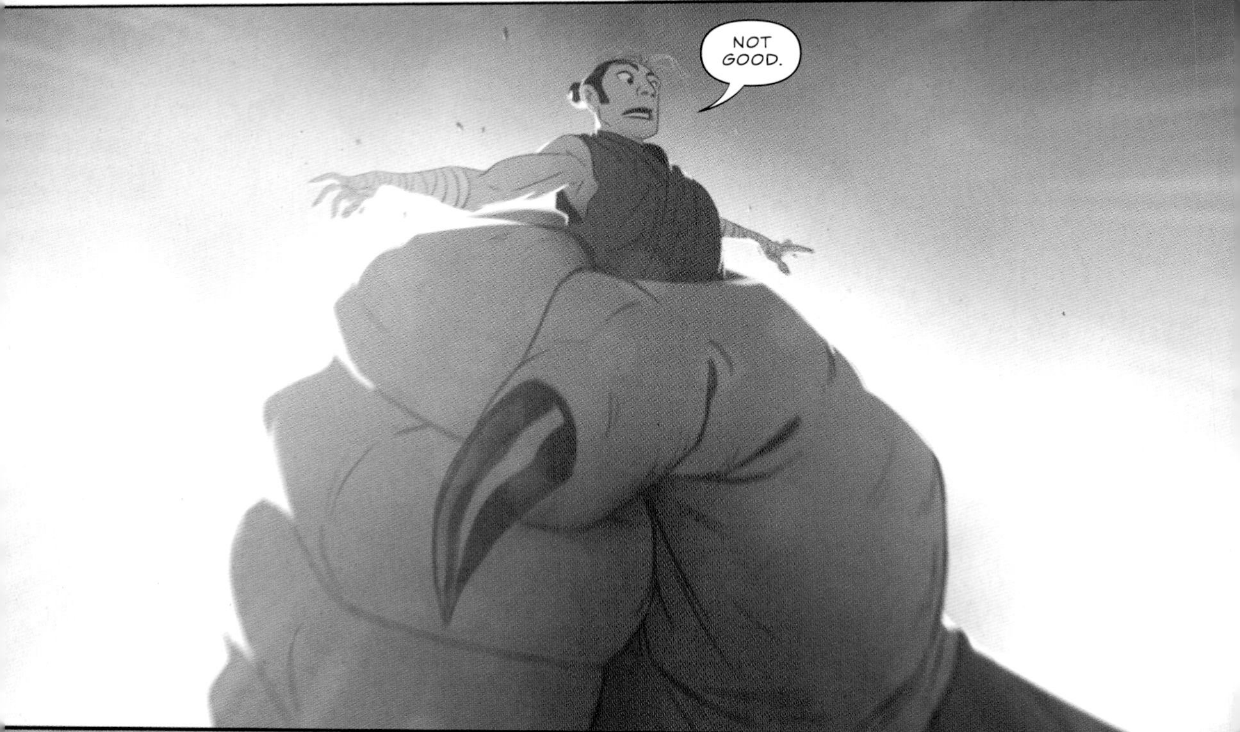
NOT GOOD.

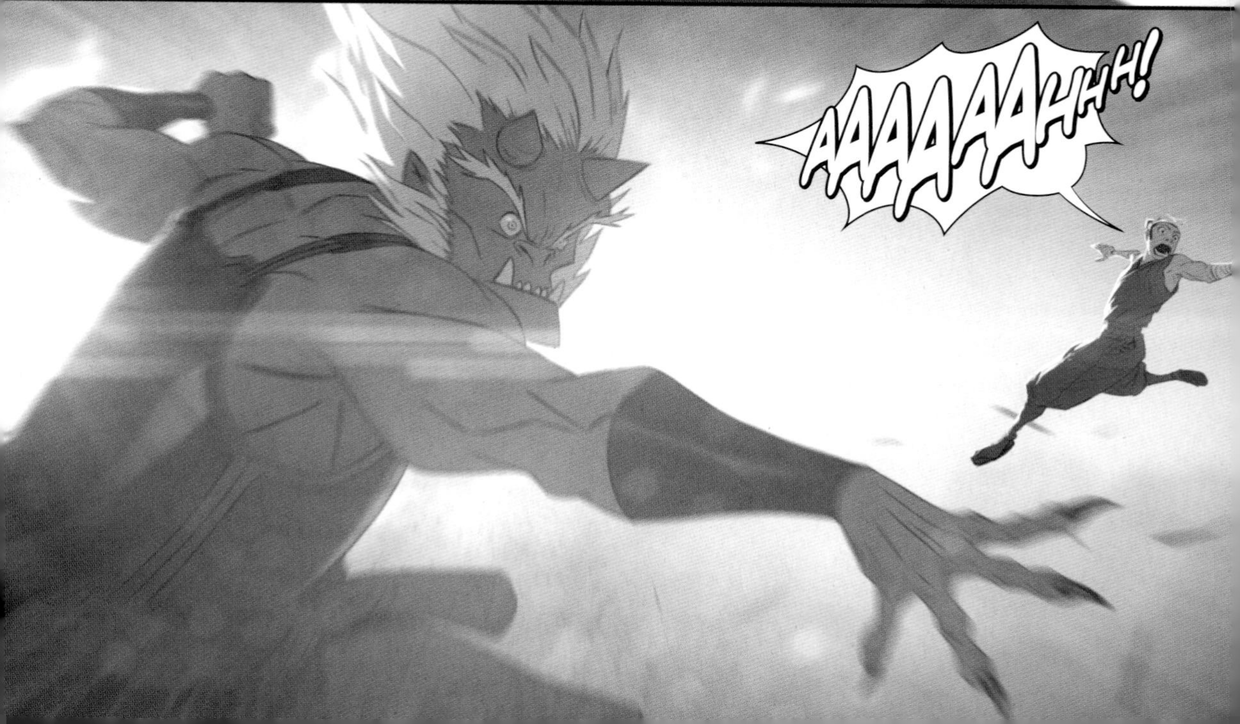
AAAAAAHHH!

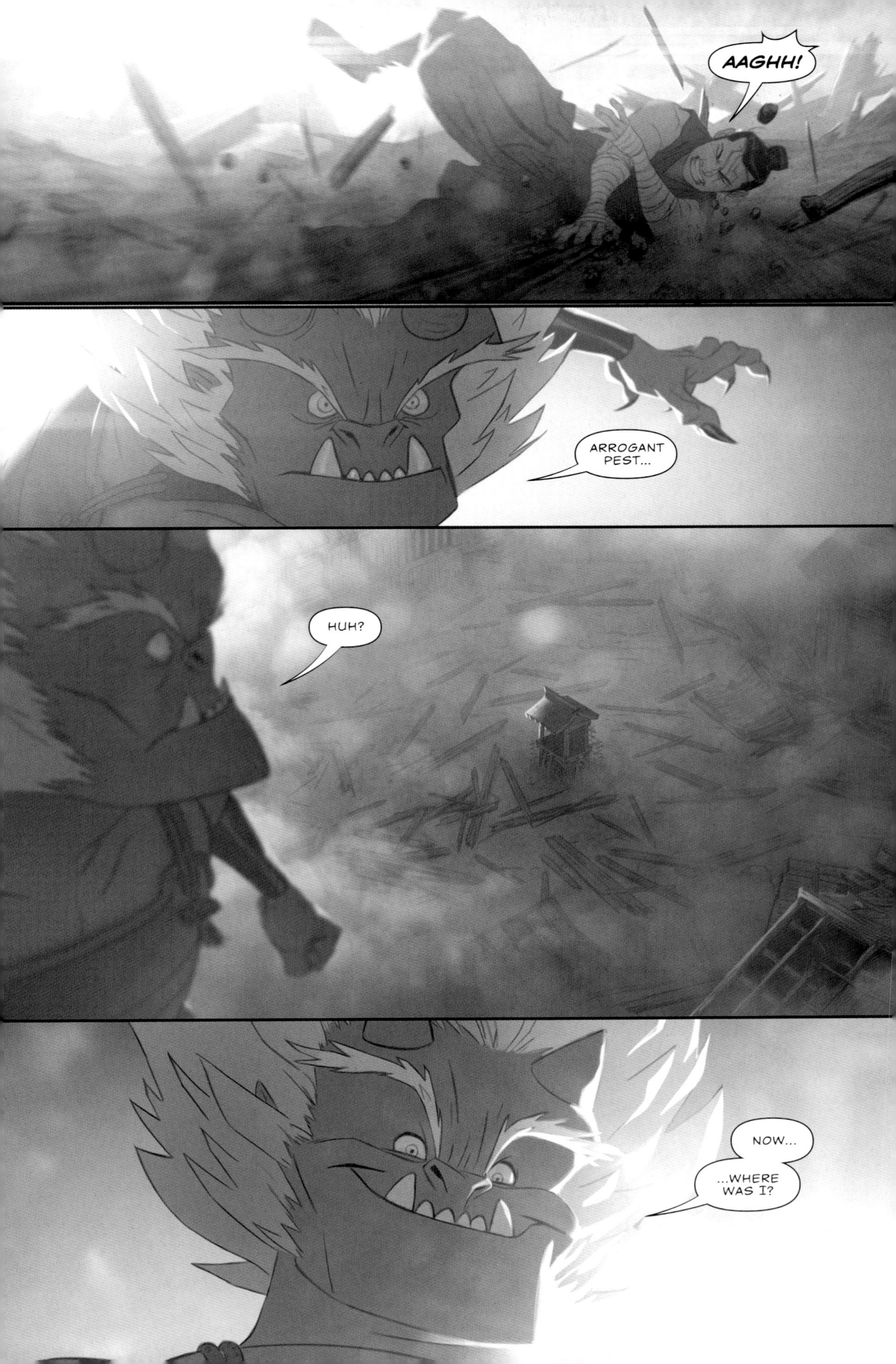
AAGHH!
ARROGANT PEST...
HUH?
NOW...
...WHERE WAS I?

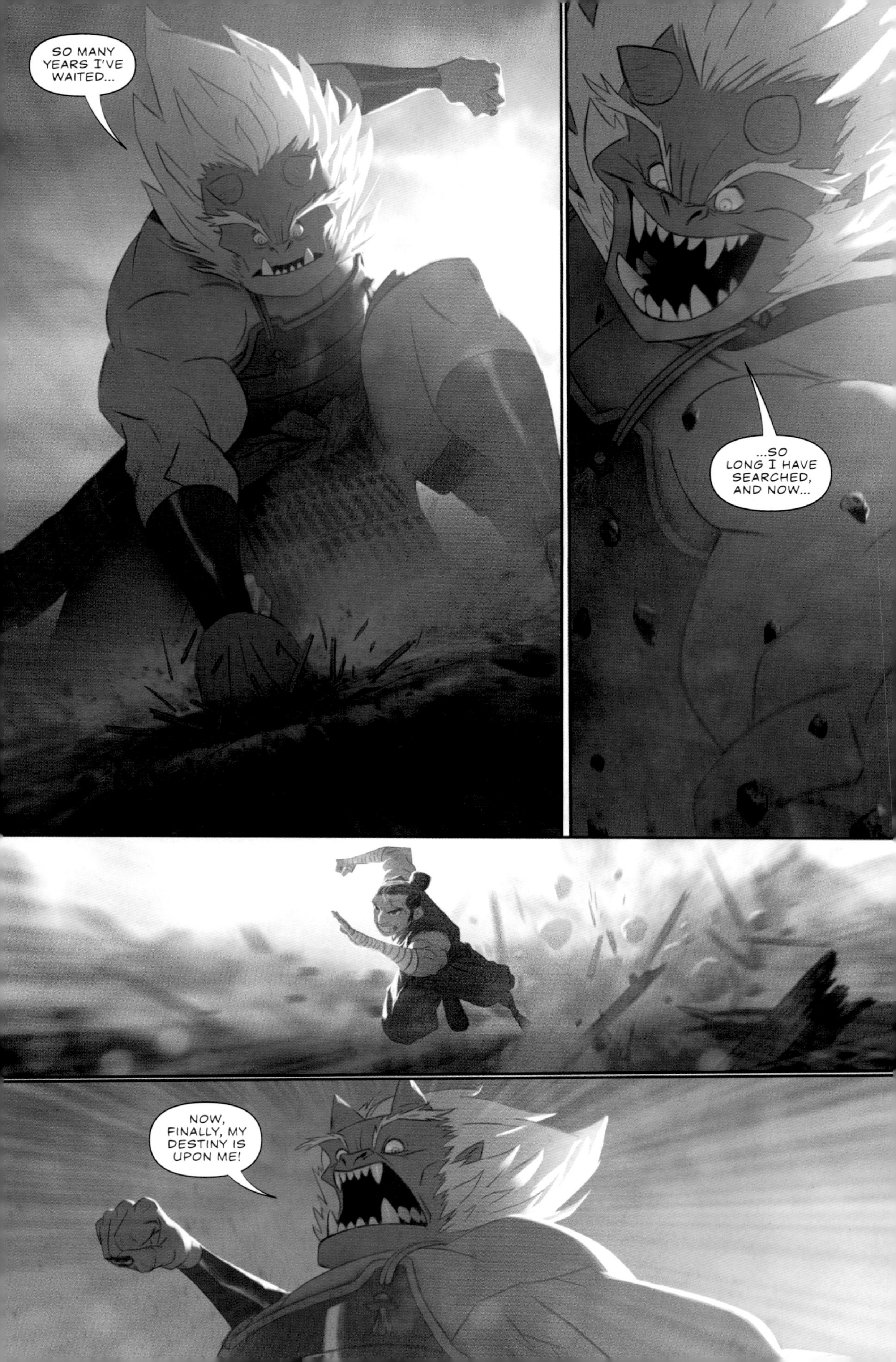
SO MANY YEARS I'VE WAITED...
...SO LONG I HAVE SEARCHED, AND NOW...
NOW, FINALLY, MY DESTINY IS UPON ME!

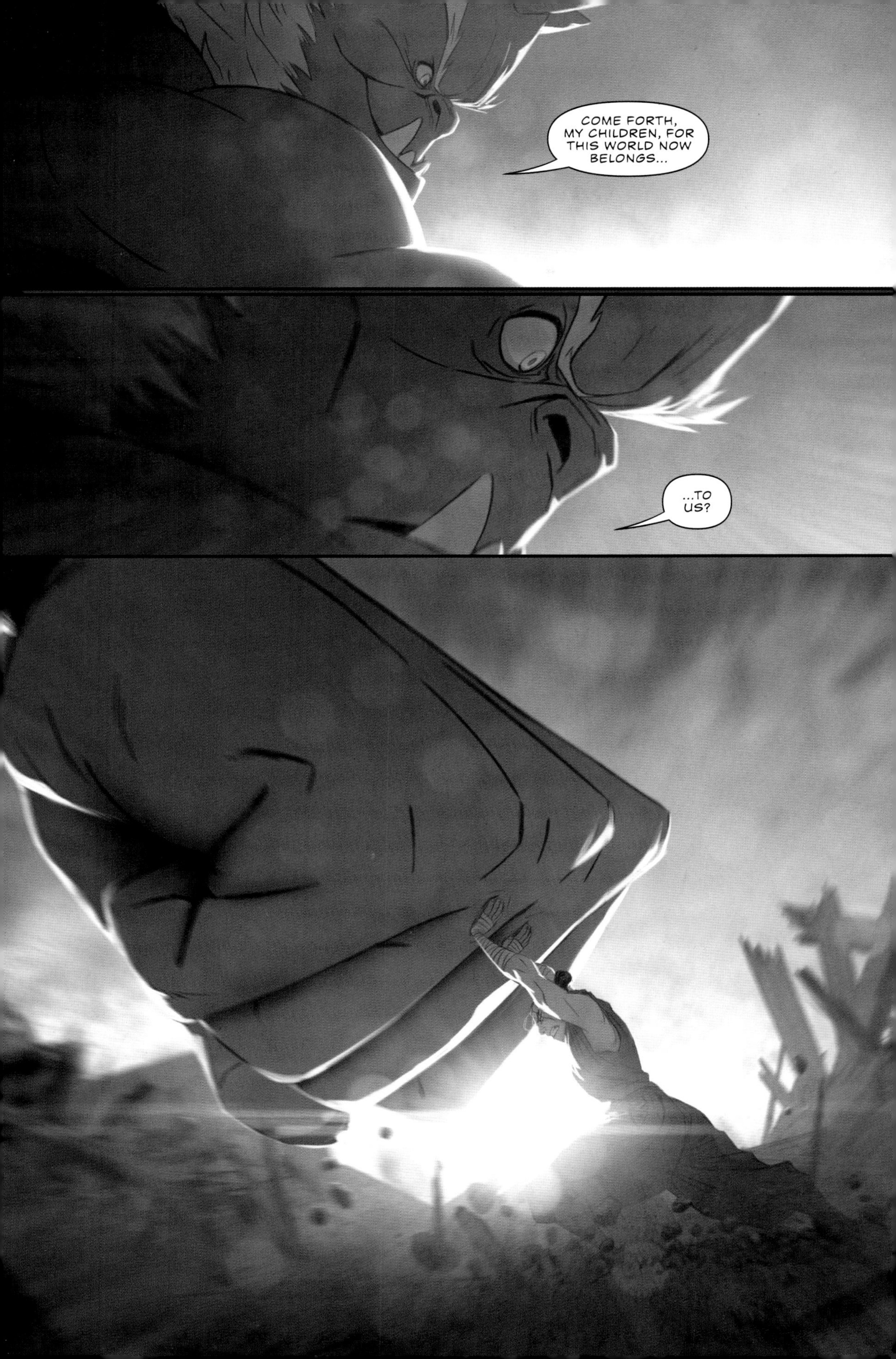
COME FORTH, MY CHILDREN, FOR THIS WORLD NOW BELONGS...
...TO US?

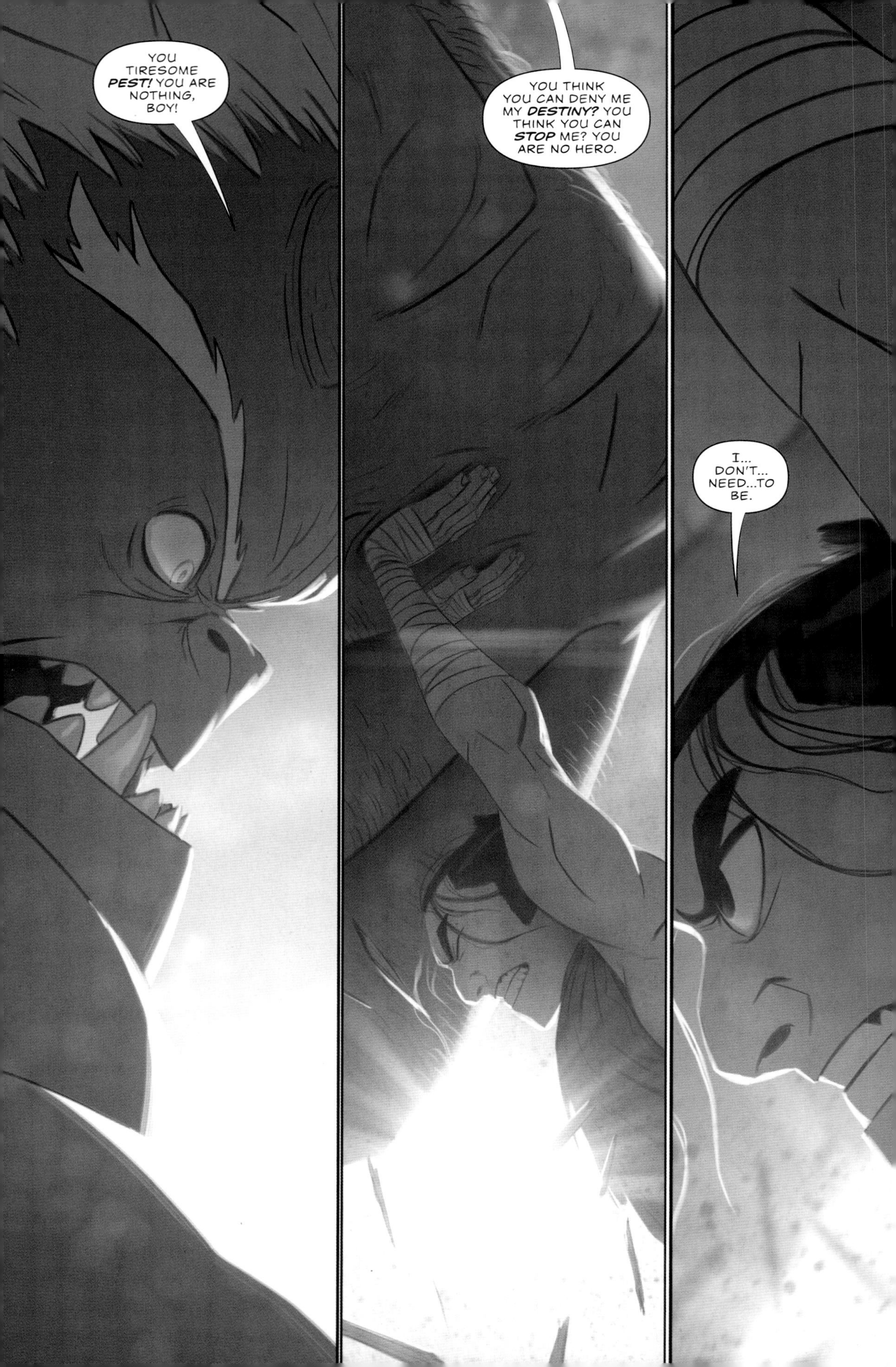

YOU TIRESOME **PEST!** YOU ARE NOTHING, BOY!
YOU THINK YOU CAN DENY ME MY **DESTINY?** YOU THINK YOU CAN **STOP** ME? YOU ARE NO HERO.
I... DON'T... NEED...TO BE.

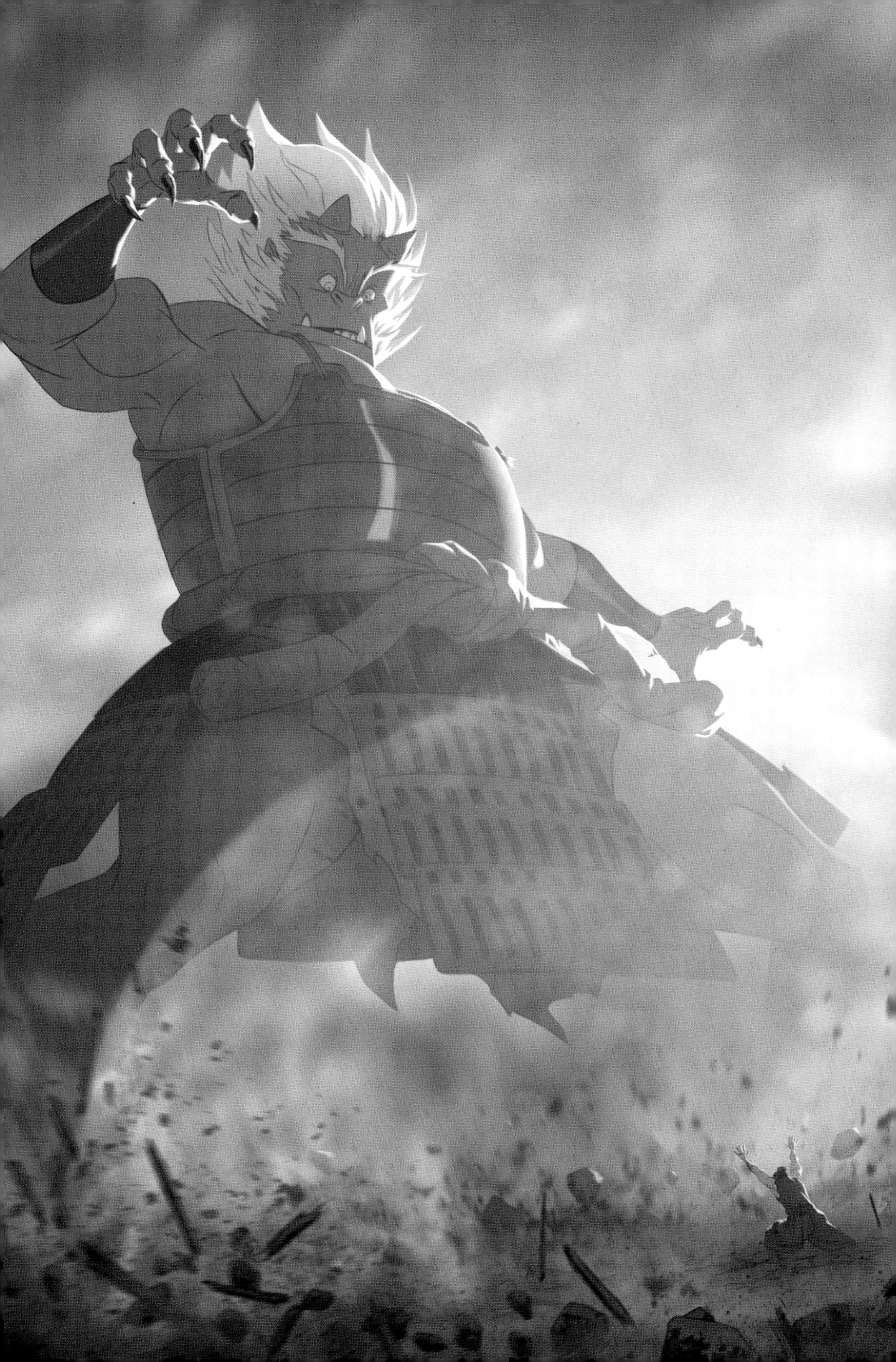

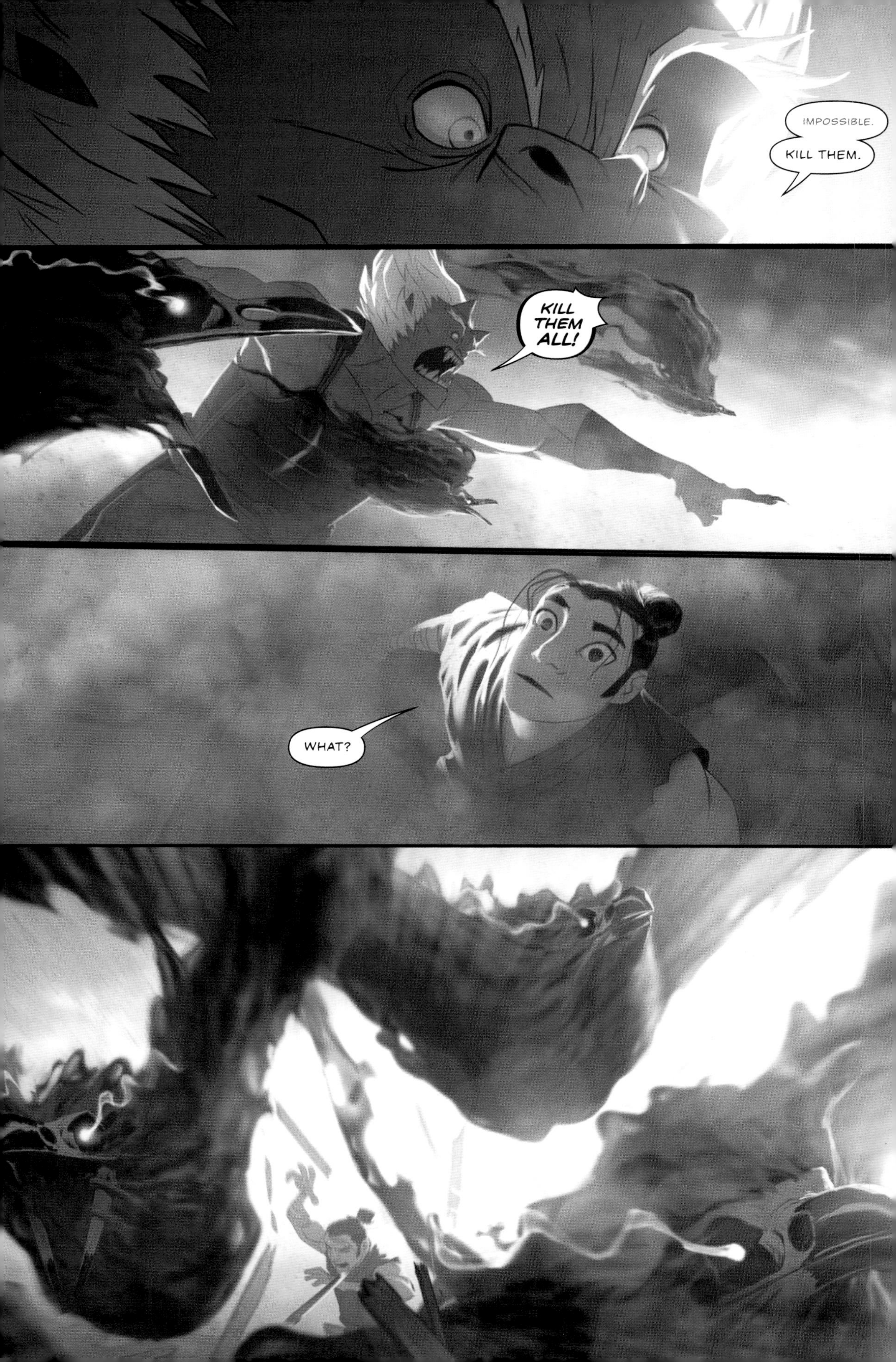
IMPOSSIBLE.
KILL THEM.
KILL THEM ALL!
WHAT?

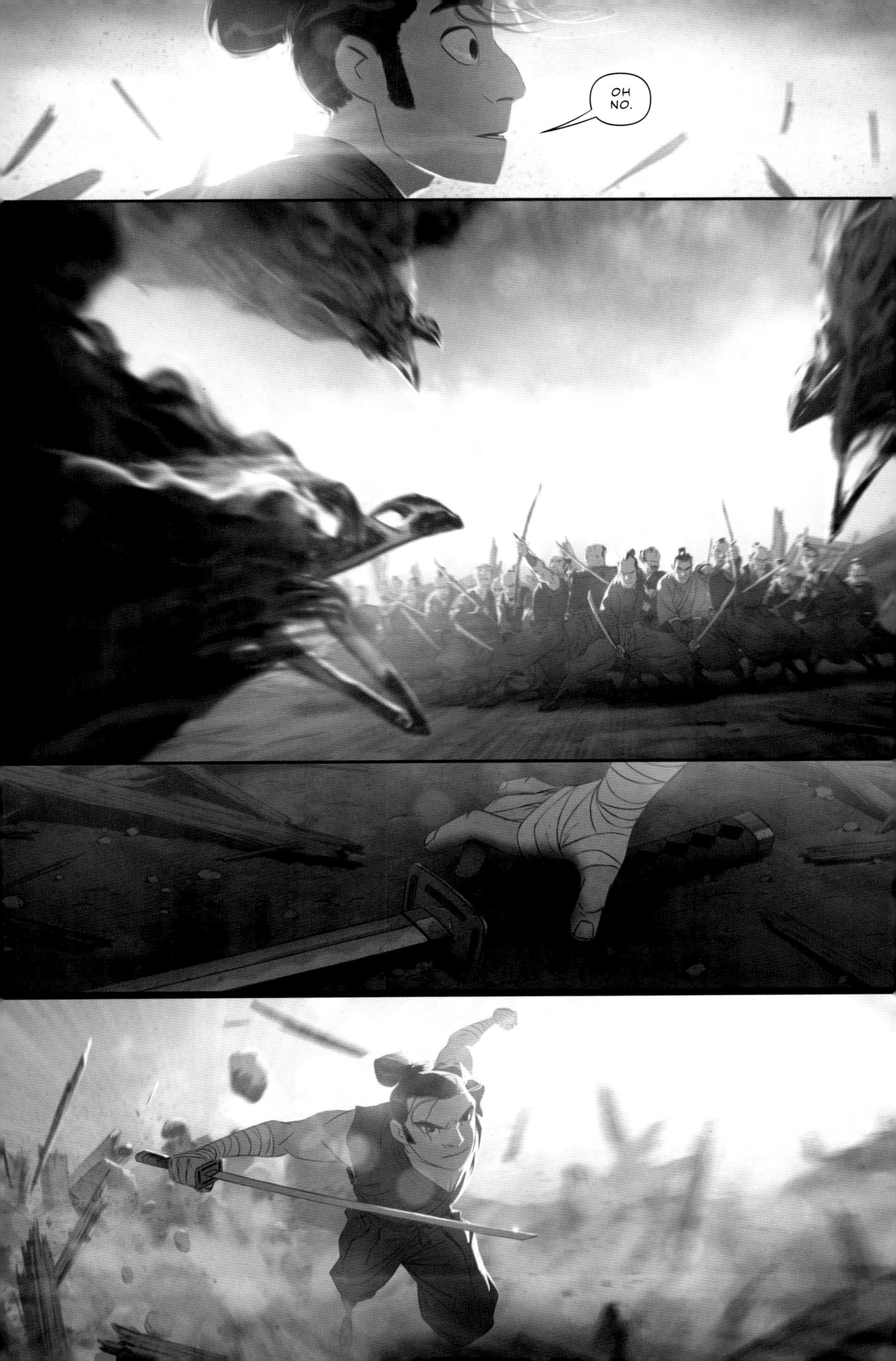
OH NO.

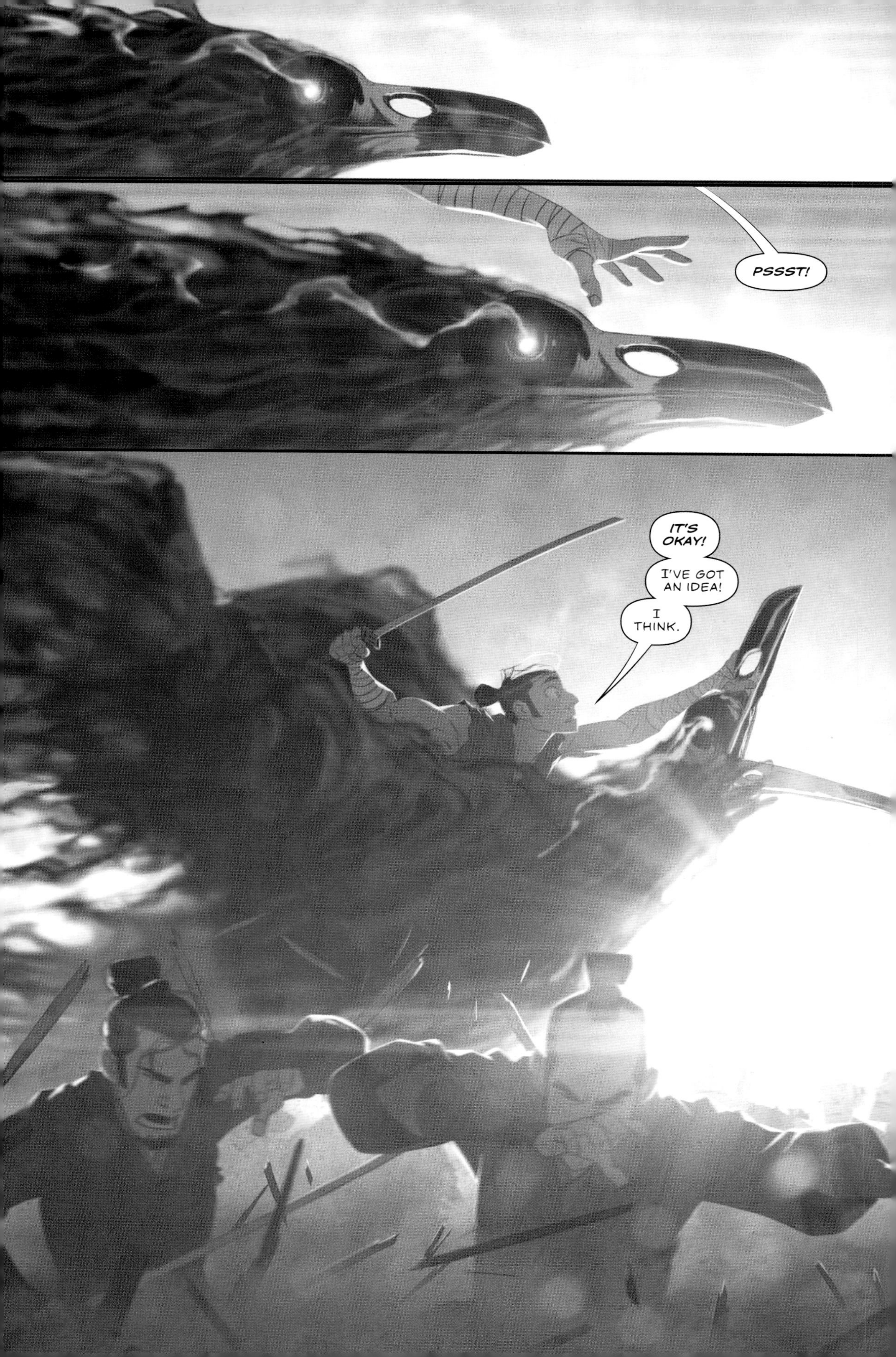
PSSST!
IT'S OKAY!
I'VE GOT AN IDEA!
I THINK.

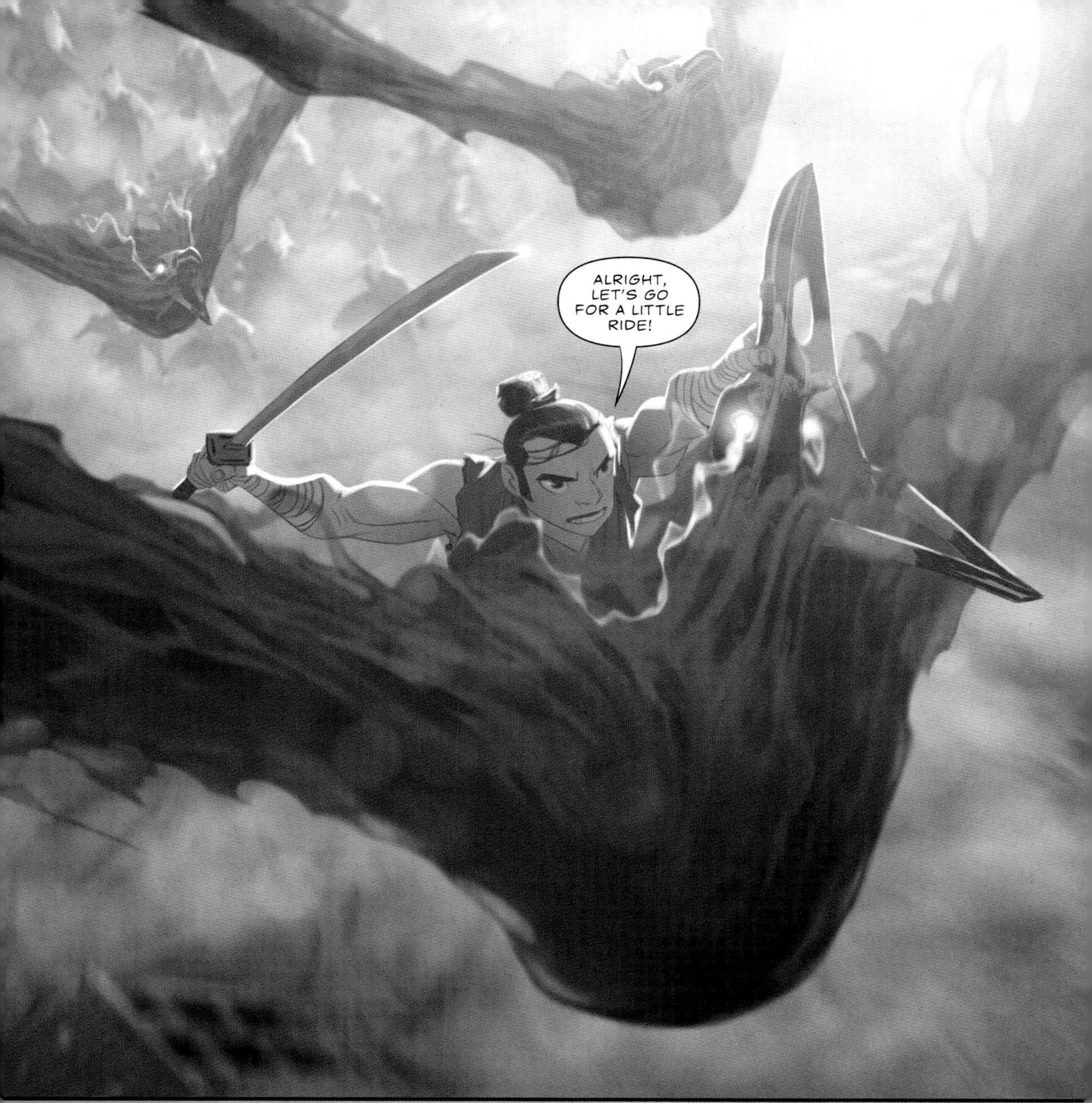
ALRIGHT, LET'S GO FOR A LITTLE RIDE!

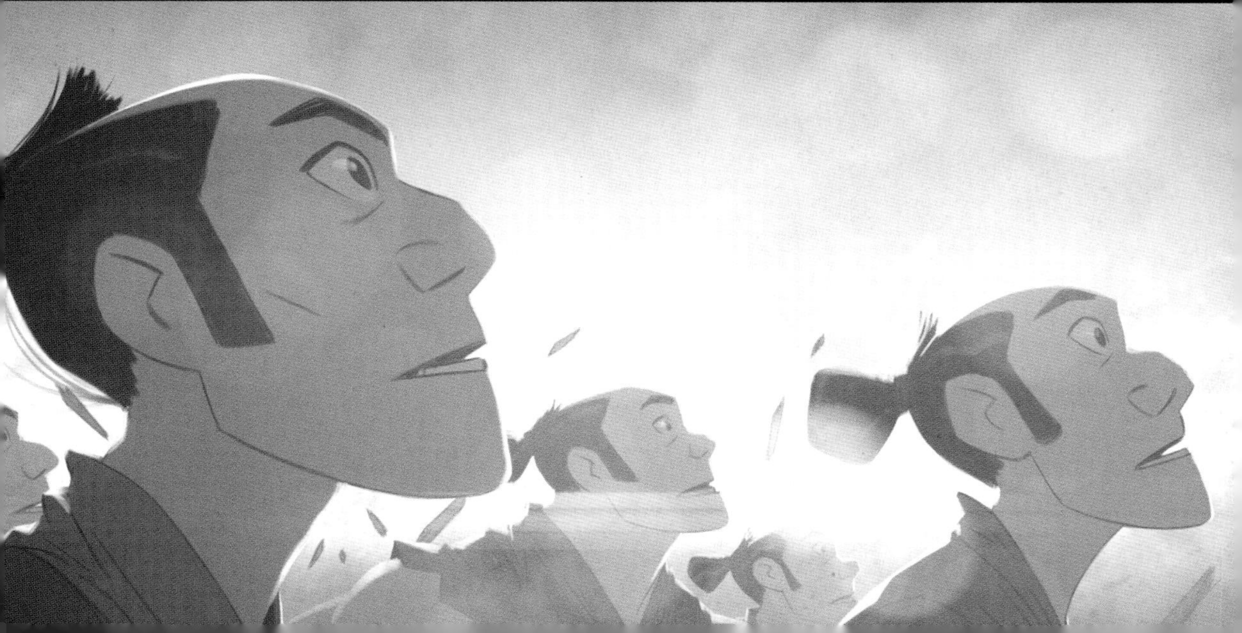

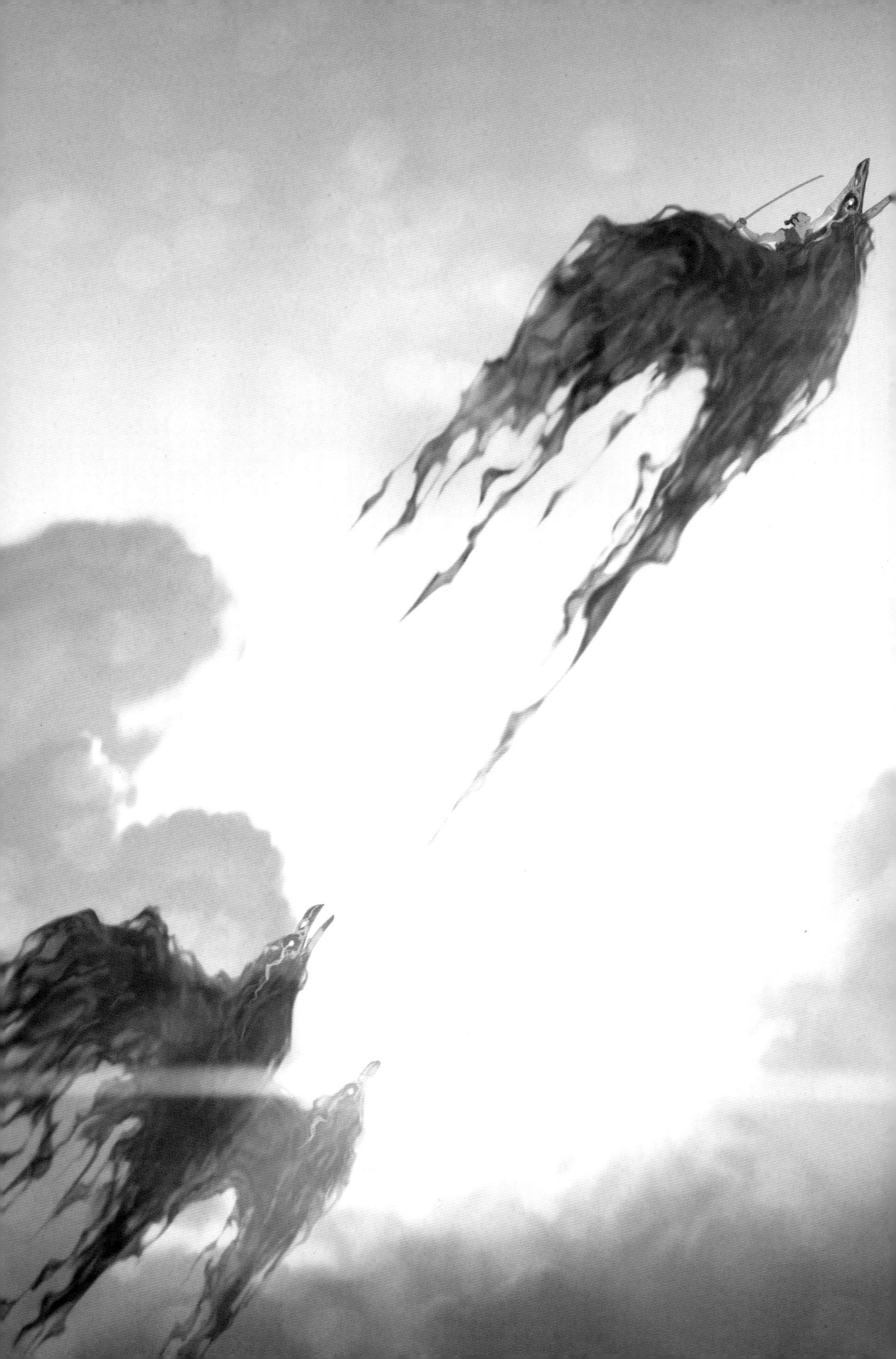

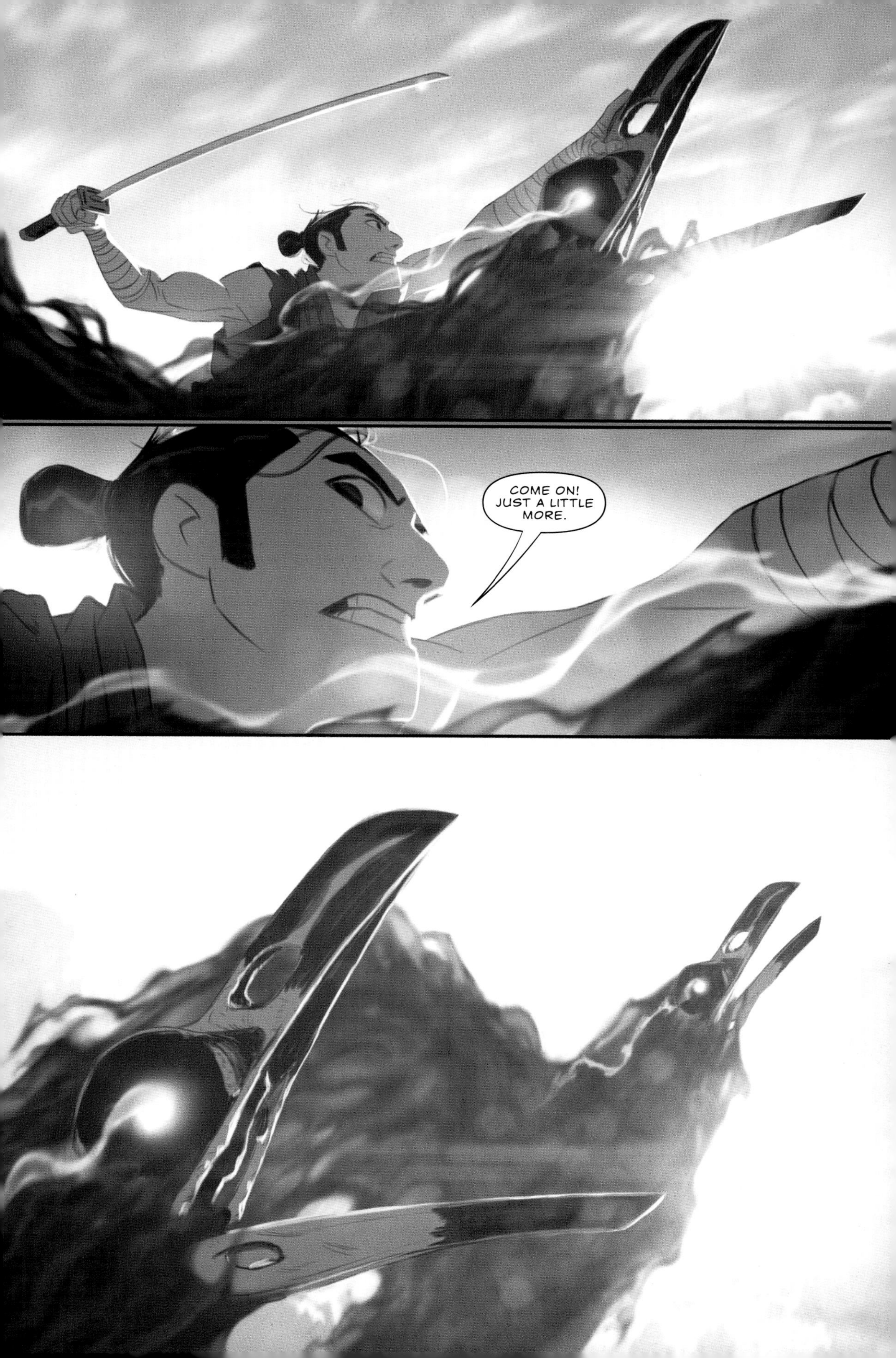
COME ON! JUST A LITTLE MORE.

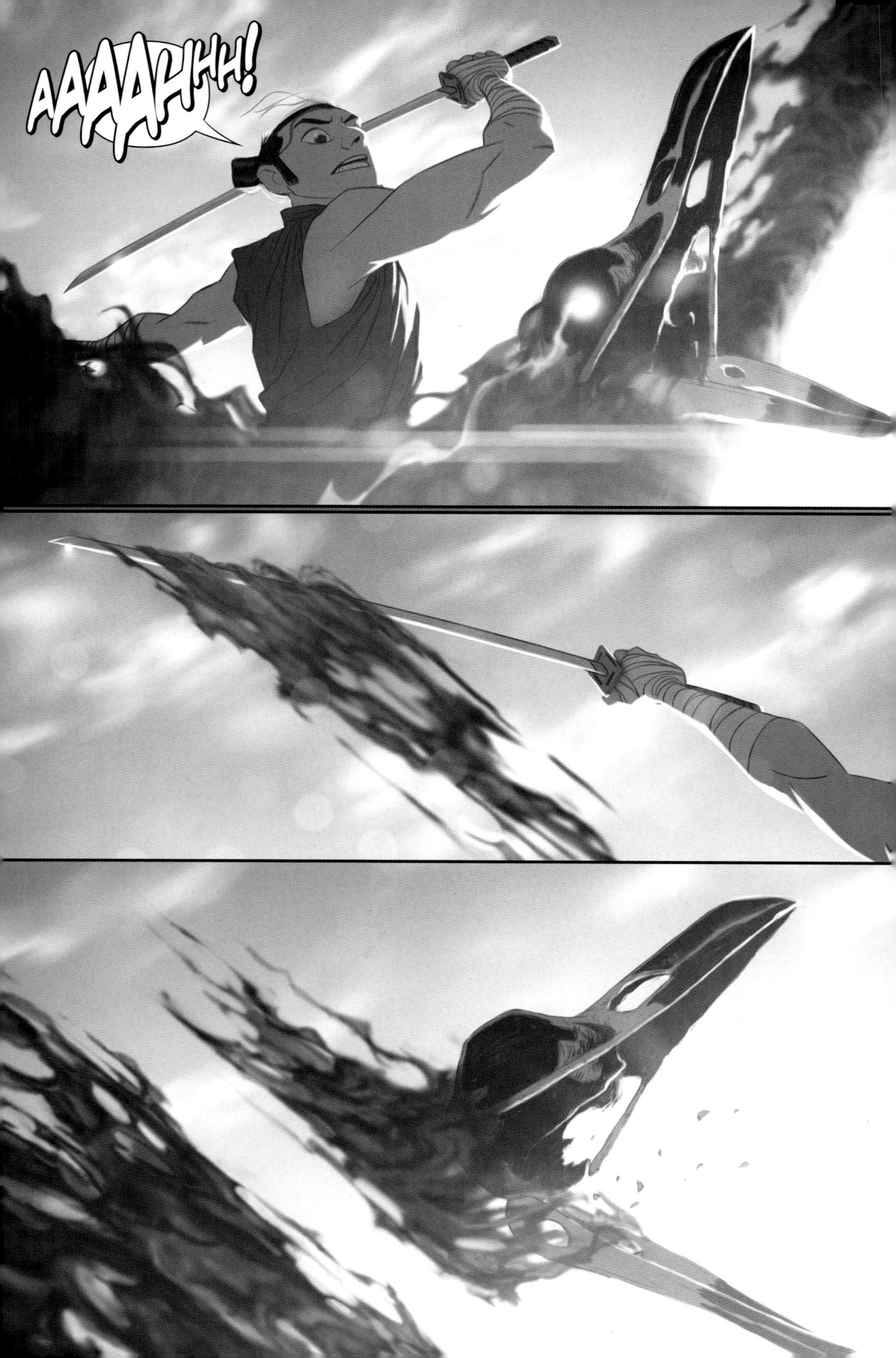
AAAAHHH!

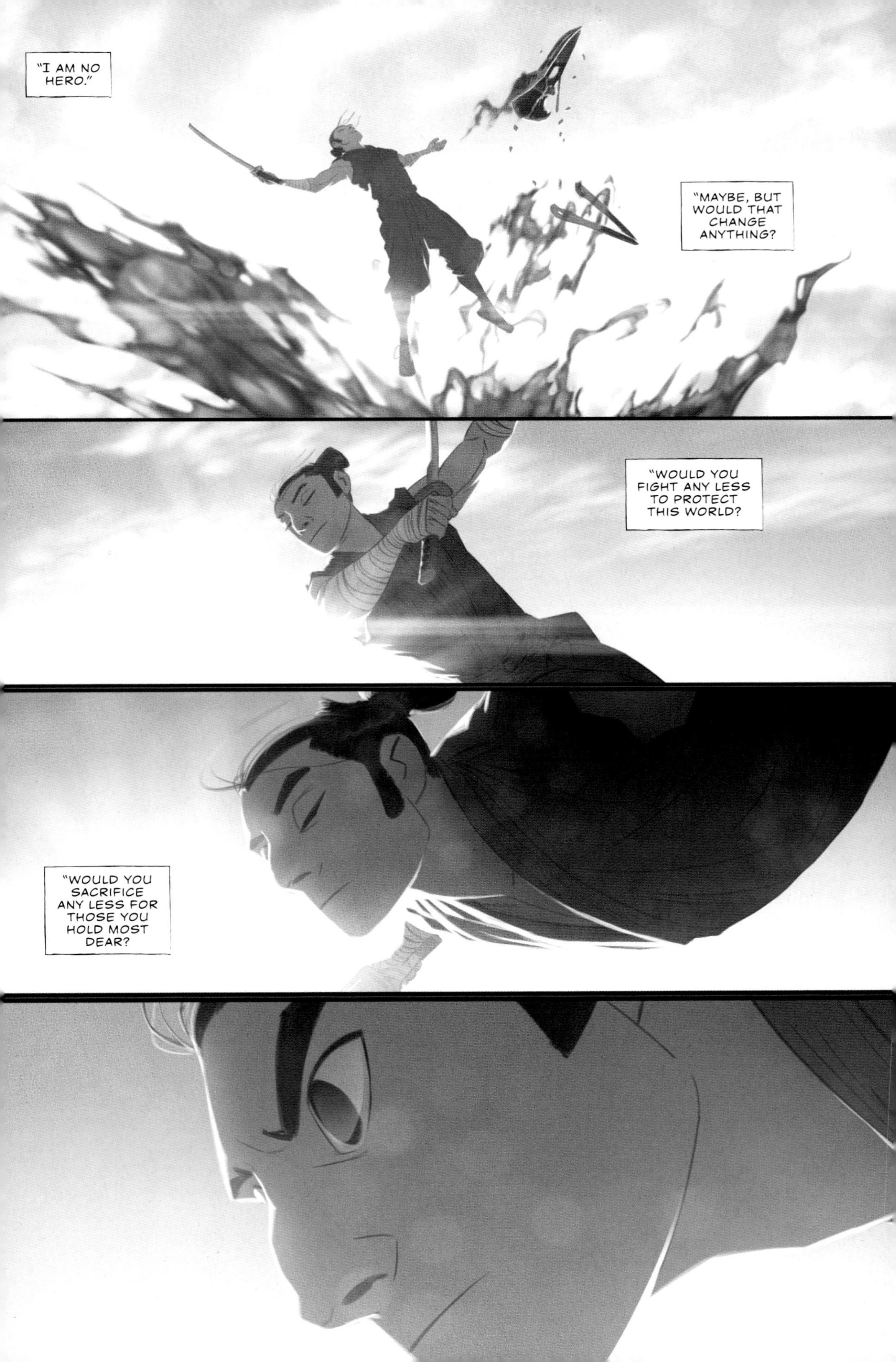
"I AM NO HERO."
"MAYBE, BUT WOULD THAT CHANGE ANYTHING?
"WOULD YOU FIGHT ANY LESS TO PROTECT THIS WORLD?
"WOULD YOU SACRIFICE ANY LESS FOR THOSE YOU HOLD MOST DEAR?

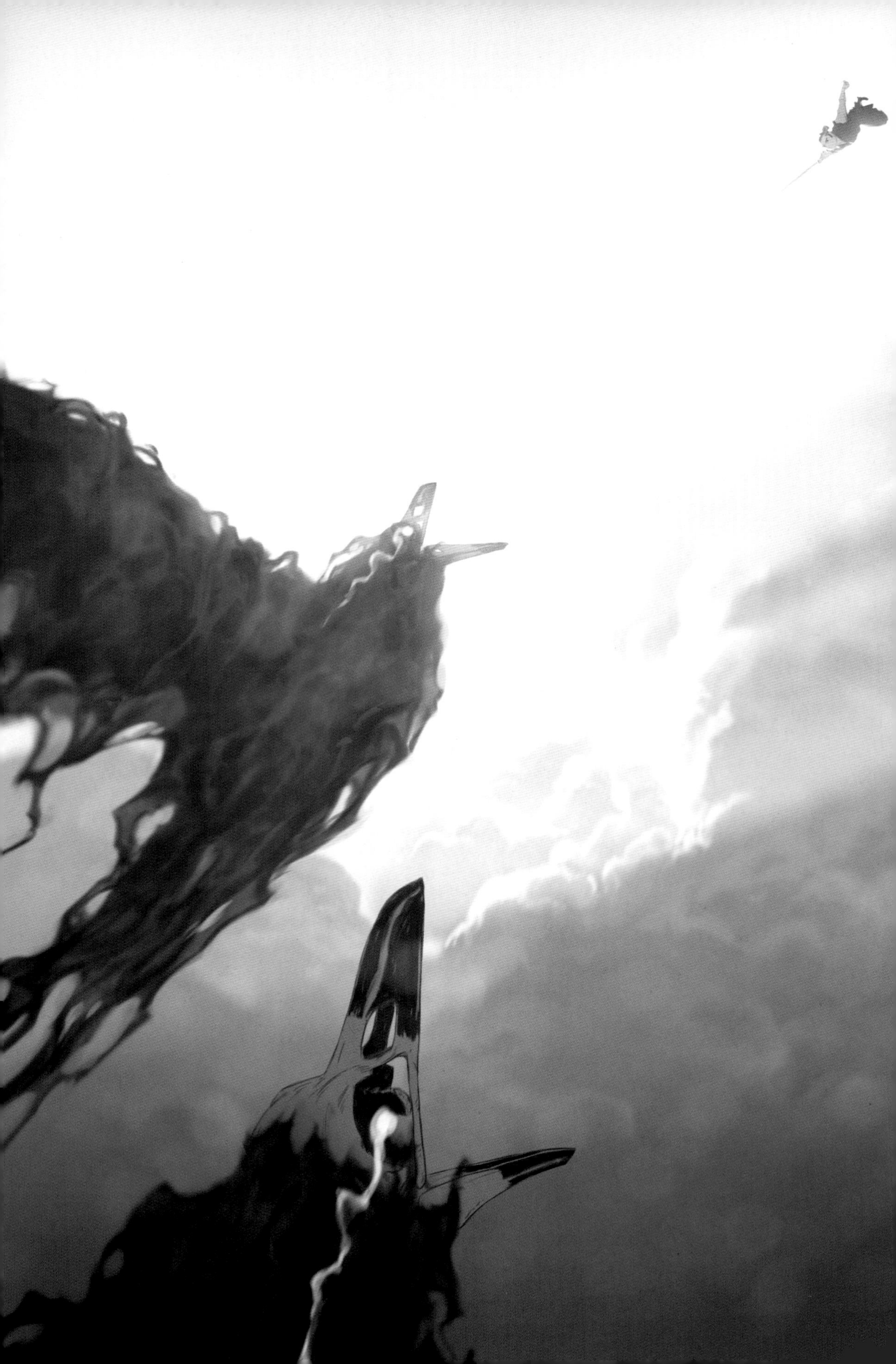

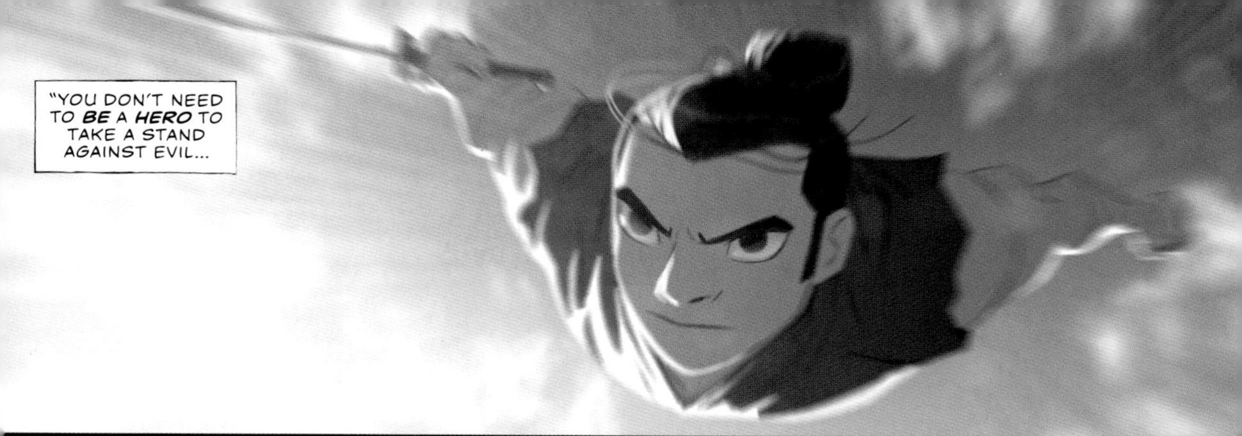
"YOU DON'T NEED TO **BE** A **HERO** TO TAKE A STAND AGAINST EVIL...

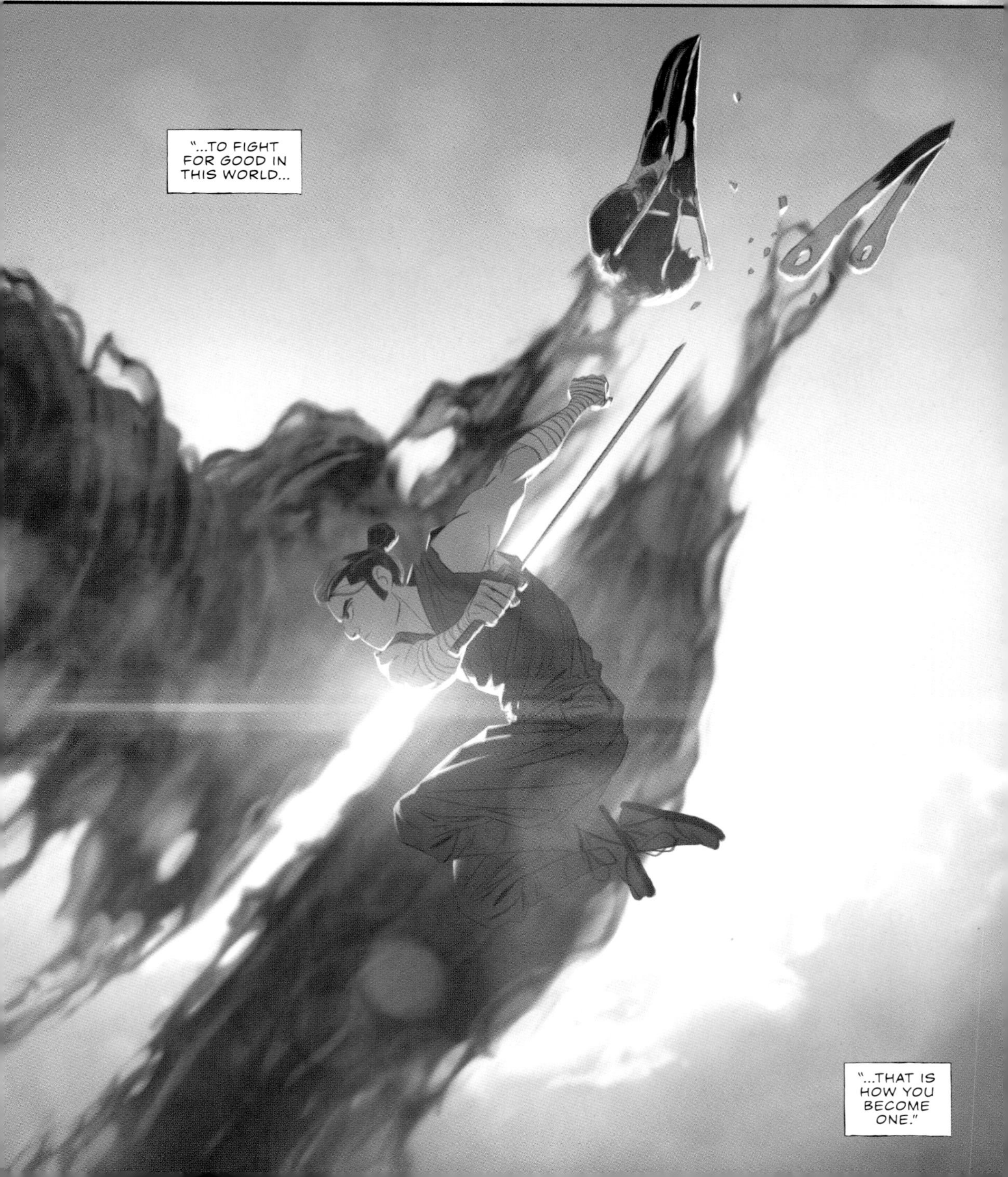
"...TO FIGHT FOR GOOD IN THIS WORLD...
"...THAT IS HOW YOU BECOME ONE."

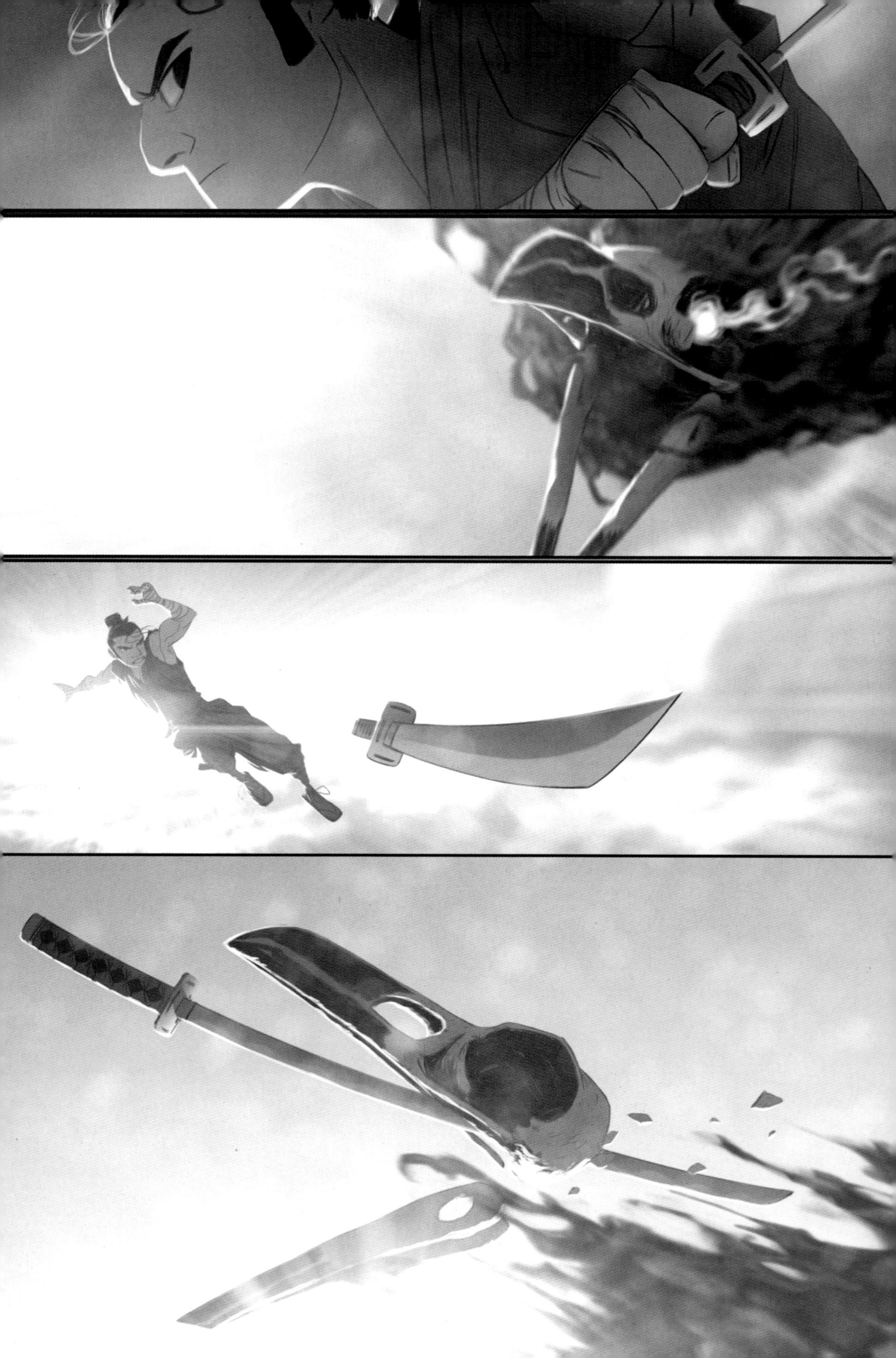

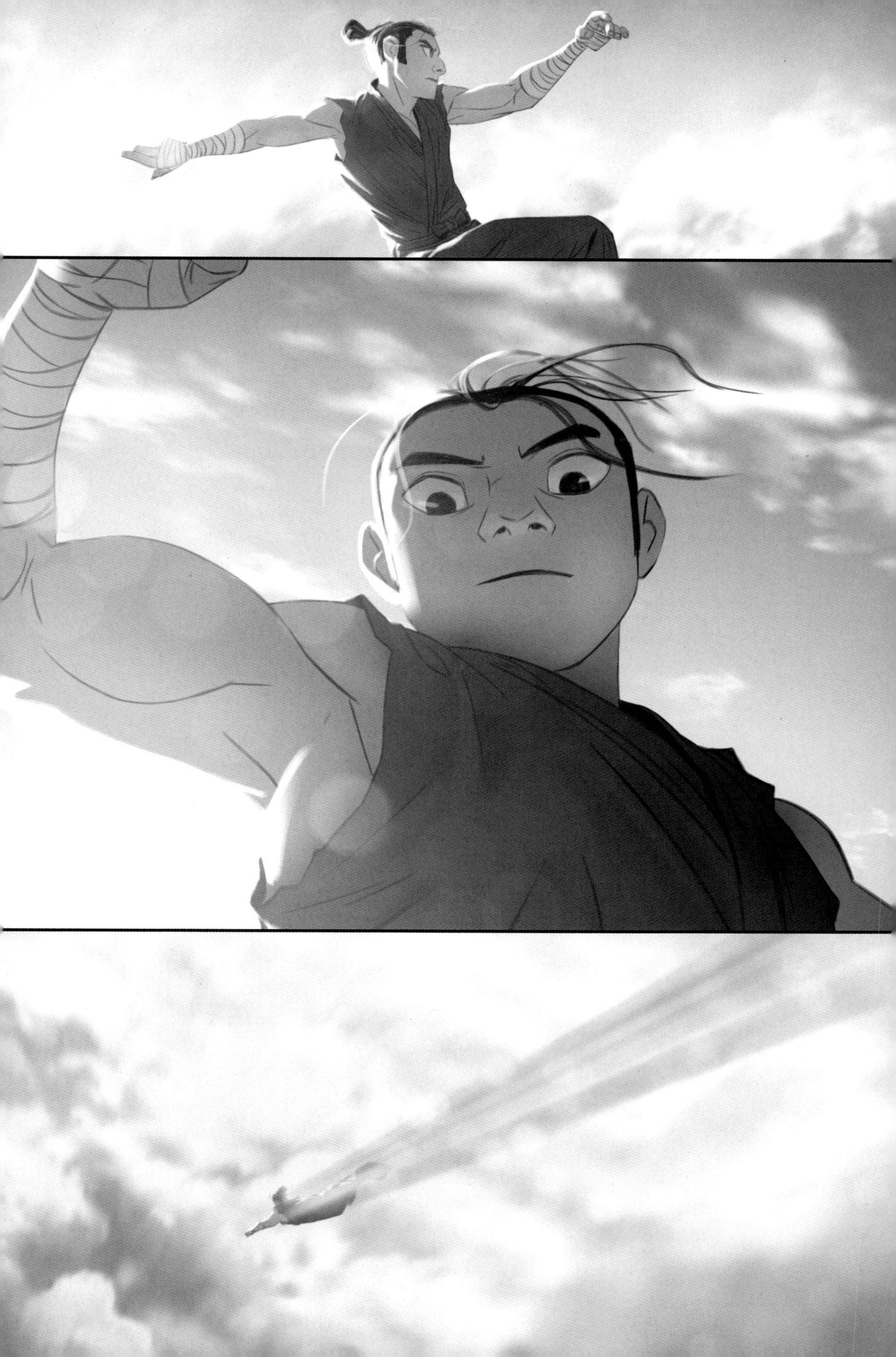

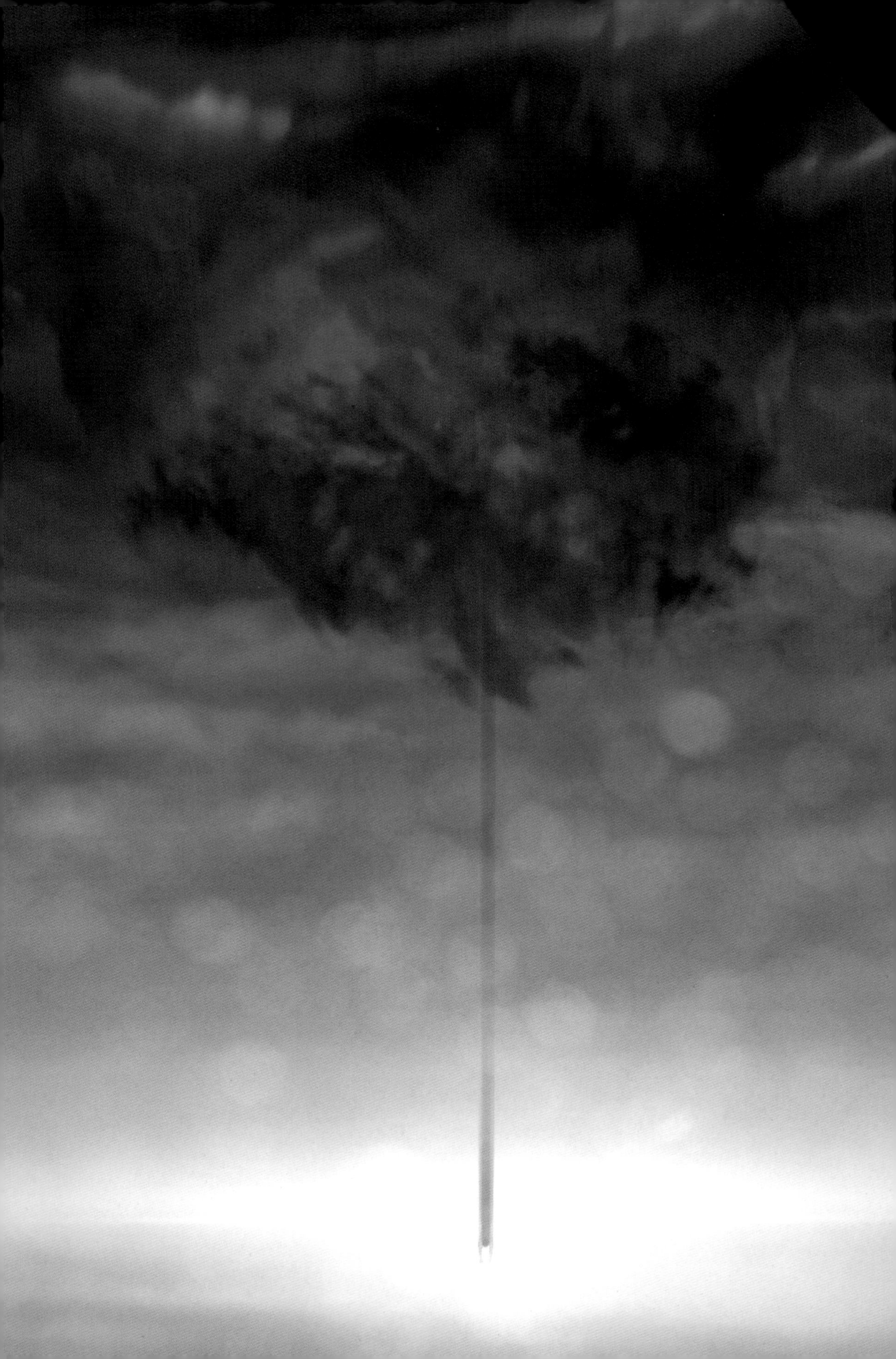

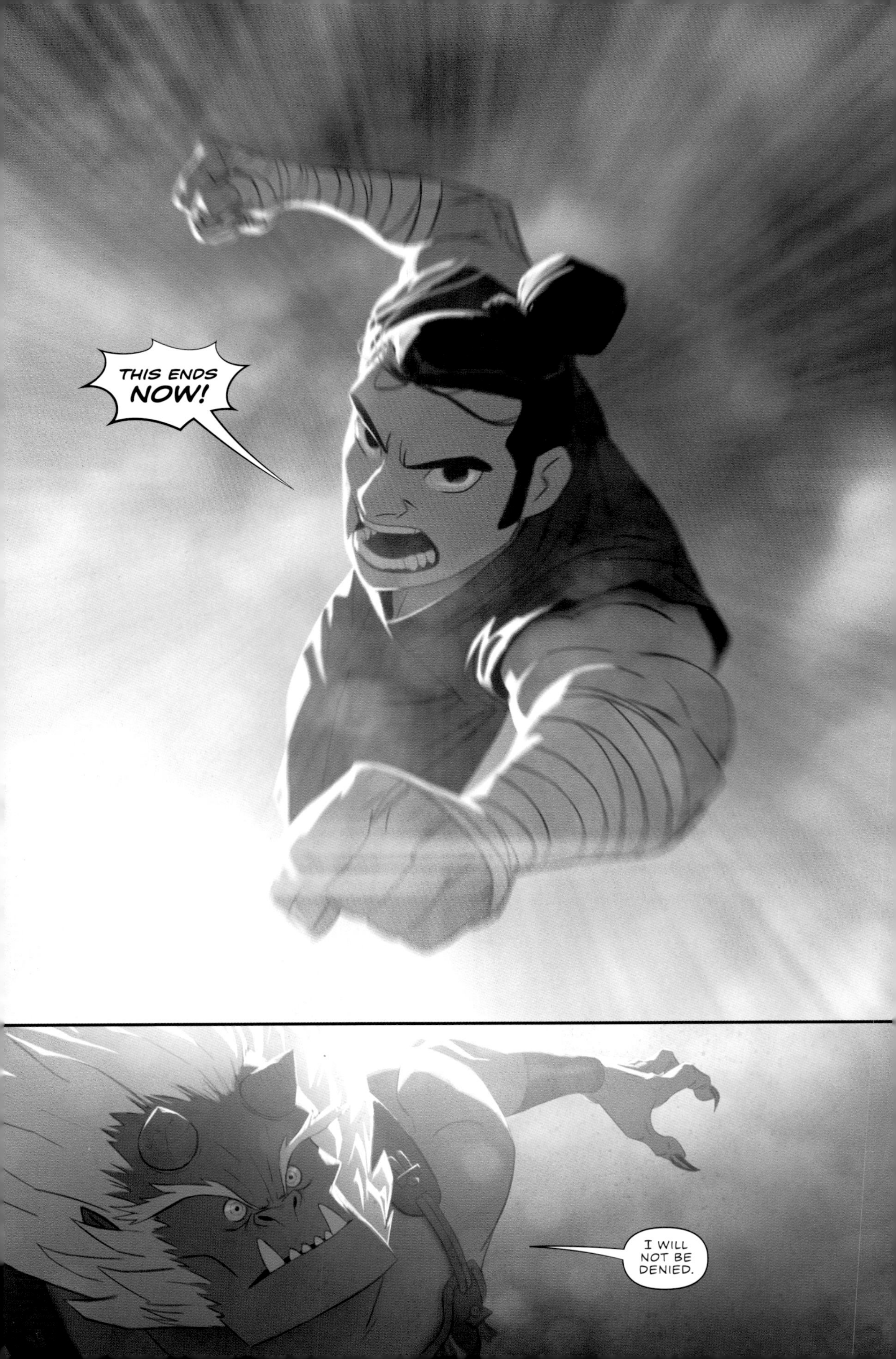
THIS ENDS NOW!
I WILL NOT BE DENIED.

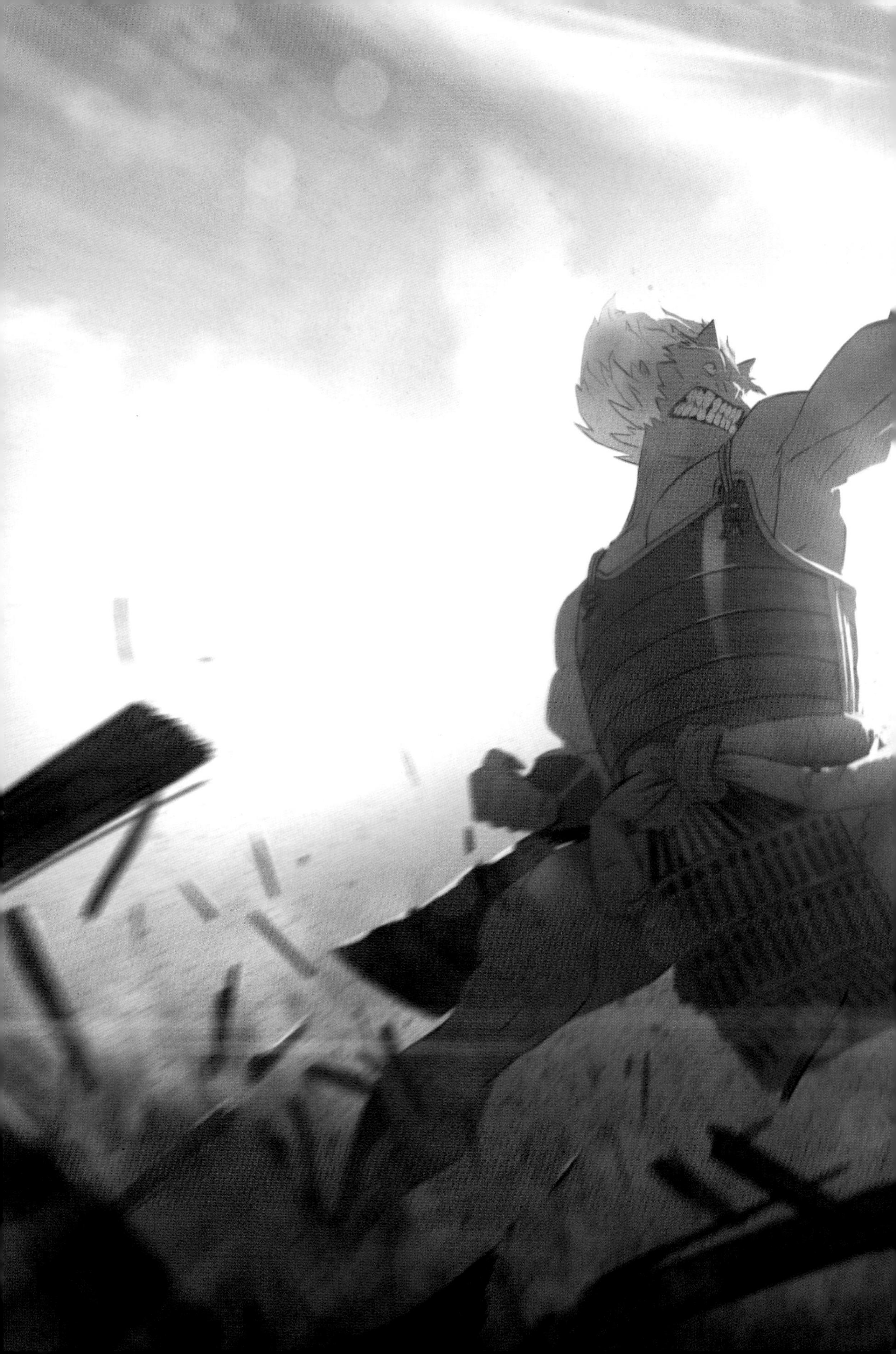

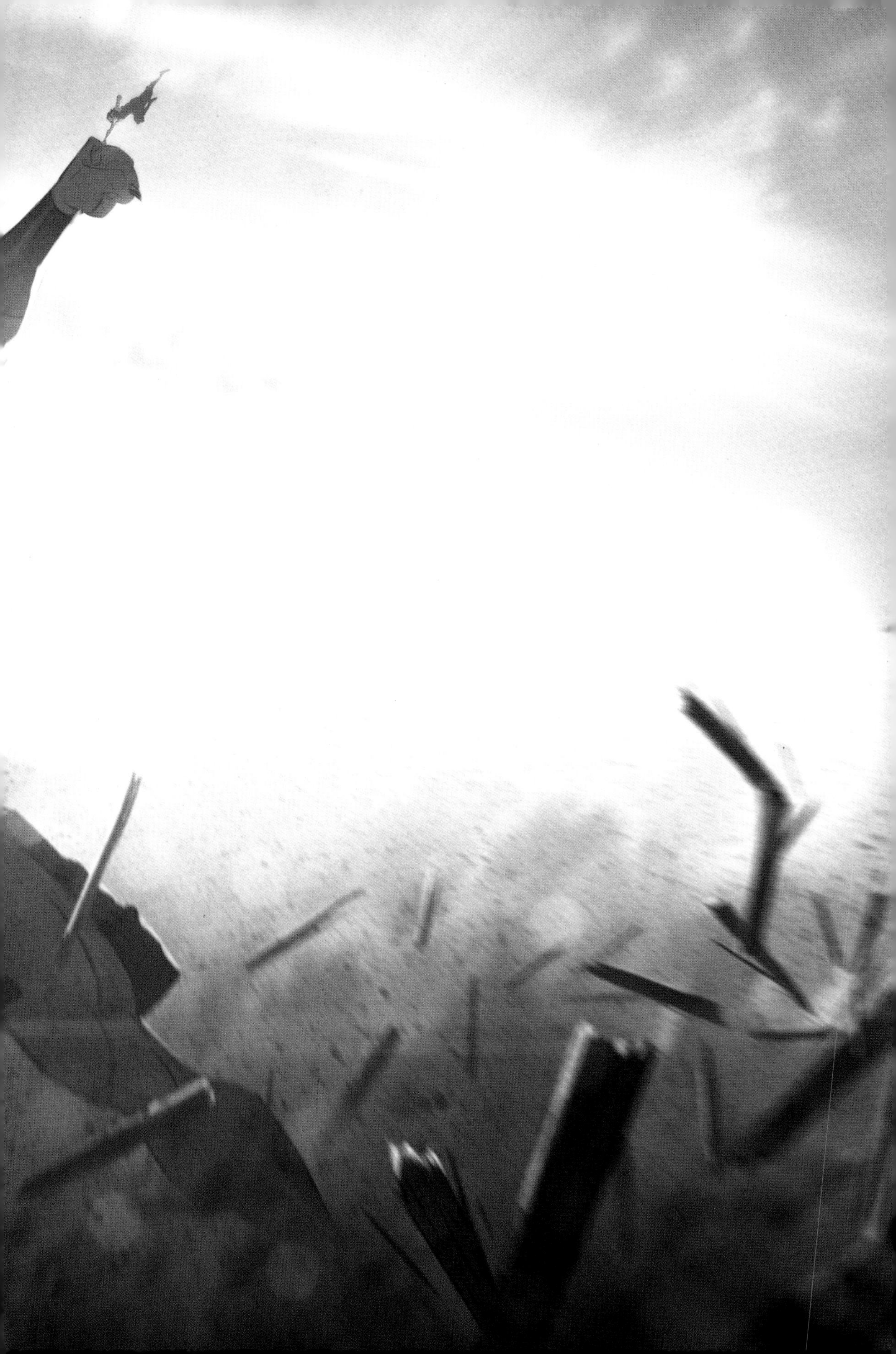

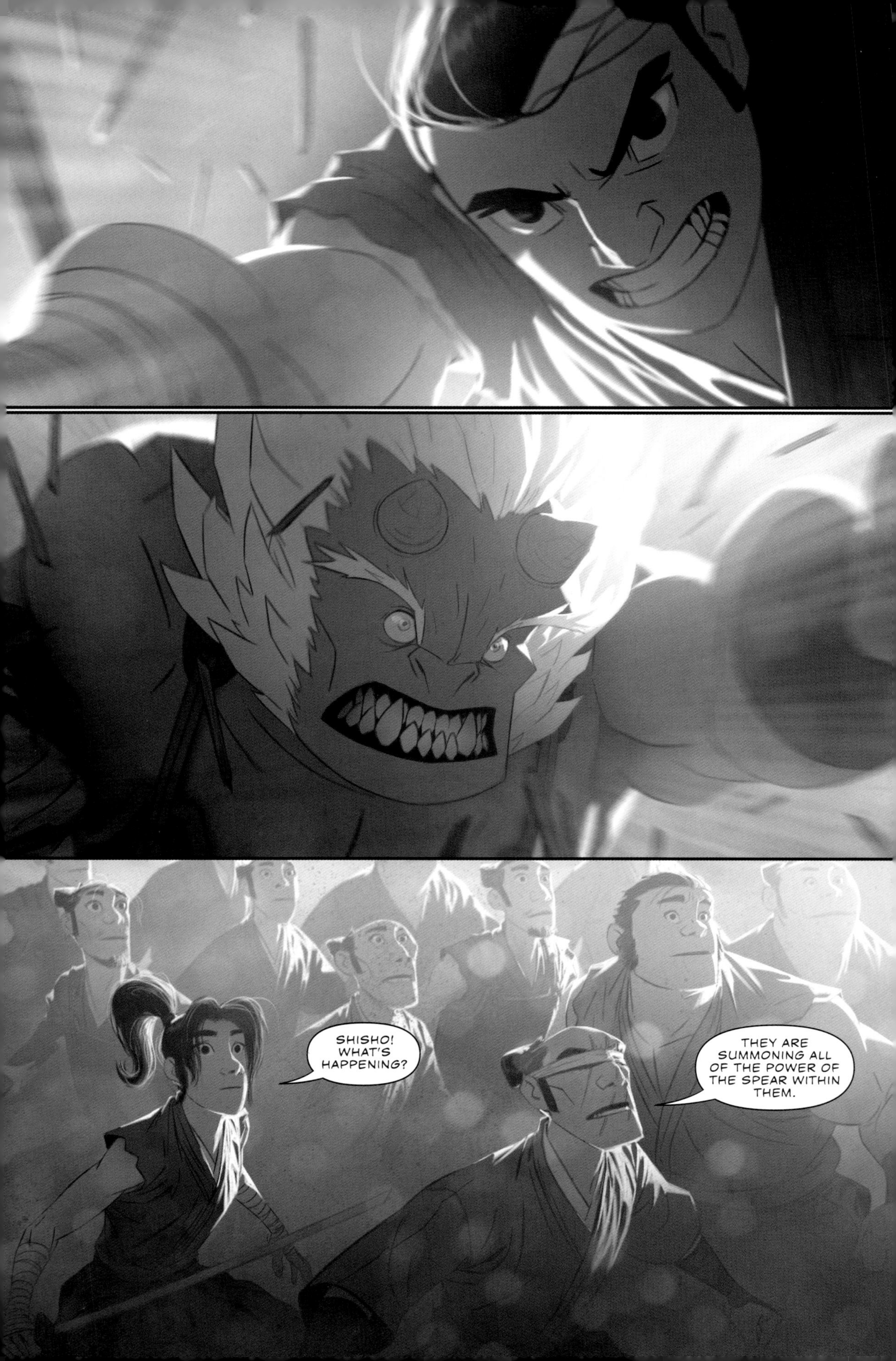
SHISHO! WHAT'S HAPPENING?
THEY ARE SUMMONING ALL OF THE POWER OF THE SPEAR WITHIN THEM.

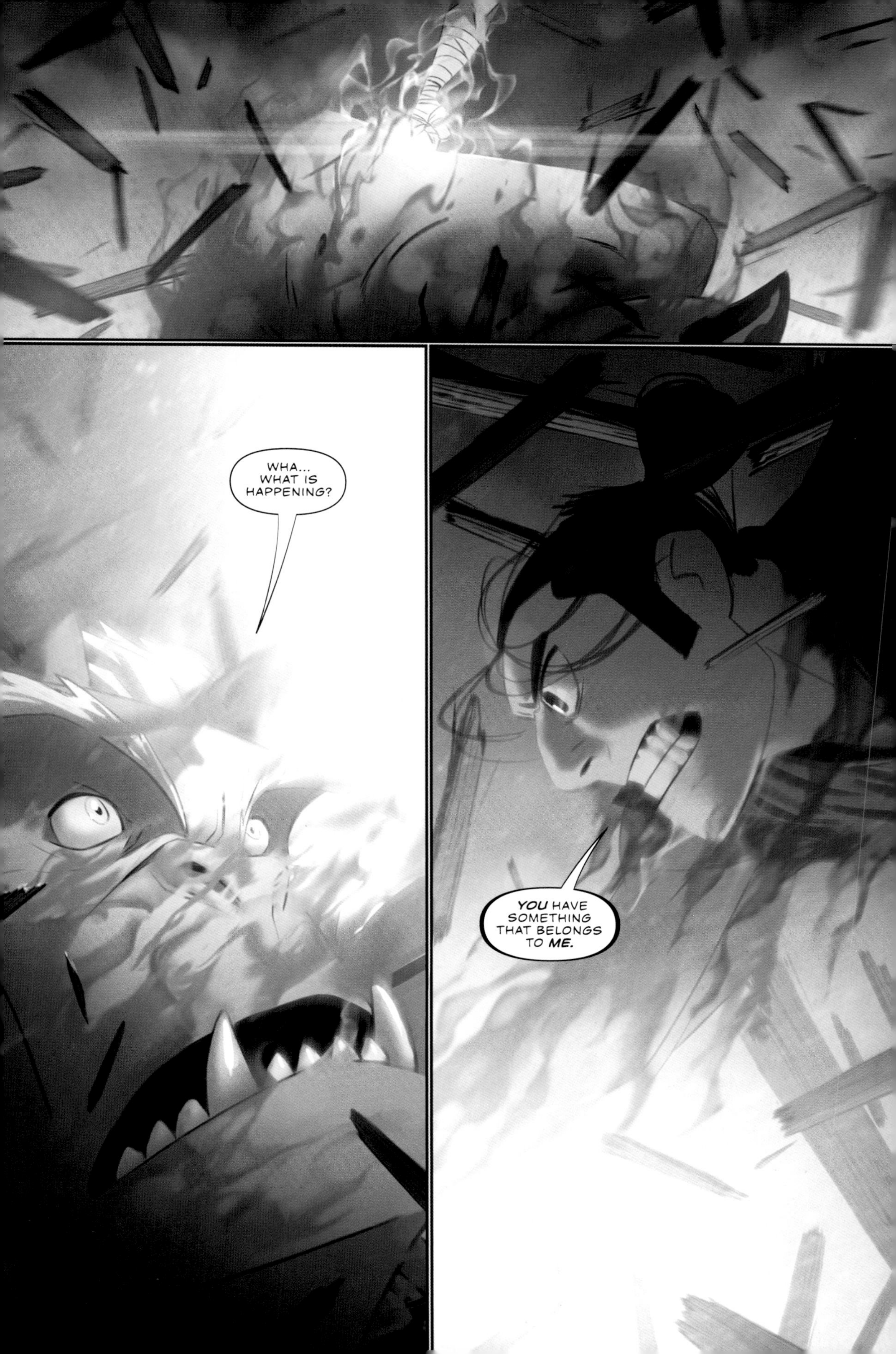
WHA... WHAT IS HAPPENING?
YOU HAVE SOMETHING THAT BELONGS TO ME.

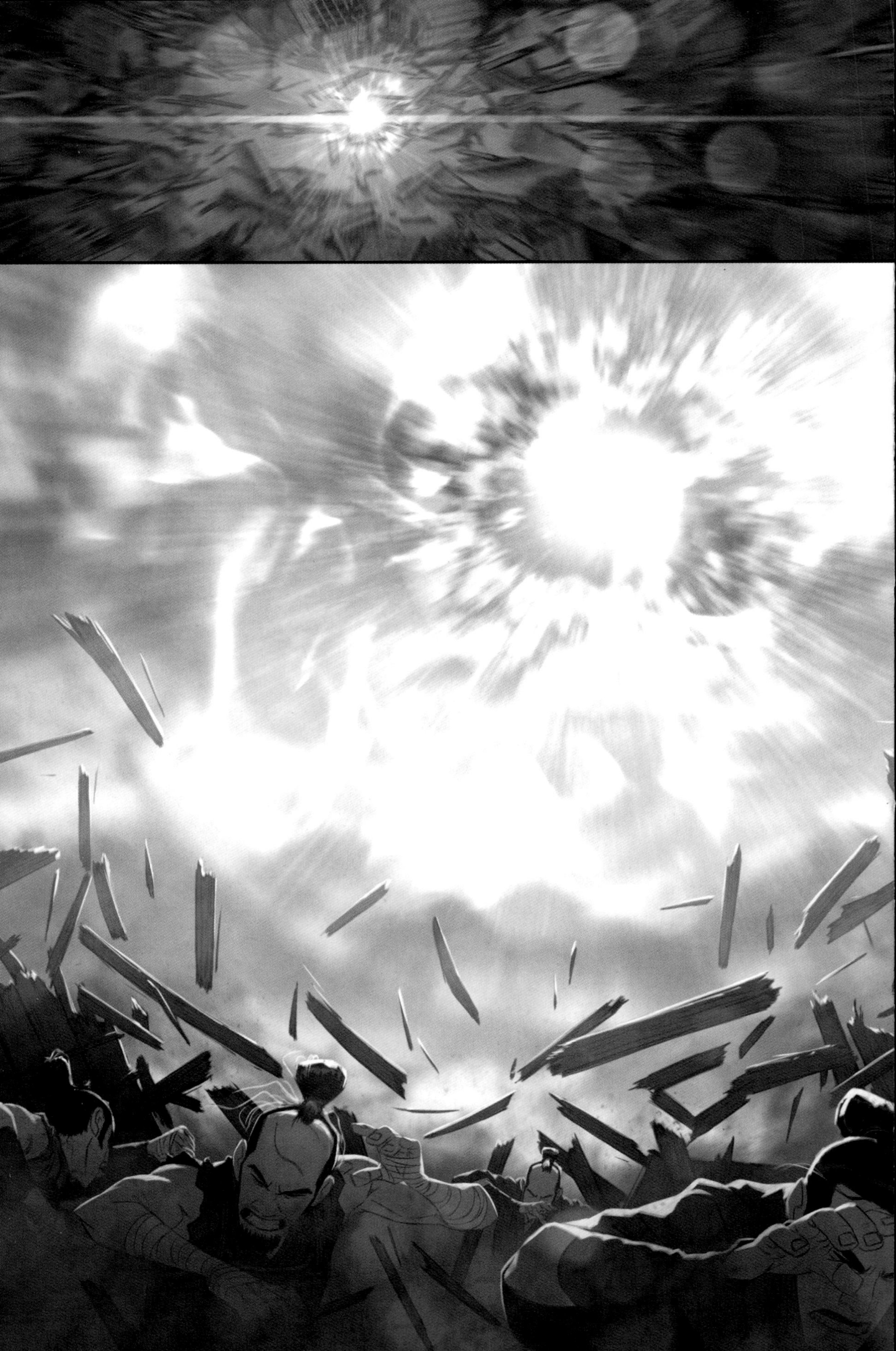

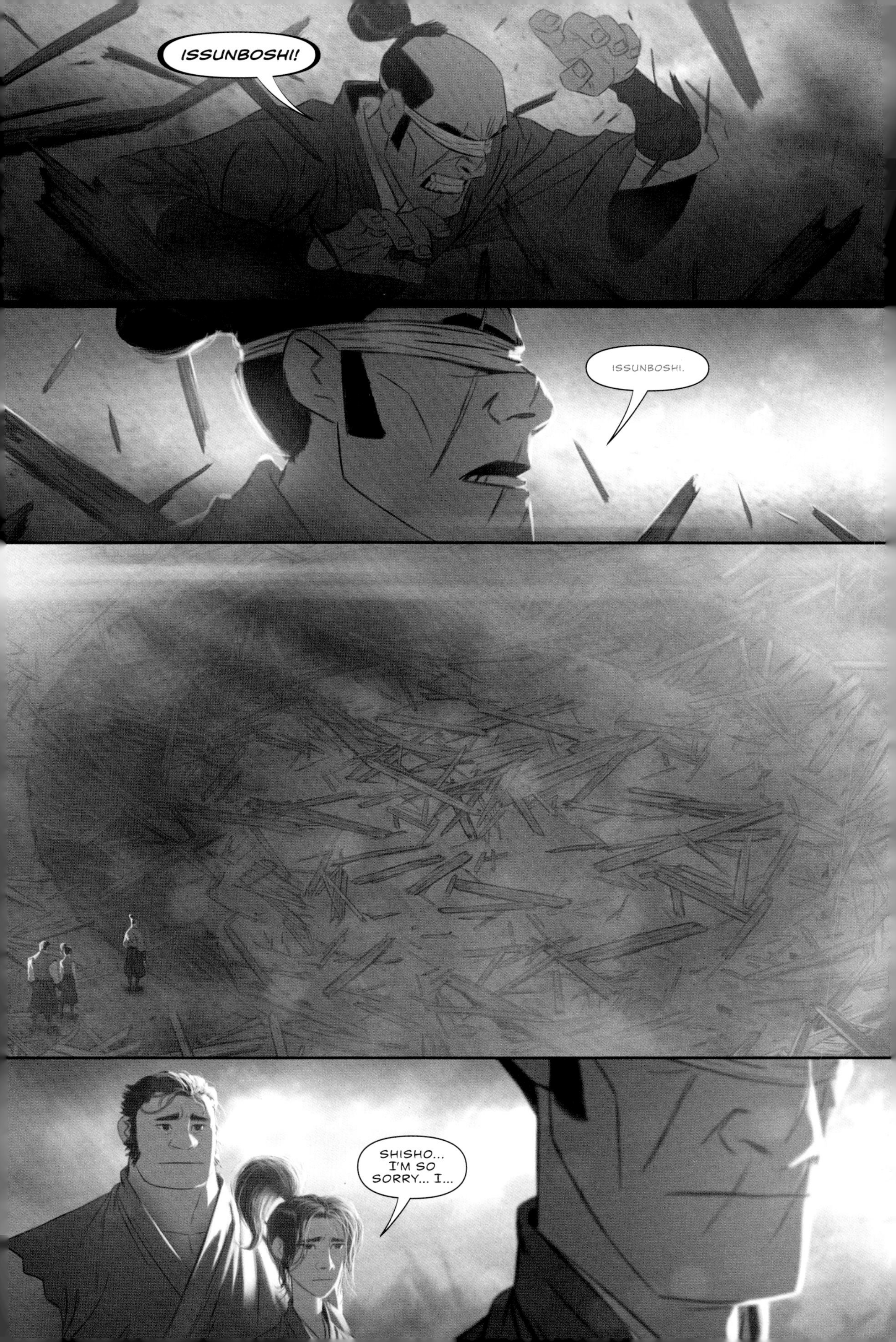
ISSUNBOSHI!
ISSUNBOSHI.
SHISHO... I'M SO SORRY... I...

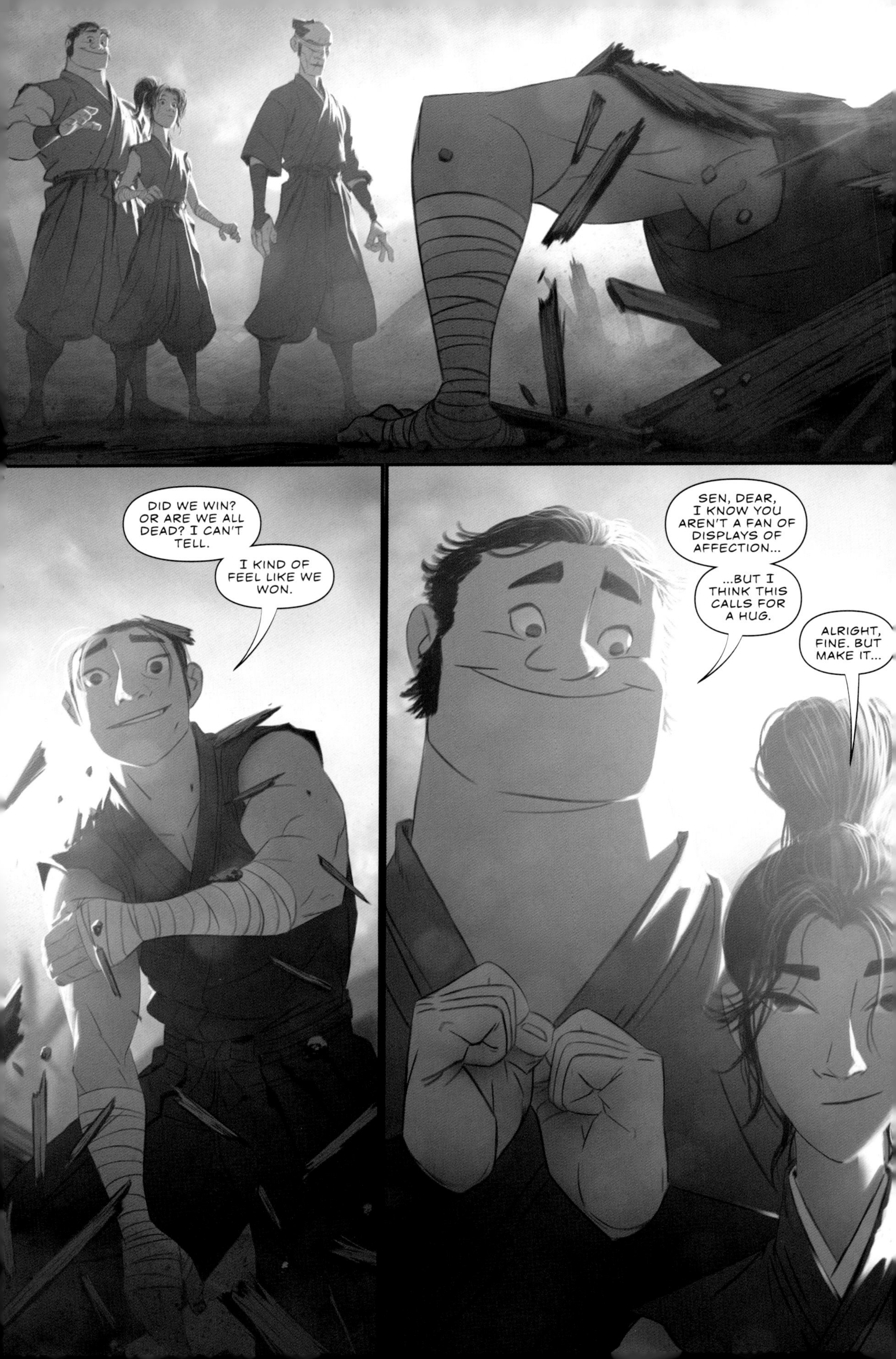
DID WE WIN? OR ARE WE ALL DEAD? I CAN'T TELL.
I KIND OF FEEL LIKE WE WON.
SEN, DEAR, I KNOW YOU AREN'T A FAN OF DISPLAYS OF AFFECTION...
...BUT I THINK THIS CALLS FOR A HUG.
ALRIGHT, FINE. BUT MAKE IT...

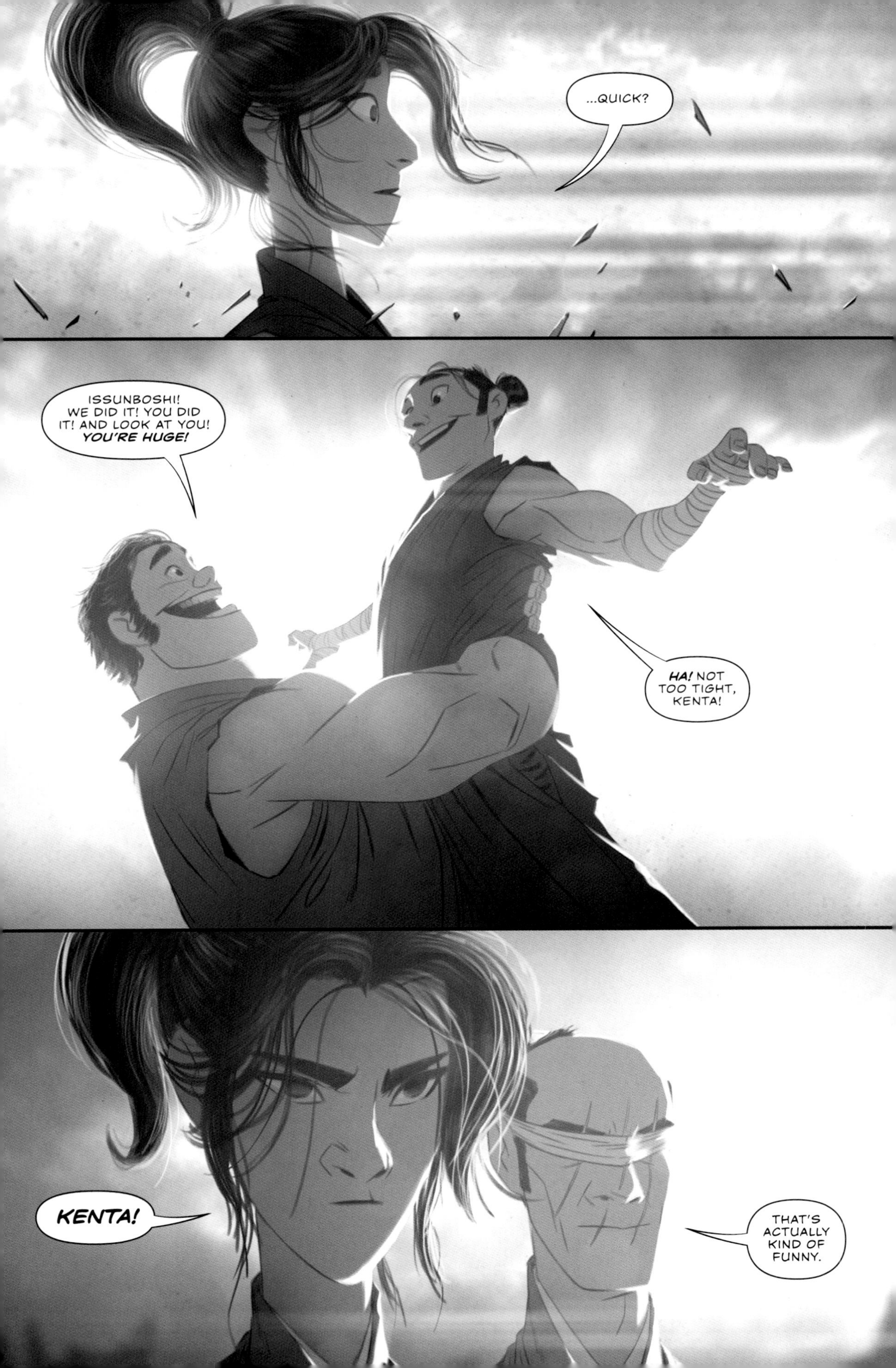
...QUICK?
ISSUNBOSHI! WE DID IT! YOU DID IT! AND LOOK AT YOU! ***YOU'RE HUGE!***
HA! NOT TOO TIGHT, KENTA!
KENTA!
THAT'S ACTUALLY KIND OF FUNNY.

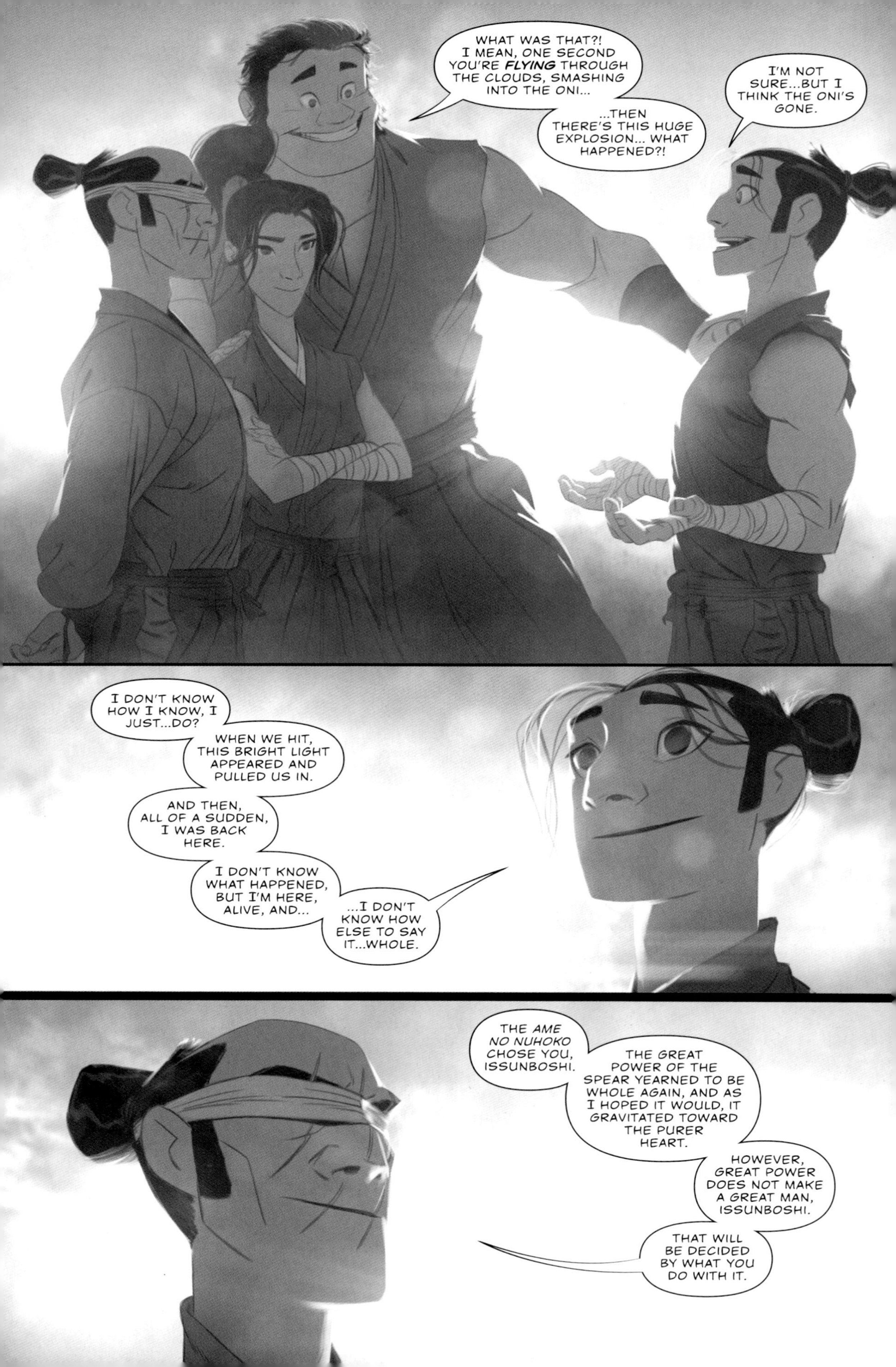
WHAT WAS THAT?! I MEAN, ONE SECOND YOU'RE *FLYING* THROUGH THE CLOUDS, SMASHING INTO THE ONI...
...THEN THERE'S THIS HUGE EXPLOSION... WHAT HAPPENED?!
I'M NOT SURE...BUT I THINK THE ONI'S GONE.
I DON'T KNOW HOW I KNOW, I JUST...DO?
WHEN WE HIT, THIS BRIGHT LIGHT APPEARED AND PULLED US IN.
AND THEN, ALL OF A SUDDEN, I WAS BACK HERE.
I DON'T KNOW WHAT HAPPENED, BUT I'M HERE, ALIVE, AND...
...I DON'T KNOW HOW ELSE TO SAY IT...WHOLE.
THE *AME NO NUHOKO* CHOSE YOU, ISSUNBOSHI.
THE GREAT POWER OF THE SPEAR YEARNED TO BE WHOLE AGAIN, AND AS I HOPED IT WOULD, IT GRAVITATED TOWARD THE PURER HEART.
HOWEVER, GREAT POWER DOES NOT MAKE A GREAT MAN, ISSUNBOSHI.
THAT WILL BE DECIDED BY WHAT YOU DO WITH IT.

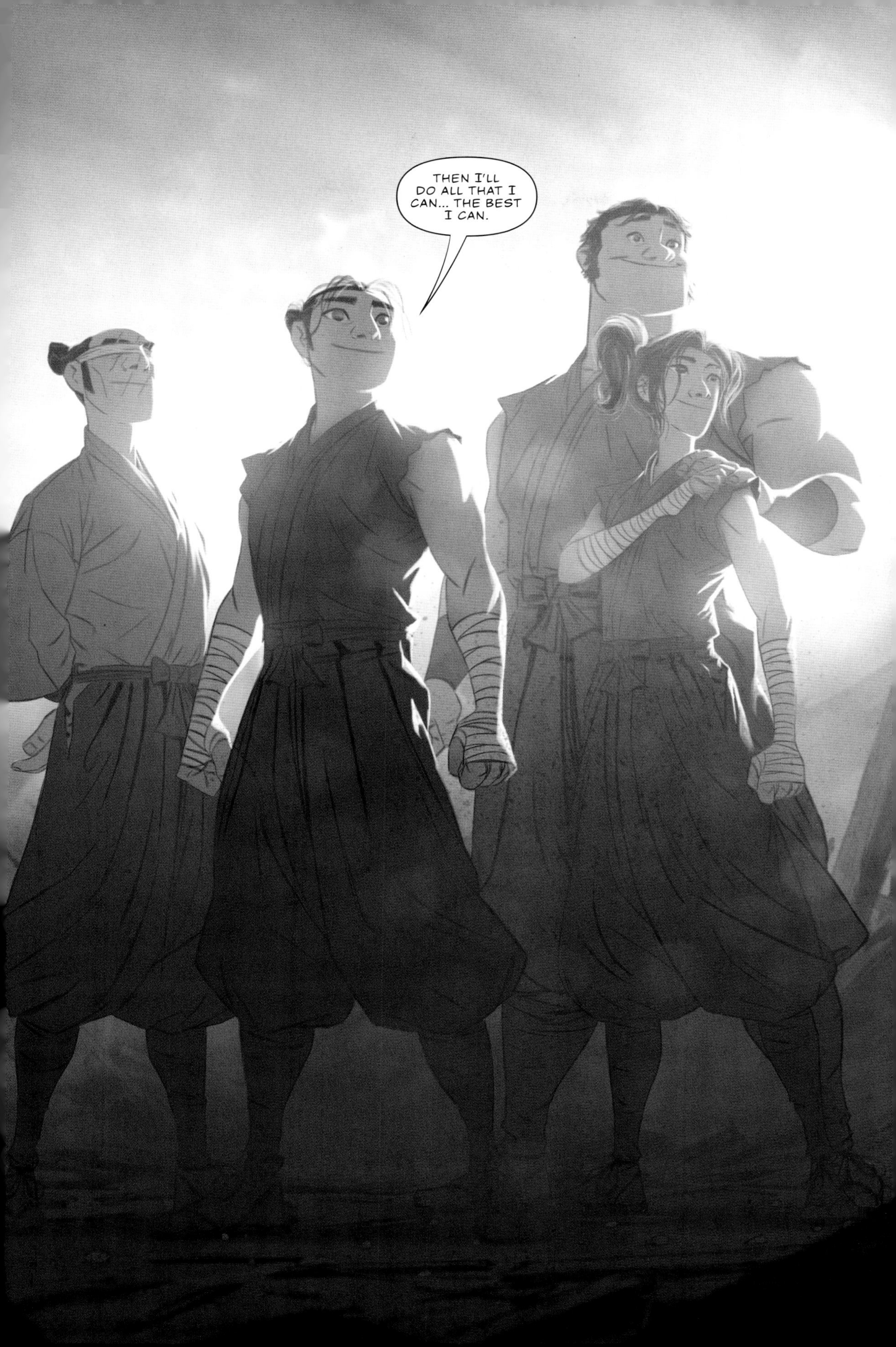
THEN I'LL DO ALL THAT I CAN... THE BEST I CAN.

EPILOGUE

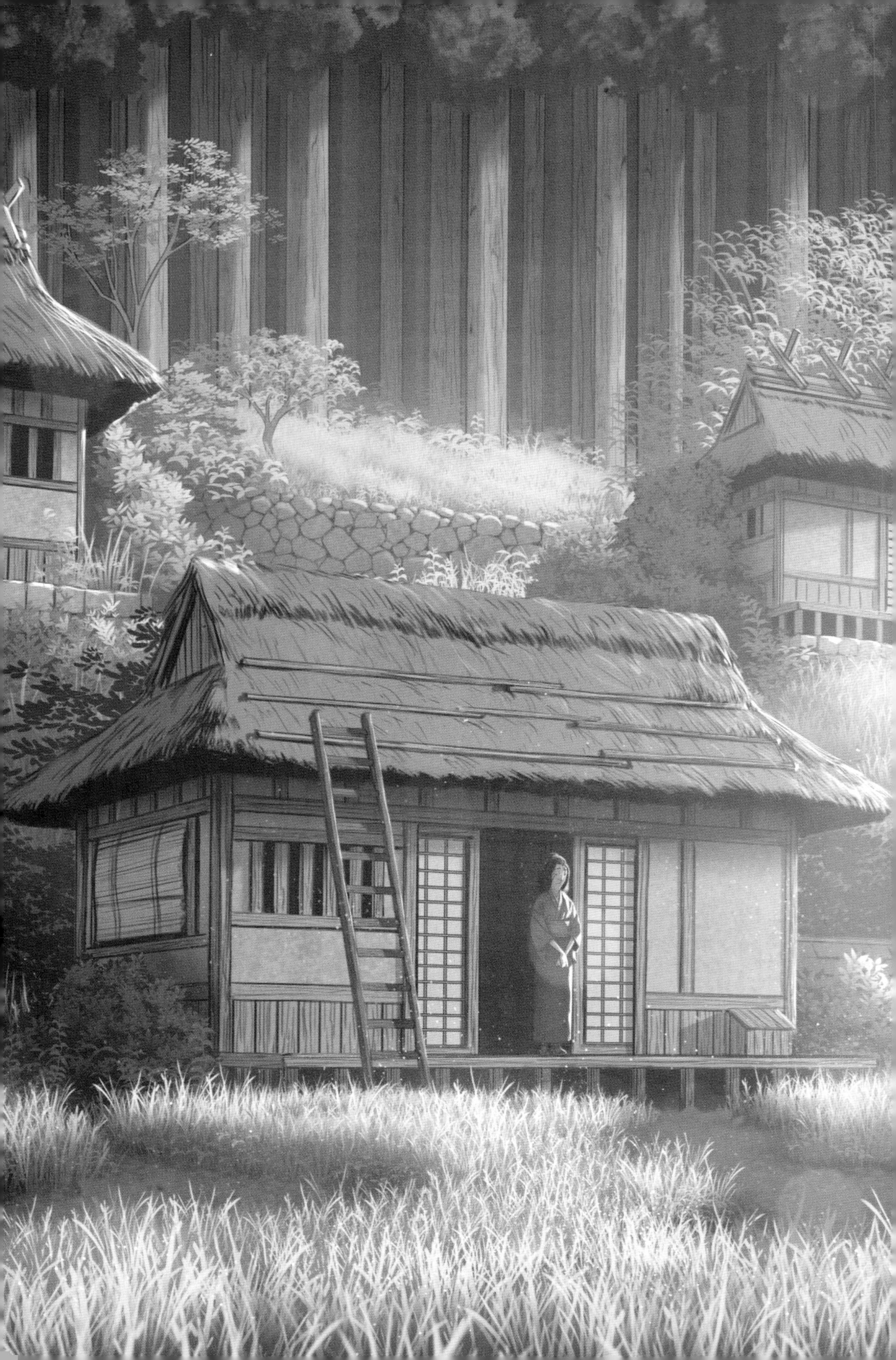

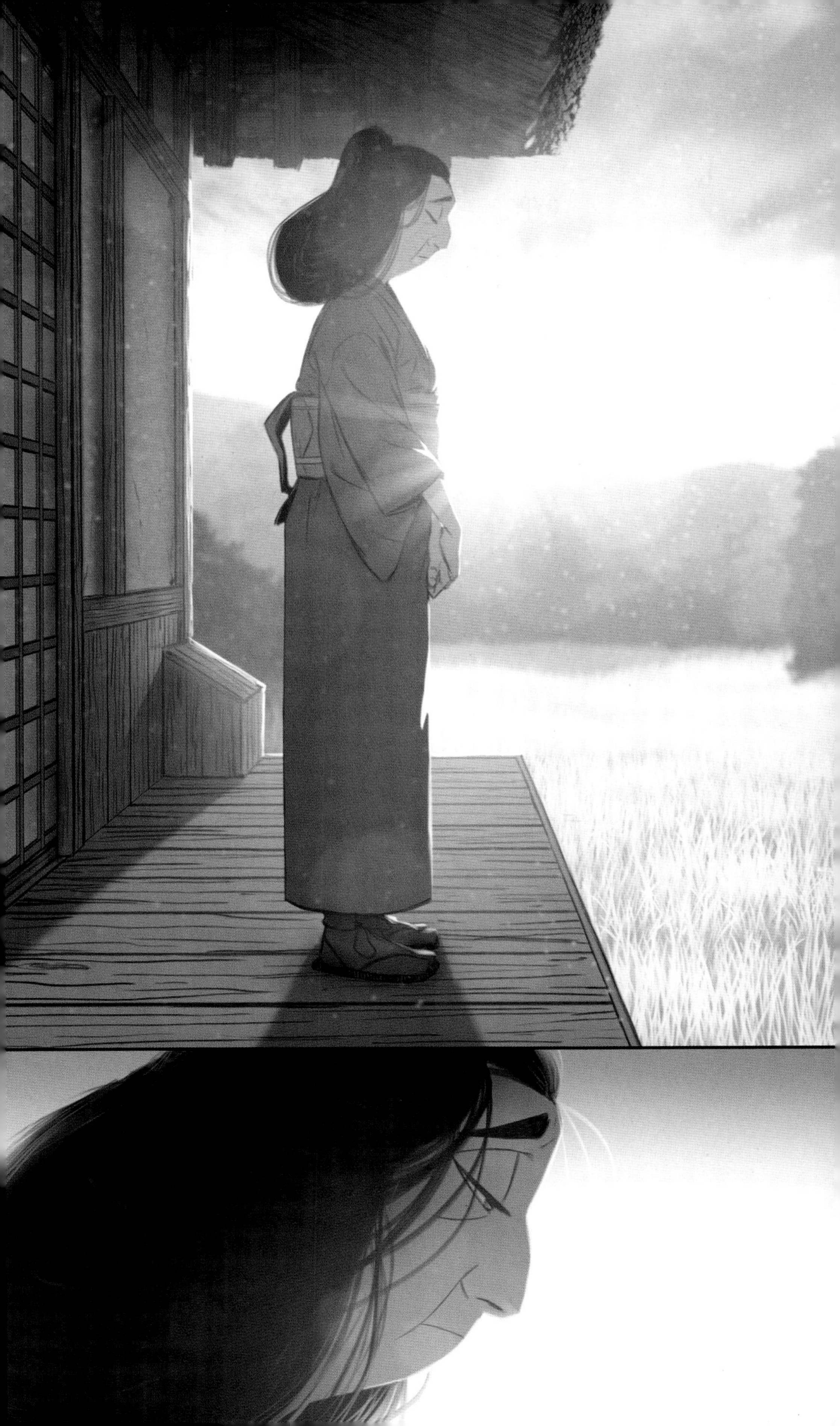

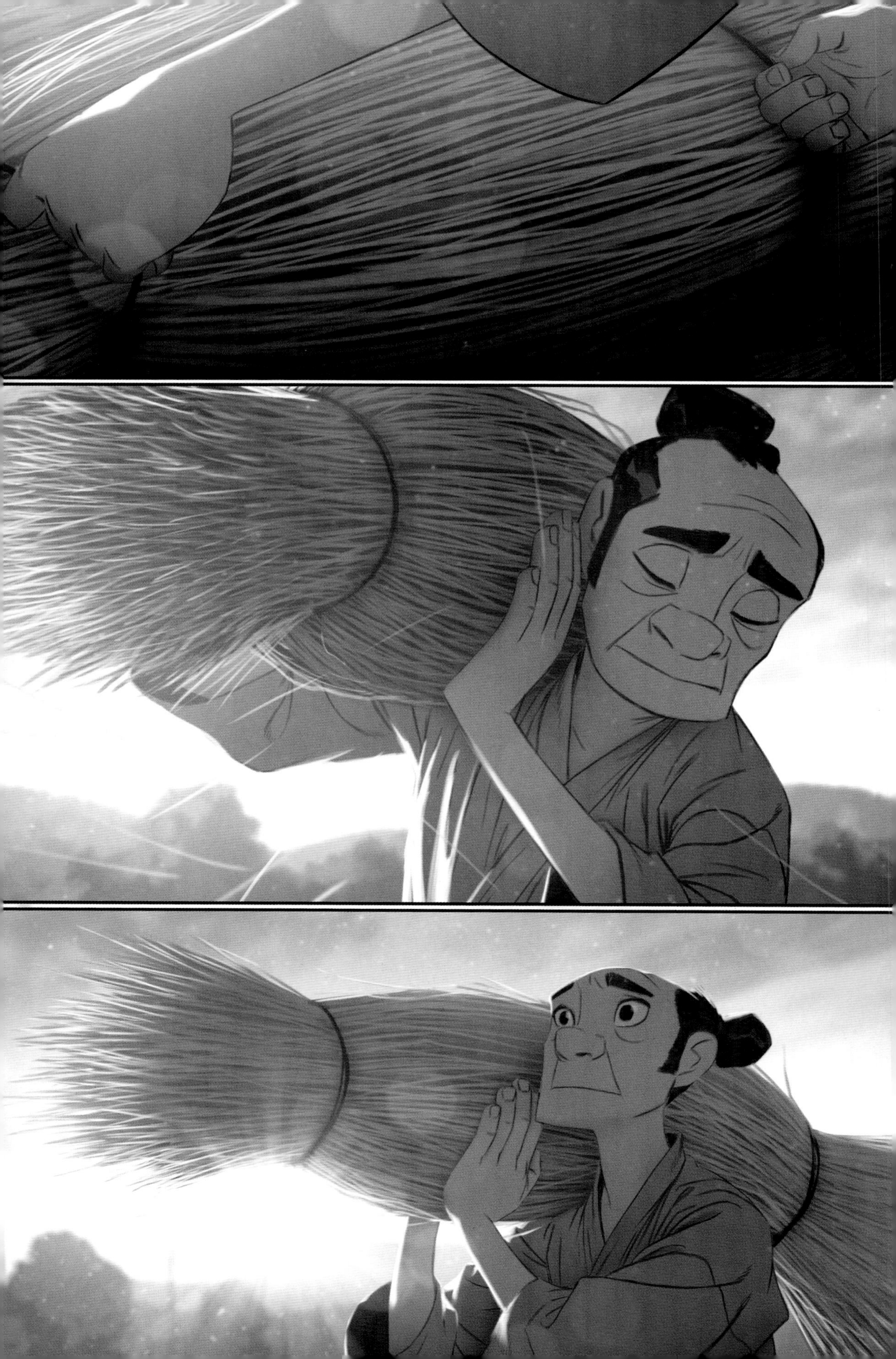

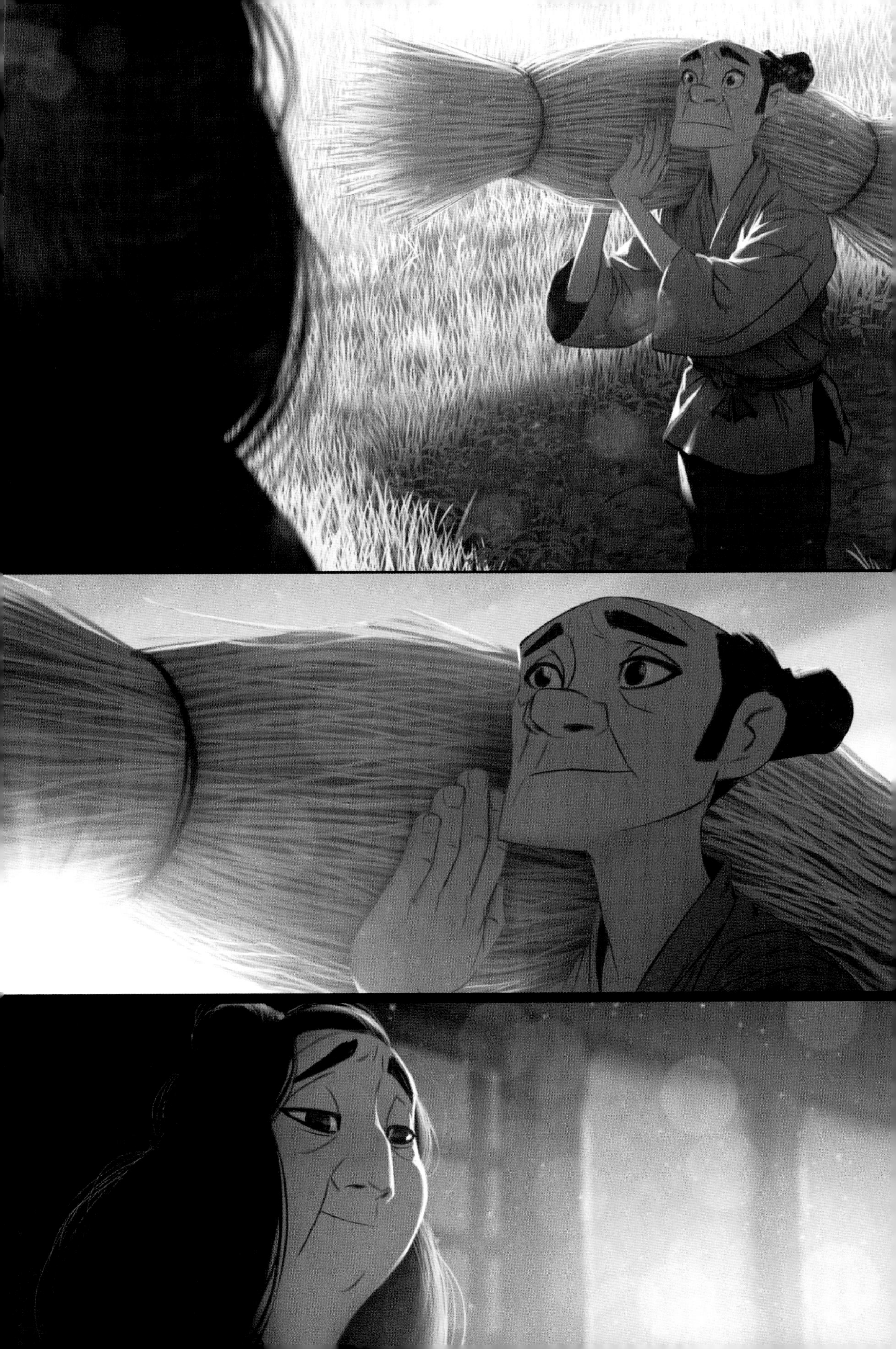

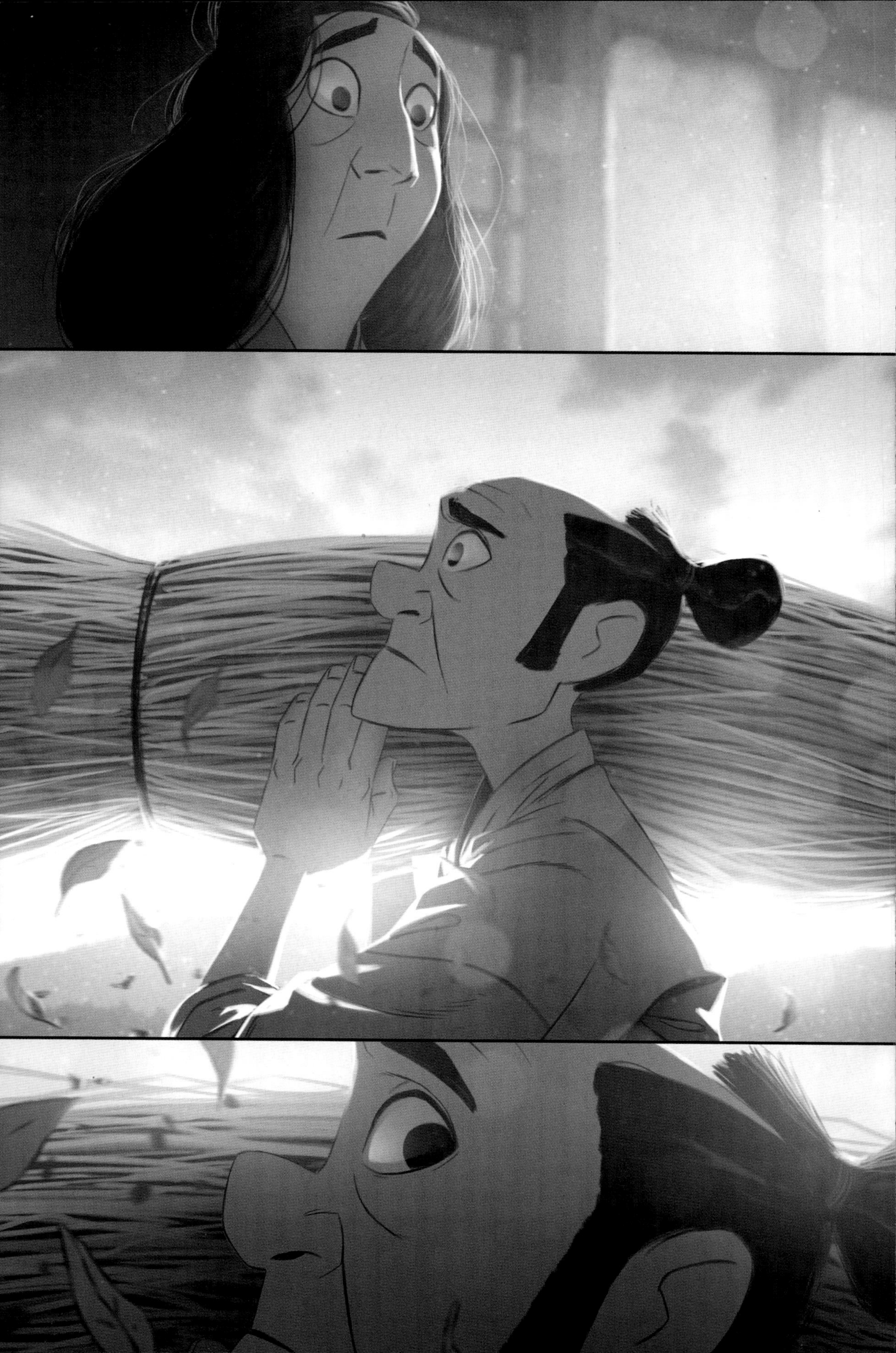

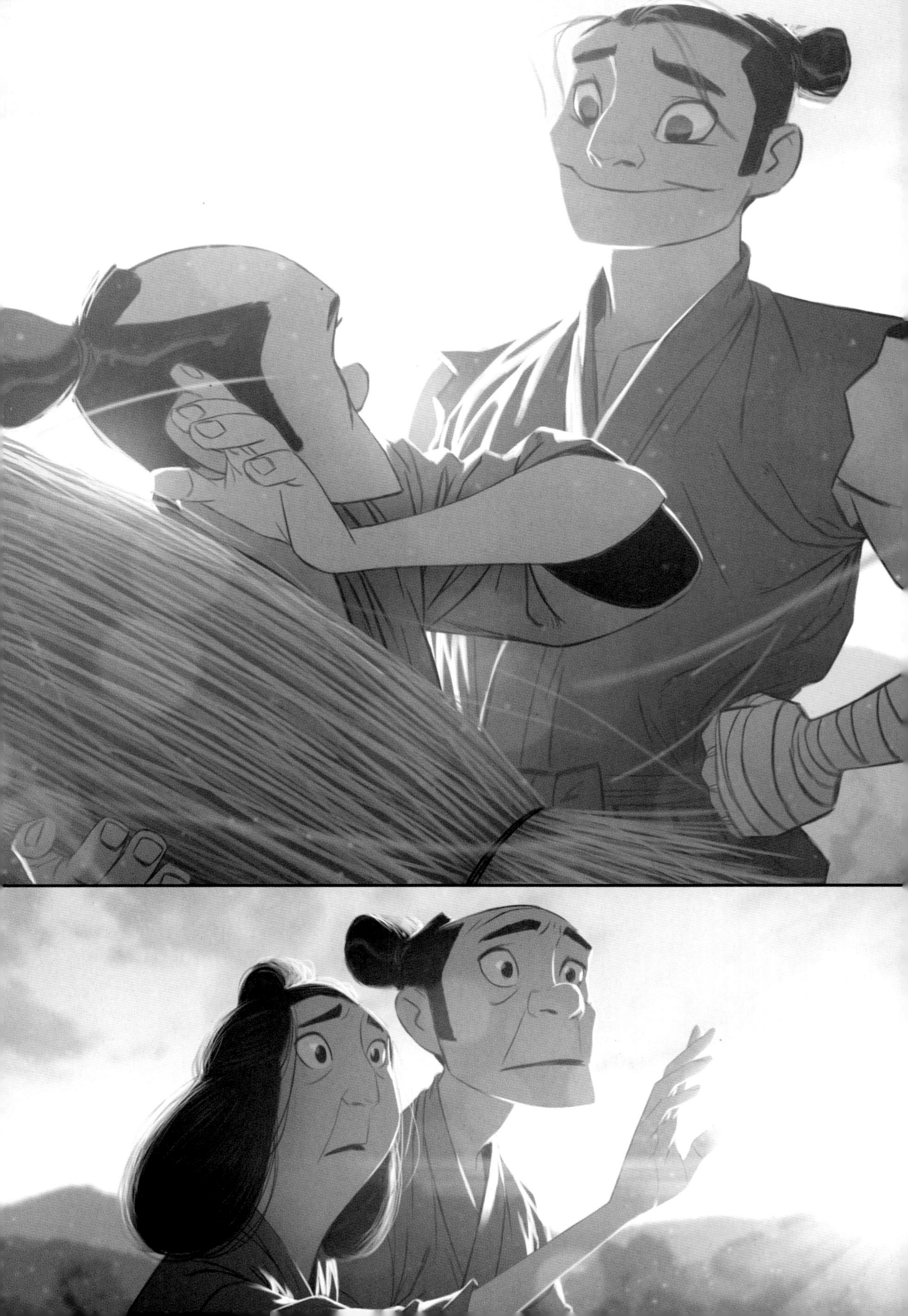

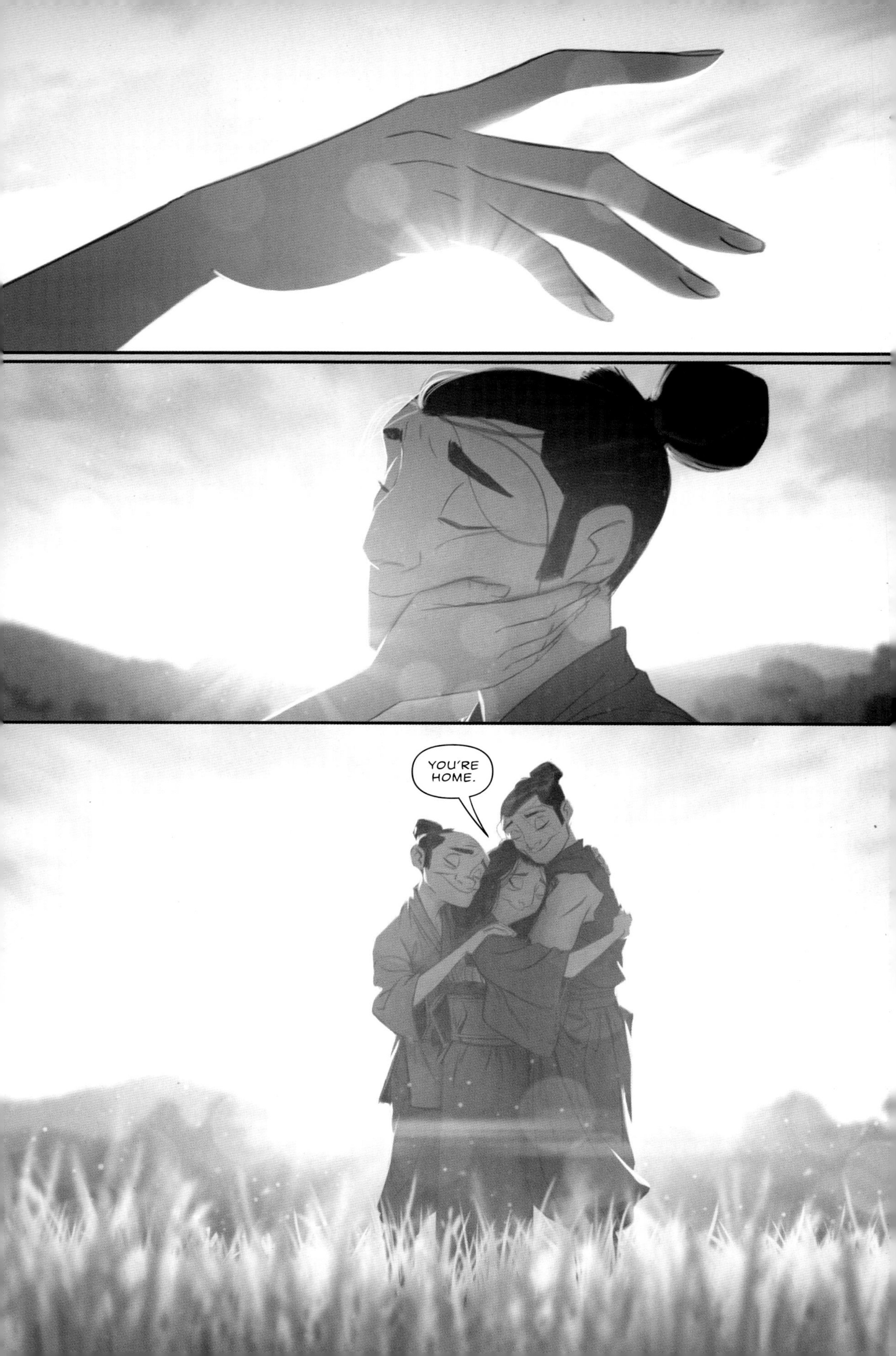
YOU'RE HOME.

the end.

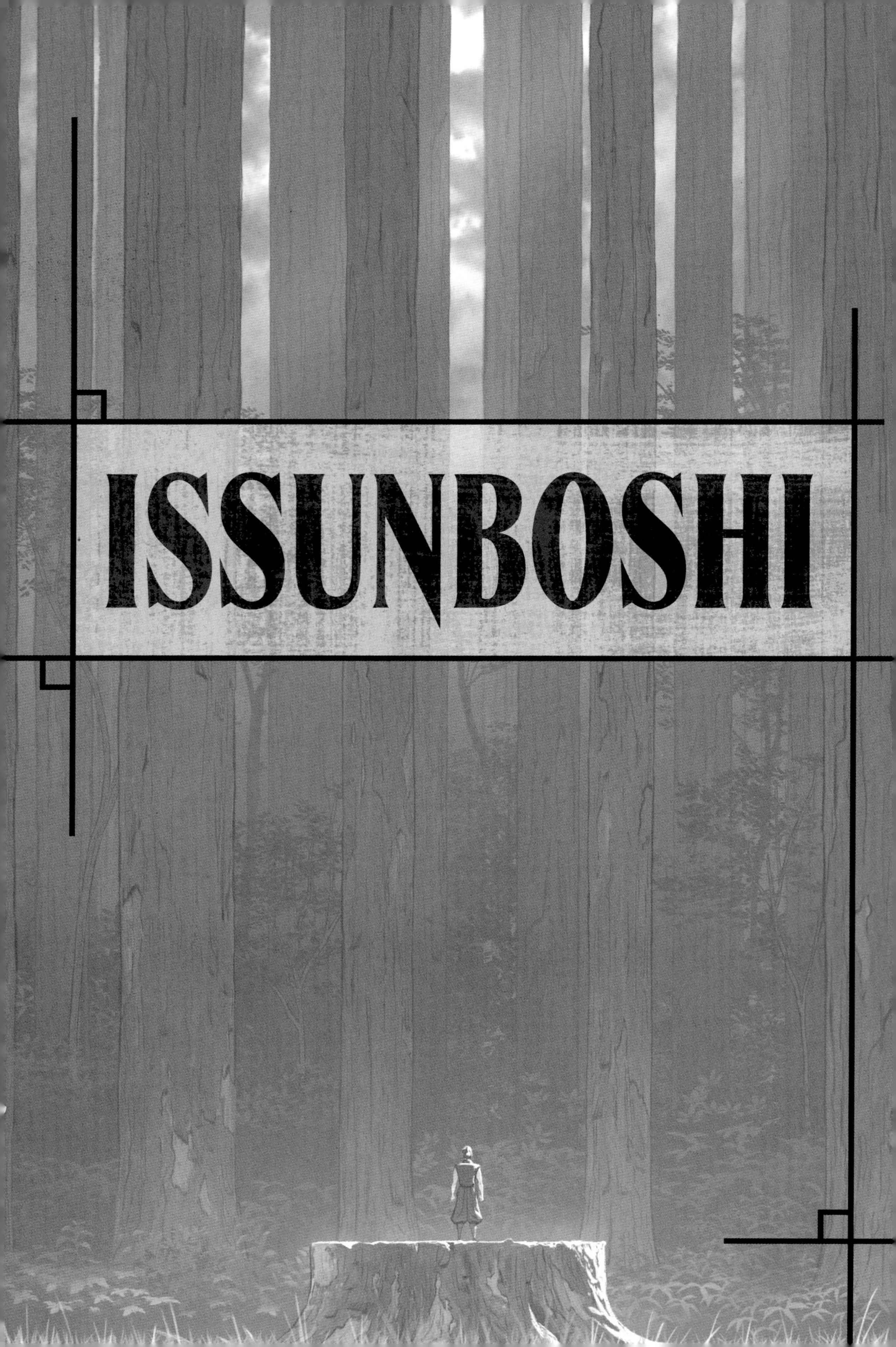
ISSUNBOSHI

A SPECIAL THANKS TO...

Rune Bennick
Andrea Blasich
Linda Chen
Phil Craven
Andy Cung
Duncan Fegredo
Maggie Kang
Cory Loftis
Rad Sechrist
Angela Smaldone
Kate Spencer
&
Makiko Wakita

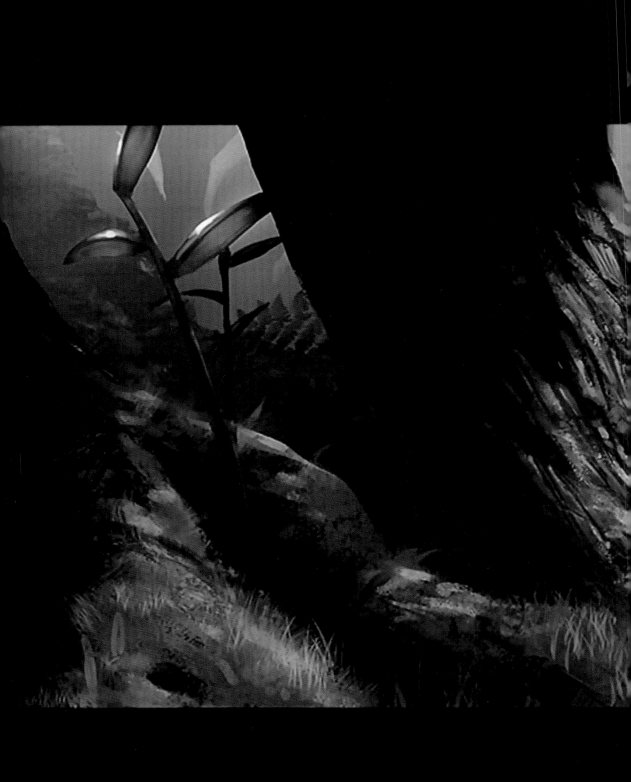

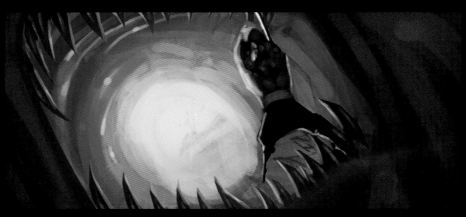

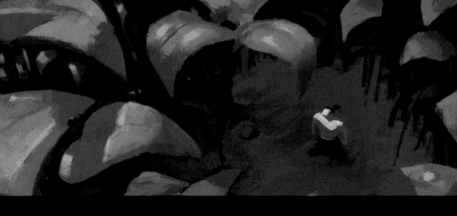

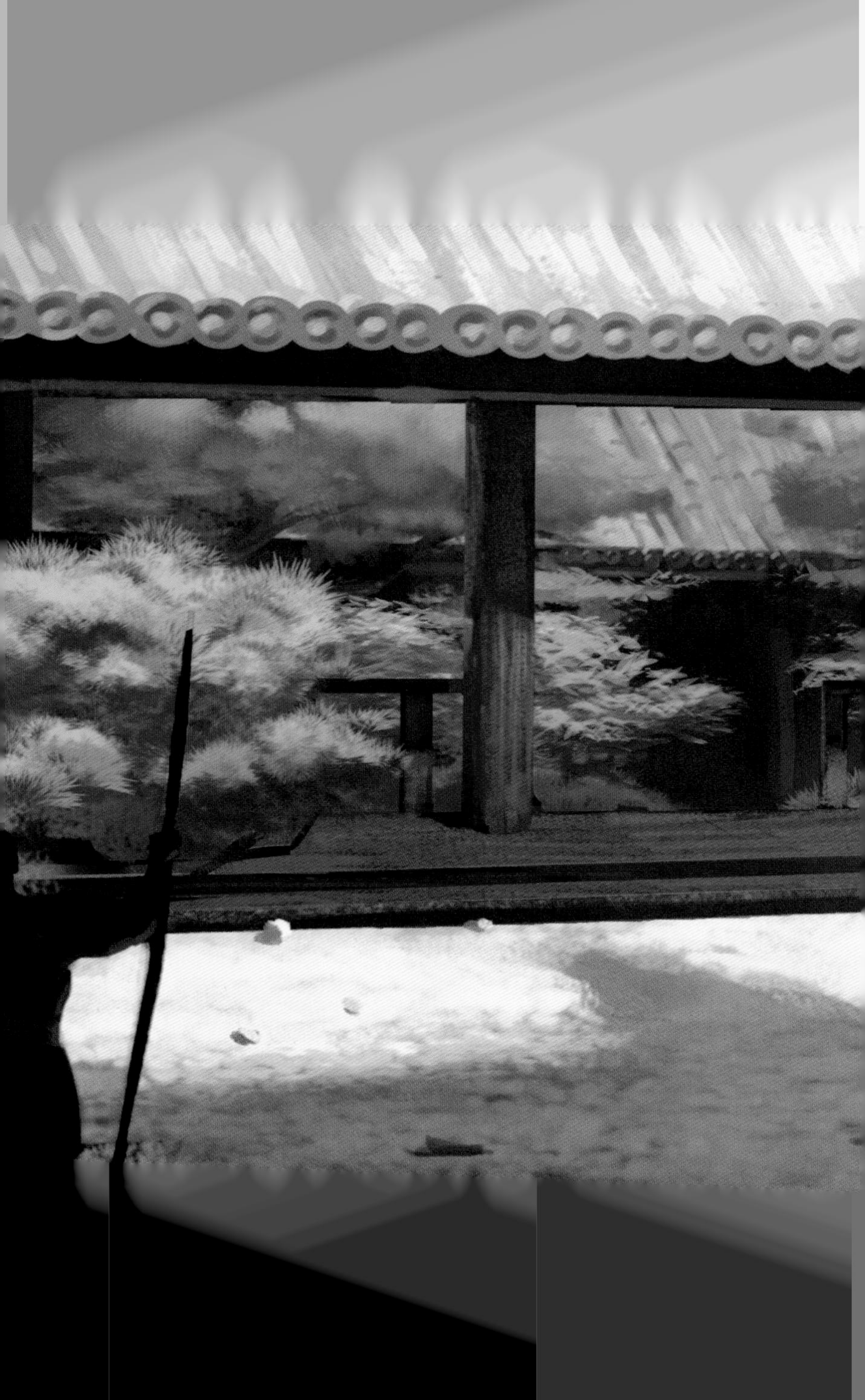

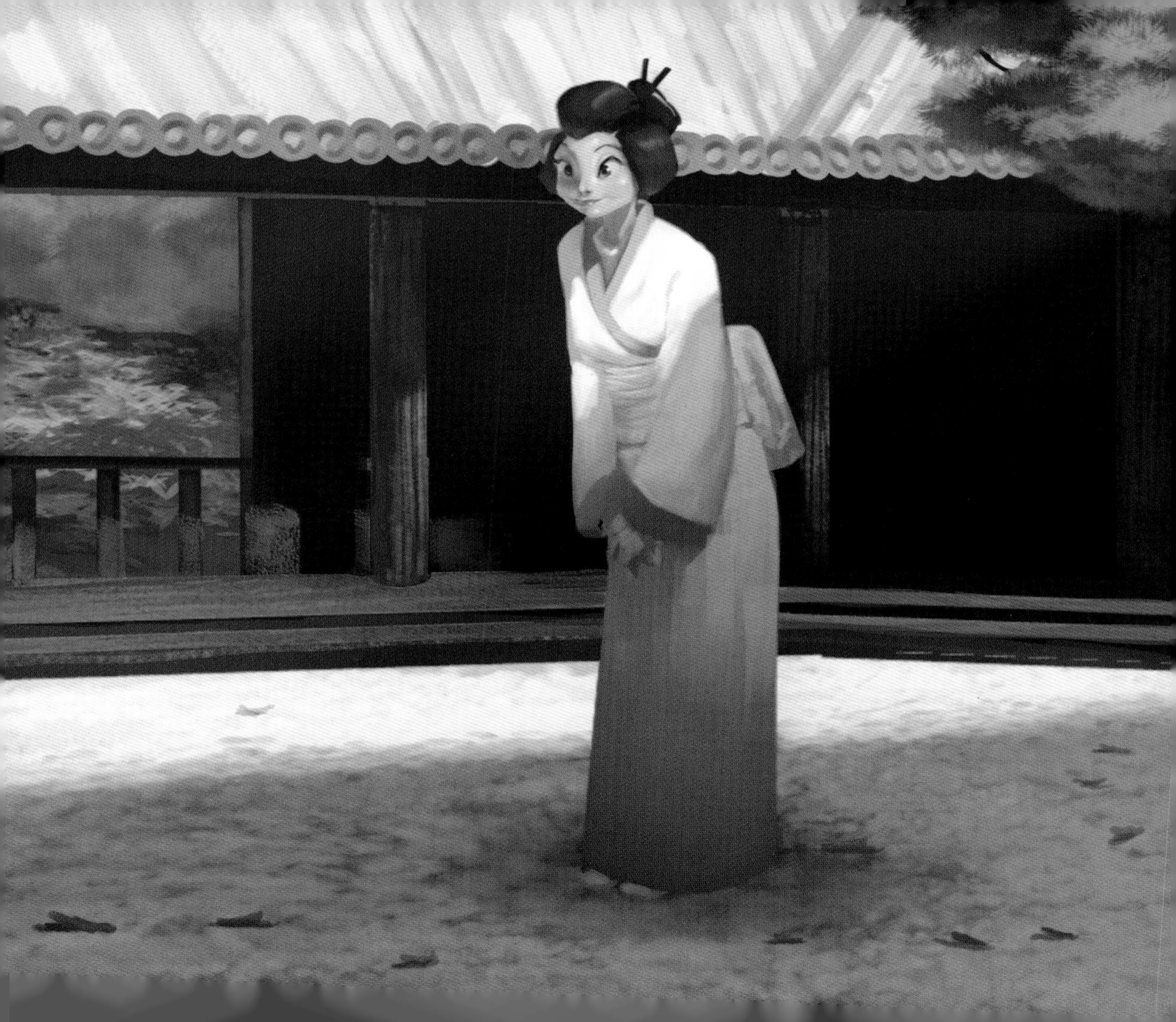

Ryan Lang is a Los Angeles–based production designer and visual development artist who was born and raised in Hawaii. At a young age, he fell in love with the art and storytelling of comic books, which eventually led to a career in both animation and live-action. He has contributed to such films as *Wreck-It Ralph*, *Moana*, *The Mitchells vs. the Machines*, *Doctor Strange*, *Avengers: Infinity War*, and *Avengers: Endgame*. *Issunboshi* is his first graphic novel.

Issunboshi was one of the first folktales Ryan Lang heard in preschool and has stuck with him ever since. *Issunboshi: A Graphic Novel* is an epic amalgam combining one of his favorite folktales, his love for animation, and his passion for stories about what it takes to be a hero.